Rough Diamonds

**THEY CANNOT BE EATEN AND
THEY CANNOT HAVE CHILDREN**

GUY HALLOWES

National Library of Australia Cataloguing-in-Publication entry

Creator: Hallowes, Guy, 1941—author.

Title: Rough diamonds: They cannot be eaten and they cannot have children / Guy Hallowes.

ISBN: 978-0-6484790-9-3 (pbk.)

Subjects: Zulu (African people)—Fiction.
Diamond mines and mining—South Africa—Fiction.

Dewey Number: A823.4

Cover design by Designerbility www.designerbility.com.au
Layout by OMNE www.omne.com.au

Published by OMNE www.omne.com.au

Contents

(For words in *italics* see glossary at the end of the book)

Chapter 1

Utterly exhausted, Mapitha Ndwandwe found a vantage point on a small hillock overlooking Kwa-Bulawayo, the great kraal of the Zulu Kings. He was dressed in rags—an old pair of khaki trousers and a shirt. His feet were bare. He carried the Mauser rifle he had taken from the Boers more than three summers before, and his spear: the short, stabbing spear called "*ixwa*" by the great Zulu King, Shaka, this being the sound it made when it was withdrawn from the body of an opponent. Hung from his person was a cartridge belt, still with several shells in it, a small food bag, which had been empty now for many days, and the kaross he had been given three years earlier, at the start of his journey. The kaross was now rather moth-eaten but still kept the night chill out. He also carried, well hidden next to the skin in a small animal skin pouch, a collection of diamonds.

Kwa-Bulawayo, the great kraal, was built on a gentle slope facing the sea; its more than one thousand neat and orderly beehive huts glistened in the sunlight. The establishment was dominated at the top of the slope by the *Isigodlo* or King's royal enclosure. Surrounding the kraal were large herds of cattle, tended by boys too young to be in the King's *ibutho*.

Mapitha could also see the occasional much smaller kraal: these he had deliberately avoided on his return home; he had intuitively felt that he had better make his way to the King's kraal first.

Judging from the dust, smoke, and noise, there was a major celebration in progress at the kraal. Only the celebration of a great victory or the King's birthday would warrant such an event. Despite his weariness, he hurried along through the long grass and thorn scrub, and soon after the sun reached its zenith arrived at the mighty entrance of the kraal. Mapitha had expected to be greeted like the long lost hero that he was, but his ragged appearance and complete lack of Zulu identity immediately raised the suspicions of the guard.

"Son of a thieving jackal, who are you and where are you going?" challenged the guard.

"I am Mapitha of the Ndwandwes, returning from a secret mission for the great King Mpande," responded Mapitha.

"The great King Mpande made his journey to the land of our ancestors almost three summers ago," countered the guard.

Mapitha was silent. News of Mpande's death had reached Kimberley almost a year after its occurrence. He had assumed that the new King would wish him to continue his critical mission.

"You are a stinking, thieving Swazi who has come to spy on the celebrations for our great King Cetshwayo. Die, you dog!"

The guard raised his spear, but the guard captain came out of a nearby hut and yelled, "Stop! Perhaps he is telling the truth. There was a mission to the great river in the west more than three summers ago, but nobody returned and we thought they were all dead. I will take him to the King."

Cetshwayo was seated outside the *isigodlo* surrounded by his *indunas*. Mapitha's eyes nearly popped out of his head when he saw that the positions of honour, one to the King's right and one to his left, were occupied by two bearded white men. He and the guard captain had crawled on their stomachs the last fifty yards to the foot of the King's seat.

"What is your business?" growled the King. "Can't you see we are busy enjoying the celebrations?"

"O great King..."

"Get on with it, get on with it," growled Cetshwayo.

"This stinking, thieving piece of hyena turd was found entering the gate," stammered the guard captain.

"Is he a spy? Then kill him," answered the King.

"He claims he was sent on a secret mission by your mighty father to the great river in the west."

"I know of no such secret mission," growled the King. He addressed Mapitha: "What is your name?"

"Mapitha of the Ndwandwes, O lord, O great elephant," answered Mapitha.

The King laughed.

"The Ndwandwes have just started their homage; we'll soon see if you are indeed an Ndwandwe or not," he said. "Go, go join them."

Mapitha was of course aware that five hundred men of his *ibutho* were assembling fifty yards away. They looked magnificent in their ceremonial dress, which consisted of a fan-shaped ostrich feather headdress surrounding the face, short animal skin skirts plus armlets and anklets made from monkey skins and, of course, their six foot high, cow hide shields. All had their "*ixwa*", short stabbing spears. Mapitha had led this homage dance many times in front of Mpande and now, with his "*ixwa*" in one hand and the Mauser in the other, much to the surprise of the whole regiment, he took his place in the very front of the throng, rags notwithstanding. There were one or two hisses before Mapitha began.

"Usuthu!" he bellowed, stamping his right foot, and then the regimental discipline took over.

"Usuthu!" they bellowed in return and five hundred right feet stamped in unison.

To start there were a few surprised looks among his fellow warriors, and then for an hour they entertained the King to a mighty display of dancing and discipline, led all the while by Mapitha.

The King was astonished, to say the least. He had been expecting another victim to be marched off to the execution mound outside the kraal, to be killed with one spear thrust to the heart and then left to be picked clean by the vultures.

When the Ndwandwes had finished and withdrawn in good order, Mapitha was mobbed by the other members of his regiment, especially his age group. They stripped off his rags and quickly dressed him in regimental finery. Mapitha made sure that his little cache of diamonds went unnoticed and he kept the Mauser within his grasp.

Then they noticed the scars on his back. One of his old friends fingered them.

"It looks as if you have been gored by one hundred buffalos and mauled by fifty lions," he said.

"Worse," said Mapitha.

"Worse?" was the question.

"This was done by the white man. See those two mongrels sitting there with the King," said Mapitha amid nods from his fellows, "that type of white man."

They all looked.

"And you have a firestick like the white man," another said quietly. "Can you show me how it works?"

"Maybe I should show the King first," said Mapitha diplomatically, "but I need some food and water beforehand."

In the middle of his meal a messenger came from the King.

"The one who is called Mapitha is instructed to pay his respects to the King," the messenger droned.

Mapitha took a mouthful of ox that was being roasted whole over a large fire nearby. He gulped down some *utshwala*, picked up his Mauser, his spear and shield and went with the messenger to the great hut.

As was customary, he approached the King on his belly.

"Stand, honourable Mapitha of the Ndwandwes," the King called quietly.

He did as he was told and approached the King on a gesture from him.

"Mapitha, one of my *indunas* indeed remembers the mission that my father, the great King Mpande, sent you on more than three summers ago," said the King graciously.

Mapitha nodded.

"There were two others sent with you?" said the King, more in the form of a question than a statement.

"The great Kulaan, he died from the gunshots of the stinking, thieving white horsemen so that Nzobo and I could report to the mighty King."

"And Nzobo?" asked the King.

"Nzobo was badly wounded when stealing the horses of our white pursuers. I left him in the care of a friendly *Ibhunu*. He will return when he is well again."

"Trouble, I sense, O'Hara," muttered one of the whites to the other one.

The King glared at him.

Mapitha translated for the King.

"You speak this heathen tongue?" the King looked surprised.

"*Yebo, Nkosi,* I worked with the stinking whites for three summers and may the souls of their ancestors plague them forever," said Mapitha. "There was one exception, an American," he added guiltily.

"Tell us the story," said the King quietly, "but first sit and have some food and beer."

"The story must be for your ears, oh great *Nkosi*, and for other Zulu ears, not for the ears of the stinking whites," advised one of the *indunas*.

The King was just about to dismiss the whites when Mapitha said, "Great *Nkosi*, let them stay for just a few moments, while I show you what these people treasure above all else. Just watch them; it is as if they are taken over by some sort of spirit, some sort of devil." Mapitha then produced his pouch of diamonds and proceeded carefully to spread them out on a cowhide in front of the King.

There was a sharp intake of breath from both the whites; they both leaned forward and their eyes glittered and their hands shook.

"Jesus, Flynn!" muttered the one who was called O'Hara. The King glanced at Mapitha, who shook his head. "He is just calling on his heathen god," said Mapitha.

"Get your hands on that little package," said Flynn, "and we'd be set up for life in the old country; no more stumbling about among these savages and their heathen ways."

Mapitha translated for the King, who glared at Flynn.

O'Hara stuck out a trembling hand, as if to pick up one of the diamonds. It was withdrawn rapidly when Mapitha stuck a spear in his face, without touching him.

"See the expressions in their eyes…" Mapitha started.

"Stop chattering like a pregnant baboon," growled the King. "Do you not think I have eyes like you?" Then he went on more gently, "but you are right. When I show them my royal herds of cattle and talk about my many wives, they pretend to be interested but they are not, yet these silly stones which do nothing—they can't have children, they can't be eaten—seem to have a magic and dangerous power over these people."

Mapitha nodded and put the diamonds back in the pouch and handed the pouch to the King.

"Now the story," said the King.

"Would you like me to demonstrate the firestick first?" said Mapitha. "This will also frighten the whites."

They all trooped through the massive kraal: King Cetshwayo, Mapitha, about one hundred *indunas*, plus Flynn and O'Hara.

Mapitha was looking for something to shoot at when a warrior came up, holding a thirteen-year-old boy by the arm.

"What do you want?" growled the King.

"This boy, he allowed your precious cattle to stray and one of them was killed by a lion," stammered the warrior.

The normal punishment for this type of transgression was a spear through the heart.

"Use the firestick," ordered the King.

"He will die," said Mapitha.

The King nodded.

The boy, on Mapitha's instructions, was taken about 100 yards away and held by the warrior.

Mapitha levered a round into the well-oiled breach of the Mauser, took careful aim and fired; the poor boy dropped down dead, and after a moment's stunned silence there was a cheer from the King and the *indunas*.

"Jesus Christ, the murderous bastards," muttered O'Hara.

"Keep your bloody mouth shut, O'Hara, or we'll be next," whispered Flynn.

Mapitha reloaded and the King went up to examine the dead boy. He couldn't understand what he had just seen. The warrior, meanwhile, had taken fright and was running away. He knew in the scheme of things that he would be next on the list. A shout went up and the King said to Mapitha, "That one too."

The man was almost one hundred yards away, running fast. Mapitha took careful aim and tried to remember all the lessons he had learnt from his mentor in Kimberley. He squeezed the trigger. The man's arms went up over his head and he fell down in a crumpled heap, amid another amazed cheer from the assembled *indunas*.

There was no thought for the hapless victims, or their families. Their now lifeless bodies were hauled away to the execution mound. The vultures would look after them.

The King's entourage returned to the kraal. Flynn and O'Hara were dismissed and they uncertainly made their way back to one of the many beehive huts that were part of Kwa-Bulawayo. One of the King's *ibutho* had been detailed to look after them. Their every need was provided for, but they were virtual prisoners.

The King was greatly troubled. The power of the rifle truly astounded him. Although he made Mapitha show him how the weapon worked, he barely understood; the concept was so far from anything he had experience of. One thing he did understand: if somehow he could harness the power of the weapon, he could secure the Zulu nation from the increasing depredations of the *abelungu* (whites)—the *amaBhunu* (Boers) in the north and the *amaNgisi* (British) to the south. Cetshwayo again settled his large frame down in the front of the King's hut. He ordered beer for himself and his *Indunas*.

"Now tell me your story," he commanded Mapitha.

Chapter 2

The year was 1867, the place, a drought stricken, decrepit little farm not far from the banks of the Vaal River in the Northern Cape. In time, that unlikely looking place was to become Kimberley, the centre of the world's diamond industry.

Fritz Koekemoer sat at his rough-hewn kitchen table, staring at what could have been a glass bead about the size of a very large marble. He pinched himself: he had a diamond, the biggest diamond the world had ever seen, sitting in front of him on his table. He was now absolutely sure it was what he thought it was. For him, this meant untold riches and escape from this hellhole of a place.

Fritz and his young wife Petronella had come north from the "fairest" Cape three years earlier. He had bought land dirt-cheap from the Cape Government. He didn't like the British, who had now controlled the Cape for more than half a century, but he had not had the courage to join his fellow Boers in the great move north to the fledgling republics of the Transvaal and the Orange Free State. He and his trusting Petronella had dreamt of making themselves rich on the sheep they would raise, and then returning in triumph to the Cape. They had built a small lean-to shack, which consisted of a bedroom and a small kitchen. The toilet was a long drop fifty yards away in the treeless veld. Water came either from a stone tank that Fritz had built to collect water from the corrugated iron roof of their shack, or it had to be laboriously carted from the river in their small scotch cart, which meant inspanning his two oxen.

Fritz owned twenty thousand acres of the driest, dustiest part of the Northern Cape. The land was almost flat. The waist-high, brown grass grew sparsely and appeared to Fritz to have little or no nutritional value. There were no trees but the desolate landscape was dotted with stunted thorn bushes. The nearest neighbour was almost half a day's ride away, since all the landowners had to have large pieces of land to be viable. The Koekemoers had a few *Griqua* herdsmen who looked after the sheep and cattle. The place was lonely and utterly desolate, with baking hot summers and harsh cold winters. The little rain that fell came down in a few fierce summer storms, which had the little *spruits* gushing for a few hours. The sun then came out and parched the landscape once again.

Towards the end of winter there were fierce winds from the west, which created monstrous sand storms. The harsh red sand got in everywhere; right through their little shack and all through the fleeces of those sheep that survived.

The place was desolate and, as far as Fritz and Petronella were concerned, held out no hope of escape.

"This is just temporary," he had promised Petronella when they first arrived. "Just for a few months until we get properly established."

Now, three years later, he was, like most of his fellow settlers round him, almost broke, or worse, almost destitute. Two little graves out in the veld testified to the harshness of the environment. Both children lived little more than a year, and then succumbed to one or other of the innumerable diseases that he and his wife had no idea how to treat. Petronella had changed from a bright, cheerful, optimistic wife to a prematurely aged frump, who took no care with her appearance and treated her husband as a semi-idiotic irrelevance. Although they shared the same bed since there was only one bed, she hadn't allowed him to touch her in months. The *Dominee* wasn't much help. In any event, the low price of sheep and wool, the drought and the fact that the local population stole everything they could from the settlers, was hardly the *Dominee's* fault, even if he did claim that he and God, in that order, would fix everything.

Fritz loathed this place and everything it stood for. He hated the Tswana, "thieving *kaffirs*" as he thought of them, who stole his sheep and cattle and then drove them off into the distant veld, never to be recovered. The *Griquas* were not much better, although they spoke the same Afrikaans *Taal* as the Koekemoers did. They had horses and guns, and had no compunction in driving off settler stock and shooting the settler should there be any resistance.

Petronella came in from her daily ritual of placing some veld flowers on the graves of her children, and then spending an hour praying over them. She dumped a cup of coffee in front of Fritz, spilling some of its contents on the table, and then started busying herself around the kitchen.

"You realise we got diamonds here, on this farm," said Fritz sharply.

"Pffuh," responded Petronella contemptuously, "I heard you gave that little *kaffir* boy a sheep for a glass bead; they're all laughing at you."

"Here *vrou*, look at this—it's a diamond, the biggest the world has ever seen," said Fritz firmly. "Look, hold it up to the light; see how it sparkles. I am sure it is a diamond, not a glass bead."

She ignored him. "You and your stupid dreams. Soon all the sheep will have been stolen by the *kaffirs*, and you will still be sitting here dreaming of riches. How many more children will we have to bury?"

Fritz stood up. He had the diamond in his hand and he roughly pulled Petronella to him.

"Just look *vrou*, just look in the light. This is a diamond; this will be our salvation," he bullied.

Something in his voice had changed. It was no longer the whining, defeated Fritz of the past year or so, but something much closer to the confident, ebullient Fritz that she had married, so she looked.

This was certainly no ordinary glass bead. She was thrilled by the way the light sparkled through the stone, but she wasn't about to give way, not just yet.

"Pffuh, maybe, so what will you do about it?" she asked.

"I now have a collection of more than twenty of these stones, and a few smaller ones as well," said Fritz, "but this one is the best. We will take them to the Cape, and I will sell them after registering claims."

"Twenty stones!" exclaimed Petronella. "How long has this been going on?"

"A few weeks, maybe a couple of months," said Fritz.

"And you didn't say anything?" she asked, exasperated.

"Ag, *vrou*, I wasn't sure, I didn't want to raise your hopes," he responded almost kindly.

Rough Diamonds

"And now?" she asked.

"Now I am sure, we will go soon, tomorrow maybe," he said.

"Fritz, I will not go to the Cape with you, not yet. Not when I look like this. I have nothing to wear and they will all laugh at me, saying, 'Here's the mighty Petronella now, coming back here with her tail between her legs.' Hetty Nel will come to stay. Her no good husband has gone off hunting again, to shoot elephant in *Kgama's* country. Maybe he will be back in a year. You go, and if this is a real diamond, you can come to fetch me, not before."

He hadn't had a speech out of her like that for more than twelve months. What she said made sense. He wondered a little bit about how she and Hetty Nel would manage but he hoped to be back soon. He had two good ponies and had checked them out, and they were sound and well fed. He'd ride one and lead the other; he might make better time doing that. He glanced at his wife; her eyes almost had a sparkle to them again. Perhaps it was not too late for the two of them. Anyway, he knew what he had to do.

Fritz set off early the next morning. He had decided the safest thing to do was to join the main track to the Cape, and then travel together with a wagon train or one of the occasional British military convoys for the four week journey to the Cape. He was completely self-sufficient. Apart from the two ponies, he had a bedroll, a sack of food for the ponies and a quantity of *biltong*, some cooked *mealie-pap* and half a sack of uncooked maize meal, some coffee, and a canister of water.

He was a tall, well-built man with reddish hair. The beard he had grown was black. Few of the farmers shaved, they just trimmed their beards occasionally. He dressed in khaki riding breeches, a khaki shirt and a good pair of riding boots. A waistcoat and jacket and a battered felt hat made up the ensemble. A pair of fierce, almost black eyes looked out from under the hat. The harsh veld had made him tough and strong. Fritz had a Mauser rifle, favoured by many of the Boers, and a bandolier full of cartridges for the rifle. Hidden away underneath his waistcoat was a thirty-eight Smith and Wesson revolver, and strapped firmly to his thigh was one bag of diamonds, which he would never take off, even to wash; he also had another bag of the smaller stones in a jacket pocket. The bedroll and food and water were firmly strapped to the spare pony, and Fritz took his heavy coat and strapped it onto the front of the saddle on his mount. Petronella had let him have a kettle and some pots and pans. He had a good, sharp, bush knife on his belt.

The first few days of the journey were uneventful. He shot a springbok on the second day, which gave him some fresh meat. On one occasion he came uncomfortably close to a pride of lions. The horses bolted when they saw the lions, and it was all Fritz could do to stay in the saddle until the horses exhausted themselves and he was able to bring them under control again. The track was littered with human debris: broken wagon wheels and the bones of dead animals, mostly oxen and horses. Once he saw a complete tent, and on several occasions graves, often with crude, wooden crosses over them.

Some time late in the first week he overtook a small wagon train, consisting of two covered wagons owned by a white driver, who was helped by three coloureds from the Cape. They transported much needed supplies to the Northern Cape area, where the Koekemoers had settled.

On one occasion, when they were sitting round the campfire after their evening meal, Karel De Wet engaged him in a conversation that troubled him greatly.

"Things not too good up in that Northern Cape region?" De Wet said, more as a question than a statement.

"*Kaffirs* and *Griquas* steal everything that moves and the drought has been bad this year," responded Fritz.

"Much slower for us too," said De Wet. "There used to be ten people I knew transporting goods up there; now there's only me and one other."

Fritz, squatting comfortably on his haunches, took a long pull on his tobacco pipe, spat into the fire and said nothing.

"There's rumours of diamonds being found up there," De Wet looked at Fritz speculatively.

Trying to control his churning stomach, Fritz spat nonchalantly into the fire again.

"*Ja*, I heard those rumours too. Like many others up there, I spent weeks panning for gold and diamonds in the riverbeds. Nothing," Fritz responded as calmly as he could.

"Panning, never heard of no panning," De Wet responded. "Maybe next trip I should take some panning equipment."

Fritz shrugged as if it were of no interest.

When De Wet asked where his farm was, Fritz gave him rough directions to a farm some forty miles from the Koekemoer place. Fritz did not mention his name.

De Wet looked at him shrewdly. He turned the discussion to other matters. Fritz told him that his father had died, and he had to return to the Cape to clear up his affairs.

"Maybe there's even a small inheritance," he offered. "Could keep us going until the better times come."

He also made sure that De Wet knew his wife had been left to look after the farm. He just wanted De Wet to forget about the diamonds.

Fritz stayed with De Wet for another day or so after the diamond conversation and then, at night, when he thought everyone was asleep, he crept off into the veld and travelled for the rest of the night and all the next day to put as much distance as he could between himself and De Wet. He wanted to get as far away as possible from this man who seemed to know too much.

De Wet, in the meanwhile, could not get the conversation with Fritz out of his mind. He wondered whether Fritz was the rumoured diamond carrier. Fritz had behaved quite oddly after the conversation and had unnecessarily waved his pistol around as if to give De Wet a message. Even a small cache of diamonds would make all the difference to De Wet's life; there would be no more of this traipsing backwards and forwards to the dusty, miserable Northern Cape. He imagined himself owning a wine farm near Stellenbosch. Maybe he should kill Fritz and dump his body in the veld, where the wild animals would look after it.

Something woke him in the middle of the night and when he got up to investigate he found Fritz and all his equipment had gone. He was now convinced that Fritz was indeed the diamond carrier and he decided to try to follow him, so much to the surprise of his coloured helpers they were on their way long before the dawn.

Almost two weeks had passed since Fritz left Petronella, and he estimated that he was about half way to the Cape. He'd hardly given Petronella a thought since the journey began, he remembered guiltily.

Two days later, Fritz was just considering making camp in a dry, boulder-strewn riverbed, when a platoon of British dragoons clattered up.

"This looks like a good place to camp," said Lieutenant North, who was in charge, and then he noticed Fritz.

"Oh! Mind if we join you?" he asked.

"Help yourself," said Fritz. He hoped that the diamond rumours had stayed within the Afrikaans farming community and that the hated British would have heard nothing of it.

There were a few scraggy trees around the campsite, which had obviously been used by many other travellers. Fritz had already made a small fire, which the soldiers shared. They ate their respective meals from their own sources.

Normally such a gathering would have been quite jolly and an attempt would have been made to share stories round the fire over coffee. There was, however, a curious tension among the men, which Fritz could not put his finger on.

Fritz then made a show of taking a small shovel he had with him and his water canister.

"Just going for a crap," he said.

The soldiers watched him go without saying a word.

Fritz made a point of crashing through the bushes and then, using his considerable bush craft, crept back towards the fire. He stayed just outside the firelight and hid behind a boulder, out of sight but within easy earshot of the group round the fire.

"This must be the fucker," said one of them.

"Doesn't look like a diamond hunter to me," said another.

"Look, there was a strong rumour that there was a man carrying a fortune in diamonds riding to the Cape." said the lieutenant.

Fritz's heart nearly stopped beating.

"This fellow said his name was Stompie something," said another.

"I think this is our man," said Lieutenant North. "All we need to do is to keep a cool head and we'll be rich. When the man is asleep you, corporal, will shoot him. We'll find the diamonds and then take the corpse off into the veld, where the hyenas and jackals will deal with it. We'll scatter his goods and chase his horses away. The man will simply disappear. Is that clear?" They all nodded.

Fritz was paralysed for a few seconds. He wondered how he could escape and how many other predatory people were on his trail. As he went back to the camp he heard a disturbance and a bedraggled and tired looking De Wet and his wagons rumbled into the camp.

Despite his clandestine escape from De Wet only two days earlier Fritz greeted him like a long lost friend. Much to De Wet's surprise, Fritz helped him settle his oxen and set up camp. When Fritz thought that they were out of earshot of the British soldiers, he whispered:

"*Meneer* De Wet, I need your help. These people have also heard the rumours about diamonds being taken to the Cape and they think that I am the one carrying them. I overheard them discussing how they would shoot me and leave my body out in the veld."

"Are you carrying diamonds?" asked De Wet.

"No, *meneer*, no. I told you my business."

De Wet looked at Fritz shrewdly. He was certain that Fritz was lying and

 Rough Diamonds

he was the diamond carrier. Still, he wanted the diamonds himself and he was not about to let a bunch of British soldiers steal them from under his nose.

"O.K. I'll help you, but you had better listen to me or we'll both be shot."

Fritz nodded, thinking that he would make a run for it as soon as he could and leave De Wet to face the music.

They returned to the fire and De Wet ate his meal under the watchful and impatient eye of the soldiers. Having said very little, Fritz and De Wet moved away. Fritz moved his own bedding to where De Wet had his camp and looked at him expectantly.

"We need to get out of here as soon as we can," said De Wet. "But I must let the oxen rest for a day at least. They are very tired."

Nothing had been said about Fritz leaving De Wet's camp in the middle of the night. Nothing needed to be said; it hung over them like a swirling mist, with both of them floundering around wondering what to do and not trusting the other.

"One of us two and one of my men will stay up and keep watch all night," said De Wet calmly. "You take first watch." That suited Fritz, he couldn't possibly have slept anyway.

Over at the soldiers' camp a long discussion ensued on the subject of how they could lay their hands on the diamonds.

"We'll keep an eye on the situation," said the lieutenant. "It should be easy enough to get rid of one person, but now this tradesman has arrived, it makes things much more complicated. We will just have to track this fellow and see how we get on. Does anyone know his name?"

There was silence for a few moments.

"I think we should go and sort the two of them out now," volunteered Corporal Jones. "Take them by surprise. It won't take us long to make everything disappear. They have no reason to suspect anything."

"Go over there, then, and see if they have a watch on. If they don't, then they probably suspect nothing. If they do, then that tells us they are careful, at least, if nothing more. And Corporal," Jones looked up, "Don't do anything stupid, just come back and report."

Corporal Jones carefully walked the one hundred yards to the Afrikaners' camp, using the dim light of a half-moon. He made sure that he was visible; the last thing he wanted was a surprise bullet. Fritz saw him coming and moved into the shadows. "Make sure that he sees you," he whispered to the Coloured wagoner.

The Coloured spoke only Afrikaans and when Jones approached, asked him what he wanted. He made sure that Jones could see the rifle he was carrying.

Jones didn't understand, but said: "Just came to make sure that you were OK."

All he got was a scowl.

Fritz knew what the soldier had come for and knew that if he wanted to survive he would have to take drastic action. He had no doubt that the soldiers would have killed him if De Wet had not been there, and he thought that De Wet would probably do the same thing given half a chance. His mind strayed to the decrepit shack that was his home—it now looked like a haven and he longed for the safety of his drought stricken farm. He knew his only chance was to escape during the night; if he fell asleep he would be killed.

Jones reported back to the others that there was indeed a watch on and they had no chance of taking the Afrikaners by surprise during the night.

"We'll keep an eye on the situation; things may change," said Lieutenant North. Two of the men were instructed to keep watch on the Afrikaners' camp. "Make certain that you can't be seen," he directed.

Fritz waited until he thought both camps were quiet. He told his Coloured companion to stay on one side of the De Wet encampment whilst he watched the other. In particular he told the man to watch out for the soldiers and to make sure that they stayed where they were. He quietly packed up his bedroll, crept over to where his two horses were tethered and strapped everything on ready for his escape.

Fritz returned to his camp to check that he had left nothing. He was sweating despite the cold night air of the Great Karoo. In a panic, he wondered what to do: should he leave and make a run for it? That was surely the safest thing to do; maybe he would get four or five hours' start and then with his bushcraft he should be able to lose the soldiers, whom he felt would have limited skill in the South African bush. Perhaps, before he left, he should release the soldiers' horses and lead them off into the *veld*. On the other hand, he pondered, perhaps it would be better to stick with De Wet and hope that together they could see the British soldiers off.

The matter was taken out of his hands. De Wet came out of the shadows with a rifle pointed straight at Fritz.

"Where do you think you are going this time, you *skellum?* You think that you are going to run off again and leave me to deal with the lousy British, don't you? What are you so scared of, if you don't have the diamonds?" The questions, more in the nature of statements came out quietly, but Fritz had no doubt of De Wet's determination, and that one false move would result in his death.

"You say you have no diamonds!" De Wet continued. "What the hell are these?" He produced the small packet that Fritz recognized came out of his jacket pocket. He instinctively reached down into his jacket. De Wet raised the rifle threateningly. "Keep your hands up, or I really will shoot you. Yes, that is where I found them." Fritz remembered leaving his jacket hanging up while he was helping De Wet set up camp. "So now what do you have to say?" asked De Wet.

Fritz remained silent. He hoped that De Wet was now satisfied and would leave him alone; he doubted that the man had any knowledge of the modest value of what he was trying to steal from Fritz. Comforted by the feel of the other, much more valuable, package, strapped to his leg, which neither De Wet nor the soldiers had any knowledge of, Fritz just stared at De Wet. The stand-off lasted no more than ten minutes, with De Wet trying to provoke Fritz into a false move and Fritz just staring him out and staying silent.

There was an eerie silence and then the sound of a twig breaking, followed immediately by a barked order which Fritz recognized as the voice of the British Lieutenant: "Hands up and don't move!" Since he already had his hands up, he did nothing. A ring of red-coated soldiers emerged into the pale moonlight and three or four rifle barrels were jammed into his ribs. He could see the same happening to De Wet, and the packet of diamonds was found and snatched away.

"We now have the diamonds, sir," said Corporal Jones, after examining the contents of the packet "Shall we finish these people off, sir, as we agreed?"

"Patience, Corporal, patience," answered North.

Ignoring his senior's words, Jones moved quickly towards De Wet with his rifle at the ready. Then there was the crack of a rifle shot and Jones slumped down into the dusty *veld* howling, and clutching his leg. The soldiers had forgotten the presence of the Coloured wagoners, or had not realized they were armed.

De Wet slipped behind a tree and loosed off a fusillade of shots; two of the soldiers were hit and lay writhing on the ground in agony, and the rest scattered. The soldiers holding Fritz left him and dived for cover.

Unseen by DeWet Fritz flattened himself behind a small rock. With the soldiers focused on personal survival, he was able to slip off unnoticed into the darkness and sneak over to where his horses nervously waited. Everything was ready for departure: his rifle was in its scabbard, and he still had his revolver. The only thing that was missing was a small packet of diamonds, and whoever had them now as welcome to them. One problem remained—the danger of pursuit. Running the fifty yards to where the soldiers' horses were tethered, he released them all; mounting his own horse he herded them all off into the *veld* at a canter.

He made good time on the main track heading south, then at daybreak he left the track and by noon he camped in a clump of rocks. From now on he would avoid all contact with people until he arrived in the Cape. It was clear that he could trust nobody and he wondered where all the rumours had come from that were plaguing him. Petronella had probably told Hetty Nel what he was up to and the story had spread from there.

The sparse grasslands of the almost waterless Northern Cape had given way to the saltbush of the Great Karoo. Fritz avoided all other travellers like the plague. Whenever he saw a plume of dust, he diverted off into the veld and made sure he was not seen. During the long days, he wondered about the soldiers and De Wet and what they would do.

Piet Koekemoer was sitting on his stoep in the little village of Stellenbosch enjoying a small glass of brandy and his pipe, when he noticed something familiar about a very ragged, dirty man riding up the street, leading another pony. Piet, as usual on a Sunday, had spent the morning in church and was still dressed in his Sunday best, including his top hat. He was idly wondering what the morrow would bring to his substantial legal practice, when, to his horror, the man stopped in front of his house and dismounted. He was about to ask him to move on when the man greeted him.

"Hello, *Oom* Piet, its Fritz," said the man.

You could have knocked him down with a feather. That no good schemer of a nephew of his, who had taken that pretty Petronella to some hell hole in the Northern Cape. Piet got up.

"Fritz, my goodness, so it is! You really do look a mess; please come in," said Piet.

He made Fritz take the horses round the back and watched while he unsaddled them and watered and fed the animals.

Not much was said. Piet wondered what sort of tragedy had befallen his nephew, but he held his tongue. Besides, Fritz gave off an air of anticipation rather than tragedy.

Piet had been widowed these many years and lived quite simply. He did for himself on Sundays; this being God's day of rest, even his coloured maid had the day off. He showed Fritz to a spare room and said, "Make

Rough Diamonds

yourself at home. When you've had a wash, come out onto the stoep and tell me your business."

One glance in the mirror was enough for Fritz. Forty minutes later he came out on the stoep looking slightly better; but he was still in his dirty old clothes, since he had no clean ones, and although he had done his best with his beard and hair, he still looked like someone who had just spent a month in the *veld*.

Piet poured him a *dop* of brandy and asked politely, "How's the beautiful Petronella?"

"Fine, when I left the farm about a month ago," said Fritz.

"And the farm?"

"Bad drought, *kaffirs* steal everything," was the response.

Piet waited.

"Oom Piet, what do you know about the diamond business?" Fritz asked eventually.

"A little; I've registered a few claims for people," said Piet. Fritz nodded; his eyes glittered. If he had anything to do with it, Piet would register many more in the next few days.

After much fumbling in his ragged trousers, Fritz eventually produced the pouch of diamonds. He laid them out carefully on the table in front of his uncle. Piet's jaw nearly dropped to the floor.

"*Vragtig* Fritz, where," he could hardly get the words out, "where the hell did these come from?"

"From the farm, *Oom*; they were picked up by the *Griqua* herd boys on the farm."

"These are priceless," said Piet, "and that big one, I've never seen anything like it." Piet was cautious, he didn't want to excite Fritz too much; he also doubted that Fritz knew the real value of his hoard of diamonds.

Fritz nodded.

"Aren't they pretty, *Oom*? They will make men go crazy."

Piet Nodded

Piet had a feeling that Fritz was holding back on something. He felt that enough had been said for one day, but he was determined to find out more. Fritz had always been devious and Piet had often found him wanting in his past dealings with him.

The next morning, being a Monday, Piet said to Fritz at breakfast, "First things first—we can't let you run around a respectable place like Stellenbosch looking like one of your precious *Griquas*." Fritz could see the sense in that;

but he was more concerned about the incident with De Wet and the soldiers and he wanted to change his appearance as much as possible to avoid the chance of detection should anyone start looking for him.

"I don't have much money," was Fritz's response.

Piet looked at him. This nephew really was na ve, he thought. He has a fortune wrapped up in that that rag of his tied to his leg and he makes remarks like that.

"That's O.K.,"he said neutrally. I'll lend you whatever you need."

Looking like a real man about town Fritz, now clean shaven and attired in a fancy suit with shiny riding boots, rode together with his uncle the twenty miles to Cape Town and went to the department of mines to register claims.

Together they registered dozens of claims throughout he area surrounding the Koekemoer farm. Where possible they used their own names, but they used the names of every imaginable relative as well.

"We may lose a few of these claims," said Piet, "because we can't work them all, but I suspect we will also be able to sell many of them."

Fritz nodded. Piet suggested that they register the claims in blocks; they might be more valuable then. Fritz had no idea; he went along with whatever Piet said.

They called a family gathering and explained the situation, and also showed them the diamonds. Amid the excitement, almost all the men decided to make their way to the Northern Cape and join the search for diamonds.

Frank Devereaux, an American, had briefly joined the California gold rush some years earlier, but no luck had come his way. Some instinct had sent him to South Africa to seek his fortune, and he happened to be staying with one of the Koekemoer relatives, so he was invited to the meeting.

When Fritz displayed the diamonds, Frank could barely contain himself. This was it! This was the way to restore his fortune.

Once the excitement had died down, Frank managed to address the throng. He told them he was a mining engineer, which was only partly true. His studies had been interrupted by a family crisis, and he had not completed them. He also told them that he had been involved in the California gold rush, and his experience during that episode would materially help the Koekemoer clan in their new adventure. Frank was very engaging, and it seemed almost natural that he would be part of the expedition.

Frank came from what had been a wealthy Virginia family with large cotton plantations and many slaves. Everything had been destroyed in the civil war. His parents had been killed, the big house burnt to the ground and there was nothing left of the plantations. All the slaves had now been freed, of course. Frank's elder brother was vainly trying to re-establish the place. Frank was committed to finding a way to help him find the money to achieve that. The discovery of diamonds seemed to fit the bill exactly.

Within two weeks, Frank and a group of a seventeen Koekemoer relatives had embarked in five wagons, loaded with everything they could think of for the trip north and the search for diamonds. So far as a leader was needed, Frank became the unofficial leader. Piet had funded the entire expedition, but he really wanted Fritz to be part of the group that went north. Although he still had his doubts about Fritz, he thought that wealth might have a steadying influence on the man, and Fritz had, after all, actually found diamonds and had lived in the Northern Cape for three years.

As soon as the family meeting was over, Frank had helped them draw up lists of required supplies.

"All I ask is 10% of whatever you find," Piet told them. "I expect some of them will pay gladly and some not," he confided in Fritz later. "All in all, I expect to become quite a rich man when all is said and done." He had also helped Frank register some claims in his own name.

When the wagons pulled out of Stellenbosch on their way north, Piet told Fritz that they could now sell his hoard of diamonds.

"When news of this gets out, this place will become a madhouse, but now our people have a head start. There are already rumours, as you know," Piet said. He didn't know whether there were rumours or not, but he wanted a reaction from Fritz.

Fritz looked completely uninterested.

Fritz had already written to Petronella, suggesting she return post haste to the Cape. He spent the next few weeks looking at wine farms in the Stellenbosch area. He couldn't believe how his life had been transformed in the past few weeks. From an almost hopeless situation, he thought that shortly he would be in the position of owning a substantial wine farm quite close to the very pretty town of Stellenbosch. He admired the town's Cape Dutch style houses, with their rounded, white gables contrasting attractively with the dark thatch of the roofs. Stellenbosch was mostly Dutch speaking, so he wouldn't have to worry much about the hated English. With all the excitement he had almost managed to forget the unpleasantness of the incident in the Karoo.

Piet had taken charge of the diamonds. "I will keep them in a safe I have in the office," he told the trusting Fritz. "They can't come to any harm there."

Unbeknown to Fritz, while he was looking at wine farms, and dreaming of his new life in the Cape, Piet had taken the diamonds to a dealer called Minski in Cape Town, whom he had known for many years.

"Come in, come in. Coffee?" Piet was ushered into the man's small, untidy office.

Both waited for the other to speak.

"How's business?" asked Piet.

"O.K." was the non-committal response.

"Any new developments?"

"Not really."

Minski waited; he knew that Piet would not have come all the way into Cape Town for nothing, but he was not one for just giving out information.

After a lengthy silence Piet pulled the packet of diamonds from his pocket and spread them out in front of Minski, who unsuccessfully tried to maintain his composure.

"*Meneer* Koekemoer, where…where in God's name did you get these from? This, this one in particular"—he held up the big stone, and spoke in a strangled voice "is probably the biggest and best stone I have ever been privileged to see."

"What is it worth?" asked Piet.

Minski shrugged. "I don't know, I may need some help in valuing it. A stone like this will have a high profile in the market. I trust that it comes from a registered claim."

Piet nodded.

"Will you tell me where these came from?"

"Can I trust you to keep this confidential?"

"Of course, you know me *Meneer* Koekemoer."

"Northern Cape. Maybe one of the first from there."

Minski raised his eyebrows.

Piet looked at him shrewdly. "You have had others? It is important to me to know. This is obviously a major find," he said, waving his hand over the diamonds, "and I am trying to keep it quiet as long as possible, for reasons which I am sure you understand." Piet smiled thinly.

"I had a small packet brought to me yesterday," Minski said. "I think that the man was an army officer. They came from the same place as these, although they are of lower quality."

"Can we compare them?"

   Rough Diamonds

"They are no longer here," answered Minski. "However as I said they are from the same source."

"Do you know how an army officer came to be owning diamonds?" asked Piet.

Minski shrugged. "Maybe he stole them; he was very nervous and he accepted a low price; clearly he knew nothing of their value."

"How much for these?" asked Piet.

"As I said, I need help with this. You do not need to worry though; nothing will go outside this room. Stay here and I will call my friend."

He left Piet alone in the room and ten minutes later returned with another fat little man, who had a pair of piggy little eyes peering out from under a brown bowler hat. Piet was not introduced and the man virtually ignored him but spent a good half hour peering at the diamonds with an eyeglass.

"Magnificent, magnificent," the man repeated from time to time.

There was a hurried conversation in a language that Piet did not understand and the man left.

"Three hundred," offered Minski.

Piet shook his head, and after another hour they finally settled on one thousand and fifty pounds.

Minski said nothing and gave Piet two receipts and two cheques, one for seven hundred pounds in Piet's name and one for three hundred and fifty pounds in Fritz's name. Piet gave him all the details of the claims from which the diamonds came.

One evening over dinner a few days later Piet asked Fritz whether he had had any luck finding a farm that he liked.

"*Ja*, plenty, plenty," said Fritz. "But I don't know whether I can afford any of them yet. It will depend on what we can get for the diamonds."

"What sort of prices are they asking?" Piet knew the answer perfectly well, but he wanted to see what Fritz's perspective was.

"They seem expensive," answered Fritz, I saw one at one hundred and fifty pounds and another at one hundred and seventy-five pounds. Can we really get that sort of money for the diamonds, *oom?* I hope that we can but I don't want to over commit myself."

"Ja, Fritz, maybe the farms are expensive, but I have some good news for you and maybe some not so good news."

Fritz looked up expectantly.

"I sold the diamonds for three fifty. Here is your receipt and bank deposit."

Fritz looked stunned. "Is this real?" he said almost to himself.

"It is as real as I am sitting here, you can get the money at any time. So you can probably afford a good farm."

"*Dankie, dankie, oom,* you have saved my life. I will buy you a nice present." He tried to hug his uncle.

Piet waved him away. "It's all in the family Fritz, I would do it for any of the family, but I told you that there was some other not so good news. Do you want to hear about that too?"

Saying nothing, Fritz looked up; he had an idea what was coming.

Piet really needed Fritz to be part of the family expedition to the Northern Cape and it was clear that all Fritz wanted to do was to settle down to a life of leisure on his wine farm somewhere in the Stellenbosch area. Piet had been racking his brains to find a way, by fair means or foul, to persuade Fritz to be a part of the family search for diamonds. Instinctively he also wanted Fritz out of the way, since he had swindled him out of two thirds of what was rightly his; Piet did not want to be reminded on a regular basis that part of his own wealth was the result of stealing from his relative.

After he had sold the diamonds Piet had spent another two days in Cape Town, looking for something, he was not really sure what. He knew from Fritz's demeanour that he was hiding something. He also wanted to buy every wagon and team of oxen that he could lay his hands on, since he was sure that there would be a rush to the north when the news of the diamond discovery emerged. So he trolled some of the coffee shops and drinking houses he knew and talked to as many friends and acquaintances as he could.

At first he came up with nothing. The town was going about its normal business and there were certainly no rumours about a major diamond find. When he enquired about wagons for sale he was told that there was another person, whose business was transporting goods to the Northern Cape, who was in the market for wagons and maybe he should talk to him. Piet was directed to a rough and ready yard on the outskirts of town and found Karel De Wet busy repairing a wagon with the help of a coloured employee. There were two other almost new wagons in the yard.

Piet tried to engage him in conversation and after the normal greetings said to him:

"Business must be picking up in the north there." It was more a statement than a question. De Wet shrugged, as if it was of no interest.

"If you want to sell me some of your wagons, I would pay you a good price."

"What do you want them for?" was the suspicious answer.

"Transport, I am in the transport business."

"I know all the people in the business, why haven't I seen you before?" De Wet was becoming increasingly uncomfortable and wanted to get rid of his visitor.

"I am acting on behalf of a few private investors; they think that there may be opportunities opening up in the north."

"Drought is bad and there are fewer operators now than there were a few years ago, so business is not so good at the moment."

"I see two new wagons over there." Piet gestured. "Business can't be that bad."

De Wet shrugged.

Piet could see that the conversation was going nowhere, so he decided to take a chance.

"There are rumours of a diamond find in the north, is that what you want the wagons for?"

There was a momentary look of panic on De Wet's features, and then he recovered his composure. He said nothing.

"I have some funds to invest in wagons and other transport equipment," Piet continued. "I actually have no interest in looking for diamonds, but if the rumours are true—and they are getting stronger—there will be a fortune to be made in transport and supplies. I may need someone with your experience to help me manage the business from this end. There will be a major rush, if there really has been a diamond find."

"I know nothing of any diamonds," said De Wet cagily. "But, *meneer*, what have you heard?"

"I have a friend, a diamond dealer, who told me that he had been offered a small package of diamonds from the north. He wondered if it was the start of a new find?"

De Wet looked startled.

Piet continued: "You travel up there often enough. Have you heard any of these rumours?"

"*Ag, meneer*, there are always rumours. You hear something here and something over there."

"And you don't know anything about the package that my diamond dealer friend was offered? Maybe from an army officer."

Without saying anything De Wet shook his head.

Piet took his leave saying: "Maybe you will think about what I have said. I will be back in a few days to see if you have any interest."

He then went round to a small, undistinguished house in district six, to see a Coloured acquaintance, who had helped him in the past.

Piet was always treated with due deference by his host, one Tertius Neethling, who was a small man with a shrewd expression on his face Although they were not on the same social plane Piet had always paid him well and more importantly treated him with respect, which contrasted deeply with the way he was treated by most whites. He listened carefully while Piet explained what he needed, which was some more information on De Wet's operations and why, in particular, he was investing in more wagons when due to the drought, business in the Northern Cape was quite bad. Piet sipped the cup of very sweet coffee he had been given by Tertius' wife.

"There are two or three Coloured helpers in De Wet's outfit. See what you can find out from them." He handed over a few coins. "This should help loosen their tongues."

Fritz looked up expectantly at Piet.

"The rumours are already out; the dealer that I went to had already purchased another package from a man he thought may have been an army officer. He said that there was no doubt the package I sold him and the other one came from the same source. You don't know of any other finds up in that area, do you?"

Fritz felt his gut tighten.

"No," he cautiously replied.

"Anyway, the dealer said he would try to keep everything quiet for as long as he could, but as soon as he sold the big stone there was bound to be a rush up north."

Piet was watching Fritz and at the start of the conversation and noticed his nervousness. He was obviously hiding something.

"Anyway, I am buying up all the wagons I can find and I am trying to persuade a man called Karel De Wet…"

There was a big intake of breath from Fritz, which stopped Piet in mid-sentence.

"You don't know this man do you? He runs a transport business up to the Northern Cape. To your part of the world."

Fritz shook his head.

"Well, I have said I will go back and see him in a few days, and I think you should come with me. As you know I am buying up as many wagons as I can lay my hands on; once the news gets out there is going to be a mad rush and I expect to double my money. I need a person like De Wet to help find the wagons. You should put some of your own money into wagons as well, and the same will happen to you."

Piet noticed that Fritz had gone a shade paler.

"Is anything the matter, Fritz? You look as if you have seen a ghost. Are you sure that you don't know De Wet?"

Fritz shook his head. He wondered if he should tell Piet the whole story about De Wet and the soldiers. After all, he had actually done nothing wrong, except perhaps drive the soldiers' horses off into the *veld*, although in his heart of hearts he knew that if either De Wet or the soldiers told the story, somehow he, Fritz, would end up in the wrong. They had stolen a packet of diamonds, but he wanted no trouble and since he now had more than enough money, had put it all out of his mind. He felt that that packet of diamonds had actually saved his life and he wanted nothing more from them. Now nothing must upset his dream. He had money in the bank, Petronella would be here soon and then they would buy their farm and quietly forget all about the Northern Cape, diamonds or anything else from the recent past. In any case it was too late to confess to Piet; he had told too many lies already and he wanted to maintain the new respect that Piet seemed to have for him. If he said anything now, Piet would think badly of him, and he didn't want that.

After Piet's visit De Wet had rushed round to the area near the Castle and found Lieutenant North just entering one of the drinking establishments.

He looked at De Wet coldly: "I thought we had agreed that there would be no contact," he muttered.

"We did, but this is important. Can we find somewhere private?"

They found a dark corner in a Pub down an alley.

"Be quick," said North. "I don't want to raise suspicions."

After Fritz had left the encampment and because the soldiers only managed to recover three or four horses, both parties had come to their senses. De Wet had agreed to provide transport for the soldiers to Cape Town, including the wounded ones, and they had agreed to share the proceeds from the diamonds. De Wet had eventually negotiated for a twenty percent share and the soldiers took the rest. The proceeds were what he had used to buy the extra wagons. They also agreed to put the blame on Fritz for shooting the soldiers; if he were ever caught and charged he would be lucky to escape the gallows.

De Wet told North of Piet's visit.

"Well what are you worried about? The man only seems to be

fishing for information, from what you have told me."

"I don't like it," answered De Wet. "Between him and the dealer they had identified you as an army officer, and where do army officers get access to diamonds? I can tell you, it is very dangerous. If people start asking questions, the story will come out and then what?"

"Just keep your head and don't tell anyone anything. I expect it it will all blow over. Don't come back here unless it is absolutely imperative."

They left the pub separately.

On three or four separate occasions Piet made arrangements for Fritz to accompany him to Cape Town to see De Wet, and on every one Fritz found some reason why he was unable to go. He urgently had to see a farm; he feigned sickness and so on. Piet patiently cancelled his visit and made other arrangements; there was now no doubt in his mind that Fritz probably knew De Wet and for reasons yet to be discovered was very reluctant to see him. He tried questioning Fritz on more than one occasion but Fritz denied all knowledge of the man.

Piet paid another visit to Tertius Neethling on his own. Tertius had provided De Wet's Coloured assistants with copious amounts of cheap Cape wine and after several visits managed to extract the full story of the confrontation in the *veld* between Fritz, De Wet and the soldiers.

"De Wet and the soldiers took a packet of diamonds from this other *oke*, who was travelling alone. They were going to kill him, but somehow he escaped and drove all the soldiers' horses off into the veld. Three of the soldiers were wounded and *meneer* De Wet agreed to transport them back to Cape Town. They argued about the split most of the way back here, apparently. De Wet used his share to buy more wagons. He thinks there will be a rush up to the Northern Cape area as soon as the news gets out." As always Tertius' reports were accurate and to the point.

"Did you get a description of this other *oke* as you describe him?"

The description he gave could have fitted Fritz as he was when he first arrived in Stellenbosch. "He was riding one horse and leading another, you say?" asked Piet.

Tertius nodded.

"And they are going to put all the blame on this other traveller, the one they stole the diamonds from."

Again Tertius nodded.

"This traveller, did you find out whether he fired any of the shots that wounded the soldiers?"

"No, he did not have a gun with him when they were shot."

As usual Piet paid Tertius more than they had agreed and returned to Stellenbosch. He now thought that he had most of the story, but he failed to understand why Fritz had not confided in him. Piet didn't really care, he never had had much time for his nephew and he now thought that he could manipulate the situation to suit his own ends. Piet was concerned about the expedition he had funded, now going north with his inexperienced relatives, and led by that American. He really wanted Fritz to be part of the venture and now he thought that he had the ammunition to persuade Fritz to make himself scarce for a few years at least, until the matter had been forgotten.

Fritz had now run out of excuses and he and Piet rose early and found their way to De Wet's yard on the outskirts of the bustling metropolis of Cape Town. Piet noticed that Fritz had taken great care with his dress and he looked almost foppish, in great contrast to his appearance when he first arrived on Piet's doorstep a few short weeks earlier. He also wore a wide brimmed hat, which partially kept his face in shadow.

During the visit it was all that Piet could do to prevent himself from bursting out laughing. De Wet kept looking at Fritz with a worried expression on his face, as if there was something familiar about him and Fritz kept his mouth shut after a very brief and perfunctory greeting. Fritz would not take his hat off even when they were inside. De Wet after some persuasion on Piet's part agreed to act as Piet's agent, buying up all the wagons and equipment that he could lay his hands on for a generous commission. Fritz had wandered outside at the conclusion of the discussions and Piet then had a few minutes on his own with De Wet.

"*Meneer* De Wet," said Piet in an unmistakably threatening tone, which made De Wet suddenly sit up and take note. He had been busy thinking about how he could maximize his earnings from this windfall on top of the bonus he had received from the diamonds. "I am about to tell you a story, which I know is true; if you try to deny it, I can promise you that you will be in deep trouble." He then related the tale that Tertius had told him, with De Wet going very pale but keeping silent. "If this story gets out, the discovery of diamonds in the north will become well known sooner than is necessary and that suits neither me nor you. We will make a fortune if we can keep it quiet and buy up all the wagons and so on as we have discussed. You will tell that Lieutenant North that he had better take the next available ship back to England and forget that any of this ever happened. If the police start asking questions he and you will be in the dock, not that poor sod from whom you stole the diamonds. Remember I have all the evidence to put both of you away for a good many years."

De Wet started to protest but Piet held up his hand. "I don't want to hear it. You can make a fortune if you and North keep your mouths shut, and if you don't, you will end up in jail. You have quite an easy decision, I think."

A few days later De Wet had an unexpected visit from Lieutenant North. "This is a surprise," said De Wet, "actually I have some news for you." He told North of the visit from Piet.

North was dismissive. "I have resigned my commission and a few of us from the troop have decided that we will go and look for diamonds up there in the north. We must go ahead of the rush though. When the news gets out there will be a rush, I am sure of that. What I want from you is a wagon or two and we will be off in a few days."

"What have you done about the wounded soldiers? What have you told the army?" asked De Wet.

"There will be an enquiry, which will take months. I thought about it and when I decided to try to be one of the first up in the north I just told them a cock and bull story, which has kept them off my back for the moment. When they wake up I will far away. Nothing has been mentioned about the diamonds."

North happily acquired the two wagons that De Wet had just bought for double what he had paid in the first place.

A day or so later just when Fritz was feeling more comfortable about his situation, Piet decided to tackle him about the incident in the *veld* with the soldiers and De Wet. Fritz now beleived that his new appearance would effectively disguise him and since neither De Wet nor the soldiers knew his name, he felt safe. Petronella would be in Stellenbosch within a week or so and then they could settle down quietly and enjoy their new-found good fortune.

They were enjoying a brandy on the *stoep* when Piet decided to drop his bombshell.

"Fritz, there is something that you should be aware of; the police are looking for a man who looks very much like you," he lied. "Some soldiers were shot in the *veld* and they say he also drove off their horses and they almost died; luckily a man with some wagons came along and helped them."

Fritz shook his head; he could see his dream going up in smoke there and then. "Nothing to do with me."

"Fritz, I am your uncle, you can trust me; I have helped you with many things including selling your diamonds. If you try to deal with this on your own, as sure as I am sitting here you will go to the gallows or spend many years in jail. I know the story is true and now you are lying to me." He pressed home his advantage: "Fritz, I am very disappointed in you, I thought that you had turned over a new leaf, with your new found wealth, but I see it is still the same old Fritz sitting there in front of me."

Fritz hung his head.

Piet then calmly told him the full story, as he understood it.

"Well?" questioned Piet.

Much to Piet's surprise Fritz burst into tears.

"Those bastards, De Wet and the soldiers, they wanted to kill me and take the diamonds. Luckily I had the good ones strapped to my leg and all they got away with was the smaller packet. They wanted to kill me, *oom*, and I did not touch a hair of the head of any soldier."

"I know that, but that is not what the police are saying. Why the hell didn't you tell me this earlier?"

"They were always going to tell lies about me, *oom*. I don't know why I didn't tell you; I didn't want anything to spoil the dream. I'm sorry. Is there anything you can do to help me? I do not want to go to jail, especially for something that I did not do."

"Well you can't stay here in the Cape for much longer, but I'm sure the police are too busy to send their officers very far out of the Cape area, so you should probably leave the area altogether."

"What about Petronella? She will be here in a day or two."

"*Ja*, you can buy the wine farm that you had in mind and leave her there, until all this has blown over. I can help you with all that. You won't be able to return for five years at least, maybe more."

"Five years!" Fritz was aghast. His dreams shattered there and then. "Five years," he whispered.

"There is a solution," said Piet.

"What's that?"

"Well, I'm certain that the police won't be looking in the Northern Cape, it's too much trouble. So the best thing would be for you to join the family there. You will probably find more diamonds; after all, you are the one person who has already found diamonds up there. You could be very useful to the expedition."

Fritz thought in horror of the hardships he would again have to face. He almost couldn't bear it. His dreams shattered, he wept again.

It was a very subdued Fritz who greeted Petronella when she arrived a few days later. She didn't really think about it, with all the excitement of rushing round the dress shops and being taken to the farm that Fritz had chosen.

When they had finally decided on the farm, Fritz introduced her to a wizened little man, with large ears.

"This is *meneer* Visagie," said Fritz. "He will be the manager on the farm."

"Manager, what do we need a manager for? What do you think you will be doing all day you big *pampoen,* drinking brandy?"

Visagie was one of Piet's finds and he was an expert on making wine, according to Piet. He stood there looking uncomfortable. He would always be faithful to Piet, who had kept him out of jail for many little transgressions.

"I will explain later," replied Fritz.

When the situation was explained to Petronella afterwards she first burst into tears and then said:

"You don't expect me to go back there, to that hell hole, do you?"

"No, *vrou,* there is no need for that. You can stay here and enjoy the farm."

Petronella made the most of her new situation and almost ignored Fritz in the last few days that they were together. She certainly wouldn't let him sleep with her, much to his disappointment. He was so downcast by the turn of events that he just stumbled from day to day and left Piet to handle everything.

Making sure that he was well set up for the journey north lifted Fritz's spirits a bit. He could see that with the resources they now had he would be much better off and more comfortable than on his previous hellish journey.

Petronella didn't even watch him ride out through the gate, with his two very grand horses, accompanied by his young nephews Frans and Vic Koekemoer, together with two Coloured servants, also well mounted.

Frans and Vic, close to each other in age in their very early twenties, were a last minute addition to the expedition. Their parents, Fritz's brother and sister-in-law, had a successful wholesaling business in Cape Town and had no intention of embarking on what they saw as a wild goose chase into the interior. Their plans were for their two sons to develop in the business and in a few years take over and provide their parents with a comfortable retirement.

Piet had originally suggested the trip to Fritz's brother. He had seduced the young men with romantic stories of the riches they would find. He persuaded the parents that a year or two in the interior under Fritz's care would do Frans and Vic the world of good and would make them ready to settle down.

"If we find the riches we think we will, that will help secure funds to develop the business here in the Cape," Fritz had added diplomatically.

Piet's main motivation for including the young Koekemoers in the venture was to ensure that there would be energy and commitment to the venture. He now felt he was certain to collect a fortune from the family endeavours.

Fritz's brother was a clever businessman and he had grown apart from Fritz. He distrusted Fritz's inconsistencies and his judgement, but after much discussion, reluctantly allowed his sons to go on their adventure.

"Just behave yourselves," he urged them both. "Make sure the family name remains well respected."

◇◇◇◇◇◇◇◇◇◇◇◇◇◇◇

Chapter 3

The festival of the fruits in the year of 1872 turned out to be Mpande's last. Apart from a few skirmishes with the Swazi to the north, the bloody clashes that his half brother Dingane had had with the encroaching Boer were now distant memories, and somehow his diplomacy had kept the British south of the Tugela River.

The *amabhunu* had moved off north and were now giving the Zulu a wide berth. Mpande was however concerned; he had heard rumours of thousands of whites converging like ants on an anthill at a place near the banks of the great river in the west. He had heard they were looking for the hard, sparkling stones, which Zulus now called *idayimani*. To him these stones were useless. He had also heard that they used these stones to decorate their women. He had never seen a white woman but he wondered why they couldn't use coloured beads like his good Zulu women did. He would have to send some of the young men to the great river in the west to find out what it was all about. The idea of thousands of white men, all with their powerful firesticks, almost frightened him.

Once every year at the festival of the fruits, all the Zulu

clans gathered at the great kraal of Kwa-Bulawayo to pay homage to the great King Mpande. There were ten thousand of the very finest and fittest Zulu warriors from all parts of Zululand: the Quabe and Cele from the south, the Ngwane and Kumalo from the west, the Ndwandwe from the north, and even the slightly rebellious Mabhuda from the far north had each sent regiments, and many others.

The three days of dancing and feasting had almost come to an end. Mpande was so fat and prosperous that he was unable to walk, and he was carried from the *Isigodlo* every morning to oversee the proceedings. The Zulu expected their King to be fat—it was a clear sign of the prosperity of the nation; a thin King would have been a very bad sign.

Mapitha of the Ndwandwe's, now approaching his prime, being just out of his teens, felt he had excelled himself and had led his regiment in many fine dances. He and his colleagues were in the process of packing up, so at first light the next day they would make the two-day jog across the Mfolozi River back to their own villages, wives, and cattle. Mapitha had certainly felt inspired by the week's festivities. Kwa-Bulawayo, with its more than one thousand neat beehive huts, was looking its magnificent best. The rains had been good that year and the King's cattle grazing near the kraal all looked fat and well. The maize and sorghum crops were also bountiful.

A breathless messenger came running up to the Ndwandwe encampment some way outside the kraal and called, "Mapitha of the Ndwandwes is to pay his respects to the King."

Mapitha was still dressed in his finery, and he picked up his six-foot, cowhide shield and his *ixwa* and jogged back to the King's kraal. He wondered what misdemeanour he had committed and what the punishment would be. Mapitha crawled on his belly the last fifty yards to where the King was seated.

"Mapitha of the Ndwandwes," said Mpande majestically.

"*Nkosi*," was the response.

"Have you ever seen a white man?"

"No, *Nkosi*."

"There are many white intruders to the south, to the north and the west," said Mpande.

"If the *Nkosi* says so, then it must be so."

"In the west, near the great river, these white people are gathering like ants after a rainstorm," Mpande continued.

"And what are they finding?" asked Mapitha.

"They look for the little white stones that sparkle in the light."

"And what do they need these stones for?" asked Mapitha.

"They tell me they decorate their women with them," said Mpande.

Mapitha was silent; he didn't really understand.

"There are many of these whites," said Mpande.

"So the *Nkosi* has said."

"You will go and join these people there and understand their ways, and then you will return and tell us about them," said Mpande breathlessly.

"I am but a humble Ndwandwe; what do I know of these white people?" Mapitha was shocked. All he really wanted was to settle down in his village on the banks of the Mfolozi River and have as many wives and cattle as he could manage.

"Mapitha, I have watched these past days; you jumped higher and danced better than anyone in all the other clans. I have selected you for this important task; go now, take two others." Mapitha was dismissed.

On his return to the Ndwandwe clan area, Mapitha sought out his *induna* and discussed it with him.

"The great King also told me of this plan," said the *induna*.

Mapitha looked at him expectantly.

"Select two other warriors and then, three sunsets after we have returned, you will go on your journey. The *sangoma* will throw the bones and give you her wisdom."

Mapitha was troubled. Where was the river in the west? He needed practical help.

On the way home he discussed his mission with his friends Nzobo and Kulaan. If Mapitha was going, they would go too.

The *sangoma* told the prospective travellers that the best time to start their travels would be any time in the next month. She gave them each a small animal skin pouch in which she placed various ground herbs and animal parts. This was a protection against evil spirits. She didn't really know when the best time to travel was, but she did not want to fall foul of the King, so the sooner the travellers left the better as far as she was concerned.

Eventually Mapitha found an old man who had been with a war party in Dingane's time.

"The great river to the west, she rises in the southern mountains. Do not go there; those treacherous Sotho will kill you and take everything. You must go north first to the lands belonging to the Ndebele, who are our cousin tribe and speak our language. They will help. Then you travel west, and before you come to the sand country, you must go south again. Then you will find the river you seek," said the old man. "And stay away from the *amaBhunu*," was his final piece of advice.

Mapitha and his companions left the well-watered banks of the Mfolozi just as the dawn broke. They were dressed in the traditional loincloth made from animal skins and all had the Zulu head ring *isicoco,* signifying maturity. They had each been given an animal skin kaross to protect them from the cold winters on the highveld. They each carried a small shield (the six-foot battle shield would have been too clumsy), a bow and a quiver full of arrows for hunting, their *ixwa* short stabbing spears, and an *isagila*, plus a small food bag and a calabash of water. Everything except the weapons were wrapped up in the kaross and strapped on their backs. The weapons were carried separately, with the quiver full of arrows strapped across the back.

Mapitha was tall and athletic looking and had a ready smile. Nzobo was thin and wiry and always thoughtful. Kulaan was big and strong; he had once wrestled with a leopard and lived to tell the tale.

The haphazard nature of the directions made Mapitha cautious. He had decided to make his way along the banks of the northernmost (Black) branch of the Mfolozi River. To start with the scenery was familiar, with the tall grasses now greenish from the summer rains and the low acacia thorns providing cover and some shade during the heat of the day for the many wild animals. Dotted around the countryside was the occasional Zulu kraal. Nothing of course on the size and scale of Kwa-Bulawayo, but the sight of the familiar neat beehive huts was a comfort to the travellers. Some of the villages had as few as a half a dozen such huts, and there were one or two which had fifty or more.

Mapitha and his companions were always able to stay the night in one of these villages and however humble the village, the travellers were treated with courtesy and given a large meal of *utshwala*, *putu*, meat and vegetables. Directions were hard to come by but most of their hosts pointed in a northwesterly direction. The first few nights were spent with people from their own Ndwandwe clan, and then they moved into the area occupied by the Ngwane.

After ten days the party had traversed past the headwaters of the Black Mfolozi River and they were moving into the northern extension of *Ukhahlamba* (Drakensberg) Mountains. They were fairly certain that the Sotho of King Moshoeshoe would not venture this far north out of their territory, but when they came across a large village with the familiar beehive huts, they approached with caution. The chief, as usual, once they had identified themselves and their business was generous with his hospitality. One of the elders knew the area beyond the chief's territory, since he had been a member of many raiding parties during Dingane's reign. He again directed them northwards.

"You can find the great river you seek not more than five dawns away, but if you go too far to the west you will find many *amaBhunu*, and the *amaBhunu* are all trouble. They will try to kill you with their firesticks or take you as slaves," he said solemnly.

Nzobo came up to Mapitha towards the end of the meal and whispered, "There is some treachery afoot. Many moons ago the chief's brother was killed by an Ndwandwe and now he thinks the Gods have delivered us into his hands so he can take his revenge. I think they will try to kill us, maybe tonight."

Mapitha nodded. The Zulu clans were notorious for harbouring grudges that required some sort of tribute to be paid, often in the form of a life, long after the reason for the dispute was completely forgotten.

Some time in the middle of the night when all was quiet, Mapitha and his companions gathered up their few possessions and crept out of the hut. The normal summer rains were in full swing and the sky was dark with thunderclouds.

"Good," thought Mapitha. "A heavy rainfall will cover our tracks."

Mapitha had no wish to further extend the feud between this clan and the Ndwandwe. For this reason he had told the others their job was just to escape, and when their lives were threatened they should try not to kill anyone. He fully understood the sentiment though; he would certainly seek revenge for any wrongs done to his clan.

A dog barked at the far end of the compound and the cattle that were always driven into the village at night mooed nervously as the three Ndwandwes crept through the village. Mapitha had determined that the safest thing to do would be to find a way through the thorn bush fence. The main entrance would probably have someone on watch. He was hopeful that there would be no other guards about. The group quickly and skilfully moved in the shadows from hut to hut. They made no noise with their bare feet and, as with all Zulu kraals, the compound was meticulously swept every day, so there were no sticks or other obstacles lying about. They were just a few yards from the fence when suddenly there was a movement ahead of them. Someone was crawling very silently through the fence in their direction, coming back into the village. At first they thought it was only one, but then another figure appeared. Mapitha almost laughed out loud; it was one of the young *ibutho* and a maiden from the village. They were obviously returning from an assignment in the *veld* outside. Mapitha made a hand signal and having crept closer to the couple, Kulaan, in a second, had silently wrestled the man to the ground and Nzobo had silenced the woman.

"Listen, you Ngwane dogs, one sound out of you and you will get a spear in the ribs," whispered Mapitha fiercely.

The terrified couple needed no further prompting. If they had been caught that would have been their fate anyway.

Mapitha signalled to the gap in the fence. Kulaan led, followed by the terrified *ibutho*, then Nzobo followed by the girl, then Mapitha.

Once the party was out of the kraal Mapitha led the way northwest. They ran for about an hour. It started to rain, big single drops with rolls of thunder. Mapitha stopped. Normally he would have killed the hapless couple, but because of the blood feud he let them go. They ran off like startled rabbits as fast as they could.

"They will not raise the alarm," said Mapitha to the others, "and anyway, once the dawn breaks, the Ngwane will know we have already left."

They ran through the rest of the night, mostly in the rain. They rested up during the very hottest part of the day and then ran on. Within two days they had covered more than sixty miles.

The Ngwane lived on the south slope of the *Ukhahlamba* mountain range and once Mapitha and his companions crested the range and started to run slightly downhill they knew they were out of the Ngwane territory and it was most unlikely they would be followed. To be on the safe side they kept going and Mapitha, ever mindful of the advice he had been given, now set a more northerly course.

The group was now more watchful than ever. If the Ngwane had wanted to kill them, what fate would befall them if they fell into the hands of another, probably hostile, tribe? At every possible vantage point they scoured the landscape, which was now transformed into the brown, rolling hills of the highveld with very few trees and bushes and endless swathes of tall, lush grass. In the distance they glimpsed two raiding parties who looked like Zulus.

"This is Ndebele country," Nzobo told them. "The Ndebele are a cousin tribe."

He proceeded to tell them that during King Shaka's time the Ndebele

Chief Mzilikazi had first joined Shaka and then broken away from the Zulu hegemony and first settled in what became the Transvaal and then when the Boers arrived in numbers moved further north across the Limpopo River. Some of the Ndebele clans had stayed behind. It remained to be seen whether they were friendly or not. They saw no sign of any Boers.

On the fourth day after leaving the Ngwane kraal, the travellers were becoming quite hungry, although they had managed to kill a small springbok. Mapitha then spotted a village with only about seven or eight huts. All the huts were in the familiar beehive shape but they looked less stable than the familiar ones in Zululand. "Maybe because the trees are smaller," thought Mapitha.

They approached the small kraal openly and while the sun was high in the heavens, so as to allay any suspicions as to their intentions. They were extremely wary, being ready to fight or to flee if the reception turned out to be hostile.

Once it was clear that the intentions of Mapitha and his companions were benign, they were made very welcome, and the garrulous old chief entertained them royally for two days.

The clan seemed content enough, but they certainly did not give off the air of wealth that the clans on the southern side of the mountain had. The chief said they never went near the Ngwane and knew nothing of them, when Mapitha told him of the planned treachery and their escape.

When Mapitha asked about the great river the chief gave him directions. He also told him to be careful because many Boers had settled along the river. When asked about diamonds, the chief was intrigued but knew nothing. The travellers left and the chief gave them directions to another small Ndebele clan on the other side of the river; the chief was anxious to make contact with the clan, as he had not heard from them since shortly after the summer rains had started. All three travellers realised, when they left the scrappy little kraal that the hard part of their journey had just begun. The difficulties they had so far encountered were likely to pale into insignificance. They were now going into hostile territory and few, if any, people would treat them as anything but enemies.

When the travellers found the river, they weren't even sure that it was what they were seeking. They were expecting something like the mighty Tugela, which at the mouth was more than three hundred yards wide. This river was barely fifty yards across and, although due to the rain it was flowing quickly, they had their doubts.

"Is this the great river in the west?" asked Kulaan.

"Maybe; it is certainly flowing west," answered Nzobo.

The peaceful scene was suddenly disturbed by a volley of shots from across the river. Then came the sound of thundering hooves, some more shots. They heard cries of pain and anguish and then after no more than ten minutes, the sound of hooves heading into the distance. Then there was silence. Clouds of smoke appeared above the trees.

Mapitha and his companions had hastily gone to ground behind some bushes when the firing had started. When it was clear that the attackers, whoever they were, had disappeared, they cautiously emerged. Mapitha started to make his way gingerly across the river.

"Careful of the *izingwenya*," cautioned Nzobo.

Mapitha waved them on. "Too cold for *izingwenya*," he said.

They all managed to cross the river, hanging onto each other in the fastest flowing part. They scrambled up the steep bank, which had a few overhanging trees, and crept towards a plume of smoke now winding its way into the clear blue sky.

Not more than five hundred yards from the river they came across what had been a small village. All the huts were burning fiercely and the bodies of ten or more men, women and children were strewn around, as if a hurricane had blown them there. Mapitha stopped behind a bush and with his companions watched for twenty minutes. The only sound was from the crackling of the fire.

"Ndebele," said Mapitha at last, indicating the shattered village.

Despite the fire, they could still distinguish the shapes of the now almost destroyed beehive huts.

The group crept uneasily into the village and started to collect the bodies, all of whom had been shot where they stood.

Nzobo suddenly dashed off into the bush and a sharp cry was heard. He returned with what turned out to be a young girl. She was shivering in fear and when she saw the bodies, started wailing. Nzobo said to the others, "This is not an Ndebele or a Zulu. You see the colour of her skin: this skin is brown like the antelope from the plains, not black like the hide of a buffalo, like a Zulu."

Mapitha tried to speak to the girl, who was dressed traditionally, with a small animal skin skirt. She was too upset to say anything.

The three Zulus collected up all the bodies and in the absence of any digging implements, as gently as possible put them into the burning huts.

They then added more wood from round about until the bodies were completely consumed by the flames.

The girl after a while started to say over and over, "*amaBhunu, amaBhunu*" Mapitha understood.

"This was the work of the *amaBhunu*," he said. "We had better go."

All the food in the village had been destroyed in the fire, and when they were satisfied that the spirits of the dead had been properly attended to the Zulus, now accompanied by the girl, made their way back to the river.

The girl kept shaking her head.

"*Amabhunu*," she said and pointed away from the river.

Mapitha had no wish to encounter the Boers and he followed the girl's direction, through the long grass away from the river. A small camp was made some distance from the river and they shared what food they had. It was clear from her dress and demeanour that the girl was still a virgin, and the tribal taboos were such that no Zulu male would ever take advantage of the situation. No physical contact with the girl was possible without the permission of the parents.

Mapitha lent the girl his kaross to keep the highveld cold out during the night. He shared Nzobo's with him. Kulaan's kaross was barely large enough to cover his large frame, so he was left alone.

The group spent two days in the camp, which was protected by two large boulders, which they all climbed periodically to check for any dangers. Kulaan went out early the morning of the second day and came back with a small springbok, which he had stalked and taken down with his spear.

Mapitha made it clear to the girl that she would come to no harm while she was with them and she gradually relaxed. Her Ndebele or Zulu language skills were rather ragged and sometimes she slipped into another language, which the Zulu could not understand.

After much coaxing the girl's story was eventually told.

She was actually a Tswana from the west, "at least thirty dawns away," she said. She had been captured by an Ndebele raiding party two years earlier. All the male members of her family had been killed and she had been brought to the now burnt out village by one of the *ibutho* from the raiding party. In time she would have become the wife of the *ibutho* who captured her. She didn't really mind being in the Ndebele village and had been treated well.

During the past six months a large party of Boers had camped on the river, half a day's travel from the village. There had been trouble from the start: it was clear that the Boers had come to stay and their objective was to get rid of anyone in the way. The Ndebele had fought back and had driven off many Boer cattle. Eventually the Boer had settled on a policy of extermination and they set out to raid the small Ndebele villages and kill the inhabitants or chase them away. They took all the cattle. The raid on the village that the Zulus had witnessed was part of the process.

The Zulus told Tutula (they had eventually coaxed the name from her) that they were making for the place near the "great river in the west" where the *abelungu* were digging for *idayimani*. She shook her head, indicating that she had heard of no such place, although when diamonds were described to her she had seen the occasional stone cut from the crop of an ostrich. She could not understand why anyone placed value on such an item.

Having determined that the river nearby was the "great river in the west" or at least flowed into it, Mapitha decided that the best course was to follow it. When she was told of the plan, Tutula shook her head violently and persuaded the men that the *amaBhunu* had settled all the way along the river, and therefore to follow its course would mean death or enslavement.

When they set off they therefore went north for seven days and then headed due west. Food and accommodation was found at the occasional Ndebele village. Although the Ndebele looked speculatively at Tutula, none of them so much as touched her; she clearly belonged to the Zulus.

In the early part of their travels the party was very wary and kept a sharp lookout for *amaBhunu*; so they were able to avoid trouble on the one or two occasions when they saw horsemen on the horizon.

After several days when they had seen no horsemen, they started to become careless. As far as Mapitha was concerned, they had left the river and therefore the *amaBhunu* far behind. Unbeknown to the travellers, however, the river actually flowed north-west for about five days' travel, therefore as they made their way west, they started to get closer to the river.

One early morning, as they started on their daily trek, suddenly they came upon three *amaBhunu* horsemen just two hundred yards away, who immediately spotted the Zulus and galloped towards them. Mapitha guided his party quickly to a nearby rock-strewn *kopje* and took cover. The horses would have to slow to a walk here and Mapitha hoped that his group would be able to take cover in the rocks and avoid the horsemen. The Zulus spread out, with Tutula staying close by Mapitha's side. The Zulus crept behind the rocks and stayed in the long grass; they could hear the *amaBhunu* crashing about on the *kopje* cursing. Mapitha and Tutula were lying behind a rock when one of the horsemen came within a few feet of them. As the horseman spotted him, Mapitha flung himself up at the man and before the *iBhunu* could bring his rifle to bear, Mapitha had stabbed him in the heart with his *ixwa*, yelling "Bayete!" at the top of his voice. The man fell on top of Mapitha, dead, and the horse bolted in fright. Kulaan, having heard the noise, used his great strength to wrestle another of the horses to the ground, but the rider miraculously escaped and was almost magically lifted onto the back of the third rider's horse, which then dashed off the *kopje* and clattered off. After having made sure they were alone again on the *kopje*, the Zulus examined their spoils: one dead *iBhunu*, whom they would leave to the hyenas or the other *amaBhunu* if they were quick enough, a rifle and a bandolier full of ammunition. Mapitha had no idea how the weapon worked but he took it and the bandolier. They also had a nervous-looking horse and all its equipment. The Zulus knew nothing about horses but Mapitha reassured the others, "They seem rather like zebra, and if the *amaBhunu* can manage them, so can we."

The Zulu knew they had to get away quickly, before the rest of the *amaBhunu* came back for their fallen colleague. They persuaded Kulaan to ride the horse with Nzobo leading it; Mapitha and the girl jogged on ahead. As they came off the *kopje*, Mapitha turned round to see how his colleagues were doing, and he accidentally tripped on a small rock; the rifle went down with a clatter and went off, the bullet flying harmlessly into the air. His Zulu colleagues got a terrible fright, left the horse alone and hid behind some rocks. Mapitha eventually gingerly picked up the rifle. The horse was completely unconcerned and went on grazing until the Zulus had pulled themselves together, and the party returned to its rapid progress northwards. They jogged for most of that day and long into the night; they knew if the *amaBhunu* ever caught up with them they would be shown no mercy. The three men took it in turns to ride the horse; Tutula would have nothing to do with it.

They slept for a few hours and then continued on their way. After three days on this routine with no sign of pursuit, they eventually slowed down and travelled as before during the day. The Zulu knew enough about stock to make certain that the horse had time to graze properly every day, and to make sure that it had sufficient water; they even worked out how to remove the saddle and after some days they were able to remove the bit from the horse's mouth so that it could graze. Soon *ihashi* became an established part of the group.

  Rough Diamonds

Mapitha was determined to find out how the firestick worked. Since it had accidentally gone off, he had carried it without touching the mechanism. He went by himself behind a large boulder away from their camp and took a careful look. After about ten minutes he managed to work out how to lever the breach open, which he did, and the empty cartridge case fell into his lap. Instinct told him to compare the case with a full cartridge in the bandolier, so he could see that the small piece of metal at the top of the case was somehow shot up the barrel of the rifle and away. Without thinking he closed the breach again and then started playing with the trigger mechanism; in his impatience he pulled the trigger and of course the gun went off noisily. Mapitha dropped it and ran away ten yards. He very carefully returned to the gun, picked it up again and pulled the trigger again. Nothing happened. He then levered the breach open again; another empty case fell out. He closed the breach and pulled the trigger again. The gun went off. This time Mapitha did not run away. He opened the breach again and the empty case fell out. He closed it and pulled the trigger; just a sharp click. He opened the breach again and could see it was empty. "Ah," he thought. He pulled one of the cartridges from the bandolier and, with much fiddling, managed to load it into the breach. He then pushed the bolt forward and pulled the trigger. "Bang." The gun went off. He now thought he understood how the weapon worked. Aiming it was another problem. He assumed it would be like an assegai, which one threw up in the air towards a target. It was only months later, after they had got to the diamond fields, that he was shown how to aim properly. During the rest of the trip, whenever he wanted to use the weapon he levered a round into the breach and, holding the gun at forty-five degrees pointing roughly in the direction of the quarry, pulled the trigger. He was altogether frustrated that he never managed to hit anything, and the game always scampered away at the unfamiliar sound of the shot.

Once Mapitha was satisfied that they had escaped the Boers, the party turned west again. They sensed that gradually they were moving to a lower elevation. The land was drier, the grass not as lush and the bushes smaller. Game was not as plentiful and they had to be certain that they conserved the water they carried. Ndebele *kraals* petered out and they came into Tswana territory. Mapitha and the other Zulus were suspicious of the rough, unkempt appearance of the huts but Tutula was quite at home. When they came to the first Tswana kraal she pacified the inhabitants, and after a long, painful explanation the Zulus were reluctantly housed and fed. By this time the Zulus were two months into their travels and looked dirty and unkempt. Tutula advised them to smarten themselves up, which they did. The Tswana were generally a peaceful people, and when it was obvious the Zulus meant no harm, they were the subject of much discussion. They were much darker than the Tswana people, and the rifle and the horse caused much interest. The Tswana had only seen these items in the possession of the occasional Boer trekker.

As the travellers made their way through Tswana territory, they gradually heard rumours about the diamond diggings. They were directed southwest until they found the river. Tutula had been asked by Mapitha if she wanted to return to her village, but she said she no longer knew where it was. In truth she found being with the Zulus much more fun and had decided to find out for herself what all the fuss about *idayimani* was about.

Mapitha was very wary of the Boers, who had started to establish themselves along the river. The country away from the river was semi-desert, sparsely grassed, with stunted thorn trees scattered about. It seemed to Mapitha that if the Boers saw them with the horse and gun, they would know that these items had been taken from a Boer and any Boer would try to take them back. Since the Zulus were in no particular hurry, they kept one establishment under observation for two days. On both mornings, after what the Zulus thought was the morning meal, they saw a black person take a path two hundred yards to the river and wash some pots and pans, collect some water, and return to the settlement. Mapitha decided to approach this person at the river and ask for directions.

Mapitha went down to the river, now two hundred yards wide, under the watchful eye of the other three in the party, who were ready to move off at a moment's notice. He approached the person at the river cautiously, but as soon as he came into view the woman at the river screamed at the top of her lungs, dropped everything and ran back up the path to the settlement. Mapitha was non-plussed but he soon gathered his wits and ran off down river to join up with the others. None too soon, because shortly afterwards two horsemen came out of the settlement and spent half an hour galloping about and shooting wildly into the surrounding bush.

They made rapid progress for a day and then decided to find a place to cross the river, which was becoming wider and wider. They also had no idea whether the river had hippo and crocodiles in it. After many attempts, they found a place where wagons and cattle had crossed. Kulaan made his way across with some difficulty; he wasn't much of a swimmer and he had trouble for about fifty yards in the middle of the river. He ended up about two hundred yards downstream but scrambled back long the heavily wooded riverbank to the ford, where Mapitha and the other two were waiting on the opposite bank. Tutula was very nervous; she had no idea how to swim and had never seen such an expanse of water. *Ihashi* came to their rescue. Mapitha put the girl in the saddle and he and Nzobo held on upstream of *ihashi*; the animal had no hesitation in walking into the river and then swimming across to the other side when the river became deeper. Everything they had was soaking wet but it soon dried out in the sun.

Their experience with the Boer settlement made them wary of approaching any other signs of habitation. In the end, they just followed the wagon tracks for three days, and they almost stumbled on the town now called Kimberley.

Mapitha pointed out the dust that already hovered over the town. '*Iday-imani*' was all he said, and pointed.

The Zulus were not really certain what they had expected, but nothing prepared them for Kimberley. The biggest settlement any of them had ever seen was Kwa-Bulawayo and none of them had ever seen a wheeled vehicle, such as a scotch cart or wagon, before. On their way into town they passed close by what turned out to be some diggings, where dozens of people of every colour under the sun were feverishly digging away at the grey-coloured earth. The party were still dressed in loincloths and very little else, and as they made their way down what was to be the main street in the town, they looked increasingly out of place among the bearded white men with large hats and boots and rough shirts and trousers. Nobody took much notice of them though; the town had attracted all sorts during its three years of existence. Mapitha's first instinct was to find the chief. He could not envisage any place at all without a chief; certainly in such an important looking place there had to be a chief. Nothing was familiar; there was no obvious *isigodlo*. "Surely in such an important place there must be a very important chief," he said to the others.

As they made their way warily down the street, they noticed many men going into one particular building. None of them could read, but there was a rough sign outside hanging lopsided, announcing "Cora's Saloon". This building was also the largest among the hodgepodge of buildings in the rough, dusty streets.

Mapitha halted his nervous little party outside the saloon and they waited and watched for nearly one hour. The absolute disorder of the place was what struck them hardest. It appeared that anyone could go into the chief's house (since this was what they had determined the saloon to be) unannounced;

and people often came out appearing to be drunk. Although Mapitha had noticed that the many black people about were wearing tattered versions of the clothes the whites wore, he was not the slightest bit conscious of his own nakedness.

After an hour Mapitha was still as confused as ever. "I will just go inside and find the chief," he told the others.

Carrying only the rifle he had taken from the Boers, he marched confidently up the steps and through the bat-wing doors of the saloon. He hadn't taken two steps into the place when he was grabbed by two white men standing near the entrance, who unceremoniously tossed him into the street. "No naked *kaffirs* in here," one shouted. Before Mapitha could do or say anything Kulaan, who knew of no person stronger than he was, coolly walked into the saloon and one by one picked the two bouncers up and dropped them face down in the street. Men poured out of the saloon, expecting to witness a spectacle. This was not to be; Mapitha had picked himself up and Nzobo quickly made sure that the Zulus were armed again with their *ixwa* spears, *isagila* and their small shields. The Zulus advanced on the two bouncers, who scuttled back into the hotel.

Frank Devereaux had been watching all this with some amusement from the other side of the street. In the four years he had been in Kimberley he had worked his claims hard. He had found a few diamonds, which kept him going, but he had yet to strike the riches he dreamt of. He had just acquired some more claims and he needed labour for those claims. He led his horse over to the now truly angry Zulus, who were just about to attack him when he used the two words of Zulu he knew. "*Sakubona, Nkosi* (hello, chief)," he said.

The Zulu were dumbstruck; they hadn't heard a word of Zulu from a stranger since they left the Ndebele country months earlier.

"*Sakubona,*" they chorused.

Frank quickly led them out of the town to his own little encampment on the outskirts, where he made it clear to them that they could make themselves at home.

✧✧✧✧✧✧✧✧✧✧✧✧✧✧✧

Chapter 4

Charles Lawrence was a wild young man. His parents were hard working farmers who had established themselves in the Greytown area. As well as timber, they had a large acreage under sugar, the new industrial crop of the fledgling colony of Natal. They also had a few cattle, but sugar had become the mainstay of the farm and indeed the colony. For sugar they needed labour. Over the years both Charles and his father had developed good relationships with the local Zulu chief Magaye, whose domain lay south of the Tugela. Magaye was actually a Cele and although he nominally accepted Cetswayo's authority as Zulu King, he and his people bore long standing historical resentments against the Zulu hegemony since Shaka's legions had conquered the Cele some fifty years earlier, making them vassals. Magaye, therefore, in some ways welcomed the advent of the new white settlers. He was able to play the ever-increasing power of the whites off against the might of the Zulu King.

Magaye respected the Lawrences and encouraged his people to work for them, since he saw they were just. Charles had spent many happy days at the chief's kraal and spoke Zulu fluently. Magaye loved him like a son and he was always welcome as a visitor. Magaye could see the way the political wind was blowing, and he had determined that to preserve his own authority he needed to cooperate with the whites. He was also conscious of the fact that, because of the deep reluctance of the Zulus to labour in the cane fields, the British Administration had imported hundreds of East Indians, mainly from Gujarat, to plant and cut cane. He did not want the Indians to come into the Greytown area. Dealing with the *amaNgisi* and their God was difficult enough; he found the thought of having to deal with the *amaNdiya* and their array of Gods too difficult to contemplate.

Magaye and his fellow neighbouring chieftains also encouraged their young men to join the British Military and Police. They did this in droves. The idea of working in a cane field had no appeal to most Zulus, but the idea of strutting around with a rifle and being part of a military operation appealed greatly. Under Cetswayo's hegemony that is what they would have been expected to do; now their chief was encouraging them to join the British.

Charles Lawrence spent much of his time tearing about the Natal countryside on horseback, attending parties in Pietermaritzburg and throughout the surrounding farming districts. He was a tall, handsome man with fair hair and blue eyes and he rode like the wind. His parents despaired of him. As he was an only son, they wanted him to settle down on the farm, marry, and provide them with grandchildren and a comfortable retirement. Charles had left many broken hearts among the eligible white farmers' daughters in the district. He was quite unconcerned and was enjoying himself. He worked on the farm as little as he could get away with without completely alienating his parents. He maintained his relationships with Magaye and the Cele by attending regular beer drinks with the men there, and he went to as many parties in the settler community as time would permit. Charles was aware of certain tensions between the increasing number of whites living south of the Tugela in Natal and the apparently restless Zulu and their King Cetswayo north of the Tugela. He took little notice of this and assumed that his amusing, energetic lifestyle would continue indefinitely.

Then he met Alice. It was the end of a cricket match at which, as usual, Charles had excelled. His team had narrowly won the match against the more fancied opponents from Durban. He wandered off the field, laughing with his teammates. There was this slip of a girl, with clear, pale skin under a large brimmed hat. She was exquisite, with high, firm breasts and a beautiful face. She wore her hair in the long tresses that were the current fashion.

Charles was immediately surrounded by admirers, which did not include

Alice. Having changed his clothes, he frantically tried to find her and introduce himself. She had disappeared. He asked around. He was told she would be at the dance that evening, and he went back to his uncle's house and washed and scrubbed and put his finery on. The dances he had attended in the past had never caused him any anxiety whatsoever; he usually danced all night and went home when the fun was over. This time, however, he was very apprehensive; he arrived early and paced up and down, waiting anxiously for Alice to arrive.

When Alice did arrive, without thinking he rushed up to her and asked her to dance.

"Well, no," she said. "We haven't been properly introduced." Charles did not notice the gentle, amused sparkle in Alice's eyes. Charles could have kicked himself. "What a clumsy fool," he thought, and he dashed off and found his aunt, who made the proper introduction.

"Well, let me see," she said. "I have one space left in the programme, a waltz." She smiled and wrote his name on her card, and then continued with her conversation as if he did not exist. Charles shambled off feeling like a naughty schoolboy. If he had turned around he would have seen her amused eyes watching him over the top of her fan.

Charles tried to smother his inner turmoil by dancing with absolutely everyone. He could not help noticing Alice apparently enjoying herself. She had no shortage of dancing partners. When it came to his turn to dance with Alice, he was really surprised at how strong she was, despite her apparently small, spare frame. They danced magnificently together, so well that unnoticed the floor cleared and by the end of the dance, much to their embarrassment they found themselves alone on the floor. Everyone clapped. Alice had tried to ignore this man, but during the waltz her body had responded almost with a will of its own to the proximity of the male body holding her. Despite herself she had a feeling of desire deep in the pit of her stomach. Charles was ecstatic after the waltz and asked if he could call on her the next day.

To say that Charles was besotted would not have been an exaggeration. He found out that Alice's parents had a farm in the foothills of the Drakensberg and that she spoke Zulu at least as fluently as he did. He called on her every day and when she went home (to an uncle and aunt in Pietermaritzburg) arranged to call on her there. After a few visits, Charles realised that there was much more to Alice than he could conceivably have imagined.

Charles' relationship with the Cele clan of the Zulus was totally straightforward and uncomplicated. He attended beer drinks with the men and listened to their innumerable stories, but they had their place in society and he had his. He never questioned the fact that the whites had come to stay in Natal and that in the nature of things the whites held power, at least south of the Tugela, and the blacks were their servants.

Alice, however, viewed things differently; as the trust between the pair grew, she started to discuss with him the loss of power and identity suffered by the Zulu clans. "Our neighbours the Hlubi managed to fend off the depredations of Shaka and remained unconquered by the Zulu *impis*," she said.

Charles nodded. He had very little idea where this was leading.

"They kept their cattle, they kept their women and on the few occasions that the Zulu tried to attack them, they drove all their stock into the mountains and hid in caves. Any Zulu that got lost in the mountain stronghold was slaughtered. Eventually the Hlubi chief came to some sort of accommodation with Shaka and paid him a bounty of a few head of cattle each year. The Hlubi were then left alone."

Charles had some vague awareness of this. "The Hlubi have not been so lucky when it came to dealing with the whites," Alice went on.

Charles nodded.

"They managed to accumulate some wealth, including guns, by working in the diamond mines in Kimberley," said Alice.

Charles had seen a few guns in Zulu hands. Most of them did not really know how to use them.

"Shepstone tried to get the Hlubi to register these guns but they were concerned that this would result in confiscation, so the Hlubi tried to flee over the Drakensberg. This was the last thing that Shepstone wanted. He wanted control." Alice was now flushed and showing some anger. Charles was surprised. He'd heard about the Hlubi and the trial and imprisonment of Langalibalele their chief, but the settler community had generally accepted the government line and had not questioned the action taken against the Hlubi.

Alice told him the rest of the story.

"Langalibalele and most of the tribe had long gone, they were over the mountain and into the Free State, but there was a skirmish in one of the passes and a few British soldiers were killed, so the British pursued Langalibalele, captured him and imprisoned him on Robben Island. The Hlubi have been made to pay a fine of eight thousand head of cattle, which has forced many of the young men into the work force here in Natal, precisely what Shepstone wants, but it is causing great anger and resentment." Alice hesitated; she had not told this part of the story to anyone and her father had sworn her to secrecy. If the word got out both she and her father could be prosecuted. She glanced at Charles, who was looking at her speculatively; she nodded, almost to herself, and then she instinctively went on as if the question of trust between them could never be an issue, even though she had known him for such a short time.

"I haven't told anyone what I am going to tell you now, and you will see in a minute why you can't tell anyone else at all." Charles raised his eyebrows, but said nothing and Alice continued: "The farm is quite close to a Hlubi village and we keep in constant contact with them."

On that particular day, Alice's father Tom Cuthbertson had woken her early as usual and they had set off for one of their regular visits to the local Hlubi village, as the dawn broke in the east. Mid-winter mornings in the mountains were always cold and they both snuggled into their warm sheepskin coats and gloves. Alice always treasured the mornings up in the 'Berg', the air was clear and crisp, she could see that it was to be one of those bright cold winter days. Nothing much was said until they came to the gully where there were always two Hlubi warriors on guard. Tom called but there was no answer, he called again with the same result. "Strange, "he muttered and they clattered on, now more urgently. When they came to the village they found a frenzy of activity, with everyone appearing to be packing up ready to leave. Alice and her mother had for years run a makeshift first aid clinic at the village, but on this day, unusually, Alice had only one or two minor ailments to attend to; normally she would have been mobbed, especially by the women. Strangely none of the people she dealt with would answer any of her questions, they just had their ailments attended to and then scurried off. Tom found the chief and after a very long discussion he eventually told Tom that they were moving over the mountains: "To escape that *Somseu*, who wants to take all our guns and cattle," said Mahbule aggressively. Both Tom and Alice had tried to reason with them but to no effect. "All the Hlubi will go," added Mahbule, as if to ensure that there was no misunderstanding.

"What about the land that you have here?" asked Tom.

"There is more land over the mountain; we have been there and looked," answered Mahbule. "Our cattle will come with us; we will be gone by tomorrow or in a few days." He then looked down and hesitated for a few moments. "Our only regret is that we will leave you *Nkosi* Tom here and the *Nkosikasi* Alice. We have been good for each other, but now you must go," he was uncharacteristically blunt; "we have much to do if we are to leave soon."

Tom tried other arguments to no avail and within less than two hours of arrival they were on their way home again. Tom was worried; it seemed a rash decision and could only bring hardship to the Hlubi. He also wondered how he would run the farm without their help.

A few days later their breakfast was rudely interrupted by a platoon of mounted British soldiers led by a lieutenant, who, without much ceremony, demanded that Tom act as a guide for his troops into the mountains.

"I'm told by the people in Estcourt that you know these mountains like the back of your hand, and we need to get going quickly," Tom was told.

"What is the issue? What are you trying to do?" asked Tom innocently.

"Don't you know, the Hlubi are trying to escape over the mountain, and it is our job to prevent that." The officer appeared to assume that Tom's loyalties would always lie with the authorities and had no inkling of the close bond that existed between the Cuthbertsons and the Hlubi.

"O.K., just give me a minute to saddle up and I will be with you. I suggest that you all dismount and relax here in front and I will be as quick as I can." Tom disappeared into the house. Alice was waiting for him; she had instinctively not gone out to greet the visitors.

"Alice, you probably heard all that. You need to get to the village unseen by these people and warn Mahbule what is going on. I will take the soldiers round the long way and delay as much as possible; I might be able to give them two days, but they can't bank on any more than that." Tom and Alice went out to the stables, making sure that Alice had her bedroll, rifle and some food, and within minutes Alice led her horse out the back way and when she was out of sight of the farm buildings she mounted and cantered up the well-worn path. Tom gave her a few minutes and then rode his horse round to the front of the house.

"I need some time to get all my mountain equipment together," he said to the Lieutenant. "This visit has rather taken me by surprise."

Half an hour later the troop moved out of the farmyard and led by Tom took a path straight up the mountain, away from the Hlubi village.

Alice raced as fast as she could to the village in the hope that the villagers had not yet left. There were no warriors on guard, and when she reached the village it was completely deserted; it looked as if the people had indeed

                                                                    Rough Diamonds

left a few days earlier as they had promised. "With all those cattle they will make slow progress and the trail should be easy enough to follow," she thought. She did not consider returning to the farm, without delivering the message. She cantered along the wide trail left by the cattle and the villagers; by nightfall there was still no sign of them although the signs of fresh cattle dung meant that they were not too far ahead. She made camp off the main trail next to a little stream, fed and watered her horse and then collected firewood and made a small meal. She was tempted to swim in the deep clear pool nearby, but thought better of it since it was getting cold and dark. Alice was not afraid, as she had spent many nights up the mountain on her own, with her father, or with the *sangoma* from the village collecting medicinal plants. Nevertheless she kept her rifle nearby and made sure that a log was kept burning all night, to deter any wild animals. At dawn she was on her way again, making good progress, and by midday she caught a glimpse of the Hlubi cattle entering a gully far up the mountain. During the afternoon she came up with rear of the caravan and was immediately recognized. "Quick, take me to Mahbule! The soldiers are coming and you will need to hurry if you want to get over the mountain before they get here," she told them. They found the chief in the middle of the group. Alice told him about the soldiers and that Tom had been ordered to guide them but was deliberately taking them round the long way to give the Hlubi more time to escape. Mahbule questioned her at length and then said: "We will be over the mountain by tomorrow, with all the cattle. We should be a long way from the mountain by the time they get here, but we will leave some of our best warriors in the pass to stop the soldiers from following us. We thank you for what you and your family have done; it will not be forgotten."

Alice spent the night with the villagers in their encampment and when they continued on their journey the next day, she returned home. Alice had always felt comfortable and safe in the mountains; they were almost part of her. She arrived at her campsite of two nights previous at about midday and this time, having made sure that her horse was well tethered; she stripped off her now dirty clothes and swam for a few minutes in the icy cold water. Having dried herself off, she lay down on a flat rock in the warm winter sun. She had enough food for herself and the horse, so she decided to spend the night there. She had been away in the mountains for much longer at other times, so she was certain that her mother would have no fears for her safety especially as there had been no snow. She arrived home at dusk the following day.

Alice continued the story: "My father succeeded in delaying the soldiers for the promised two days and he thought that the Hlubi had got clean away, but Shepstone ordered the military to pursue them, illegally, over the border and when some soldiers were killed he sent reinforcements and returned Langalibalele and all the Hlubi to Natal. I've told you the rest of the story. I don't need to tell you that the fine has impoverished the tribe.

"Many Hlubi and members of some of the neighbouring clans lost their lives. None of it is their fault. Shepstone and his cronies are murderers and thieves. And this is just the start. You wait and see what they plan for the Zulus. Our actions, however, have helped to cement our relationship with Mahbule and his clan, who are of course now back where they were, minus their part of the cattle fine. If we hadn't helped them as we did I think we would have been chased off the farm-or worse. I don't know." She looked away; there were tears of frustration in her eyes, which she impatiently brushed aside.

Charles was absolutely silent. Suddenly his view of the world had been turned upside down. Eventually he said, "So what do you think can be done about this?"

"We have to help; we have to help the Zulus, otherwise they will be trampled just like the Hlubi," she said.

"How?" he asked.

Alice was waiting for this.

"The only people who are trusted by both the Zulus and the government are the missionaries," she said. "The only people who can really help are the missionaries."

Charles was incredulous.

"But..." He wasn't allowed to finish.

"They need education," said Alice, "and nobody will be allowed to go in there and start schools. Neither Shepstone nor the King would have anything to do with a scheme like that."

"And they need hospitals and doctors," responded Charles. It was as if a light had been turned on in his head.

She nodded.

"So far the only people that have been allowed to operate are missionaries and traders. Traders won't do, so the only option is missionaries."

They let the subject drop. Both of them felt that almost too much had been said already. No commitments had been made either way and they hardly knew each other; they hadn't even shared a kiss.

Alice went home to her parents' small farm in the foothills of the Drakensberg, with the massive peak of Injasuti towering over their little homestead, and a little further away, the more gentle slopes of Giant's Castle. She said nothing but Charles said he would call. The farm was a mere three days ride from Greytown.

Charles went home and told his parents at dinner the first night he was home, "I'm going to become a priest, a missionary; I want to be able to help the Zulu."

His father nearly choked on his soup.

"Are you sure?" he asked.

"Yes, they need help, education, medicine. I will set up a mission station with all that," said Charles.

"But what about the religion? You hardly ever go to church—don't you have to be a committed Christian to be a missionary?" his mother asked.

"Well," said Charles defensively, "I do go to church at Christmas and Easter."

"All the priests I know were educated in England; will you have to go there?" asked Charles'mother innocently. He just glanced at her; he had no idea.

"Well, think about it, son," said his father kindly. "This place will be yours one day if you want it." He waved his hand expansively. The farm was indeed a gem and would provide a handsome living.

No more was said; privately Charles' parents thought that nothing would come of it.

They were used to Charles tearing about the countryside, so they were unconcerned when he announced that he was going off to visit a farm in the mountains west of Estcourt. Charles mentioned Alice and his parents just smiled. They were used to their wayward son chasing round the country after attractive girls.

Charles arrived at the Cuthbertsons after almost three days' hard riding from Greytown. He never had any fears for himself; he always carried a hunting rifle in a scabbard attached to the saddle, and his language skills enabled him to find shelter and a meal with the local Zulu clans or with the occupants of one of the outlying white farms.

The Cuthbertsons' house appeared to be deserted when Charles arrived, so he tied up his horse and went round the back, where he found Alice's mother feeding chickens. She started when Charles spoke and told her who he was.

"Oh," she said, "You gave me a terrible fright. We don't get many visitors here, you know, it's a bit out of the way. Alice did say she thought you might pay us a visit; she'll be pleased to see you, I expect. Fix your horse up and put him in the paddock over there." She pointed. "There's some feed in the store."

Charles spent some time making sure his horse was properly watered and fed and brushed. He cleaned the animal's feet and once he was sure all was well, turned him out into the paddock. During the summer months the horse would be fine outside at night. He was just about to go inside when Alice and her father rode up. Somewhat to Charles' surprise, Alice was wearing riding breeches and rode astride instead of sidesaddle as women were expected to do. Tom Cuthbertson was a tall man, with bushy eyebrows and a steely expression on his face. Although his hair showed tinges of grey, he was the epitome of strength and determination. Charles could see that he would do well to stay on the right side of this man. Alice introduced Charles and then said, "Dad, you go inside; Charles and I will see to the horses."

Tom nodded and left them.

Alice was obviously pleased to see Charles and they chatted about inconsequential things as they watered and fed the animals. They brushed against each other once and were both surprised and thrilled by the electric shock that produced. The African dusk was setting in, and they let the two horses into the same paddock as Charles' horse and watched for a few minutes to make sure there wasn't any unpleasantness toward the strange horse. After much whinnying and some play-acting on the part of Tom's horse, the animals seemed to settle down. They couldn't be seen from the house and Alice, after making sure that the horses were going to behave, returned to the stables, followed by Charles. She was surprised by the way her body responded to Charles proximity, it was the same reaction as had happened on the dance floor and she wasn't sure how to deal with it. In her embarrassment she took her large hat off and shook out her reddish brown curls.

"Mum always insists I wear this," she laughed. "Keeps the sun off."

Charles moved closer; he loved the sweet scent of her. He had almost plucked up the courage to kiss her when there was a yell from the house. It was Alice's mother Meg. "Supper's ready."

Alice glanced at Charles as they made their way to the house, he was slightly flushed and breathing harder than any recent exertion warranted.

The house faced north to make the most of the sun in the winter when warmth was at a premium. The front veranda looked down a tree-lined valley, which had a stream running the length of it away from the mountains. Behind the house was the majesty of the Drakensberg, towering eleven thousand feet or more above sea level and five thousand feet above the house.

The talk over dinner was about routine farming matters; it was assumed that while he stayed Charles would make himself useful round the farm.

Charles had heard rumours concerning the Cuthbertsons and their origins: that Meg had been a barmaid and Tom the eldest, now disgraced, son of a prominent and wealthy family. None of that mattered to him and it all seemed irrelevant in the remote reaches of the new colony. As far as Charles was concerned he was completely smitten with Alice, and her parents went out of their way to be pleasant and hospitable.

Charles was put in a room as far away from Alice as could be managed in that little house. Alice's room was right next to that of her parents. Before ten o'clock they were all in bed and the hurricane lamps had been extinguished.

There was a rap on Charles' door at five thirty a.m. It was Alice.

"There's a cup of tea in the kitchen," she called.

"O.K."

Charles scrambled out of bed. He poured water from a large enamel jug into an enamel basin and splashed the almost freezing water onto his face. He dressed quickly.

He found Tom Cuthbertson and Meg sitting at the kitchen table drinking tea. Meg poured him a cup and smiled.

"Sleep well?" Meg asked.

Charles nodded. A few minutes later Alice appeared. Looking fresh and beautiful she was dressed as she had been the day before in riding breeches and a shirt. She gave her parents a peck on the cheek each and poured herself a cup of tea, and looked fondly at Charles.

Tom got up.

"I'll just go and rouse the labour." He looked at Charles. "We normally do a few chores, come back here for breakfast about eight and then go out again. I need to see Mahbule the Hlubi chief this week some time. We also have to brand the calves over the next few days."

"Fine," said Charles. "I'll help wherever I can."

The next few days saw Charles and Alice working together branding calves, castrating male calves and male lambs and tailing all the young lambs. They helped with the milking and repaired some fences that had been knocked down. They worked well together and with the Hlubi labourers, who enjoyed Charles' banter. They were quite used to Alice, who had been helping out ever since she was a child and who worked as hard as any of them. Charles marvelled that Alice could transform herself from an unsophisticated farmer's daughter into the cultured, beautiful girl he had met only weeks before in Pietermaritzburg.

One morning they got up earlier than usual and ensuring that they had food and water in the saddlebags, they set off into the mountains. Both Tom and Alice had similar hunting rifles and Alice had her saddlebags full of bandages and medicines.

"Dad and I pay a visit to the chief about once a month. We help them as much as we can. I trained as a nurse, for a few years in 'Maritzburg, and we tend to their ailments, as best we can" said Alice simply.

After a steep climb into the mountains, they rode their horses through a narrow pass and emerged into a protected, fertile valley. After a brief conversation with two warriors in the pass, they were allowed through.

"They are always suspicious of strangers," explained Tom. "Your language skills immediately put them at ease." Charles had greeted the guards formally in their own language.

The valley was well watered and at this time of year was green with freshly planted crops. The cattle looked fat and well although there weren't many of them.

"The herds are slowly building up," said Tom. "They were unjustly forced to pay a fine of eight thousand head a year or two back."

Charles nodded.

"Alice told me the full story," he said. Tom looked sharply at Alice who said nothing. On reflection she thought that she had been indiscreet and half wished she had not told Charles how she and her father had helped the Hlubi; if the story ever got out the family would suffer, she knew.

When they arrived at the chiefs' village they were greeted like old friends. Alice was immediately mobbed by the women, and she spent half an hour admiring new babies and catching up on the gossip.

Tom and Charles were taken to an area outside the chief's hut and they, together with the menfolk of the village, passed round a calabash of *utshwala*. Charles was familiar with the process. It would take some time before any business was discussed, and Tom had explained the things that would be raised: the depredations of a local leopard, more help with raising the quality of livestock and on Tom's side, the shortage of young men willing to work. Halfway through the discussions, Alice came over and asked if Charles would come and help with the clinic. None of the other women would have dared to interrupt the men, but Alice being white was able to get away with it.

The clinic had been normal. Alice had dealt with colds, cuts and bruises. She had examined all the new mothers and their babies and had dished out appropriate medicine.

Now there was a boy, in his early teens, with what looked like a broken leg, lying on a rough-hewn table. He was obviously in pain. "What are you going to do?" asked Charles. The situation looked really difficult and there was clearly an expectation from the assembled women that Alice would be able to do something.

"I will try to straighten it out and then he needs to be kept still for at least two weeks, but what I really need is for some splints which I can tie up to keep the bones in place."

"O.K. maybe I can help with that," said Charles. "How long do they have to be?"

Alice showed him.

Charles went away and with the few tools they had brought with them, within half an hour he had fashioned four splints, from branches of a nearby tree.

"How will you keep him quiet, won't this be terribly painful?"

"I've made him chew a leaf that the *sangoma* showed me, which should sedate him a bit. If it gets too bad they will give him *dagga* to smoke, or chew."

"Now you must help me hold him down, this will be painful."

Charles held his good leg, and two women held his arms, with another holding the broken leg above the knee.

Alice laid out her bandages and the splints on the table. She had examined the leg carefully. There was no sign of a break in the skin.

"The trick is to try to set the leg straight."

As soon as Alice held the leg, the boy screamed in pain and then fainted.

Alice went about her business and as best she could, straightened the leg out. She and one of the women then bound the splints tightly onto the leg with the long length of bandage that she had with her.

"He is not to move for two weeks," she told the boy's mother.

"We now need a pair of crutches," said Alice looking at Charles.

"Where did you learn to do all that?" he asked.

"The hospital in 'Maritzburg."

"Should he now go to a doctor somewhere?" asked Charles.

"They won't go, it is a long way and since the Langalibalele affair they want nothing to do with the white settler community. They trust us though, and a few others here in the mountains, but the Government, no, they will have nothing to do with them."

Charles made the boy some crutches.

Alice spent a few minutes making sure that the mother understood her instructions.

"They don't always listen," she confided to Charles. "If he moves much during the next few weeks he will always walk with a limp."

By this time it was late afternoon and the cloud had come right down over the mountain and the village, shrouding them in mist. Chief Mahbule walked out with Tom, looked up the mountain and said, "You cannot go home, *Nkosi,* much too dangerous. It will be fine in the morning."

Charles made sure the horses were looked after and tethered inside the village, which was protected by a large fence made from bushes piled on top of each other. The huts were the usual beehive type huts seen throughout Zululand and Natal.

Charles was still intrigued by Alice's activities.

"What happens if the boy dies?" he asked.

"I don't think he will, but if he dies, he dies; it happens all the time here: snakebites, lions, various diseases, Zulu raids," she answered.

"What do the authorities think? Do they know you run this clinic?" asked Charles.

Alice laughed.

"They know very little about what goes on around here," she said. "And certainly now, nobody volunteers anything."

Alice was included in the men's meal in the chiefs' hut in deference to her white skin. The conversation was general and centred around the weather and the prospects for crops.

The chief directed the conversation towards the Langalibalele incident, which had changed his whole perspective on the advent of the white people in his country:

"*Nkosi,*" he said respectfully, "since you have come here you have helped us with medicines given to us by *Nkosikasi* Meg and now she has grown up by *Nkosikasi* Alice here." He smiled fondly at Alice, who was a favourite in the village. "We have also helped you and some of my people come and work with you."

"Yes," said Tom.

"When you first came we could have chased you away or even killed you; we did not know anything about why you were here or what you wanted. We had no knowledge of what new things you could bring to us to help us."

Tom said nothing. He remembered the long discussions he had had with Mahbule's father, the previous chief, who had eventually agreed to cooperate with the Cuthbertsons.

"But you and my father had good vision of the future and you decided to work together and both you and my people have benefited. Our cattle are fatter and have more calves and our crops give us a better harvest. And you, *Nkosi,* now have a good farm."

Tom looked uncomfortable. He was well aware how vulnerable the farm was if the Hlubi turned against him.

"Now this *Somseu,* he seems to want to own us, almost like slaves. He has forced us to come back here and we have to pay his taxes, so our young people they have to go to the farms or to *Thekwini* to work, to collect money so I can pay the taxes. When they are here these young people are educated in our ways, the wise ways of our ancestors, but when they go away, they forget those ways and they lose respect for the elders of this village. I also hear stories of excessive drinking and paying for sex with loose women. These are against all our ways. It seems that *Somseu,* who calls himself the 'white father of the Zulu people' just wants to destroy the Zulu and us the Hlubi, who as you know are not Zulus although our language is similar."

Tom in his heart agreed with the sentiments of Mahbule but felt obliged to offer some sort of counter argument:

"*Somseu* and people like him will not be here for ever, *Nkosi;* we must all hope that people of goodwill like your father and you and me will continue to help each other for the benefit of all the people."

Mahbule looked somewhat mollified, he wanted the cooperation with the Cuthbertsons to continue, but he went on:

"That stinking Zulu King Cetswayo, he has many *ibutho,* just waiting to fight. His father Mpande, a wise old man, managed to keep the peace with the whites, but I can see that Cetswayo will chase all the whites into the sea and then we will have trouble again like we did with Shaka and the *mfecane,* when the Zulu tried to make slaves of all of us, almost the same as *Somseu.*"

Tom could see the conflicts in Mahbule's mind, it seemed that despite the recent past he thought that it was probably in his long-term interests to cooperate with whites.

Charles was fascinated; this was deeper conversation than he had ever experienced with his friends the Cele, although he supposed the arguments would be much the same.

Alice kept her own counsel. Although, because of her white skin she was included in the men's meal, she thought that any comment from her, being a woman, would be considered inappropriate.

Towards the end of the meal, on a lighter note, some of the older men told stories handed down over the generations about deeds of past heroes. Many included myths relating to the wild animals that were part of their lives. Later, Alice was ushered off with the women to sleep in one of the women's huts. Charles and Tom slept in the chief's hut. This was all completely normal for Charles, since he had spent many such nights with the Cele clan near his home.

The chief had questioned Charles politely about his background, and the information about his associations with the Cele clan was stored away for future reference.

The cloud had lifted by dawn the next day, and after an early breakfast they set off back to the Cuthbertsons' farm. Alice had seen the boy with the broken leg and all appeared to be under control.

"I think I will take Charles the long way back," said Alice to her father. "It's Saturday today and it's going to be really spectacular up there with the weather clearing like it has."

Tom nodded. He didn't really try to control his headstrong daughter any more and Charles had made a good impression on him.

"Be sure to be home before nightfall," he said gruffly, glancing at Charles.

"Of course," said Alice smiling.

Tom really had no fears for his daughter. She knew these mountains intimately and had spent most of her youth riding and walking through them with him and with the Hlubi. He worried a little about Charles but he knew his daughter would never do anything she didn't want to do.

Tom trotted off unconcernedly and then Alice, leading the way, headed up the mountain. Charles was looking about him, admiring the mountain in all its glory and wondering where the path was leading when Alice indicated an almost invisible path, which traced its way round a bush and into a narrow gully with steep sides. The horses were allowed to find their own way among the rough stones and after a lengthy scramble up the steep path they found themselves on a small but spectacular upland plain.

"I would never have found that opening on my own," remarked

Charles when they had stopped to give the horses a breather.

"The village *sangoma* showed it to me some years ago. We were trapped up here in a snowstorm for three days before we were able to return home," she said.

The plain extended to the base of a buttress, where a thin spray of water tumbled off the rock into a still pool. There were a few small trees and bushes round the edge. "This is my private place," said Alice. "Nobody much knows about it although I've been here once with my father." She looked at him knowingly. "In the summer I come up here and swim sometimes," she said. "We can tether the horses so they can graze over there, and we can picnic here next to the water." She showed him the cave where she and the *sangoma,* had once found shelter in the snowstorm she had talked about earlier.

Charles organised the horses and put their saddles out of the way. He collected some sticks for a fire and Alice produced a loaf of bread and some meat from the Hlubi village. She had a few tomatoes from her mother's vegetable garden. They sat on the coats that were part of their equipment and nibbled at the lunch. Charles could think of nothing but his desire to kiss her but wondered what her reaction would be. When dealing with the Hlubi she had seemed completely self-assured, now she seemed hesitant almost as if she wondered whether she should have brought him to this place at all. Just as he had plucked up courage to lean over and kiss her she stood up and moved away slightly. He was very surprised when she said: "I'm going for a swim and you must promise not to look, so turn your back. You can swim later. It is such a beautiful day."

There was a great deal of rustling as Charles sat virtuously with his back to the pool and then he heard a splash. "You can turn round now," she called laughing. He noticed her clothes in an untidy pile near the water and Alice was swimming strongly out in the middle. "Your turn," she caught him by surprise again. "I'll look away." She swam away from where he was and after a moment's hesitation he tore off his clothing and ran into the cold water. As soon as Alice heard the splash she turned around and swam back towards him. He was conscious of the outline of Alice's pale naked figure in the clear water. She stayed a few feet away from him and said: "I'll race you to the other side and back." Before he realized what was happening she was off and he only managed to overhaul her a few feet before they reached the shore near their picnic place. After some more swimming around and playful splashing she said: "It's getting a bit cold. If you look away again I'll get out and dress behind that bush and I'll come back when you call me."

He looked away and heard her getting out of the water, but he couldn't resist and he turned around just in time to see a flash of shapely pale white buttock and the outline of an upright breast fast disappearing behind a nearby bush.

Charles emerged from the water and dried himself as best he could with his shirt. When he had dressed, leaving off the shirt, he called and a few moments later Alice emerged from behind a bush looking fresh with her damp hair. Her wet shirt accentuated the shape of her firm upright breasts. He hung his own shirt on a bush.

"More lunch," he offered.

As Alice approached, rather to her surprise, he clumsily reached out and planted a kiss on her mouth. She stood still for a moment and then gently pushed him away saying nothing. "Kiss me Alice, please," he pleaded. "I want to kiss you, you are so beautiful." She tried to pull away but Charles was not that easily put off and he held on round her waist. Within a few short seconds he could feel her resistance weakening and soon she was pressing her body into his and had returned the kiss with a passion that he found exhilarating. They fell on the coats and the kiss was deepened, with their tongues seeking out each other. Charles was now lying almost on top of her with Alice's arms around his neck. He started to undo the buttons of her shirt and pushed her vest up to expose her big firm breasts, which stood erect right there in his face. Charles thought he was in heaven, he kissed one then the other; Alice showed no resistance, she appeared to want it to continue, so he kissed her again and then moved his hand down to the top of her riding breeches. She tried to pull away: "No, no, Charles not that, please. Just kiss me some more." So he did. After half an hour they lay back exhausted lovingly looking each other in the eye.

"Do you know about *hlobonga?*" asked Charles.

He had been encouraged by Magaye to participate in the teenage rituals of his age group, which also involved *hlobonga,* where the girls and boys of the age group are encouraged to lie together without full penetration taking place. The girl keeps her legs together to give the man sexual pleasure and the girl takes her pleasure as she can. So Charles had had some sexual experience with his Zulu age group and more than once with a willing white girl from one of the outlying farms.

"I know about *hlobonga,* but you can put that out of your mind. I will wait until I am married as is the Christian tradition."

He kissed her again and happily fondled her breasts, which stood erect with all the attention they were receiving.

As the sun lowered itself towards the horizon they reluctantly packed up, saddled the horses and returned to the farm, arriving at dusk.

There was time for a quick kiss as they tended the horses before they were called in for supper.

Meg looked speculatively at Alice's sparkling eyes and happy face, but the discussion centred round their visit to the village and the majestic beauty of the mountains.

The next day being Sunday, only a few essential chores were completed on the farm, the most important being milking the cows.

Charles spent another two weeks at the Cuthbertsons; he made himself useful around the farm and he and Alice returned to the Hlubi village where the boy with the broken leg had listened to Alice and looked as if he would make a good recovery.

They also spent many happy hours at their special pool high up in the Drakensberg, swimming as before and kissing, with Alice always in charge, and not allowing Charles any more liberties than he had already taken.

They had had a few desultory discussions about the future, which Charles found inconclusive and unsatisfactory. He was due to return home the next week and when they rode up to the pool on the Sunday he was determined to somehow bring the issue to a head. They swam as usual and spent a happy hour kissing and fondling each other. Charles was convinced that they were in love and all he had to do was propose to her and she would marry him. He still had in the back of his mind the question of really helping the Zulu, but he was uncertain how to go about it and whether he could become a missionary priest.

He knelt in front of her with her clothing still in disarray and said:

"Alice, I love you more than any other person I have ever met. I want you more than anything else in the world."

"I love you too," she said in a very quiet voice, looking away.

"Alice, then will you marry me."

She looked him straight in the eye and said firmly but quietly:

"Charles, no, I can't marry you. My life's work is with the Zulu and as we have discussed if I am to help them in any way I will have to be the wife of a missionary, in Zululand. He'll then run the mission, with all that involves and I will run a proper clinic."

"What's wrong with what you are doing here, you seem to be doing a great job here, well accepted and appreciated by the local people."

"This is rather part time, what I had in mind was a full time clinic, even a hospital maybe, in time."

"What about us, you and me? I can't just forget you, you know. I can't think of anyone else or anything else, I love you and nobody else. You want me to just go away. Who is this missionary you will marry?"

"There is no missionary right now, but my belief is that I have been put here to do some good and if that is my destiny then I have faith that I will marry such a person and spend my life with the Zulu, north of the Tugela."

"But you said that you loved me; is that not more important than anything else?"

Alice cried but said through her tears: "The only person that I will marry will be someone who can help me fulfill my destiny. If it is not you then maybe I will learn to love him as well."

"You think that it could be me?"

"If you become a priest and then if the Church will let you go to Zululand to become a missionary, then yes."

"How long will you wait for me?"

Alice shrugged.

They kissed, gently at first and then with more passion. Soon it was time to pack up and return to the farm.

The evening meal was a rather subdued affair with Meg looking from Charles to Alice to see if she could detect any signs of tension. She had half expected that Charles would ask for Alice's hand, but to her disappointment nothing had transpired.

Alice rode with Charles for an hour to see him on his way. They kissed passionately before parting. Charles had very little idea of how to go about becoming a priest and wondering whether he would ever see Alice again turned for home with a heavy heart.

When he arrived home he discussed his dilemma with his parents. They had never seen him so smitten with any of the young women in the district. He awkwardly explained the situation.

"Are you certain that you are cut out to be a missionary in Zululand? It will be very tough and in any case, so far, the King has refused anyone permission to establish a mission station. It may just be a pipe dream, you may have to wait forever and then what will you do? Your whole life could be wasted waiting for something that is unattainable. If you want my advice I would forget all about Alice. From what I hear she comes from a peculiar background anyway, with her father being a remittance man and her mother a low-class barmaid. As I have said you can take over this place and in time you will find a very nice girl who will make you a good wife and can help on the farm, like your mother has here."

Charles didn't rise to the bait, and just forlornly looked at his parents: "I will never be able to forget Alice, not as long as I live. I understand what she is trying to do and I would be able to help with my knowledge of the Zulu."

"Think about it, son," was all his father had to offer. "In a few months Alice will be nothing but a dream."

A week later he asked his father: "The least I can do is to go and see the bishop and see what is possible. Maybe I could go to England and train as a priest, but I don't know what that involves."

His father reluctantly agreed to accompany him to see the bishop.

The bishop regarded the local settlers rather disdainfully and thought of them as poorly educated louts, who misunderstood and mistreated the local blacks. He was curious about Charles and his father and listened with half an ear to what they had to say. He could see the value of having Zulu speakers as missionaries but was concerned about their levels of education. As they went out an Archdeacon, who had been in the meeting offered them a cup of tea and showed much more interest in their situation. He made Charles read a few passages from the bible, which he did quite competently, much to Archdeacon Green's relief. Many of the locally born would have had trouble even doing that. He tried to establish why Charles wanted to become a missionary and found Charles reasonably convincing, although he thought that there was more to the story than Charles was letting on; Charles had not mentioned Alice of course.

"I suggest that you become familiar with the bible and I will send you some references to passages that will help with that; I will also lend you some of my Shakespeare and this new author Dickens which will help with your general education. Come back in six months and we will see how you have progressed." As Archdeacon Green ushered them out Charles' father asked: "We could send him to England if that was necessary, but would it help?"

"It would be difficult," said Green evasively. "Do as I suggest and we will see."

Charles was elated and during the next months he did all that was asked of him.

◇◇◇◇◇◇◇◇◇◇◇◇◇◇◇◇

Chapter 5

By the time Fritz and his entourage had left the Cape the Koekemoer family expedition had been on the road for more than a month.

It took Frank a few days to firmly identify all the members of the expedition and very quickly he helped them establish a routine where they were all up and ready to go when the dawn broke.

The Koekemoers were as motley a crew as Frank had ever had the misfortune to be involved with. There was Elsie, whose husband Stompie had been employed for some years by her brother, a baker in Fish Hoek, who found him lazy and incompetent. "Good riddance," he thought, when Stompie and Elsie told him they were going to the diamond fields.

"We'll be rich, rich like Fritz," Stompie told his brother-in-law uncharitably, "and you'll still be penny pinching in that old bakery of yours."

Kobus had a clerical job in the Cape government offices. Almost all of his colleagues were English speaking and looked down on Kobus for no reason other than that he was different. It had been made quite clear that he had no chance of promotion within the service. After considering the matter long and hard, he and his wife, Cora, decided to accompany the expedition. "We will never get another chance like this," he told Cora, "and if that *skellum* Fritz can find diamonds, we should also be able to." They had some concerns over their seventeen-year-old daughter Hannelore, but thought that it was best for her to accompany them so they could keep an eye on her. "Besides," said Kobus, "if what Fritz says is true, we will only be up there a few months and then we can return here and live comfortably. Hannelore can then find a nice, rich husband and settle down here in the Cape."

Pik had a very small wine farm in the Stellenbosch area, on which he and his wife Anna barely scraped a living; in fact Anna often helped out in a dress shop in Stellenbosch to make ends meet. "Maybe we will find some diamonds like Fritz did and be able to buy a bigger place," said Pik. The farm was left in the hands of a coloured overseer and Uncle Piet Koekemoer said he would look in from time to time to see that all was well. As far as Pik was concerned, he was giving nothing up and if the worst came to the worst he would just return to what he was doing.

P.W. was the foreman on a large wine property near Paarl. He was happily married to Hannetjie and they had three children. He was competent at what he did and was well provided for. It had been one of his ambitions for a long time to buy his own place and this seemed the ideal opportunity. He had little regard for Fritz and assumed that if Fritz could find diamonds, anyone could. Hannetjie was dead against the arrangement. "You have a perfectly good job here," she said. "We're comfortably off; our three children are being educated; this is a wild goose chase and it could be very dangerous. You have always thought that Fritz was no good and now you want to follow in his footsteps." But the diamond bug had bitten P.W. badly; he gave up his job and the house they lived in went with the job. His family had no choice but to leave and accompany him.

Magnus was unemployed more often than not and he did odd jobs in and around Stellenbosch to keep him and his wife, Mimi, and their two children from starvation. They lived in an old shack owned by Uncle Piet Koekemoer. For them the decision was easy.

Piet had provided five wagons for the Koekemoer family, together with horses, oxen and provisions for the journey and all the equipment needed for exploration. Although Frank was part of the expedition, he had provided his own horses, wagon, provisions, and equipment and two coloured wagoners. From the very beginning the organisation was chaotic. Frank had thought he had identified each and every Koekemoer after the first week. Well into the second week, he came across someone the others referred to as *Oom*. It was early morning and *Oom* was paralytically drunk and had just fallen down whilst trying to climb out of his wagon to relieve himself. When Frank enquired, he was told that *Oom* had been like he was for fifteen years "And anyway, who else is going to *blerry* well look after him?" said Elsie defensively.

"It's going to be tough up there," said Frank. "*Oom*, as you call him, won't survive, and besides, we need people to look for diamonds, not to sit around clutching a brandy bottle."

"You, Mr. fucking Devereaux, mind your own *blerry* business, this is a family matter," said Stompie, who Frank had gathered was Elsie's husband. He came up and tried to push Frank away but he didn't budge. Stompie glared at Frank.

"This is no picnic, Stompie," said Frank evenly, "and don't come running to me looking for help." Stompie spat a stream of tobacco juice at Frank's feet, being very careful not to actually spit on him.

Frank was concerned that few of the Koekemoers seemed suited to enduring the hardships the enterprise would entail. There were also half a dozen children, who flitted from wagon to wagon; these varied in age from the seventeen-year-old Hannelore, to a young boy of no more than six or seven. Hannelore peered shyly out from under a large sunbonnet and had a pretty, freckled face. "Trouble," thought Frank, as soon as he set eyes on her.

One evening early on he decided that he had to take the matter firmly into his own hands. So after dinner he addressed the throng:

"We are making very slow progress," he said. "Piet said he would try to give us some breathing space before the news of the diamond find was general knowledge, but if we go on at this pace others will overtake us and any advantage we might have by being there first will be lost. And another thing, when we get there we are going to have to dig to find diamonds. You people seem to think we can just wander about in the veld and pick up stones."

There was silence, then Stompie spat in the fire and said, "If that big *pampoen* Fritz can find diamonds, so can anyone."

They all laughed and the chatter started again. Frank interrupted, "Just listen to me; it's still six hundred miles to the diamond fields, most of that is through dry dusty and dangerous bush. We have to get on. We need to leave at dawn each day and have some well-planned stops so the oxen can graze and keep their strength up. Here's a map; I've marked all the stops

　　　　　　　　　　　　　　　　　　　　　　　　　Rough Diamonds

and what we need to cover in a day. This will get us to the diamond fields in three months. The way we are going now it will take more than a year, if we ever arrive at all."

There was a stunned silence. In their previous lives only Pik and P.W. had ever had cause to see the dawn, and they all preferred to take life at a leisurely pace.

"So we get up at sunrise?" said Stompie hopefully.

"No Stompie," said Frank firmly. "We leave at dawn. That means you have to be ready and packed by then with the oxen inspanned. I will be getting up at four."

"Four?" asked Stompie with incredulity.

"Yes, for some of you it may need to be earlier," said Frank.

They all stared at Frank.

"And a few other things, while we are about it. All this equipment was lent to you by Piet; I am sure he expects to be paid for it sometime," said Frank, looking about. There were a few leery grins; he wondered if any of them had the slightest intention of ever paying anything back. "I'm going to the diamond fields and I'm going to be one of the first there; if you people can't pull yourselves together, I'll go on my own."

The party broke up early that night and apart from some mutterings, the camp was quiet by ten p.m. The next morning Frank rose at 3:30 a.m. and noisily woke everyone up. By sunrise they were on their way. Frank had thought of trying to throw away all the alcohol he could find but he thought better of it. "Anyway" he mused, "the way these people plan they will run out before we are halfway."

Fritz and his party met up with rest of the group, who were camped near the small hamlet of Beaufort West, which Frank thought was about half way to the diamond fields. On the journey they had passed one other wagon train, which to Fritz's amazement was manned by Lieutenant North and some of the men from his troop. North showed no sign of recognizing Fritz, who really bore little physical resemblance to the very ragged man they had encountered in the veld now some three months earlier. Fritz was surprised at the strength of the emotion that struck him when he realized who he was talking to and he and his people moved rapidly on. It was clear that North was going to search for diamonds as well, although neither party was willing to divulge their true intentions. All Fritz could think about in the days that followed was how he could wreak revenge on North and the British for what they had done to him.

In the five days they spent at Beaufort West, Frank helped the Koekemoers with minor repairs to their wagons as well as replenishing some supplies. They were also able to swap some of their teams of oxen with teams that had had a few weeks to recover from the ardours of the trek from the Cape.

When Fritz arrived he noticed that a wagon was missing.

"What happened?" he asked Frank.

P.W. and Magnus took him by the elbow and explained the situation.

They were about to camp by the side of the Buffalo River when Frank had suggested that because of a threatening storm, the river might come down in flood during the night, and probably sweep them all downstream. Most of the party took notice of Frank's good sense, but Stompie, who objected to being given directions by anyone, let alone an ignorant foreigner, left his wagon where it was, while the others all moved their wagons to higher ground. As Frank had predicted, there was a storm and the river came down in flood. Stompie had been woken by the noise and had managed to crawl out of his wagon and had just saved himself, but he was unable to save Elsie and *Oom*.

"We spent two days looking for them down the river," explained Magnus. "But it was no use, we found some broken pieces from the wagon and other bits and pieces, but nothing else. Most of the oxen had already been moved to higher ground, so we have a spare team."

"What does Stompie have to say about all this?" asked Fritz.

"He has said almost nothing since the accident, he's too shocked. We just leave him alone. He rides with us now," said Magnus. "Don't say anything to him, he's really not himself."

Fritz rode with the party for a few days and then started to fret with the slower progress of the wagon train against the much faster horses that he had become used to.

"Maybe Frans, Vic and I should just push on and start to set things up for when you arrive," he said reasonably. The other members of the expedition said nothing; they felt that they had an established way of operating and Fritz was a disruptive influence, so they were quite happy for him to move on.

Hannelore had remained fairly quiet during the trip but continued to make eyes at Frank. He had no intention of getting further involved with any of the Koekemoers and he gave her no encouragement whatsoever. Twice he had found her in his bedroll when he turned in at night. The first time he gently told her to return to her own wagon, the second time he gave her a good hard whack on her naked buttocks and sent her on her way.

Rough Diamonds

A few days after the conversation about Fritz moving on, nothing further was said; then Frank noticed that Hannelore was now riding Fritz's spare horse.

"You stupid, stupid bugger," muttered Frank to himself. He kept his eyes open and sure enough, once the camp had settled down that night he saw the slight figure of Hannelore creeping out of her wagon and making its way to where Fritz and Vic and Frans had set their bedrolls. He saw her crawl into Vic's bedroll, which was strategically placed away from the others behind a small bush. This had the potential to cause more trouble. "Dammit," he thought, "Surely he has enough authority to stop this. She is his niece; he should be protecting her not encouraging his nephews sleep with her."

When they were on the road again the next day, Frank managed to get Fritz on his own.

"I thought you were going to go on ahead," said Frank.

"*Ja*, well, I'm quite enjoying being here with the wagons, maybe I'll go in a week or something," answered Fritz.

Frank sighed and said, "Look, it's pretty obvious that Hannelore is sleeping with Vic. When the parents find out there will be big trouble; there's been enough trouble already on this trip, with the death of Elsie and *Oom*."

Fritz shrugged and tried to pretend that he knew nothing.

"I've seen her leaving her wagon and getting into Vic's bed; it's no good trying to deny it," said Frank. "You must be as aware of it as I am."

"It's got nothing to do with you," responded Fritz angrily.

"Fritz, I have a big stake in this expedition and all I can see is trouble; I don't need any more unnecessary disruption. The journey gives us all the trouble we need. Fritz, you know this is wrong. Just go ahead with Frans and Vic, as you had planned and maybe she will have forgotten all about the affair when the rest of us arrive in the diamond area."

"Vic says she came to him, if she wants it that bad who am I to interfere?" said Fritz.

"Yes," said Frank. "She tried that on me; I just gave her a big whack on the bum and told her to behave herself."

"So you want me to leave so you can have her to yourself?" said Fritz.

"No, you stupid bugger, I want nothing to do with her, but you are responsible for your nephew, surely you can sort this out so that nobody gets hurt. He needs to be told that what he is doing is wrong." said Frank in exasperation.

Fritz was in a bind, he had already knowingly turned a blind eye to the situation, he could hardly now tell Vic that it was all wrong.

"What do think Kobus and Cora will say when they find out, and it won't be long?" asked Frank.

"They can say what they like, I found the diamonds in the first place, they didn't have to come on this trip." answered Fritz harshly. Fritz rode off.

The matter came to a head that night. Frank was woken up by a lot of shouting, then a shot. He scrambled into his clothes and ran over to where the fracas was.

Kobus was standing over a now cowering Vic, with a revolver in his hand. Hannelore, wrapped in a blanket, was being firmly marched away from the scene by her mother Cora.

"Tell me why I shouldn't put a bullet through your thick skull" said Kobus through his teeth. "You are a no-good piece of dog shit, just like your uncle Fritz here."

"No, no, please Kobus, leave him alone, let me explain," said Fritz, trying to dress. Frank went firmly up to Kobus and gently took away the revolver. Fritz recovered; he and Vic now made a move towards Kobus.

"Both of you stay where you are," said Frank, "or it will be me that puts a bullet in you."

He was relieved to see that nobody was injured.

By this time the whole camp was awake and the fire was rebuilt. When they found out what had happened Vic and with him Fritz was abused by all.

"You must have seen what was going on, Fritz, are you so weak that you were unable to stop this?" asked Kobus. "Or are you just too stupid to care?"

The abuse went on with Fritz bearing the brunt of it.

"All right, all right," said Frank. "Fritz, I think that you, Frans and Vic should go ahead to the diamond fields as planned. That will give everyone a chance to calm down. I think Stompie should go with you."

"Stompie?" said Fritz in horror.

"Yes," said Frank. "He can ride your spare horse; I think you should go right away."

Fritz looked nonplussed. Frank took him back to his bedroll and told Fritz's servants what was happening.

"I found the diamonds, if it wasn't for me none of this would have happened." said Fritz defensively, waving his arms about indicating the whole wagon train.

"Yes you did, but you can't run around behaving as if these people belong to you. You need them too, you know. You keep a tighter rein on those two nephews of yours and tell them to keep their hands off Hannelore. Now go before we bury you here."

Within half an hour Fritz and his entourage rode off, with a rather bewildered Stompie accompanying him.

Once they had left Beaufort West the country became drier and drier and they found that the caravan became a target for scavengers and then predators, mainly lions, who saw the oxen and horses as legitimate prey. Frank insisted that the men all took it in turns to keep watch at night together with one of the coloured wagoners and during the day from time to time some of the men rode out and fired shots in the air to scare the lions away.

The precautions all worked, if the lions came too close they were chased off with volleys of rifle shots over their heads and they found that if they chased the lions far enough away in the afternoon they were not bothered during the night.

There was a discussion one evening round the fire about organising a lion hunt. Frank urged caution:

"Do any of you have any experience at all, hunting lions?"

There was silence.

"What is our main purpose in going on this trip?"

Again there was silence; they all knew the answer to that.

"Then please, don't do anything foolish. We will need all the hands we can get when we arrive on the diamond fields. There are going to be injuries and deaths a-plenty if my experience in California is anything to go by. I hope that it all won't start sooner than that."

They all went to bed as usual with Frank assuming that he had made his point.

Unbeknown to Frank there was a hurried discussion among the four remaining men: Kobus, PW, Magnus and Pik.

"Who the hell is this foreigner to tell us what we should be doing. This is our country and he is taking over. I for one am going lion hunting in the morning and I will be leaving camp at 5am. Is anyone coming with me?" said PW forcefully.

There was some hesitation and then both Kobus and Magnus said they would join him.

"There is really no danger," said Kobus, "we will just go out there shoot a couple of lions and come back, that's it. We have all seen how they run away."

"Frank has been right most of the time, we would still have Elsie and *Oom* with us if Stompie had listened to him," said Pik uncertainly.

"*Ag*, Stompie, we all know that he is really stupid. Nobody takes any notice of him anyway," said Kobus dismissively.

"Come on Pik, it will be fun, we have had no fun on this trip, it's just work, work, work. What difference will it make if we arrive at the diggings a day or so later," said Magnus.

Pik always wanted to be one of the 'boys', so he said: "OK, but I will just watch, you can do the shooting."

Frank woke at the usual hour to find the camp virtually deserted, none of the men and few of the coloured wagoners were visible.

"They went hunting?" he asked Hannetjie.

She nodded.

"You had better keep some water boiling and get out your dressings and bandages then. That is what I will be doing."

She looked at him uncertainly.

"Hunting lions is dangerous," said Frank. "If they don't know what they are doing, someone will get hurt."

At about midday a very sorry little party arrived back at the campsite.

Kobus was dead and PW badly mauled, he would be lucky to survive and certainly would be unable to work for a number of months. There were no lion trophies.

Frank said nothing. He just helped Hannetjie clean PW's wounds and set his broken arm and leg. He also helped her set up a bed in the wagon in which PW could travel.

Pik tried to explain: "It was so quick…"

Frank held up his hand.

"Save it, I don't want to hear."

They buried Kobus that afternoon and the next morning a very subdued party continued on its way north.

At the start of the twelfth week they came upon the first few of the diamond hunters that would soon be migrating in their thousands to what was to be known as Kimberley. They were directed to Fritz's little shack, which was much as he had left it only six short months earlier. Fritz said nothing when he was told of the further tragedy that had befallen the expedition.

◇◇◇◇◇◇◇◇◇◇◇◇◇◇◇

Chapter 6

Despite the start on the Koekemoers had had on their journey from the Cape to the diamond claims, already, in dribs and drabs, people were coming to the area to search for diamonds.

Fritz and his nephews had marked out the Koekemoer claims as well as all of Frank's claims.

"It's not going to be easy," Fritz confided in Frank. "At the moment it's very hard pick and shovel work and the local *kaffirs*, the Tswana, are lazy, they will not do any work, man."

"Do you think your Koekemoer relatives will be prepared to work?" asked Frank.

"I hope so," said Fritz wryly, "what's left of them."

Within days, much to Frank's surprise, the whole Koekemoer clan set out to work their claims. Fritz had unloaded the wagons and set out the picks and shovels. At Frank's insistence he had included in his loads some big, hand held sieves. Within a few days they had dug up a large pile of sand and rock, and Frans and Vic were then detailed to sieve it all down to the finest sand. They loaded the sieve and with Frans holding the handle at one end and Vic at the other, rocked the sieve backwards and forwards so the fine sand dropped through the wire mesh.

It was back breaking work and for those expecting instantaneous results, not very rewarding.

Before Frank started any laborious digging he decided to spend a few days exploring. He knew there were diamonds in the area, but before he started digging he thought he would make certain that he was putting his resources and efforts into the right place. The *Griquas* he came across were basically hostile; they had escaped the already racially segregated Cape to create a homeland for themselves in the wasteland of the Northern Cape, and the last thing they wanted was an incursion of whites. They could see that in time the same attitudes would start to prevail. In a weak moment, after a smoke and half a bottle of brandy, one of them did say to Frank, "If you want diamonds, look in the hard, grey earth." Frustratingly Frank couldn't get any more out of him, particularly where this hard, grey earth was.

After some fruitless searches near the area where Fritz had settled, Frank decided to explore further afield, and he made his way uncertainly across a huge river and to the outskirts of what appeared to Frank to be a well-established village. He was greeted somewhat suspiciously by the chief, but after a few days of gift giving the chief became friendlier. Frank had provided himself with some appropriate gifts, based on the experiences of the American pioneers. The chief had seen a few whites before but the interactions had often been confrontational, especially with the Boers. After a day the chief gave an instruction to one of his assistants, who brought out a small collection of rough diamonds.

"Are these the stones you seek?" asked the chief through a *Griqua* whom Frank had employed as an interpreter. Frank was disappointed with the quality of what was in front of him but didn't show it.

"Yes, this is what I seek," he answered.

"And what will you do with these things when you find them?" asked the chief.

"I will sell them to people, who will take them over the sea and cut them and make special decorations and ornaments, mainly worn by women," answered Frank.

"And when you have done that, will you come back for more?" asked the chief.

"I have a home in America across the sea; it was burnt down in a war we had and I will use the money from the diamonds to help build up the house again," said Frank.

The chief didn't understand all he was told, but he did understand the fact that Frank was only in the area temporarily.

"Maybe you will also buy some cattle and wives," said the chief helpfully.

Frank smiled.

"Cattle, yes, and possibly one wife," said Frank.

"Only one wife?" asked the chief. "I have six wives," he said proudly.

Frank did not want to get into a long discussion on the benefits or otherwise of polygamy. "One wife, big trouble," he said smiling. "Two wives, very big trouble, six wives…?" Frank threw his arms up in the air as if to say, "This is far too much trouble."

The chief laughed appreciatively. After some more discussions an old man joined the group.

"These diamonds are mostly from the crops of ostriches," the chief explained. "This old man says there are many more and bigger stones in the grey rock on the other side of the river."

Frank's eyes lit up.

"I have heard of this grey rock, but can he help me find it?" asked Frank.

"Maybe," said the chief.

After two more days of haggling, with the promises of more gifts, the chief agreed that the old man should return with Frank, together with two of the young men from the clan to help with the digging.

The old man showed Frank the grey stone area that they had been talking about. Over two days he and the old man broadly marked out a large area in the dusty brown veld.

"This is where the *Nkosi* will find what he is looking for," said the old man.

"Thank you," said Frank.

"But the *Nkosi* must be very careful," added the old man. "Many summers ago when I was still a very small boy, some people came here from the east, not the south as you have done. They were dressed in long white robes and they also sought the hard, shiny white stones you seek. They all died: this one from snakebite; that one was killed by a lion. Not one of them returned to the place they came from, not one climbed back on to the big white birds that swim over the water. All were buried here; all were buried in the soil these stones come from. Maybe the same will happen to all those who seek the stones."

"How do you know all this?" asked Frank.

"My father, he told me; he also told me that other men would come from the south and seek the same stones," was the response.

"How did he know?" asked Frank.

The answer was just a shrug and the old man waved goodbye and went back home.

Frank supposed the men described were Arabs. He was also aware of the many rumours surrounding King Solomon's Mines. His heart raced in anticipation.

When Frank returned to the Koekemoer encampment there was great excitement.

"We've found it, we've found it!" yelled Fritz.

"Well, what have you found?" asked Frank.

"Diamonds, man, diamonds, right here," was the excited answer.

And indeed they had found two small stones, which were definitely diamonds, as Frank could see. The Koekemoers looked as if they had been partying for the last three days and their encampment was in chaos.

Frank told Fritz of his own discoveries.

"Don't take any notice of what those thieving *kaffirs* tell you," said Fritz. "This is the spot; I'm staying here."

Frank had brought elaborate maps with him and he proceeded to register as many claims as he could, dispatching the documents quickly to the claims office in the Cape.

"I'll register a few for you, Fritz," said Frank.

"No thanks, I have plenty here; this is where the riches are."

It was quite a relief for Frank to move his own encampment the two miles to the new site. He was tired of the goings on in the Koekemoer establishment.

The women had almost gone into shock when they realised that this was the god-forsaken place where they were to spend the next many months or even years. Cora, especially, was at her wit's end. She had now lost her husband, and her wayward daughter Hannelore was found in all sorts of compromising situations, mainly with her own kith and kin. The latest episode had occurred when, hearing a lot of noise coming from their wagon, Cora had looked in and seen Frans pounding away on top of Hannelore, with her making all sorts of squeaking sounds. Cora put a very quick stop to the activity by shoving a shotgun up Frans' backside. As she told Hannetjie and Anna later, "There's nothing that brings an erection down quicker than the feel of a cold, hard piece of steel against the testicles."

How was she to make a living? Her man was dead; he was not looking for diamonds. If and when any of the rest of the clan found stones she would be left out in the cold. Then she had an idea.

She spoke quietly to Hannelore. "You can have as many men as you like, but they're going to have to pay for the privilege. I'll also sell them a *dop* of brandy and, well, I could be part of the package too in some circumstances."

After some initial doubts, Hannelore joined in the spirit of the new venture with great gusto. Cora showed her how to douche herself after each visitor in the vain hope that she wouldn't become pregnant. Cora also managed to get hold of most of the remaining liquor left in the Koekemoer wagons, and sold that too.

Within weeks Cora and her daughter had a roaring business. Their activities were, however, too much for the other Koekemoer women, who made them move away. Cora then set up her wagon in what was to become the main street of Kimberley. She had visions of the hotel she would build, and when she could afford it commenced the construction of what was eventually to become a solid two-storey building. The liquor ran out quite quickly but she then arranged a regular supply from the Cape via uncle Piet.

After Frank had moved his own camp to a choice spot overlooking what was to become the big hole in Kimberley, he measured out all his claims and started digging, together with the labour now provided in twos and threes by the Tswana chief. This favour was granted in return for an on-going supply of gifts, although Frank paid his labour relatively well.

Within weeks of the arrival of Frank and the Koekemoer clan, many other people started to arrive, mainly from the Cape but also from the east where the British had established the thriving colony of Natal, and from the neighbouring Boer republics of the Orange Free State and the Transvaal. More and more of the people coming from the Cape were actually from all over the world; a number of them had chosen to seek their fortunes in the American and Australian gold rushes earlier. There were some who had resources, but most were poor and had only the strength of their backs to help them.

To their credit, Fritz and his Koekemoer relatives worked very hard for more than six months. Fritz's enthusiasm attracted many of the other fortune hunters to the area he was exploring, so apart from the few cooler heads, Frank found he was left alone to dig in the grey stone. After the first two small diamonds, Fritz and his crew found nothing, absolutely nothing, for three months; then they found two more stones on the same day. It was almost as if the gods were playing games with them. Efforts were redoubled and Fritz even managed to recruit a black African to come and work with him. Fritz didn't ask his name; he simply put a pick in his hand and told him where to dig. Fritz was already paranoid about "thieving *kaffirs*" and assumed that anyone he employed could not be trusted. Within days of taking the man on, Fritz thought he saw "the *kaffir*" as he called him lean down into the area he was digging, pick something up, and put it into his mouth. To his amazement Masisi (for that was his name) saw Fritz descending on him in a fury. Fritz grabbed him in a headlock and tried to force his mouth open.

"Open your *blerry* mouth, you thieving black bastard, I saw you put a diamond in your mouth," he shrieked in the *Taal*.

Masisi was none the wiser as to why this giant of a man had descended on him in such a fury, since he understood none of the language. When Fritz eventually forced open the man's mouth and found nothing he beat Masisi mercilessly with a *sjambok* and then chained him to the wheel of his wagon.

"Force feed him," he instructed Frans, "and then examine his crap; I want that fucking diamond."

Masisi was terrified by all this and when he was released, after three days, he ran away. Despite the fact that there was no evidence that Masisi had even seen a diamond, Fritz still believed that something had been stolen. Anything that went missing in the camp was blamed on "thieving *kaffirs*", even though, after the treatment meted out to Masisi, none of the locals would go anywhere near the Koekemoer establishment.

P.W. and Hannetjie were the first to crack. PW was unable to work because of the injuries received from the lion. The living conditions were appalling. They used the wagons they had travelled in from the Cape to sleep in. Food was scarce and expensive apart from fresh meat, which was kept in regular supply by one or other of the group, who shot a springbok whenever it was necessary. The toilet was the one built by Fritz in the early days on the farm and water had to be carted from the river. It took a whole day to inspan the oxen, drive the scotch cart down to the river, fill up the containers and return. P.W. and Hannetjie also had three children, who ran absolutely wild round the camp; they were permanently dirty had had taken to stealing small items from other fortune hunters. Also, they were receiving no education. The weather was a trial. The summers were hot and generally dry but punctuated with the occasional torrential downpour. The winters were dry and very cold and the wind blew dust into everything. None of this would have mattered if they were finding diamonds, but the few diamonds they found barely kept them going. The last straw came when their eldest child stepped on a puffadder and was bitten in the leg; he died in agony within an hour and there was nothing anyone could do.

When they told the others they were leaving, Fritz would not allow them to take their wagon or anything Piet had provided, and they were forced to cadge a lift from one of the many empty wagons going south. They were destitute, but Fritz was quite unsympathetic. "I never told you this would be a picnic," he shouted at their retreating backs.

Having seen the treatment meted out to their relatives Magnus, Pik and their wives waited until Fritz was away for a few days, and then sold as much of the equipment as they could to new arrivals, took one of the wagons and some spare oxen and headed back to the Cape. When Fritz returned he was furious and ranted and raved for a few days, but he did not dare pursue them. He knew they were waiting for him and if he as much as appeared on the horizon he would be shot.

Stompie had been a liability since Elsie and "*Oom*" had been killed, and spent most of his time drunk. Fritz was at his wits' end as to what to do about him, and he was trying to negotiate a fare back to the Cape, when Stompie ended up in a fight at Cora's now famous pub and someone hit him over the head with a brandy bottle. He died two days later.

Fritz and his two cousins fruitlessly continued to dig, but the output was low and all Fritz could think of was returning to his wine farm in the Cape. Other people were finding diamonds and Fritz was aware that Frank was finding a regular supply, not enough to make his fortune but sufficient to keep his hopes up. Fritz's operation eventually came to a stop when Frans and Vic received a letter from the Cape telling them that their father was dangerously ill. They left with the promise that they would return.

Frank had heard about Fritz's troubles and more out of a sense of obligation than anything else, he went over to Fritz's camp, to find the normally ebullient Fritz sitting outside his little shack with a letter in his hand. Frank poured himself a small brandy from an already half finished bottle in the kitchen.

"What's up?" he asked.

"It's that bitch of a wife of mine," he said thickly. "This letter is from one of my friends; he says and she is carrying on with some *oke* in Stellenbosch; according to this letter she wants the farm and she hopes that I stay up here in the diamond fields."

"Well, can't you just go back and sort it all out?"

Fritz thought about his conversation with Piet.

"No, there are reasons that I cannot go back, not just yet."

Frank looked at him curiously as if asking for more information. Fritz just shook his head and said nothing.

After a few minutes' silence, Frank could see that he was not going to get any more information, but he felt that he owed this man something. "You can still come and work with me if you like; we can share the profits somehow." A deal was quickly worked out, by which Frank ran the mining operation and Fritz the sorting. The deal was generous to Fritz, who from then on became unswervingly loyal to Frank. Fritz had also been again told by Piet, untruthfully, that the police were still looking for him and that he would have to remain where he was for the foreseeable future. Piet was furious with his relatives, having lost most of his investment in the wagons and equipment that he had bought for the Koekemoer party; his only hope really was to keep Fritz digging in the hope that he would recover something.

Frank's relationship with the local Tswana chief ensured a reasonable supply of labour. Besides, the growth of the mining operations in Kimberley were attracting indigenous people from all over Southern Africa: the Basuto from Moshoeshoe's Kingdom to the east, Shangaans from Mozambique, Xhosa from the Transkei, a few Zulus and even people from as far away as Nyasaland and the country that was to become Rhodesia.

It turned out that Frank had identified one of the better areas for finding diamonds and although it did not produce instantaneous riches, the diamonds he found kept him solvent.

Soon after Fritz had moved to work for Frank, he became aware that Lieutenant North was working claims that were very close to where he and Frank were operating. Nobody except Piet had been told the story of the escapade in the veld with the soldiers, and because Fritz thought he was a wanted man in the Cape he wasn't about to tell anyone else, not even Frank. Fritz was fairly sure that North would not recognize him; there were many men of all shapes and sizes in the diggings, with more arriving each day, and North had only seen him in the late evening and at night. Whenever he saw North or heard his voice Fritz was reminded of his ordeal and he thirsted for revenge. At some stage he would get his own back, he would make sure of that.

When Fritz sold the first diamonds he had found he was pleasantly surprised at the price he received but he thought no more about it. He maintained a good relationship with Frank, who tried to calm him down with little success. He was also a regular visitor to the hotel; but Cora and Hannelore ignored him as far as possible.

◇◇◇◇◇◇◇◇◇◇◇◇◇◇

Chapter 7

Frank Devereaux's encampment consisted of a large tent in which he himself lived, the wagon, which he had driven up from the Cape four years earlier, and two very decrepit huts, which were used by his labour. All this was contained on a rocky slope east of the diggings and about half a mile from the main diggings in Kimberley. Water was fetched at periodic intervals from the river in large drums, and the toilet was a lean-to shed over a pit on the corner of the property.

Since he was one of the first to arrive in Kimberley, Frank had established himself in the prime location. Apart from Fritz, Cora and her daughter Hannelore all the members of the Koekemoer family who had accompanied Frank to the diggings had returned to the Cape, having given up the search for riches in frustration and disappointment.

The Zulus were thankful for a place of refuge and they made a small fire and prepared a meal from what they had with them. They slept as they had in the past few months: in the open, covered with their karosses against the winter cold.

The next day Frank suggested to Mapitha that they should find a way of building themselves a hut on the property, and when that was done, they could work for him in the diggings at the rate of one shilling per day. Frank considered the rate of pay to be generous, and he also provided full rations and of course accommodation; all this was explained to the Zulus, but it meant very little to them. The concept of money was unknown to them and the idea of being paid for work was completely alien. Frank had made the overture through a Tswana who also worked for him and Tutula was able to help convey the words to the Zulus.

Frank had through his personal circumstances become tough and thick skinned, and after four years he was still convinced that he would eventually make enough money in this rough, dusty outpost of the British Empire to restore his family fortunes in America. He was not insensitive to people though, and he liked what he saw of Mapitha's party. Mapitha, for his part, saw a man of five-foot-ten, physically tough from the hard manual labour he had done, firstly in the California goldfields and then in Kimberley. He had wavy, brown hair and kindly green eyes that belied his toughness; he always wore a .45 colt revolver on his belt. Nobody had ever seen him use it, but as he said in his southern drawl, "When you need it, you need it durn bad." Through contact with the local blacks, Frank had learnt a few words of Tswana and South Sotho and acquired the reputation of being a good employer. He had some sympathies with the blacks, but he was absolutely determined that nothing would get in the way of his objective of making a fortune and then returning in glory to the green hills of Virginia.

Mapitha determined a suitable place for their hut and then sent the others off to gather the appropriate materials. He had seen people working in the diggings, and asked Frank with a set of hand signals for a pick and shovel; he then dug a pit long enough to accommodate the rifle and about four feet deep and two feet wide right in the middle of what was to be their hut. He found a few planks of wood lying about, which he carefully fitted over the hole: the planks were then covered in earth. By the time the others had returned, it was not obvious that there was a hole there. Mapitha had already hidden the rifle and ammunition in the hole.

As the Zulus were energetically constructing their hut, Frank had come over from the diggings and watched and tried to converse. He was curious about the rifle, which he could no longer see, and the horse. After some fruitless exchanges, he went away and collected his Tswana headman Molefe. Mapitha knew perfectly well that he was asking where the horse and gun had come from; he was not going to tell anyone that, if he could help it.

While Frank was away he rapidly told the others that the story he would tell Frank was that the horse had just appeared one day in camp, and if he asked any other questions they should all look stupid.

Frank, Mapitha, Molefe and Tutula then had a very long and involved conversation. All that Frank was able to get out of it was that the horse had wandered into camp months earlier when the Zulus had barely left their own territory. He was unable to get any sense out of Mapitha about the rifle, which was now nowhere to be seen. After a while Frank wondered whether he had imagined things or not. After the conversation had concluded he muttered to himself, "Likely bloody story." He was, however, convinced that the horse had indeed been in the care of the Zulus for some months and that Mapitha was probably telling the truth when he said that they had acquired the animal soon after they had crossed into the newly formed Republic of the Traansvaal. This meant the local Boers from the Orange Free State would not be coming around looking for the animal and possibly the people who had killed one of their comrades.

Frank's own horse had recently died and he could see that *ihashi*, could if fed and looked after properly be a perfectly good replacement. The horse's tack certainly looked as if it had been uncared for in the bush for months, but again, with a bit of looking after it would be perfectly serviceable. So Frank approached the Zulus again and through Molefe and Tutula managed to communicate the fact that he wished to buy the horse. Frank offered ten pounds for the horse and all its equipment; the real value was probably about double that but Frank reasoned that the Zulus had no way of looking after and feeding the animal and in any event they had acquired the animal for nothing. The Zulus had never seen money before and had absolutely no concept of its value; however when Frank proffered two five pound notes they all fell down laughing.

"A horse for two small pieces of paper," Mapitha said. And they all fell about laughing again.

Frank was rather taken aback by this response, but then he showed them some coins he had and although the Zulus were unfamiliar with coins, they took them more seriously and examined each one closely. The only real yardstick of value the Zulus understood was cattle so, whilst pretending to be interested in the coins, Mapitha asked Tutula to ask Molefe how many cows he would get for his horse.

"Three," was the answer.

"And how many pieces of coloured paper for each cow?" he asked. He made Frank produce the five pound notes again.

"One," was the answer.

"So I must get three of these pieces of paper for the horse," said Mapitha triumphantly, "and then I can go and buy three cows."

"You're not going to bring these cows here?" asked Frank apprehensively.

"Well, what else is there?" asked Mapitha. "Maybe I could buy a wife with the cows."

Things were definitely getting out of hand, thought Frank. Then he had an idea and he took them all up to the general store in the main street.

Frank, dressed in his usual clothes, Molefe dressed in rags and Mapitha, Nzobo, Kulaan and Tutula, all still wearing only their loincloths, marched into the store. The Zulus were still carrying all their traditional weapons. The store owner, Mr. Shapiro, was momentarily taken aback, then he said, "*Kaffirs* out at the back; I can't serve naked savages in here."

"But they're with me," protested Frank. "I'm trying to help them be less naked."

"Can't help that Mr. Devereaux sir, that's the rule here. *Kaffirs* out at the back," replied Shapiro.

Frank led the bemused Africans out of the shop and once the Zulus got the idea, they spent a very amusing hour deciding what to buy. They decided on a khaki shirt and a pair of trousers each for the men and a pretty floral dress for Tutula. Tutula, who had been perfectly at home wandering about almost naked, suddenly became shy and giggly when she put on the dress, but nothing would get her to take it off again. They had a great deal of trouble finding something to fit Kulaan. Eventually Shapiro found a huge pair of overalls which covered most of his large frame; he happily dispensed with the shirt. The Zulus were offered shoes but could see no point in having them; anyway none of them fitted their large, splayed feet. Frank also persuaded the men to buy a pair of shorts each for work; the other stuff, he explained was for their day off each week.

Frank eventually agreed to pay fifteen pounds for the horse. He had tried offering twelve and then thirteen, but Mapitha had got it into his head that each five-pound note was a cow and he argued that he couldn't be paid half a cow.

"After all," he argued, "half a cow is a dead cow and a dead cow is worth less than a live cow."

The clothes cost the Zulus just six pounds and they were given some change. Frank tried to persuade Mapitha to put the money safely away in the bank, and the whole party, now dressed in their new clothes, all trooped off to the bank. Frank and the teller explained to Mapitha that he could put the money in the bank and whenever he wanted it he could come and get it out again.

"What happens if this place burns to the ground?" asked Mapitha. "Then my cows will be burnt with it."

"No," said Frank. "They will always keep your money, always."

Mapitha looked doubtful.

"Look," suggested Frank, "put one cow (five pounds) in the bank and keep the rest. Then you will see."

After some thought Mapitha agreed, but he went to the bank every day for a month to ensure they still had his money.

It took another four days to build the traditional Zulu beehive hut. It was a big hut with easily room enough for four to sleep. The top of the hut was more than eight feet high, which meant that most people could stand even at the sides. The hut consisted of a frame of saplings with tightly woven grass thatch all the way from the roof to the ground. One had to bend down to enter it; the top of the entrance was only about four feet off the ground.

Once the hut was built, it was evident that Tutula would be sleeping there as well. This drew an immediate objection from Molefe, who said, "This girl is Tswana, like us. She should stay with the Tswana."

"She has not lived with the Tswana for almost three summers now," answered Mapitha. "We, the Zulus, saved her life; she will stay with us."

The Zulus all regarded her as a daughter, and they would have protected her like any father would protect his own daughter. Mapitha, in any event, was rather suspicious of the motives of Molefe, who was also rather jealous of the money the Zulus had received for the horse. Molefe was frightened by the comparatively aggressive Zulus and he didn't doubt that they would use their spears if they had to. He let the matter drop.

The area around Frank Devereaux's encampment was surrounded by similar camps for at least a mile around the newly established township of Kimberley. There was absolutely no order. People had camped there on a first come first served basis from the time that the announcement of the first diamond find by Fritz Koekemoer had been made. There was no attempt at or even thought of racial segregation. The place was a melting pot of people from all over the world and from Southern Africa itself. Whilst Mapitha and his companions found everything very strange, they had been told by their King Mpande to find out how the white men lived, and to try to understand why they valued the little, white, sparkling stones so much. This they intended to do. Firstly Mapitha decided he would try to learn the white man's language.

◇◇◇◇◇◇◇◇◇◇◇◇◇◇◇

Chapter 8

Frank Devereaux owned several claims within what was already termed the "big hole" in Kimberley. The claims were close together and were connected to the rim of the crater caused by the diggings, by a thick piece of double cable, which was attached to pulleys at each end, and a large frame at the top of the crater. The cables had large, detachable buckets, which were filled at the diggings and slowly and laboriously hauled to the top of the crater by a steam engine that chugged away all day. The sand, soil and rock that was brought to the surface was first broken up into smaller pieces and then put through a series of large sieves, with smaller and smaller mesh. Frank's sieves were operated (shaken) by another donkey engine. Many of the smaller operators still did their sorting by hand.

Frank told them that when he first started, the digging and sorting were done by hand. When "the hole" became bigger and deeper, the first cables connecting the diggings to the surface were also operated by hand. When this became impossible donkeys and mules were used to operate great capstans and now many of the diggers had donkey engines like Frank. Often the diggings were up to three hundred feet from the rim of the crater and there were hundreds of claims being operated.

Mapitha, Kulaan and Nzobo had spent their first week in Kimberley building their hut and making sure that everything was in order domestically. Tutula was detailed to look after the meals for the Zulus and in time Frank was to show her how to inspan the oxen and fetch water from the river, something that needed doing every two or three days. Frank ate in various messes that he belonged to in the town, and every few days one of the mess servants came over and washed his clothes and bedding.

As the dawn broke on their first working day, Tutula gave the Zulus their breakfast; they then accompanied Frank and Molefe and two other Tswanas, Dibotelo and Chepete who had been employed by Frank for more than a year, to the mine.

When the Zulus came over the rise that separated Frank's encampment from the main diggings, they just stopped and stared for more than a minute. None of their experiences had prepared them for anything like this. They saw an enormous hole in the ground, with numerous cables like the strands of a massive spider's web stretched from their various positions inside the hole to the frameworks on the rim. There appeared to be hundreds of men of all shapes, colours and sizes making their way quietly through the early morning chill to the mine. At that time of day the mine was cold and silent and looked almost ghostly; within the half hour it would be a cacophony of sound. The noise from hundreds of smoky steam engines driving the capstans that brought the buckets of sand and rock to the surface, mingled with the braying of donkeys, who reluctantly tramped their way round and round, operating the capstans of the less well off operations.

"Come on," said Frank impatiently and the three Tswanas and three Zulus followed him down into the pit. The Tswanas marched confidently on, but the Zulus stared around in awe and wonderment. They nearly got caught up in a cable in one place and a bucket clumsily bumped into Kulaan as a capstan at the top of the crater got going.

The Zulus were dressed in their newly acquired shorts and nothing else. Frank had persuaded them to bring food and water. Frank, of course, was fully protected from the sun with proper shirt and trousers, heavy boots and a large hat. Mapitha looked at him and thought that Frank's clothes looked very uncomfortable. Mapitha found his own shorts rather restricting; he didn't see how Frank could operate at all, let alone work in his outfit.

Frank had a number of claims, which he worked in tandem. They were all reasonably close together, and the rock and sand that had been dug out of the various claims was loaded into a cable system belonging to Frank and hauled to the surface. Fritz Koekemoer had taken on the job of running the surface operations, which consisted of a capstan run by a recently acquired steam donkey engine. The rock was hauled to the surface and where necessary broken up by Fritz's own gang of labourers. It then went through a series of sieves, where any diamonds were separated from the rock and sand. The final sieve was quite fine, so the waste product was a fine, grey dust that was carted away from all the various surface operations and dumped in the veld. These dumps grew larger and larger, and when the wind blew the grey dust from them covered everything. Fritz was totally loyal to Frank Devereaux but he treated his labour harshly and had eyes like a hawk. Any labourer who so much as touched a diamond in Fritz's area of operation was soundly thrashed and dismissed. If one appeared in a sieve, Fritz was always called to retrieve it.

The job in the mine itself was to dig holes, which Frank then filled with black powder and blasted the rock away.

When they arrived at the site of Frank's claims, the Tswana set to work. Chepete took a shovel and started to fill a nearby bucket with rock and sand, and Dibotelo picked up a large, iron crowbar with a pointed end; the crowbar was about seven feet in length and roughly two thirds of the way down its length, another piece of metal had been welded onto it as a hand hold. Frank had marked several places in the claim with a piece of chalk, and Dibotelo held the crowbar against one of the marks while Molefe picked up a 16lb hammer and hit the end of the crowbar, or crosstick as it was known. The Zulus watched this for a few minutes and could see a hole gradually developing.

Mapitha picked up another crosstick, held it against another of Frank's marks and indicated to Kulaan to hit it with one of the 16lb hammers lying about. Kulaan took a big swing but missed the crowbar altogether, and if Mapitha hadn't been quick he would have collected the full force of the hammer on his head. The Tswanas fell about laughing.

Frank then showed the Zulus what to do. It was really important that the crosstick be held very still and that the hammer hit the end with full force. After a few more tries Kulaan got the hang of things and he was hitting the crosstick almost every time. Kulaan's great strength meant that once the Zulu crew understood what to do, they drilled three holes for every two that the Tswana finished. The Zulus soon worked out a shift system, one holding the crosstick, one wielding the hammer and one resting. Frank couldn't believe his luck; the Zulus seemed to work easily as a team and Kulaan's great strength helped them far outstrip the Tswana team. By midday the Zulus had finished twelve holes and the Tswana eight. Frank stopped them and they shared some of the food and water they had.

The Zulus watched in fascination as Frank took a small barrel from a storehouse in the rock and poured out a measure of black powder, which he rammed into the back of each hole. A wad was placed on top of the powder and a piece of what appeared to be string led out of each hole. When all the holes had been dealt with and Frank had joined all the pieces of string together, he led the crew round the side of a rock out of sight of the holes. He then lit the string, which sputtered, and the little flame whizzed up the string (fuse) and round the corner of the rock. A whole series of little explosions took place, which initially terrified the Zulus. Frank had his fingers in his ears and was concentrating. He was counting, "…eighteen, nineteen." It appeared to be all over and Molefe got up; Frank grabbed him by the arm and pulled him back. There was one final explosion. "Twenty," he breathed.

The six blacks and Frank then shovelled the mass of rock and debris into large buckets. At precisely one thirty, the cable to carry the buckets to the surface started moving. Normally it took at least two people to lift the buckets onto the hooks that would carry them to the surface. Kulaan took this job on for himself once he understood what was required. He needed no help. The others were all left to do the shovelling. All around them there were little explosions going on; nobody took any notice. Mapitha couldn't help wondering how dangerous it was.

During a lull, when Frank and the rest of the crew were distracted doing something else, Mapitha noticed something shining in a pile of rubble. He quickly reached down and without anyone seeing, popped the stone into his mouth.

By late afternoon most of the rubble created by the blast had been moved to the surface. Frank called a halt. They tidied up the site, locked the tools away and made their weary way back to the surface and then home.

Nzobo and Kulaan watched while Tutula cooked their meal. Mapitha took this opportunity to dig up his hiding place and, having examined his find carefully, he popped it into a small leather pouch that he had and covered the hole up again. He came out from the hut and looked about him.

"All this," he thought, "for a few worthless stones." The diamond he had found, and he was sure it was one, was certainly quite heavy for such a small stone. Otherwise it was merely a misshapen piece of brown rock. He discovered that if one rubbed the stone it sparkled, but it was beyond his imagination to see how it could be used to decorate any woman. Of course he had not yet seen a white woman. He would reserve his judgement until he had.

A routine was soon established. Frank and his boys would go along to the mine just after dawn, work all day and return to camp by about four p.m. They worked six days a week and always had Sundays off. Mapitha didn't know whether they found many diamonds, but Fritz used to come over most evenings from his own encampment and he and Frank had long, earnest discussions that often lasted well into the night. After his first find, Mapitha managed to filch three more smallish stones over the next six months. Within his hiding place in the hut he also dug a small hole in the side wall of the pit and he placed his stones in there; the hole was covered up so nobody except Mapitha knew of the diamonds or where they were hidden.

On one particular Sunday three months after the Zulus had joined Frank, he said to Mapitha, "Bring that gun of yours; maybe I can show you how it works."

Mapitha looked blankly at him.

"Look," said Frank. "Trust me, I will help you. If it is not looked after it will be no use to you."

Mapitha had learned some English and although he did not understand all the words, he understood the gist of what was being said.

He hesitated. Could he really trust this man? Nzobo chipped in in Zulu, "You see how this man has looked after *ihashi* and made the equipment look like new. Maybe it's the same with the rifle. You know you were not able to kill any buck with it; maybe this man will help."

"Maybe he wants it for himself," said Mapitha.

"No, he has his own guns, he has no use for this one," replied Nzobo.

So Mapitha somewhat reluctantly went to the hut and a few minutes later emerged with his rifle and the bandolier of ammunition. Frank took one look at the dusty mess the rifle was in and then took Mapitha and the Zulus over to his tent and showed them how to clean it. He gave Mapitha a small bottle of gun oil and some four by two cleaning cloth and a pull through.

"Always clean the gun after you have used it; it will last forever then," Frank told them.

The four men went off into the veld and within and hour they came across a herd of springbok.

Frank said to Mapitha, "See if you can shoot one."

Mapitha rather uncertainly stalked the herd and then levered a round

   Rough Diamonds

into the breach. Then, to Frank's absolute amazement, he squatted on his haunches, and as he had done on his journey to Kimberley, placed the gun butt on the ground with the gun pointing up in the air at about forty five degrees but in the rough direction of the antelope and pulled the trigger. The antelope scattered. Frank howled with laughter; he'd never seen anything so funny in his life. Mapitha returned to the little group looking rather sheepish.

"Here," said Frank after he had recovered. "Let me show you."

He spent the rest of the day giving the three Zulus lessons on how to use the weapon: how to aim, how to load, and how to operate the safety mechanism. He adjusted the sights.

"Looks as if the rifle is throwing to the left," he said as he fiddled with the sights.

Frank bagged a springbok with his own gun, which provided fresh meat for the camp for the next few days.

The next weekend Mapitha and the Zulus went out hunting and after several attempts managed, to their delight, to bag a springbok. Thereafter they never went without fresh meat. Mapitha and Nzobo became very good shots, but Kulaan still preferred his spear.

In the early years in Kimberley no attempt was made to create racial distinction. All facilities were open to all races and most encampments were similar to the one that Frank Devereaux ran. This generally worked well, although the Boers did not like it and made a few unsuccessful attempts to have some facilities reserved for whites.

Once and only once did Mapitha and Nzobo venture into the hotel. The bar was not an elegant place. It consisted of a long bar with a few stools against it and there were rough, wooden tables and chairs scattered on the uncovered wooden floor. Most of the men in the bar wore their work clothes and they were dirty and unkempt. Mapitha and Nzobo had put on their best clothes and ordered a beer each. Nobody took much notice of them; the bar was full of white miners mainly but there were some black and coloured people scattered among the crowd. The beer came in a bottle and was clear, unlike their traditional beer. They decided it tasted quite good.

The Zulus had never seen white women except at a distance in the street. At one end of the bar they noticed a group of half a dozen white girls with long dresses down to the floor and their fair hair piled on top of their heads. They had very white faces, red lips and long earrings in their ears. Their behaviour as far as the Zulus were concerned was extraordinary. There was a man with a musical instrument that to Mapitha's ears made a horrible squeaky sound. Some men would hold the women and dance clumsily round in a small area near the musician. Then more often than not the woman concerned would disappear upstairs, followed by the man. They would come back down again thirty minutes to an hour later. Consumed by curiosity, Mapitha and Nzobo slowly moved down the bar to get a closer look. Soon Mapitha was sitting on a bar stool right next to one of the women. He reached out to touch her, because he had never seen such soft, white skin before. He did not see her as sexually desirable in any way. Quite the opposite—he could not imagine having sex with such an object. However, as he touched her all hell broke loose: both he and Nzobo were punched and kicked by what seemed like half the population of the bar and in less than thirty seconds they found themselves sitting in the dusty street.

"Keep your dirty black cocks to yourselves," someone shouted. "White women are for whites only. Go and find your own dirty black whores."

The Zulus did not really understand and went back to Frank who explained the situation.

"You mean the men pay these women to have sex with them?" Mapitha said in broken English.

"Yes," was Frank's answer.

Mapitha just shook his head in wonderment; in his experience, if you wanted a woman you spoke to her father, agreed a bride price and took her as your wife. Paying for sex seemed strange to him at that time. He could see that in the mining community there were far more men than women but the *abelungu* solution of having a few women around who made themselves available for payment was strange and abhorrent to him.

"What happens to the children?" asked Mapitha.

Frank just shrugged. He'd never really thought about it.

Some months went past and the routine continued. The Zulus, already fit and strong, became hardened by the tough physical work. They were reasonably content. Money was accumulating in the bank; they spent very little of it. Both Kulaan and Nzobo wanted guns and they agreed that it would be better to buy them just before they left to return to Zululand. When that would be they weren't sure. The King had told them to find out all they could about the white strangers and, while Mapitha felt he had learnt something about them, he didn't feel adequately prepared to return to Kwa-Bulawayo to make a formal report.

They received some news of Zululand and their homeland from the occasional Zulu who made his way to the diggings. One day they were in discussion with a new arrival, telling them:

"Maybe you should go home, if it was Mpande who sent you here then you had better be careful. The King died, now twelve moons ago, and his son Cetswayo has taken over. He may not care about the search for *idayimani* as Mpande did."

They had a long discussion.

Mapitha then decided for them all that they still knew very little about the whites and how they lived, so they would stay.

Mapitha had tried to find out from the labourers who worked for Fritz how many diamonds were being unearthed from all the rock that the crew in the mine had sent to the surface. When Mapitha arrived at Fritz's little compound, he was confronted by Fritz.

"What the fuck do you want, *kaffir*?" asked Fritz in English.

Mapitha explained that he worked for Frank Devereaux down the mine and wanted to chat with his fellow employees.

"I know who the fuck you are, I've seen you over at Devereaux's camp," said Fritz. "I asked you what did you want?"

"Just to talk," answered Mapitha.

"Not here you don't," answered Fritz. "Now fuck off, I will not have every wandering pair of thieving black hands coming in and out of my property as they want."

Mapitha left.

He met one of the black labourers from Fritz's compound later by accident in the town. The man was from Moshoeshoe's mountain Kingdom of Basutoland, so he was more than a little wary of the Zulu. When he asked him how many diamonds were being found he was told, "Two or three a week, mostly quite small ones."

Mapitha shrewdly guessed that this was enough to keep the operations going but not much more. He decided to try to have a conversation with Frank on the subject.

He approached him one Sunday, when Frank was relaxing over a beer before going to lunch with some of his fellow claim owners in town.

Since Mapitha and the Zulus had been with Frank, his operations had really gone smoothly. He was pulling out almost 80% more rock than before and although he was only just keeping his head above water financially, he had never felt more optimistic about achieving his dream of making a big enough find and returning to the green hills of Virginia. He liked and respected Mapitha, but always wondered what kept him in Kimberley and whether one day he would just quit. He looked at Mapitha speculatively and wondered if this was his mission today.

They greeted each other in Zulu.

Mapitha squatted on his haunches; Frank sat in his chair and waited. Mapitha spoke in broken English.

"The *Nkosi* has now been here many summers," said Mapitha.

Frank nodded.

"Five." He held up five fingers.

Mapitha smiled. He was well able to count in the English tongue.

"And the Nkosi has taken out of the big hole many buckets of rock and sand," Mapitha continued.

Frank nodded.

"And many *amadayimani*."

"Some diamonds, not enough though," said Frank with a sigh.

"Not enough, not enough for what?" asked Mapitha.

"Not enough to make me rich," said Frank.

"What is rich?" asked Mapitha. "You want many wives, many cattle?"

Frank laughed.

"One wife," he said. "Maybe some cattle."

Then he went on to explain about the civil war in America and the fact that he had hoped to rebuild his family's fortunes by finding diamonds in Kimberley. Mapitha was curious about the civil war. His geography was at best hazy; as far as he was concerned all white men came from somewhere overseas. He was interested that they had fought each other.

"The *abelungu*, they fight each other?" he asked.

Frank nodded.

"Here, they just fight the black people," said Mapitha sadly. He went on, "So how long will it take before you return to Virginia?"

Frank shrugged.

"One year, two years, five years, however long it takes," he said.

"And you?" Frank asked. "Why are you here?"

"I am sent here by the King of the Zulus, the great King Mpande," said Mapitha "to find out about the *abelungu*. The King has now died, but we will tell our story to the new King Cetswayo."

"To find out what?" Frank was intrigued. He thought of his Zulus as ordinary labourers, not as emissaries from the Zulu King.

"Well, we Zulus have the *amaBhunu* to the North now and the *amaNgisi* to the South. They have all taken too much of our land already.

                                                    Rough Diamonds

We want to keep what we have," said Mapitha.

"You will fight?" asked Frank.

Mapitha nodded.

"When you find your big *idayimani* what happens?" asked Mapitha, changing the subject.

"Maybe Fritz takes over the claims; anyway, I go home to Virginia," said Frank.

"Maybe Kulaan, Nzobo and I can take over the claims," said Mapitha. "Maybe Fritz will also be rich like you and go?"

"Maybe," answered Frank. He hadn't thought of that.

Fritz was still consumed with the need for revenge on North and his colleagues, he knew that it was stupid and would only cause him grief, but he just could not help himself. He spent many hours spying on the North camp trying to create a plan that would do the maximum amount of damage. Fritz also, unusually, refused to grow a beard, calculating that there would be less chance of North recognizing him clean-shaven. To start with Fritz contented himself with minor acts of sabotage. He found two cobras in the *veld* and unseen during the day put them in the tent on North's property; he made sure that he was wandering past when the Britishers returned from working their claim. Within minutes there was a flurry of shouts and yells and much thrashing about and the two dead snakes were flung out of the tent. Not much notice was taken; snakes were common. A few weeks later he started a grassfire on the North property, but it was put out before any damage was done. The following Friday when he and Frank were having a beer in Cora's hotel and Frank had gone upstairs with one of the girls, Fritz found himself surrounded by North and three of his previous tormenters. They did not waste time: "Look you ignorant Dutchman," said North quietly, "we recognized you almost the minute we arrived here, we also saw you on the journey. We decided to leave you alone, although I think that the authorities might be persuaded take an interest in you. You were seen lighting that fire in our place the other day. If that's the way you want it, that's the way you will get it." They left just as Frank returned.

"What was all that about?" asked Frank.

"Oh, nothing," answered Fritz evasively. "They think that I had something to do with the fire at their place the other day."

"And did you?"

Fritz shook his head without answering.

Fritz was not that easily put off and he kept his eyes open for opportunities to harm the Englishmen. In the hotel the next week Fritz deliberately knocked over the table where the Englishmen were playing cards. "Hey" yelled North. "You clumsy ape." Fritz was ready when North took a swing and North found himself flat on his back with a broken nose. Then all hell broke loose and Fritz and the four Englishmen were quickly bundled out of the bar by the bouncers and they continued the fight in the street. Fritz gave a good account of himself and at the end was the only one standing. He pulled North to his feet and said: "You tried to kill me in the desert there, so take this." He sent North flying again with another punch to the stomach.

Frank, when it was all over, rescued Fritz and cleaned him up in the watering trough at the front of the hotel. Despite their closeness Fritz just clammed up whenever the subject of his relationship with North was mentioned. He could get nothing out of the Englishmen either

During Fritz's time with Frank, on Fridays, both of them took the diamonds they had unearthed during the previous week to one of the dealers in town, sold them and banked the money. They then took themselves off to Cora's and had a good meal, and sometimes took one of the girls upstairs. Fritz was often surprised at the amount they received for the diamonds and over the months became aware the original haul of stones that he had so laboriously taken to the Cape had been worth rather more than Piet had let on. After a general discussion with Frank he had concluded that somehow Piet had paid him less than half what the stones were worth.

His nephews, Frans and Vic, had returned from the Cape but had decided that they would join the police rather than continue to slave away at the diggings. So without telling them the full story he had asked them to try to find out if there was any kind of mark against his name in police circles.

"Why would there be anything like that?" Vic asked innocently.

"Just before we came up here, Piet said something, he said it might be better if I left town for a little while."

"Do you know why? Surely he would have told you the reason."

"I don't really remember, I was coming up here anyway, so I didn't really bother with the details," he said lamely.

"Definitely nothing," the answer came back months later. "Nobody has ever heard of you in the police."

Fritz was now fuming at Piet. He'd been swindled out of a good proportion of his original diamond wealth; he'd been persuaded to come back to this hell-hole of a place much against his own wishes and those of his wife and

Rough Diamonds

his wine farm was possibly on some risk because he was away from the Cape. He felt that Piet had a great deal of explaining to do. Fritz considered returning to the Cape immediately and leaving everything, but he had a curious loyalty to Frank, so he stayed on.

The drinking crowd with whom Fritz became involved, were all Afrikaners, so Frank tended to avoid them. He tried to keep an eye on Fritz, though, because he needed him for his operation and he also felt a peculiar responsibility for the wayward Fritz. He knew that Fritz was liable to get himself into trouble. The Afrikaner community in common with Fritz resented the British, who treated them like second class citizens; they also thought of the blacks and coloureds as slaves or at best servants and resented the fact that there were many black and coloured claim owners who on average did just as well as everyone else. The blacks were unfairly blamed for the IDB problem and there was a move to restrict the ownership of claims to whites. Fritz told the group:

"The *kaffirs* are just a bunch of lazy, no good, thieving bastards, they stole everything I had when I was farming up here and it's the same now. But I do not stand any nonsense. The idle fuckers who work for me get searched every day, at the end of the shift; and they also have to crap once a day in front of me to make sure that there are no diamonds. I think we should also lock them up at night so they can't run around selling diamonds to the dealers here."

He persuaded some of his like-minded fellows to adopt his methods and started to generate considerable racial friction. He knew that Frank would disapprove of his methods, so he made sure that he did his searches when Frank was down the 'big hole', as the mine was now colloquially known. Frank was aware that Fritz used harsh methods to control his labour force but he reasoned that he needed Fritz, since he was sure that Fritz was completely honest in his dealings with Frank, and provided that nobody was physically injured it was none of his business. If the issue ever came up in conversation Fritz changed the subject, with the result that Frank actively avoided the subject.

At the time of the original diamond discoveries the border between the Boer controlled Orange Free State and the British controlled Northern Cape was somewhat ill defined. Fritz's group agitated to include the diamond areas in the Boer controlled areas instead of the British.

Fritz had no real political agenda of his own, but he did want his revenge. Frank became aware of his activities and the activities of the group and tried to warn him off:

"Look Fritz, what can you hope to gain by all this? The best thing for both for us is to work hard, find 'the big one' and get out. What can possibly be gained by all this agitation?"

Fritz would not listen and said lamely: "The British stole this place from us and now we want it back."

"For God's sake, what are you talking about? All that happened more than seventy years ago; who is going to get it back now? Talk sense man."

Fritz blustered on. His knowledge of history was hazy and he had no idea that the British had taken the Cape from the Dutch back in 1804; he thought of the takeover as a recent event, although he had never known any government but one controlled by the British.

Over a period of a few weeks Fritz and his gang, including Vic and Frans, made a number of plans to destroy the North outfit, none of which worked. North had in any event made enough money to return to England and retire: "Not the fortune I first thought I would find, but enough to be comfortable," he confided in Frank one day. Frank was relieved; he knew that Fritz's obsession with North would eventually lead to trouble.

During the winter period in the Kimberley there is almost never any rain, so although there was some water at the bottom of the big hole in Kimberley, most claim owners were able to operate during the winter months. In the summer, when at regular intervals the most enormous thunderstorms occurred, it was a different story. The big hole filled with the summer rains, and also the water table rose, so there was leakage into the hole from the surrounding areas as well. This meant that claims at the lower levels were inundated and could not be worked. Most of Frank's claims were above the water level, but he had three claims, which had proved to be productive, under water. Various schemes had been put forward to the claim owners to pump the water out of the mines, including one from Cecil Rhodes, but none of them had so far proved successful. Frank had found an old engine and a pump and had asked Fritz, who was good with engineering type activities, if he could try to rig something up. He and Nzobo had been busy fiddling with the equipment for a few days and now had it on the verge of working. The engine and pump were mounted on a large gantry so they could be moved about in the mine. The pipe expelling the water from the mines went up to Frank's sorting operation where it could be used to help sort the rock and sand away from the diamonds.

Almost all the claim owners used black powder to blast the rock. The unsafe storage conditions and the unstable nature of the explosive meant that blasting accidents were common.

North was about to leave Kimberley, but now that he had been bested by Fritz, he felt that somehow he should get his own back.

"I'm going to get that Dutchman, if it is the last thing I do here," he muttered to one of his partners.

There was a great deal of interest from other claim owners in what Frank and Fritz were trying to do and this gave North an idea. His colleagues thought that North was just going to blow up the pumping equipment and they left him to it. North had spent days looking for a solution and then he found it: a disused storage hole, right near the pump and not far from the Devereaux claims. Over a few nights he personally moved all the remaining powder belonging to his consortium into this facility and then he waited.

The Zulus and Tswana were filling up the buckets with rock from the previous day's blast; Fritz was fiddling with the pump engine when Nzobo noticed a lit fuse moving rapidly towards the hidden dump of explosive: "Fritz, look out, look out!" he yelled and then pulled the other Africans behind a rock. Fritz took very little notice of any Africans so he ignored the warning. There was an almighty blast and when the dust had settled the gantry had been wrecked and Fritz was lying in a pool of blood with one of the arms of the gantry lying over him crushing any remaining life out of him. The Africans rushed over to see if they could do anything to help Fritz.

"He's alive, he's alive," yelled Mapitha. Fritz was pinned down beneath a huge piece of metal.

Kulaan said to Mapitha, "I will lift, you pull him out."

They all got ready, Mapitha and Nzobo ready to pull Fritz away from the gantry, Kulaan and the Tswana ready to try to lift it. They knew they had one chance; if they lifted it and it fell back again, that would be curtains for Fritz.

Kulaan had a really good grip on the piece of metal that was crushing the life out of Fritz.

"One, two, three," cried Mapitha. Kulaan with his huge strength lifted the gantry a few inches. It was not enough.

"Just a bit more," yelled Mapitha.

With a superhuman effort Kulaan pulled the gantry up another inch. That did it; they quickly pulled Fritz to safety. By this time a small crowd had gathered and saw that Kulaan had given Fritz at least a chance of life. Fritz was bundled onto a makeshift stretcher and Mapitha and Nzobo rushed him to the top of the mine. By this time Frank had arrived and he and two of Fritz's own men took over and carried him to the hospital, accompanied by more than twenty others injured in the blast.

As soon as North had lit the fuse he quietly left the mine and joined his colleagues. Later that day they were on their way back to the Cape. Resulting from Nzobo's evidence and some other enquiries, the police managed to link the blast to North but he had disappeared and nothing much was done. Blasting accidents were common anyway.

Fritz had broken both legs and his pelvis and he had numerous cracked ribs as well as internal injuries. The surgeon told him that if he had stayed under the gantry for more than another few minutes he would have died. Tales of Kulaan's strength spread far and wide; by the following week people were saying that it took ten normal men to move the gantry. Weeks later, when Fritz had partially recovered, he did seek Kulaan out.

"*Dankie Kaffir*," was all he said.

Fritz would be unable to work for months so he arranged with Frank that he should return to the Cape while he was convalescing. He still had murder in his heart feeling that the world was against him. He had not forgotten that *oom* Piet had cheated him, and he was looking forward to sorting out his wayward wife Petronella.

◇◇◇◇◇◇◇◇◇◇◇◇◇◇◇◇

Chapter 9

Mapitha had from time to time noticed the churches in Kimberley. Most were merely corrugated-iron shacks. He noticed that much of the activity was centred round Sunday, the day of rest, and was determined to find out more. So he and Nzobo sought out the various churches and agreed to pool their knowledge later.

Mapitha had established that St Peters' Anglican Church had a Sunday morning service, so he decided to attend. When he arrived, he saw to his consternation that there were a large number of well-dressed white men and some white women. No black people at all. He waited until most of the people had gone into the church and then tried to enter. He was stopped by a white man in what appeared to Mapitha to be a long black dress.

"The Tswana service is at 2'oclock this afternoon," the man said pleasantly.

"I speak English," answered Mapitha. "I am a Zulu and not a Tswana."

"This service is not for you," said the man, this time more forcefully. "We don't have enough room."

"I can sit at the back, on the floor, if there are no seats."

The man appeared to lose patience and called out.

Two burly miners came out of the church and enquired what the trouble was.

"Troublemaker, I'm afraid," said the man in the dress.

Without a word the two men took hold of Mapitha by each arm and manhandled him away from the church and flung him into the dust.

"*Kaffir* service is this afternoon," said one of them. "Don't be here when we come out later."

Mapitha, upset at the way he had been treated, went home. Nzobo found him sitting in front of the hut, looking disconsolate and aimlessly whittling away at a piece of wood.

"What's the matter?" asked Nzobo

"These white people, they want us to go to their churches, but they still look down on us. They would not let me into the church at the same time as the white people; they say that the *kaffir* service is later." Mapitha briefly told Nzobo about he incident at the church. "I don't think that I will go to any church; the people there are bad people."

"The King told us to find out all we can about these white people. Many of them go to these churches, mainly on a Sunday. It seems to me to be important to them. Maybe we should find out why," said Nzobo. "If you like I will go with you later."

The same man in the dress looked at Mapitha suspiciously when he and Nzobo entered the church at the appointed hour, but said nothing. Mapitha was quite confused by the proceedings; the service was in Tswana, which by now Mapitha understood well enough. He quite liked the singing, did not understand the prayers and had no idea when to stand, sit or kneel. The man in the black dress then stood at the front of the congregation and told them that a person called Jesus had died for them all on a cross, to save them from their sins. Mapitha did not know anyone by that name and it seemed to him that the black congregation present had fewer sins than the bulk of the white population in Kimberley. The man in the black dress said nothing to either him or Nzobo when they filed out of the Church at the end of the service.

Over the next few weeks Mapitha and Nzobo went to all the churches in Kimberley. They were treated much the same wherever they went: they were generally not welcome to whites only services, but were encouraged to attend services laid on exclusively for the black population. Most of the denominations had this arrangement, except the Dutch Reformed Churches who only catered for the Boers.

"These people, they have all these churches," said Mapitha to Nzobo one day. "But they all seem to be saying the same thing: that this person Jesus, he died for all of us to save us from our sins. Why do they need all these churches if they all say the same thing?"

Nzobo shrugged. "Some of them talk about three Gods in one, but they still talk of this man Jesus. Maybe we should ask Frank, although he does not go to any church."

Mapitha, Nzobo and Kulaan went to see Frank, who was relieved when the subject of religion was raised. He was always worried that the Zulu might be coming to tell him they were returning to their homes. Kulaan came along although he had never been persuaded to enter a church. He said that he thought they would be full of evil spirits.

Frank laughed when Mapitha explained what they had learned about the churches and the Christian faith and he gave them a short lecture on what Christianity was about.

"So this Christianity is for all the people?" asked Mapitha.

"Yes, absolutely, it is universal," answered Frank.

"So why do we have to go to blacks only services?"

"Maybe because few black people speak English, it is better that the service is conducted in their own language."

Mapitha explained his own experiences to Frank who just shrugged.

"And who is this Jesus they all talk about? I have never heard of such a person."

"He lived nearly two thousand years ago," answered Frank.

"It is the same for us," said Nzobo. "We pray to our ancestors, but if they only talk to this Jesus, don't the other ancestors get upset and send locusts and bad rains?"

Frank felt very inadequate in the situation and felt that he was not very good at answering the questions the Zulus put to him.

"Why do they need so many churches, if they all believe the same basic things?" asked Mapitha.

"Each one has a slightly different interpretation of some of the beliefs," answered Frank lamely.

"Why do you not go to these churches?" asked Nzobo

Frank fell silent for a few seconds. The Zulus could see that he was reflecting on some painful memories. He looked down.

"These churches are not for everybody," he eventually said quietly. "Sometimes they do great evil."

The Zulus were sensitive enough not to probe too deeply.

"Will they do evil to us, the Zulus?" asked Mapitha quietly.

"Maybe, I just don't know," answered Frank.

One of the completely non-denominational and non-racial churches was run by the Reverend Josiah Potts, who was an impostor and a charlatan. His church was a corrugated iron shed behind the hotel. The church was called the United Wesleyan Methodist Church of God. Nobody had the faintest idea what that meant. Nevertheless he always had a lively congregation, who were attracted by the fiery sermons and the singing. The Rev. Potts had been born in the east end of London but had spent time in the Southern United States, where he had picked up his interest in religion. He had also been in the California gold fields and had spent two years in prison in Louisiana for fraud. "A minor misunderstanding," he always insisted.

His main interests in Kimberley were IDB (Illicit Diamond Buying), whisky and some sex, whomever he could get it from. The Rev. Potts was a large, well built man, who stood at half an inch above six feet. His heavy jowls, puce red face and bulbous nose gave away his fondness for whisky. He always wore a black, knee length frock coat with matching breeches and black buckled shoes. The frock coat partly disguised his large stomach; a top hat covered his wispy grey hair and he always wore his dog collar.

His Sundays were normally fully occupied with church services; after all, he had to keep up appearances. During the other six days of the week, he roamed the now thousands of encampments like Frank's, ostensibly to convert people to the faith. He also had a deep instinct as to where he might find diamonds that had been stolen by labourers who wanted to unload them. Diamonds could officially be sold only to registered buyers in the town, by registered claim owners. Often these claim owners were willing traders in IDB. Sometimes they just needed to make a fast buck but equally often when they wanted to sell a claim they needed to prove its value, and what better proof than some receipts of diamond sales from registered buyers. Rev. Potts had steered clear of Frank Devereaux, who looked far too honest and straightforward for him. Fritz had chased him away from his compound on more than one occasion.

"If they want to come to your fucking church, they will come," he yelled at Rev. Potts once. "But keep away from here; I don't need any God botherers or any other type of botherers, thank you." Fritz had heard rumours about Rev. Potts and thought it better to steer clear of him.

Rev. Potts had been eyeing Tutula for some time. Most of his sexual

    Rough Diamonds

needs were met by the girls in the hotel. In return he gave them absolution whenever they felt in need of it. He knew that most of the labourers who worked down the mine picked up the odd diamond from time to time, and he saw no reason why Devereaux's Zulus would be any different; he'd acquired a few stones from Molefe on occasion. As far as the Rev. Potts was concerned, a few more months in the hellhole of Kimberley would set him up nicely and he could return to a pleasant English village. That was his dream.

Making certain that all was quiet, Rev. Potts made his way, bible in hand, to the Devereaux encampment. As usual on a Wednesday, most of the residential parts of Kimberley were deserted except for some domestic servants. Tutula, as usual, was at the encampment engaged in her domestic duties, which today involved brewing *utshwala* for her menfolk to drink on Sunday.

The Rev. Potts greeted Tutula in the little Zulu he spoke. She responded shyly; she was very flattered that this important looking white man would come and talk to her so kindly. He was sitting on a makeshift stool while Tutula was grinding up her mixture of maize meal and sorghum for the beer. He asked her what she was doing, so she fetched what was left of the previous week's beer and gave it to him. He thought it was foul but managed to keep a straight face and indicated how much he liked it. Rev. Potts was fascinated by Tutula's strong young body, barely covered by her floral dress. She couldn't help noticing that his eyes went up and down with the movement of her unsupported breasts as she crushed her grains with her pestle and mortar, which consisted of a four foot pole with a rounded end crushing the grain in a hollowed out log, both of which Nzobo had provided her. Rev. Potts eventually persuaded her to come to the church service on the following Sunday. Tutula was quite looking forward to this. In the time they had now been at the diggings she had developed physically and she was beginning to find the routine in Kimberley boring.

The following Sunday, to the Rev. Potts' delight he saw Tutula at the church service, along with the one hundred or so other worshippers. Tutula was pleased with the experience; she had no idea such a world existed. The singing really fascinated her and she was determined to learn the words and the tunes. She understood not a word of the sermon but while Rev. Potts was threatening the congregation with fire and brimstone she was able to look about. There were half a dozen white "ladies" from the hotel, looking the picture of elegance as far as Tutula was concerned; a few white miners with a look of desperation on their faces; and many black miners, some of whom were IDB partners of Rev. Potts and others just liked the singing. There were one or two other black girls like Tutula but they were very much in a minority.

The Rev. Potts paid Tutula a visit on the next two Wednesdays and within a month Tutula was very much part of the Rev. Pott's little world.

Unbeknown to Mapitha, Nzobo had also been picking up the occasional diamond, from the diggings. One day, out of the corner of his eye, Mapitha saw Nzobo swoop down and pop something in his mouth. Having guessed what it was, Mapitha had a quiet word with him afterwards.

"Yes, I've been doing it for months, but then so have you," was Nzobo's answer.

Later they compared notes and hiding places and agreed that Mapitha's hiding place was possibly better. Nzobo had been keeping his collection in a little animal skin bag among his meagre belongings. They agreed to pool their collection and keep it in Mapitha's hiding place.

When they were out hunting springbok the next Sunday, Nzobo suddenly started turning stones over and looking underneath. Suddenly he pulled a forked stick out of an animal skin bag he was holding and jabbed at something that had been underneath the rock. When Mapitha came up and asked him what he was doing, he held up a healthy looking three-foot cobra; he was holding it behind the head so it was unable to bite him. He stuffed it in the bag and closed the entrance before the snake could strike.

"What's that for?" asked Mapitha curiously.

"It will protect the diamonds," answered Nzobo. "We'll keep it in your hiding place."

"How will we feed it?" asked Mapitha.

"Tutula will catch mice; there are plenty of mice about and we will keep water there in the hole," answered Nzobo.

Mapitha looked doubtful.

"Only you and I know about the hiding place," he said. "What do we need a snake for?"

"You never know," said Nzobo.

So they took *Inyoka* back with them to the hut and when some water and a few scraps of meat had been placed in the hole, *inyoka* was put in the hole and the hole closed up. Mapitha made sure that there were some very small cracks, which would provide air. Tutula was detailed to catch mice.

Rev. Potts now came and had a few mouthfuls of *utshwala* every Wednesday with Tutula. She quite liked his visits and really enjoyed the Sunday service. On the sixth visit the Rev. could not contain himself any longer, and it took very little persuasion on his part to entice Tutula to have sex with him. They both crawled unseen into the hut; Tutula removed her dress and the Rev. Potts his breeches. After a few grunts it was all over. For Tutula it seemed rather inconsequential; if it kept the white priest happy, she was satisfied. She was mighty surprised when he gave her a shilling as he left. This continued for a few more weeks and then, on other days during the week, first one reasonably well dressed white man and then another came to the Devereaux encampment and offered Tutula a shilling for sex.

During the time the Zulus had been in Kimberley Mapitha had given her money for food and clothes but nothing for herself. She found a way of putting the money she earned for sex in the bank and told nobody about it. Tutula eventually had one or two clients most days of the week and had started to accumulate a tidy sum at the bank. She felt her life was now much more exciting than it had been before. She looked forward to Sundays and she didn't really mind servicing her now regular five or six white clients. She wasn't sure what she would do with the money in the bank, but life was interesting. Much better than being married to some Tswana man in her home village, she thought. She had noticed that her monthly bleeding had stopped and that her breasts were getting larger but she took no notice. Mapitha, however, had started to notice some changes in Tutula and he spoke to Nzobo.

"Maybe she is pregnant," said Nzobo.

"Pregnant, how pregnant?" said Mapitha; he was shocked.

"She is left by herself every day, you never know. She's just a young girl," said Nzobo.

Down the mine, Frank had trained both Mapitha and Nzobo how to lay the black powder charges. He had watched them over many weeks and they never put a foot wrong. Nzobo in particular seemed, surprisingly, to have an instinct for where to drill the holes and how much powder to use. With Fritz away Frank changed his routine slightly. He always went down the mine in the early morning but now he had to run the sorting tables and sometimes he came back to the encampment for an hour or two to complete some paperwork. On one of these occasions he noticed a white man whom he had not seen before scurrying away from the encampment and a few moments later Tutula emerged from the hut the Zulus occupied pulling on her dress. She just smiled at him and nothing was said. Frank had a quiet word with Mapitha later that day.

By this time Mapitha was on full alert. He went down the mine as usual and then, having spoken to Frank, made his way back to the encampment. There was no sign of Tutula anywhere so he crept round the hut, retrieving his spear from the thatch where he had hidden it in the morning. There was the sound of some activity in the hut and he went round the side and peered in through the entrance. His worst fears were confirmed: there was Tutula lying naked flat on her back with her legs in the air, with a white man, trouserless, energetically making love to her.

Mapitha yelled "Bayete!" and gave the man a sharp jab with his spear in his little, round, white buttocks. A drop of blood appeared and the man yelled blue murder, leapt up and grabbing his trousers, rushed out of the hut. Mapitha watched him run; he fell over twice trying to put his trousers on but he soon disappeared out of sight.

Mapitha was furious. He found a stick outside the hut and went into the hut and beat Tutula until she pleaded for mercy.

"Have I not been like a father to you," he yelled, "and now you behave like this. Selling yourself to any stinking fellow that comes along. And you are pregnant, you are expecting a baby, and who is the father? One of those people who pay you to lie with them."

Tutula just cowered. She didn't know what to say.

"I have been looking for a husband for you and now what can I do, you are used up. No Tswana or Zulu will have you now."

He flung the stick at her and walked out. A few people had gathered from round about to see what all the fuss was about. Brandishing his spear, Mapitha chased them all away.

Tutula came out of the hut dressed, but shivering with fright.

"You get back to work," Mapitha told her. "I will talk to you later." He stormed off back to the mine.

Tutula, after the beating from Mapitha, had gone over to see Rev. Potts, to whom she tearfully explained her predicament.

"Pregnant you say, well we'll have to see about that," he said. "Stay here."

He stumbled over to the hotel where he found Cora, Hannelore and another of the "ladies" in the hotel.

"Got a bit of a problem, I'm afraid." He then explained Tutula's condition, leaving out his own potential role in her predicament.

"One of my flock," explained the Rev. "Got to look after their welfare you know."

Hannelore knew the Rev. Potts well, but was too smart to argue. She and the Rev. Potts had a modus operandi, which she respected. In a way they both needed each other.

Hannelore examined Tutula, noticing but not commenting on the welts left by the beating she had received from Mapitha.

"How many months have you missed?" she asked.

After a while Tutula understood and held up three fingers.

"Stay here," ordered Hannelore.

Half an hour later she came back with a tin mug containing a pint of the vilest looking and smelling concoction Tutula had ever seen.

"Drink this now and go to bed for two days. That should fix it," said Hannelore.

Tutula thought she understood but she was still scared of Mapitha.

"You must come and tell Mapitha," she said.

"O.K. I'll come over later after four o'clock," said Hannelore.

Tutula went back to the encampment and lay down.

Mapitha and the others arrived back at about the same time Hannelore arrived. She buttonholed Mapitha.

"That girl is sick, very sick; she will not work for three days. If you make her work you'll have me to reckon with," she said firmly. Hannelore had developed in maturity and confidence in the years spent in Kimberley. She and her mother were rich and somehow she had avoided pregnancy. She always dealt firmly with any man who showed any signs of getting out of hand.

Mapitha understood the sentiment if not all the words.

During the next few days Tutula thought she was going to die. She had the most terrible cramps imaginable. The men had no idea what to do, and twice Mapitha ran over to the hotel to fetch Hannelore.

"Nothing to worry about," was all she had to say.

Eventually Tutula started to bleed and, as intended, she had a miscarriage. Within a week she was back to her duties. Mapitha was concerned and over the next two months he approached Molefe and as many of the Tswana men as he could find to try to marry her off.

Molefe was jealous of the Zulus, since they had usurped the positions in Frank's operation that he thought belonged to the Tswana, who had been there the longest. Molefe was contemptuous, and he exaggerated his attitude.

"Marry her?" he almost shouted at Mapitha. "White man's whore, and having spent all that time with you Zulus. She is no longer a proper Tswana and she is not a virgin." Chepete and Dibotelo remained silent. They knew that when they went home with guns, white man's clothing and money to buy cattle they would have many potential virgin brides to choose from. There was no need to take on spoiled goods. A few of the Tswana that Mapitha approached came to see the goods, but a word or two from Molefe sent them scuttling away.

Mapitha was angry with Molefe and decided that he would find a way of dealing with him at some later date. In the meanwhile Tutula had taken the situation into her own hands.

After her ordeal she went to see Hannelore to thank her. Hannelore said to her:

"Why stay there? You would be much better off joining us girls here. Free food, board and clothes and within a couple of years you would have enough money to retire." Tutula did not understand the concept of retirement but liked the idea.

Tutula waited until the Zulus were safely at work and then moved with her belongings to the hotel. The Zulus were nonplussed when they returned and looked high and low for Tutula. A few days later Mapitha went to the hotel and saw Tutula dressed in much the same way as the white whores she worked with. He was prevented from talking to her and she ignored him. He went sadly away from the hotel.

"She was like my own daughter," he thought, "and I have completely failed her. She will surely die here." He had determined that her age was about sixteen. In his own society she would have been safely married off, as was her duty. He wondered what other horrors the advent of the white invader would visit on the blacks in his country.

The Zulus soon adjusted their domestic arrangements and life went on much as before. With Fritz away and Frank running the sorting tables, the Zulus were very much in charge down the mine.

The first day that Frank was fully in charge of the sorting tables, at the end of the shift all Fritz's labourers stripped naked and waited expectantly for Frank.

"What's this?" stammered Frank.

They said something in Sotho.

Eventually Frank gathered that this was an inspection parade to make sure that none of them had stolen any diamonds during the day. He even gathered that on occasions Fritz had conducted most intimate body searches. They then all crouched down and defecated in front of him, one of them handed Frank a stick; after his initial horror he was told that Fritz examined each individual set of faeces for diamonds. Frank was horrified and hurriedly made the men put their clothes back on again.

"Did he ever find any diamonds doing all this?"

"No!" was the clear answer. Whilst he knew that there was a certain amount of IDB activity in the town, he did not believe it was as bad as some people made out. In particular, Frank felt that the Boers were prone to exaggerate the situation to serve their own ends. What they really wanted was the complete segregation of the black labourers from the rest of the town, and this would ensure that the blacks always had an inferior position in society, almost like slaves. Frank had come to terms with his own life and the fact that his family had owned slaves, though they were now all freed as a result of the American civil war. He did not want to revisit that situation. He dealt with men as he found them and rejected the concept of society built on skin colour. He knew he would have a difficult conversation with Fritz, when he returned.

The Rev. Potts had a very successful IDB business in operation, and he was making money hand over fist by buying diamonds from the black labourers and selling them to claim owners, who in turn sold the stones to registered buyers in town. Already he was comfortably off and he could easily have afforded to retire quietly to England. He was a greedy man though, and he thought he would stay in Kimberley a few more months "just to build up an extra little nest egg," he thought to himself.

He had approached the Zulus on more than one occasion but had been rejected, and once after Tutula had gone to work in the hotel Mapitha had chased him away with his spear.

On the several occasions that the Rev. Potts had been in the Zulus' hut engaged in his seduction of Tutula, he had noticed a hollow sound when he clumped about the hut with his shoes. He was certain that this was a hiding place of some sort, and the only thing that was worth hiding in Kimberley was diamonds.

Rev. Potts kept the Devereaux encampment under observation for a few days. One morning when he was certain that there would be nobody about, he made his way to the Zulu hut and, ensuring he was unseen, eased his big frame inside. Within a few minutes he had found the hiding place and uncovered one of the boards that Mapitha had so carefully put in place. He pulled the board up, and before he could do anything else was to his absolute horror confronted by an enormous, angry snake, which sunk its monstrous fangs into his hand and then, as he tried to escape from the hut, into one of his fat legs.

Mapitha and Nzobo had nurtured the snake and it had grown, so *Inyoka* injected a prodigious amount of venom into the fat priest.

The Rev. Potts did not yell out but he tried to run away from the scene as quickly as he could. Instinctively he made his way to his church, feeling ever more faint and nauseous as he went. Collapsing unseen in the doorway of his church, he died there alone and in agony less than forty minutes after his incursion into the Zulu domain.

When the Zulus returned from the mine, as they were about to enter their hut there was a hiss and Nzobo, who was in front, jumped back just before the snake struck. As he peered into the hut he could see the snake, with its hood fully extended, swaying in the half-light of the hut. Mapitha retrieved his spear and, covering his eyes, made his way swiftly into the hut and with one thrust pinned the snake just below the head and killed it. He and Nzobo quickly examined the contents of their hiding place and determined that nothing was missing; they covered the hole up again. Nzobo had scouted round; he showed Mapitha some fresh heel marks from a shoe. They both shrugged. The Zulus ate snake meat that night.

Tutula had gone round to the church in the mid-afternoon, which was a quiet time for the girls at the hotel, and shrieked when she found the Rev. Potts' body slumped in the doorway of the church. She rushed back to the hotel and the body was carried to the hospital, where Rev. Potts was pronounced dead.

"Snake bite," was the verdict.

The funeral the next day was attended by several hundred people. Although Rev. Potts had been a self-seeking rogue many people had actually benefited from his presence in the town. The labourers had somewhere to unload their stolen diamonds, claim owners had benefited from purchases made from him and his church was well attended.

Tutula and the girls at the hotel were absolutely devastated. Although he had shamelessly exploited them, Rev Potts had treated them kindly and more importantly had looked on them and treated them as equals. They felt they had lost a true friend.

Some months later Rev. Potts' impoverished, widowed sister in England unexpectedly found she was the beneficiary of his considerable fortune. She was amazed as she had not seen or heard of her wayward brother for years.

As the Zulus had found out the blacks were tolerated if not welcomed in the main hotel in town. They did not feel all that comfortable in that environment in any event so they started to arrange their own entertainment. Frank had agreed that the Zulus could use his compound for an occasional beer drink, provided that it did not get out of hand. To start with Mapitha invited a few fellow Zulus and they drank the *utshwala* that Tutula had prepared for them. From time to time they attended beer drinks with members of other tribes but they felt more at home with their own Zulu folk so as time went by they arranged a beer drink with the relatively few Zulus who found their way to Kimberley. There were almost no Zulu women at all and they found the concept of paying for women alien so they had almost no female company during all of their stay in Kimberley. The beer drinks were congenial and gave them some news of what was happening in their homeland.

◇◇◇◇◇◇◇◇◇◇◇◇◇◇◇◇

Chapter 10

The journey to the Cape was long and to start with uncomfortable, but Fritz was young and strong and as his body healed he was able to ride his horse instead of being bumped around in the wagon. Eventually he and a servant took off on their own leaving the wagon train behind; so Fritz arrived unannounced in the Cape. He made his way apprehensively to his farm ready to do battle. He imagined himself fighting with and possibly killing Petronella's supposed lover and when he arrived at the farm he was all in a lather. As he dismounted a very surprised Petronella came out to see who had arrived and when she saw who it was rushed out to greet him. To his absolute amazement she put her arms around his neck and kissed him passionately. "Oh, Fritz, Fritz, why didn't you write and tell me you were coming, I've missed you." The horses were seen to and before he knew what was happening to him they were in bed together. Fritz was completely disarmed and spent the next few days admiring and making love to the very pretty Petronella; the Petronella that he had married and not the Petronella from the dusty Northern Cape farm. The manager Visagie had the wine farm under control and it was prospering. Fritz didn't want to let Frank down but he started to wonder whether he should return to the diamond fields at all. Still he had a few bones to pick, firstly with Piet and then there were those rumours about his wife, which he couldn't just let go, and maybe North, if he could find him.

Two weeks after his return he went to see Piet in his office in Stellenbosch. Visagie, whose first loyalty was to Piet, had of course alerted him to the fact that Fritz had returned.

"Good morning Fritz, good morning," Piet greeted him effusively like a long lost brother. Piet was still smarting about the loss of his investment in the diamond fields, for which he blamed Fritz, although he had made a fortune from the wagons and equipment that he had bought up prior to the rush north. He had almost forgotten that he, Piet, had stolen more than half of the original find that Fritz had entrusted him with. After the obligatory coffee and some talk of the family Fritz said to Piet bluntly:

"Piet, I have learned rather a lot about the value of diamonds in the past couple of years. The diamonds I brought down here which you sold were worth at least double what you gave me for them and I want the rest; I want it now." He slammed his hand down hard on Piet's desk. Piet went pale. This was the last thing that he had expected and he could not possibly match Fritz physically.

"Nonsense Fritz, you are overwrought, I gave you the full value of the diamonds I sold. I know that the price has gone up recently, maybe you are mistaken."

"Rubbish" Fritz roared. He stood over Piet and yelled: "I took this lousy piece of paper you gave me," (he produced the original receipt, in surprisingly good condition) "which luckily had all the weights on it, and had it valued by a reputable dealer in Kimberley-the one Frank and I deal with on a regular basis. He told me that without doubt I had been swindled. Also the big stone that I found is now well known. The value on here is ridiculous, and I want the rest of it. Now!"

Piet decided that attack was the best form of defence. "What about my wagons then? I trusted you to see that those no good relatives of yours looked after them, and what have I seen from all that? Nothing."

This infuriated Fritz even more: "My relatives! They are just as much yours as mine and you set the whole expedition up. You didn't consult me in any way. And all this nonsense about the police looking for me is rubbish; no police have ever been looking for me. I'll have my money or I will break your neck." Fritz moved threateningly round the desk.

"No,no, Fritz be sensible, let's talk. This is family; surely we can sort this out."

Fritz grabbed him by the shirt-front and slammed him up against the wall. Piet's breath was knocked out of him.

"I want another three hundred and fifty pounds and I want it today, or I will break your neck as I said."

"My goodness Fritz, where do you think I am going to get that sort of money from?"

Fritz slammed him against the wall again.

"You sold the diamonds, you tell me," answered Fritz.

He was about to slam Piet into the wall again when Piet suddenly went limp.He was still breathing but had gone deathly pale.

Even Fritz could see that there was something wrong and he went into the outer office and asked the very nervous clerk there to find a doctor, quickly.

When the doctor came he took one look at Piet and said: "Heart attack. We must get him to the hospital."

A few days later when Fritz visited the hospital, Piet refused to see him and the doctor castigated him.

"If he dies you will be up on a murder charge, young fellow. I heard that you had a disagreement but beating up an old man like Piet is not the way to deal with issues like that."

"He stole from me and lied to me," protested Fritz.

Petronella was aghast when she heard what had happened. She was very fond of Piet, who had really looked after their interests while Fritz had been away, possibly out of a sense of guilt in view of what he had done to Fritz. Even after Fritz explained the whole story to her she said to him:

"Isn't this enough for you? The farm, is well managed by Visagie; we will never want for anything more. Can't you just leave it alone? Piet is our friend and you go and beat him up. I was hoping that you had turned a new leaf and that now we are well off, you would just come back and stay with me in this wonderful place."

"All I want is what is due to me. He swindled me and then made up all sorts of stories that made me go back up to the diggings. Don't you understand? I could have stayed here all along."

"What is done is done, Fritz, Just leave it all alone and enjoy the fruits of your hard work. Forget about the money, we don't need it."

He just glowered at her.

Fritz also went to see the friend who had written to him about Petronella's indiscretion.

"I wish that I had not said anything," he said. "It didn't last all that long and as far as know it is all over now."

"Who is it?" asked Fritz aggressively.

"I won't tell you, it won't do any good to go and beat him up, which is what I'm sure you want to do. Fritz, just forget it. Enjoy your money and now is the time to settle down and have a family."

Fritz restlessly stayed around; Visagie had the farm under control and there was little that Fritz could contribute. He waited for Piet leave hospital but he was still obsessed by Petronella's lover. One day he asked her after they had made love:

"Petronella, there are stories around town about you and another man, what do you have to say about that?"

Petronella, in her nakedness, knelt up over him in the bed and said very firmly:

"What nonsense, these people just invent stories about us I suppose because we now have some money; if we were still poor you would have heard none of these stories." Fritz as always feasted his eyes on her pretty erect breasts and her rounded bottom and the dark patch between her thighs. Soon they were making love again and he temporarily forgot what he had been told.

After the hard work on the diamond mines Fritz, as he returned to full health, became somewhat restless and often took himself off to Cape Town, 'for business' as he told Petronella. On one of these visits he had been drinking with a few acquaintances when one of them said:

"See that fellow over there, Fritz, there was a rumour that he was your wife's lover when you were up in Kimberley."

Fritz looked up and there was a tall, handsome man gazing directly at him, almost like a challenge. He hesitated, he knew that he should walk away; he and Petronella had really discovered their old magic and whatever had gone on while he was away, she had made it very clear that she loved him. He hoped that she was pregnant. He looked away; inside he was fuming and wanted to break the fellow's neck.

His companions egged him on:"What are you going to do about it?" one asked.

Fritz just smiled: "Maybe we should just go somewhere else." He got up and they all went out to another establishment. Fritz was proud of himself, he felt very mature and satisfied with himself. His companions teased him:

"That's not like you Fritz, in the old days you would have got up and flattened him, if you had even suspected that he had slept with your wife."

They spent the afternoon drinking and then, when he was less than sober, he saw North coming into the pub going to sit by himself in a corner. A blood red rage just enveloped him, he just couldn't help himself, so he picked up a heavy barstool and before anyone could stop him, quickly moved over to where North was sitting and crashed the stool down on North's unsuspecting head. He was dragged away by his friends and they made themselves scarce. Rumours were that North would die or at best be incapacitated for the rest of his life.

Fritz went home. He knew that his actions had spoiled everything and that he would aagain have to make himself scarce, this time for a valid reason. He told Petronella the story, haltingly a few days later. After many tears Petronella went to see Piet who had recovered somewhat and already knew the story.

"If he stays here he will probably be arrested and jailed; the best thing he can do is to return to the mines. They won't bother him there; barroom brawls are quite common and the matter will have been forgotten in a year or two. Please give him this, but I will not see him; he has probably ruined my health for ever." It was an account starting with Fritz's claim for the three hundred and fifity pounds with a number of deductions, including the costs of the expedition to the mines which Piet had deducted in full, plus numerous bills for Piet's time over the years. Attached was a cheque for two hundred and three pounds ten shillings and two pence.

Fritz left a few days later with Petronella crying her heart out. She had really enjoyed having Fritz home. "I will let you know when it all blows over," she said.

◇◇◇◇◇◇◇◇◇◇◇◇◇◇◇◇

Chapter 11

In a disorganized and unstructured way the Zulus tried to learn all they could about the strange white people that had come to live amongst them. They could see that they were indeed a very powerful group, who had come from places far away and with their guns were able to dominate the local black population. Mapitha found Kimberley a haphazard and undisciplined place, and he barely understood how it all worked. He was quite happy working for Frank, who treated all his labour with respect and looked after them.

On one or two occasions one or other of the Zulus had fallen ill or had had a bad cut whilst working down the mine. Frank unhesitatingly escorted them to the hospital where their ailments were treated sympathetically and quickly.

"This hospital and these doctors can help the Zulu," he confided in Nzobo one day. "We have nothing like this. Without the doctors Fritz would have died."

"Without Kulaan, Fritz would have died," answered Nzobo. "But maybe our *sangomas* can learn from the *abelungu* doctors."

"The King asked us to find out all we could about the white man, maybe these doctors are one good thing we can report to him," said Mapitha.

Frans and Vic, being Fritz's friends and also being members of the police force, were avoided. Most of the black people had either had a bad experience from the police or knew someone else who had.

When Frank was asked about the police he said: "They are supposed to keep order."

The Zulus shrugged. The King and his *indunas* kept order in their society. They found it difficult to understand why this important task should be left to inconsequential people like Vic and Frans.

"Sometimes they lock people up, I hear," a horrified Mapitha said to Frank. "If a Zulu has done something wrong the King will order him to be killed or if he is lucky he will pay a fine to the King of some cattle. To lock people up and then feed them, we can't understand this."

"If the King decides that some one has done something wrong and then he is killed and then afterwards, they find that he had done nothing wrong, what happens then?" asked Frank.

"If the King says a person is guilty, then he is guilty. We do not question what the King says. The King is never wrong; he is guided by his ancestors to make the right decisions."

"So no Zulu has ever been killed unjustly?" asked Frank.

"What is unjustly? asked Mapitha.

"No Zulu has ever been killed who should not have been killed."

"No. What is the purpose of asking such questions? If a man has been killed by the order of the King then he is guilty, no questions will ever bring him back to life. People die all the time. If a lion kills a person we do not question whether the person died or not or whether the lion should have been there or not. A person was killed by the lion; if we can find the lion then we will kill it, if not then the Gods were looking after the lion. We would not try to catch the lion and lock it up."

"And if someone has done something small that does not deserve death, what do you do then?

"He will be beaten, or maybe pay the King a fine of some cattle. The King will always decide."

"Does the King have many cattle?" asked Frank.

"Yes, more than any other."

"Is there not some danger in this situation, I mean that the King could just take everything and kill people who try to stop him?"

"Everything belongs to the King anyway, but if he abuses his authority too much then the people will be unhappy and he will probably be killed, but worse still his family will suffer. They may even be forced to run away to another tribe and so will lose everything."

"Do you not think that there is some advantage in having a police force and an independent judge, to decide these things and to leave a person like the King out of it altogether?"

"Judge, what is a judge?"

Frank then went on to explain to the uncomprehending Zulu, the functions of a judge.

"This is not the Zulu way," said Mapitha shaking his head.

The Zulu could see that Kimberley in its shambles was a comparatively rich place, even rivalling Kwa—Bulawayo in Mapitha's eyes. The basis for the existence of Kimberley still completely baffled the Zulus, since they saw absolutely no value in the diamonds that were so laboriously being extracted from the hard gray earth. The white women in the hotel and the town, whom the Zulu only saw at a distance, were not seen as attractive in any way and the diamonds that a few of them now wore made no difference to the overall impression as far as the Zulu were concerned.

As the town grew the amenities gradually improved, so it became a place where families established themselves and schools were built by the churches, the town and the Government.

Nzobo was the first of the Zulu to become aware of the existence of the schools. In the Zulu tradition as soon as a male child was old enough he was sent out to herd cattle. He was carefully nurtured through puberty and the ceremonies surrounding that event. The Zulu youth was then inducted into his age group and became a part of a regiment until he was given permission to marry. Much attention was given to his physical development, but there was no formal education in the western sense. Girls were also formed into regiments and although they did no fighting, the discipline in those regiments was just as strict as with the men. The youth were all encouraged to practice *hlobonga* with members of the opposite sex in their age group. However if any unmarried female fell pregnant the result was instant death for both the woman and the man responsible. So when Nzobo saw a classroom full of children at desks with an adult instructing them at the front of the room he was intrigued.

"These children, all sitting down for most of the day, this will make them weak and they will not be able to fight," he confided in Frank.

"We believe that children need both physical as well as mental stimulation. They need to learn to read and write and do their sums so they can be useful members of society," responded Frank.

"What is read and write?" asked Nzobo.

Frank went and fetched a book on mining, which he explained to Nzobo. As far as Nzobo was concerned, since he was unable to read, the book was just a mass of squiggles but he could see that the pictures showed mining equipment similar to that used in Kimberley.

"You see," said Frank, "this book was written by a person in America where I come from." Nzobo nodded, he now thought that he knew what America was since Frank had discussed that with them on a few occasions. "The book tells me about mining equipment and operations in other parts of the world, I can then learn from that and use some of the information here in Kimberley. The man who wrote the book has never been anywhere near Kimberley or South Africa. So the man writes down all this information and then I can buy the book and read what he has written and then understand it. To do that I have to be able to read, that is what those children are learning now. They would not be able to function very well in our society if they were not able to read and write."

This was whole new world to Nzobo.

"If the black people do not learn this reading and writing, what will happen to them?"

"There is no reason why black people should not learn to read and write. If they don't they will have difficulty in places like Kimberley, which is run by the white people."

"The language of reading and writing, is this just English?" asked Nzobo.

Frank laughed. "No, many languages are written down."

"Not Zulu," said Nzobo.

"Maybe not yet, but I expect it will happen,"

Nzobo was greatly troubled by this knowledge. He had a feeling that there was a whole world out there that he had no way of being a part of. He told Mapitha of his conversation, who responded: "I was talking to Molefe and he told me that the people who run the churches have a place in Kuruman where they have schools teaching Tswana children in their own language. They are teaching them to read and write, like you say. They have also translated the big Christian book into that language. It seems that for the blacks the reading and writing and the churches somehow go together."

"How far is this Kuruman?" asked Nzobo.

"Maybe ten dawns away, less on a horse," answered Mapitha.

"Should the Zulus have these schools?" asked Nzobo.

"Maybe, but the Tswana are still very weak; any Zulu could beat any Tswana in a fight. Maybe they need these schools. The Zulu are strong; I think that these schools could teach the Zulu children the wrong things and that they will spend so much time learning the white man's ways that they will forget all the Zulu traditions."

"The Zulu has no guns; we cannot make guns. The Zulu could not make the engines that help us in the mine. This is all white man's doing. Should we not learn all this? If we do, maybe this learning will keep us strong. If we don't, maybe the white man will grow stronger and stronger and we Zulu will be left behind," said Nzobo thoughtfully.

"The Zulu will remain strong; any white man or Tswana or stinking Xhosa or Pondo who tries to challenge us will feel a piece of Zulu steel between his ribs. Shaka made us strong; we will stay that way if we remember his traditions," responded Mapitha aggressively.

"Maybe we should see what a Tswana school is like; maybe we can learn something."

"Maybe," said Mapitha, without much interest.

Nzobo was determined to go to Kuruman and see the Tswana school for himself. Frank gave him a few days off and allowed him to borrow *ihashi*. Molefe gave him directions and he found his way there without any trouble.

He arrived unannounced and was met by a white priest, who asked him what he wanted in a mixture of Tswana and English. The man was somewhat taken aback when Nzobo explained that he was on a mission from the Zulu King to find out all he could about the white man and on this occasion what schooling was all about.

He was taken at face value and spent two days there, spending time in classes and trying to understand the value of what was being taught. Most importantly he was treated with respect and he was very impressed with the difference between that attitude of the white priests in Kuruman and everything he had experienced in Kimberley.

"If these children spend all day here inside, don't they become all weak and so will not be able to fight and protect their village?" he asked.

"The children play games and run every afternoon. No child can spend all his time just playing games; we believe in a more balanced approach."

"Can these children look after cattle like good Zulu children have to?"

"Oh yes, they all have their duties looking after and sometimes milking the cows. They also help us grow the vegetables here." The priest showed Nzobo round the extensive irrigation scheme that grew all the maize and vegetables for the mission. Nzobo looked round politely but dismissed it all as womens work. He had no interest in growing vegetables.

"I see that you have girls in the class as well as boys. Isn't this dangerous, teaching these girls things that will put ideas into their heads that don't belong there and it will mean that their husband will have too much trouble looking after them? Maybe education is just for the boys."

"We think that both boys and girls should have the benefits of education," answered the priest.

"Maybe that's good enough for the Tswana, but I don't think that many Zulus would agree with you."

"Most of the pupils here are indeed boys, so maybe the Tswana think that way too."

Nzobo nodded.

Often during his visit he heard the names of Robert Moffat and David Livingstone, and he was told they were very well known missionaries and that Robert Moffat had started the mission at Kuruman fifty years earlier, in the time of Shaka. The names meant nothing to him.

When he returned to Kimberley he spent some time discussing what he had seen with Mapitha. Both of them concluded that the teaching and the white man's medicine would benefit the Zulu but they were unsure of the benefits of the white man's religion.

"It seems to come together though," observed Nzobo. "I think that the people who will teach us will be firstly the people of religion and maybe they will also be able to give us white man's medicine and teaching."

"Also the white people in Kuruman were not like the white people here. The white people here are caught up in the evil spirits of *idayimani*, it makes them do bad things. The white people in Kuruman were not like that, and they seemed to be really interested in me and what I was there for. Maybe all white people are not like the people here in Kimberley."

◇◇◇◇◇◇◇◇◇◇◇◇◇◇◇

Rough Diamonds

Some time into their third year in Kimberley, the Zulus trudged off down the mines with their Tswana compatriots. Frank now seldom came with them; he spent more of his time helping Fritz, who had now returned from the Cape, and he was more than happy with the way the operations in the mine were conducted. Frank could get nothing out of Fritz, although he was now more subdued and kept away from the hotels in the town.

The Zulus now had enough money in the bank to buy horses and guns and have plenty left over for cattle. They felt that they had learned enough of the white man's ways to return to the Zulu King and make a full report. Mapitha and Nzobo spoke quite passable English; Kulaan still only had a few words. They decided that they had had enough and would return soon to their beloved Zululand.

The day was sultry and hot and as usual the mine was as busy as an ants' nest. The noise was deafening and the dust rose some hundreds of feet above the mine and covered everything in the town. They had routinely completed their midday blast and were in the process of shovelling the rock and soil produced by the blast into buckets when Nzobo gave a shout. He was pointing at a particular piece of rock. The rock was studded with a number of diamonds, but right in the middle of the rock was one huge diamond. The blacks all looked at each other and concluded that the big one should be left for Frank. Without saying a word, Molefe picked up a couple of the stones, as did Mapitha, then they loaded the rock into a bucket and saw it make its tortuous way up to the surface.

Frank knew that something special was on its way up from the hand signals he had seen from the mine area. He just could not believe what he saw when it arrived, though.

"Hey Fritz, come and have a look at this!" he shouted above the din.

They both stood and stared at the rock for a good five minutes before anything was done. As far as Frank was concerned this was it; he would now certainly be able to return to America and have the funds to rebuild his family fortune. He knelt down and prayed for the first time in ten years.

Frank wasted no time. Within a few months he had sold up and had arranged to transfer his money back to America. Between him and Fritz they had cleared several thousand pounds. All that remained for Frank to decide was what to do with the claims.

"Well, I have no more use for them. Look, the blacks have worked hard, maybe we should just hand the claims over to them; they can pay us a small rent if you like," said Frank. All he wanted to do was to go home. He had completely lost interest in Kimberley.

Fritz's instincts rebelled completely against this idea. Although he could now walk away from Kimberley a comparatively wealthy man, he had never seen the blacks as anything like his equals and the idea that they could own claims and perhaps in time become wealthy was complete anathema to him. He was, of course, aware that there were several black claim owners but he preferred not to think about that. Fritz did not want to offend Frank so he said, "*Kaffirs* will not be able to manage these claims. Many of the claims are being buried by rock falls. They will need special equipment to dig anything out from their claims."

"They seem to have managed perfectly well up to now," responded Frank, surprised by the answer. Fritz realised that because the claims were marginal that it might take another five years to build the sort of fortune Frank was now walking away with.

They argued back and forth for a while and eventually Frank agreed that Fritz could have seven of the claims, but he insisted on giving the Zulus three claims. Molefe and the Tswana had already gone home contented, so they were not considered.

Fritz could easily have walked away like Frank had, but he was now obsessed with preventing the 'thieving *kaffirs*' from achieving what he himself had achieved. Besides, Petronella had told him not to return to the Cape just yet since the furore had not quite died down, although both of them wanted desperately for him to return, not least to see the baby boy that Petronella had given bith to: "He looks just like you, she wrote."

Frank eventually left with his fortune and uneasily left the Zulus to try to work with Fritz.

For a few months everything went smoothly. Mapitha and Fritz equitably shared the costs of running the steam engine and the cable system. Fritz had employed his own crew to work his claims; Kulaan and Nzobo ran the mine end of the business while Mapitha did the sorting at the surface. All went well while Fritz was pulling in more diamonds than the Zulus.

After Frank had been gone a few months, the Zulus struck a particularly rich vein and Fritz's own workers were stealing many of his diamonds before they ever reached the surface. Fritz wrongly concluded that the Zulus were part of this conspiracy. In point of fact he treated his own labour so badly that they would have done anything to harm his interests.

At about this time a great fuss was being made in regard to IDB and the laws were tightened up considerably. Many of the larger operators were also clamouring for blacks to be housed in large compounds and to be searched daily for illicit diamonds, much as Fritz had done. Fritz saw his chance to get even with the Zulus.

Frans and Vic were an established part of the police force, they had been unwilling to continue the hard labour required in the mines but were somewhat envious of some of the fortunes being made. They were readily bribed by Fritz to be part of the nefarious scheme. Fritz also knew a judge in the town, one John Jacobs who was part Boer and part English. He had a huge chip on his shoulder resulting from his ancestry, and Fritz knew that he drank too much and had embarrassingly large gambling debts to pay off. The policemen were each promised one hundred pounds to cooperate and the judge five hundred pounds.

Often on a Friday Mapitha and Kulaan would take the diamonds they had collected during the week and, as Frank had done, sold them to a well-known dealer. The money was put in the bank. Fritz knew of this practice since he often did it himself. One particular Friday after Frank had been gone six months, the two Zulus were walking nonchalantly down the street to their favourite dealer, when on a signal from Fritz the two Koekemoer policemen approached them and asked if they were carrying diamonds.

"Yes," said Mapitha, "we have a registered claim."

"*Kaffirs* do not have registered claims," said Frans. He knew perfectly well this was incorrect, but it was what Fritz had told him to say.

"Look, ask that dealer over there," Mapitha pointed to the sign. "He knows us well, he can tell you that we are owners of a claim."

"Shut up, *kaffir*," snapped Vic. He could see his hundred pounds slipping away.

Kulaan by this time was bewildered and extremely angry. As Frans tried to arrest him by putting handcuffs on him, he grabbed him and effortlessly snapped one of his arms. Frans shrieked in pain and the Zulus would have got away, but at that point a company of dragoons came by, and after a struggle the Zulus were arrested and taken to the nearby jail.

Jacobs had been told that speed was of the essence and that unless punishment was meted out quickly, the conspiracy would be uncovered.

Unusually, therefore, the Zulus were brought before the judge the very next day and, before they knew what was happening, were tried and sentenced.

"*Kaffirs* do not own claims," intoned Jacobs when Mapitha said they were registered claim owners.

Mapitha was sentenced to twenty-five lashes and Kulaan, who was carrying the diamonds, to fifty with a further fifty for resisting arrest.

"Sentence to be carried out immediately," said the judge.

Nzobo had been frantically trying to find his colleagues. He was directed to the local football field where both Mapitha and Kulaan had been spreadeagled and strapped to wagon wheels. Mapitha's sentence had been carried out and he had been cut down, bleeding and semi-conscious, from the wheel. Nzobo half carried and half dragged him away from the crowd. He managed to get a message to Tutula, who came from the hotel and was horrified to see what had been done to Mapitha.

"IDB," was the chant in the crowd.

"But he has a registered claim," said Tutula.

Nzobo persuaded her to find a hand drawn cart and get Mapitha back to the hut they still occupied.

Nzobo knew he would have a bigger problem with Kulaan. He had heard that the sentence was to be one hundred lashes. "Can anyone survive such a beating?" he wondered.

As he rejoined the crowd they were counting each lash.

"Seventy five,... eighty." Nzobo could see that even the mighty Kulaan had stopped flinching when the whip struck. The cart had come back and when the crowd yelled "One hundred," and cheered, Nzobo went forward with the cart and helped cut Kulaan down and load him into the cart. They pushed their way through the crowd and rushed Kulaan back to the hut.

Nzobo was too busy to be angry at that stage. It was clear that Kulaan was somehow still alive. Most mortals would have expired long before the final one hundredth lash had been administered. Many of the black people who knew the Zulus were incensed by the injustice and had rallied round to help Kulaan and Mapitha. They were being cared for as well as could be expected under the circumstances, but what they really needed was a doctor.

After waiting more than an hour, Nzobo was able to see a Dr. Katz who was an extremely busy physician at the hospital. He patiently listened to Nzobo. The line around Dr. Katz's mouth grew tighter and tighter as the story unfolded.

"The bastards," he eventually muttered. "And you say you all have legitimate claims which you have worked for months?"

Nzobo nodded. Katz had become uncomfortably aware that the desire of some men to consolidate all the claims under the ownership of one company was increasingly resulting in the blacks being unjustly pushed into the position of mere labourers with no other prospects. Nzobo's story infuriated him and after only a little persuasion, he agreed to accompany Nzobo back to where the injured Zulus lay.

A brief examination of the two Zulus told him that Kulaan needed hospital treatment to survive. Nzobo used the cart again and carefully moved Kulaan to the hospital. Dr. Katz spent a few minutes tending to Mapitha. He made Tutula wash the wounds down carefully and then gave her some salve to treat the wounds. He told her he would be by each day to see how the patient was faring. As long as the wounds were kept clean, Mapitha was in no real danger.

Kulaan was another matter. When he was at last at the hospital, still unconscious but breathing easily, Dr. Katz made a full examination. He personally cleaned the wounds himself, a process that took several hours. He was absolutely incensed that a completely innocent man should have been treated like this, and he was determined to get to the bottom of the situation.

Kulaan regained consciousness briefly the next day and was able to take a few sips of water. Mapitha recovered quite quickly, and within a week was up and about.

Kulaan fully regained consciousness after three days and after a week was sitting up in bed. Dr. Katz spent as much time as he could afford tending him. Kulaan was lucky he was so fit and strong. He was discharged from the hospital after three weeks, but it was two months before he could consider working again.

Dr. Katz in the meanwhile had paid a visit to a very nervous Judge John Jacobs.

"You realise that you convicted two completely innocent men, don't you?" said Katz. "They both own claims quite legitimately."

"I convicted on the evidence presented," Jacobs replied. "IDB is a very serious crime and could affect the whole industry if it is not stopped."

"The punishment was carried out with indecent haste. Both of the victims told you they were claim owners but you didn't give them a chance to prove their claims," said Katz.

"Almost everyone charged with these crimes tells me they have a legitimate claim. Anyway, they are just a couple of *kaffirs*, so why should I care?" said Jacobs.

"I will be taking this further," Katz told him.

Jacobs looked at him threateningly: "Be very careful, doctor. Do not interfere in matters that you don't understand."

"This thing stinks," said Katz. "I'm going to get to the bottom of this, I can tell you."

Jacobs just glowered at him.

It was clear to Nzobo that Fritz had something to do with the incident. He spoke briefly to Mapitha while he was still recovering. The Zulus had in any event been ready to return home before Frank gave them the claims. They knew that these claims were right in the middle of all Fritz's claims, and that Fritz's operations would be severely curtailed if they were sold to another operator. As a minimum, it would cost him more to run them, especially if there was no cost sharing.

Nzobo selected one of the major operators shrewdly, assuming that the real prize was to own all ten claims previously owned by Frank and that if anyone was able to buy the three claims owned by the Zulus, they could put pressure on Fritz to sell them the other claims. When Nzobo first appeared and tried to sell the claims to Lhodsi (Rhodes), he was laughed at and offered a derisory two hundred pounds for each claim. He politely walked out and went to Rhodes' great rival, Barney Barnato. Both parties could see the value of the claims and realised they could screw Fritz if they owned them. Nzobo's great strength was that he did not care how much he was paid for the claims. They had cost him nothing and he had no overheads; to him it was just a game to see if he could outwit the white bosses. By the time Kulaan had recovered, the price was up to three thousand pounds per claim and as far as Nzobo was concerned the game was still on. He settled two weeks later for three thousand five hundred pounds per claim, which was well ahead of the market. When the money was safely in the bank, Nzobo asked his legal adviser, one Solly Isaacs, to release the claims to Lhodsi. Rhodes was furious with the whole affair and wanted to find out how this apparently illiterate Zulu had completely outwitted him. He never had the satisfaction of finding out; after his windfall Nzobo went to ground. He left the money in the hands of the said Solly Isaacs and said he would be back for it some time in the future.

There were many long discussions between the three Zulus about what should be done about Fritz and the Koekemoer brothers. Kulaan was determined to find out what had happened and to exact the maximum amount of retribution. Nzobo counselled caution: they were all alive, he said, and the arrangements he had made with Lhodsi would almost certainly mean that Fritz would not be able to survive as a viable mining operator. This was not enough for either Kulaan or Mapitha; they wanted retribution.

Firstly they needed information, so they tracked down the Koekemoer brothers and found them as regular visitors to Cora's hotel. They waited in the shadows for many nights, and were eventually rewarded when Vic came out of the hotel one night and then went round the corner to relieve himself. Kulaan pounced and clamped a hand over his mouth to prevent him from yelling out. They tied him up and gagged him and carried him laboriously to the site of Fritz's surface operation, which at that late hour was deserted.

Koekemoer by this time was absolutely terrified and had peed his pants when he realised who his attackers were. They undid his hands and asked him what he knew about the unfair prosecution and beating of Kulaan and Mapitha. He shook his head. Mapitha in the meanwhile, had lit a small fire and ostentatiously put his spear into it. He nodded to Nzobo, who tore Vic's trousers off.

"Tell us what we want to know," urged Mapitha in broken English.

Vic shook his head.

Mapitha touched his pale white buttocks with the now red-hot spear. Vic would have screamed if Kulaan had not held a strong hand over his mouth.

Vic shook his head again.

This time Mapitha touched his penis with the hot spear.

Vic voided his bowels and then started gibbering:

"It's Fritz; he paid us; he paid the judge. He hates you so much."

The Zulus were stunned and Kulaan was furious. He said in Zulu, "I saved the man's life and this is what he did."

They then allowed Koekemoer to dress himself again and, although it was the early hours of the morning, they sought out the one person who had helped them, Dr. Katz.

The good doctor was still at the hospital when the Zulus trooped in, dragging Koekemoer along with them. Mapitha prodded the policeman with his spear:

"Speak, you son of a baboon turd; tell the doctor what you just told us."

Koekemoer looked around him, by now he was thoroughly intimidated and thought his best chance was to implicate the others.

"It was all Fritz and the judge," he stammered.

"Just explain it all," said Katz.

Vic Koekemoer then explained everything.

"Well, we had better take this up with the police," said Katz.

"Police," thundered Kulaan in Zulu. "These are the people that did all this in the first place."

"Different police," he was told.

Kulaan grunted distrustfully.

They eventually went to the police station and the next day Fritz, the judge and Frans Koekemoer were also arrested.

"See," said Mapitha, "justice will be done."

"We'll see," said Kulaan.

A few days later, to the absolute amazement of the Zulus, Fritz and his partners in crime were all released on bail.

Kulaan's response was to sharpen his spear.

Dr. Katz urged the Zulus to be patient, that white justice sometimes took longer than was desirable.

During the previous few months, ostensibly because of the IDB, there had been agitation among the white population to restrict certain facilities for whites only and to confine black labourers to their own compounds, where they could be searched on a daily basis for illicit diamonds, much as Fritz had been doing in his own operation. There was to be no room for their women folk and a black labourer would not be allowed to leave the compound for the duration of his contract except to go to work in the mine, where he would be under white supervision. The main proponents of this arrangement were the major mining companies and Cecil Rhodes. The Zulus were not at first particularly concerned with this development, since they planned shortly to return to Zululand. There was, however, panic among the thousands of black miners who had by that time converged on Kimberley.

Naively the Zulus had made the assumption that Fritz and his cronies would be brought to trial quickly and would be sent to prison. The judge obviously had his contacts however, and the trial date was delayed and delayed, much to the frustration of the Zulus.

During this time legislation was passed enforcing the segregation of the races and confining black labourers to the mine compounds. This was all going to take some time to put into place, but the Zulus were still occupying Frank's original encampment and, since Frank had been among the first to arrive in Kimberley, they had a prime location.

A week or two after the new laws had been put into place, three white policemen came to visit the Zulus and told them they had a week to move. The City Council was going to use the land.

Mapitha said to the policeman, "We are claim owners, not labourers; we will not go into any compound."

"You sold your claims; you either move or you will be moved."

After they had gone, Mapitha counselled the others: "We have now bought our horses and guns. We have some diamonds for the King. That smart lawyer has our money. We should go. Let the white man deal with white man's justice in his own time."

Kulaan grunted, "Fritz will die first."

"Forget Fritz, if you kill him then the white man will come and kill you," said Mapitha.

Nzobo chipped in, "We have horses and guns and money. You, Kulaan, can have many wives and cattle. Forget Fritz. We will go."

Kulaan appeared to be mollified by this advice. They packed up the camp and released the latest version of *Inyoka* into the veld. Mapitha carefully retrieved his diamonds and made sure they were safely attached to his person in a pouch near the skin. For some undefinable reason the Zulus had kept the diamonds they had stolen from Frank separate from the ones they had legitimately mined themselves. Nzobo had bought three good mounts and he and Kulaan had new Mauser rifles. Mapitha was contented with the one he had taken from the Boer, now so long ago.

During the hiatus while the Zulus were waiting to see if Fritz was prosecuted or not, Mapitha had managed some sort of reconciliation with Tutula.

"Come back to Zululand with us," urged Mapitha.

Tutula laughed.

"After all this," her gesture took in the hotel, Kimberley and the whole environment, relatively sophisticated as far as the average African at that time was concerned. "You want me to marry some Zulu warrior who has three other wives. *Baba*, you can see that could never be so. The great *Nkulunkulu* in the sky has brought me to this life. You can see I cannot turn back now."

"Are you sick? Sometimes you look very sick," asked Mapitha.

"No, I am not sick; Hannelore and the other girls here help me when I am sick," she said.

"We saved you from the *amaBhunu*, just to live and maybe die like this," said Mapitha. "You are like a daughter to me. Please come home."

At this stage Hannelore joined them; she had seen them and was aware of Tutula's story and her relationship with Mapitha. She put a hand on Mapitha's arm.

"Mapitha," she said respectfully, "Tutula is like a friend to me and the girls here now. We will look after her as a friend would."

Mapitha looked doubtful.

"Tutula would not be happy being married to a Zulu in some remote kraal, not after all this," she waved her hand expansively. "In a few years my mother and I will retire to the Cape. Maybe Tutula will come with us."

"The Cape?" asked Mapitha doubtfully. He had no concept of where that was.

"Yes. Maybe Tutula will have a house and servants of her own," added Hannelore.

This was almost beyond Mapitha's understanding, but he began to realise that Tutula was now so much part of the white man's world, even as a prostitute, that she could not return to the old, traditional ways. He looked at her sadly; clearly he had failed her, at least in his own mind.

"*Hamba Gahle Baba*," said Tutula. She turned on her heel, a tear in her eye that she did not want Mapitha to see.

"*Sala Gahle ndodakazi*," he said as he walked sadly out of the hotel.

◇◇◇◇◇◇◇◇◇◇◇◇◇◇◇

Chapter 13

As they set off Mapitha looked proudly on his little entourage. He would have much to show the new King. He and Nzobo spoke the white man's tongue, and they had truly, he thought, started to understand the white man's ways.

The first night away from Kimberley they found safety next to a small stream protected from the wind by some large rocks. The horses were tethered fifty yards away amongst a copse of trees. When Mapitha woke up, he immediately felt uneasy and looked about him. Kulaan and his bedroll were missing. He woke Nzobo and they rushed down to where the horses were. As expected, Kulaan's horse was missing. Mapitha looked at Nzobo and shook his head. Without saying a word they rapidly packed the camp up and retraced their steps back to Kimberley. Maybe they could catch Kulaan before he arrived there. He would certainly need their help if he did get there.

Kulaan, had, as soon as the embers of the fire died down, quietly packed up his own belongings and headed back to Kimberley. He had one objective only in mind and that was to kill Fritz. He did not understand white man's justice and was certain that their plan was to let Fritz off. Well, he was not going to let that happen. He was a proud Zulu and he was determined to get his revenge. No thought was given to Mapitha and Nzobo and what they might do or what he would do after he had dealt with Fritz.

Back in Kimberley, the encampment where he had spent almost the last three years was deserted. He fed and watered the horse and tethered it so that it would be available to ride back and join his compatriots. Kulaan was dressed as a Zulu warrior going into battle: a loincloth, monkey skin armulets and his small shield and his *ixwa* spear. He left his gun and all his western clothing with the horse. He was going to fight like a Zulu and whatever happened Fritz was going to find out what fighting a Zulu meant.

As had been the case in past weeks, Fritz had spent the evening at the hotel. He was rudely woken up at about midday by somebody kicking the side of his tin shack and yelling at him in Zulu. He grabbed his revolver, pulled on a pair of shorts and rushed outside. Fritz was a big man, over six foot; he had a big, black, husky beard and his bloodshot eyes looked out from a reddish thatch that he rarely combed. In earlier days he had been strong and muscular, but recently he had acquired a gut and was not very fit. He was barefoot, as was the Zulu.

As soon as Fritz heard the Zulu war cry: "Bayete!" he knew he was in trouble, and he knew the trouble came in the form of Kulaan. He had been expecting a confrontation with the big Zulu for months and had been pleasantly surprised when Tutula had told him the previous night that the Zulus had left.

Fritz was bowled over as soon as he left his tin shed, and he thought it was all over there and then as the Zulu lunged at him with his *ixwa*. He rolled and fired off a shot from the revolver. The spear caused a nasty gash on his left upper arm.

Kulaan suddenly realised the danger he was in and slashed wildly with his spear at the revolver, which then spun out of Fritz's hand about twenty yards away. "Good," he thought, "we are now even". Kulaan rushed Fritz and bowled him over again, his spear taking Fritz in the belly. Fritz howled in agony and blood started to pour from the wound. At that moment the Koekemoer brothers emerged and Fritz frantically indicated the revolver lying in the dust. As Frans leant down to pick it up, there was a rifle shot, which spun the weapon out of reach.

"Stay out of this," yelled Mapitha.

Mapitha and Nzobo had rushed back to Kimberley and had made straight for Fritz's establishment to save time.

The Koekemoers backed off.

Fritz pulled a large knife from his belt and lunged at Kulaan, who easily parried the blow.

Fritz moved quickly to his left and managed to knock the spear out of Kulaan's hand. Kulaan saw he only had one chance now; he rushed in, grabbed Fritz's hand holding the knife, wrenched it out of his hand and threw it away. He then used his huge strength to wrap his arms around Fritz's neck. He gave a sharp jerk, there was a crack and Fritz collapsed. Kulaan retrieved his spear and although Fritz was already dead from a broken neck he plunged the spear into Fritz's chest, yelling: "Bayete!"

The Koekemoer brothers stood there stunned for a moment. Then they ran.

Taking charge, Mapitha bundled Kulaan onto his own horse and the three Zulus rushed back to their own encampment. Nothing was said but within ten minutes they were on their way out of Kimberley again.

This time instead of going north they made their way due east. Mapitha had decided that their best chance was to make for the mountain fastnesses of the Basuto Kingdom. He wondered how long the pursuit would take to get organised and follow them. Their own horses were already tired, and it was still six hours to darkness, being the summer season.

It took less than two hours for a posse of twenty well-armed men with fresh horses to set off after the Zulus, and another two before the Zulus caught sight of their pursuers.

"Soon it will be dark," Mapitha indicated the heavens. "After that we must let the horses rest."

They kept pushing on and whilst the pursuit gained a little, the Zulus kept ahead.

The sun set quickly and soon the Zulus found a stream surrounded by large boulders where they could feed and water their horses. Nzobo whispered to Mapitha, "We need fresh horses. Our pursuers are not far away; I will take theirs."

Mapitha thought for a moment and then nodded.

Nzobo took his rifle and spear and jogged effortlessly back the way they had come. Sure enough, shortly he saw a big, blazing fire in the darkness. He knew that from the circle of firelight it would be difficult to see more than about twenty yards. He came no closer than was necessary. The horses were tethered in some trees almost seventy yards from the fire. Nzobo was sure there would be a guard on the horses and he watched for ten minutes. He was just about to move when a match flared. The guard had lit a cigarette. Nzobo crept round behind him. The guard was there to scare away wild animals; the thought that there might be any danger from humans had not occurred to him. Nzobo crept round behind the guard, who he could now see was Frans Koekemoer; he was leaning against a tree smoking a cigarette. Nzobo never had the slightest hesitation about killing the man. At this stage he was aware that it was kill or be killed. He gave no quarter and expected none. Frans never knew what hit him. Nzobo skilfully stabbed him in the throat and there was a slight gurgling sound as Nzobo lowered his body to the ground. He waited a few minutes before he crept over to the horses. He picked up what he thought were the best three and he let all the others loose. He was mounted on one horse leading the other two, one in each hand.

Suddenly there was a yell from the fire; they had seen him. He decided that attack was the best policy so, quickly driving the loose horses ahead of him, he galloped towards the fire. The horses were all rather nervous and they crashed their way through the campsite, scattering people and pots and pans and hot ashes everywhere. Nzobo thought he had got clean away, but just as he was leaving the firelight he felt an excruciatingly painful thump in his right arm and heard the crash of a gun. He was extremely hard put to stay on the horse but he kept going and within thirty minutes had returned to the small Zulu camp with the three horses. Bleeding profusely and almost falling off the horse he was riding, he pulled the horses to a stop.

Kulaan was detailed to prepare the horses for a night trek, while Mapitha tended to Nzobo's wound. The hope was that it would take at least most of the next morning for the pursuers to gather their horses, and by that time the Zulus would be far away.

Nzobo's wound was very bad. The bullet had taken him in the upper right arm, smashing the bone; every movement was absolute agony. Mapitha spent an hour tying the wound up to stop the bleeding. Nzobo really needed to stay put somewhere for a while so he could heal. There was no chance of that, however. After a struggle, Mapitha managed to cut two suitable sticks and make a splint for the arm. He then tied Nzobo to the saddle of his horse and took the reins. Kulaan would have to ride one horse and lead three. Mapitha's job was to try to look after Nzobo, who kept slipping in and out of consciousness.

Although they kept going the rest of the night and all the next day, progress was slow for the Zulus. They had to make frequent stops to tend to Nzobo and towards the end of the day Mapitha was looking anxiously over his shoulder for signs of pursuit. Two hours after dark he called a halt and they stopped in a small copse of trees where Kulaan fed and watered the horses and Mapitha tried to look after Nzobo. A fire was lit and Mapitha boiled some water and tried to wash Nzobo's wound. The Zulus had no medical equipment at all but Mapitha had, during the day, picked the leaves of a plant that he knew had healing properties and being as gentle as he could he applied the leaves and rebound the wound with the splints. Nzobo was persuaded to eat a small amount of the meal that was prepared, and then the Zulus all tried to get some sleep. They could not afford to set a watch but felt reasonably secure, since they had been unable to spot any signs of the pursuit.

The posse had managed shortly after dawn to collect ten horses together and it was decided that they would set off immediately. If the other horses could be found within a day, the rest of the posse should follow, otherwise they would return to Kimberley once they had buried Frans Koekemoer.

The tracks left by the Zulus were easy enough to follow and they made a good pace.

"They are travelling slowly," said Vic after an hour or so, "and they keep stopping. One of them must be hurt."

So they redoubled their efforts to catch the Zulus. At dusk, when they could no longer follow the tracks, they camped for the night and this time kept two guards on during all the hours of darkness.

The Zulus woke up stiff and sore and after having had a small meal they strapped Nzobo on a horse amid his protestations.

"Look, if you leave me here," he said weakly, "both of you will get clean away. If you try to take me with you, we will all die and then the King will not be able to find out what he needs to know about the *abelungu*." Mapitha took no notice. Shortly after the dawn they continued on their painful way. Kulaan had been told to look out and avoid any white owned farms, and if he saw any other people they were to avoid them if possible. Mapitha knew that Bloemfontein, the small capital city of the Boer Republic of the Orange Free State, would be to the south. He wanted to avoid that at all costs since he sensed that the Boers would be hostile.

The pursuit found the Zulu camp by about mid-morning. Vic jumped down and gingerly put his hand in the ashes of the fire.

"It's still warm," he said. "They are not more than three, four hours ahead." The posse set off again at a frantic pace to try to catch the Zulus before nightfall.

At four in the afternoon on the third day out of Kimberley the Zulus saw dust on the horizon and realised that the pursuit would catch them within the next two hours. It was impossible to go faster, although they tried; it was just too much for Nzobo. Within an hour the pursuit had caught up to within half a mile and they could hear the shouts of the horsemen, followed by an occasional shot.

The Zulus were desperate, but Mapitha would not hear of leaving Nzobo behind, despite his pleas. Then without a word Kulaan handed over the reins of the horses he was leading to Mapitha and said to him, "*Hamba*. I will stop the *abelungu*. *Hamba*, try to save yourselves." Then with his spear in his left hand and his rifle in his right he cantered towards his pursuers. Mapitha urged his horse to a canter and amid groans from Nzobo made off as quickly as possible.

The pursuit stopped for a few minutes, somewhat at a loss. Kulaan had disappeared into a gully between them and the Zulus, which was sparsely filled with bushes, small trees and head high grass, but he appeared to be heading their direction. They could also see Mapitha and Nzobo and five horses vanishing into the dusk.

Kulaan had chosen his ground well; he cantered the horse through the gully and then steeled himself for an assault on the pursuers. He knew he was going to die and in the tradition of the Zulu warrior he was determined to die bravely, causing maximum damage to the enemy. He had the advantage of partial surprise and, as he thought to himself, he had the weapons of the *abelungu*. The posse was still wondering what to do, when twenty yards to their left there was a wild yell of "Bayete!" and Kulaan emerged from the bush galloping at his pursuers. He managed to get three shots off, killing one horse and wounding one of the posse, before his horse plunged into their midst. His rifle was then flung at the nearest member of the posse, who fell off his horse and was trampled by all the other horses in the mayhem. Kulaan then got to work with his spear. From the back of his horse he plunged it into the chest of his nearest attacker, yelling "Usuthu!" He then drove his horse into the throng, knocking another man off his mount. The people in the posse were panicked by the ferocity of the attack; their rifles were almost useless and couldn't be fired for fear of hitting one of their own. Kulaan attacked another of the posse, inflicting a severe wound in the man's stomach. Vic Koekemoer kept his head and managed to fire two shots into Kulaan's horse, which collapsed under him. Undeterred, Kulaan leapt from the horse as it was going down and flung himself at Vic Koekemoer in a blind frenzy. He took two slugs as he leapt at his tormentor. This would have stopped most mortals in their tracks, but Kulaan's great strength and determination carried him through. He hauled Koekemoer off his horse, ignoring his screams, and plunged his trusty spear into Koekemoer's heart with a final, high pitched, constricted yell of "Bayete!" Bloodied but still standing, he then turned to face his attackers, who had now managed to regroup. He was struck by a volley of shots; amazingly he still stood. The next volley saw him sink to his knees and then pitch forward onto his face, blood oozing from a dozen wounds.

Shaken, the remaining seven men of the posse stood and gazed in wonderment at the carnage. Two of their men dead, one wounded and two of their horses would have to be put down. It was getting dark. They buried their own dead with a mumbled prayer. They were going to leave Kulaan to the hyenas and jackals until one of their number said, "He died like a true warrior; he may have been our enemy but he deserves more respect than being left out in the veld."

He was then buried alongside the others that fell, without the prayers. Stones were piled on each of the graves to prevent scavengers from digging up the bodies.

The darkness had swallowed up Mapitha and the ailing Nzobo. Mapitha could see the wound was festering and unless he received treatment, Mapitha was certain that Nzobo would die. During the journey they had thus far avoided the few isolated farmhouses, where Boer farmers were trying to scrape an existence from the harsh, dry environment. They had covered a few more miles when Mapitha saw the twinkling lights of a farmhouse. He thought for a minute. "This is our last chance; if the people are hostile then so be it. There is just a chance, a small chance they will help."

He cautiously led the horses directly up to the house. A man was sitting on the stoep cleaning a rifle.

"*Nkosi*," greeted Mapitha uncertainly.

The man quickly reassembled his rifle and loaded it.

"Who is that, what do you want?" he asked nervously in Sotho, peering out into the darkness.

"I need help, my friend here is badly wounded," responded Mapitha is halting Sotho, picked up in Kimberley.

"Come closer, and no funny business," said Hennie van Zyl, pointing his rifle at Mapitha's chest. "Dismount," he ordered. Mapitha did as he was told.

"Why do you need so many horses?" asked Van Zyl.

"These are from the people chasing us; we took them away so they would stop chasing us," said Mapitha hesitatingly.

"Who is chasing you?" asked Van Zyl.

"The *abelungu* from Kimberley," said Mapitha.

Van Zyl had an abiding hatred of all things English. His father had left the Cape in the mid 1830's as part of the Boer exodus now known as the Great Trek, and established himself here. He was proud of the independent Boer Republic of the Orange Free State. He regarded the discovery of diamonds in nearby Kimberley as a disaster, a prelude to further British adventure in the interior of South Africa and probable interference in his own life. It mattered not to van Zyl that the population of Kimberley was made up of many races, including Boers; as far as he was concerned, it was run by the English enemy. He would do nothing to help them.

Van Zyl was also sympathetic to the local blacks. He spoke their language and had persuaded the local Sotho chief that a "live and let live" policy was in everyone's interests. It had now been years since the Sotho had raided his cattle. Once or twice a year he went to the chiefs' kraal and took him gifts of prize cattle. He also drank beer with him and had on occasion slept with one of the chiefs' wives.

Under the watchful eye of van Zyl, Mapitha undid the ropes holding Nzobo onto the horse and gently lowered him to the ground. Van Zyl's wife, Susanna, and two teenage sons emerged from the house. Nzobo was taken on to the veranda and Susanna busily got to work on the wound.

"Hmm, this is very bad," she said to Mapitha in halting Sotho. "Would have been a lot worse if you hadn't put those leaves on the wound though."

She spent an hour bathing and binding the wound. Nzobo was then moved into a rough bed in an outhouse. She looked at Mapitha sternly.

"I will not allow him to be moved. If you move him he will die. Don't worry; no *uitlanders* from Kimberley will touch him."

"We must go to report to the King," said Mapitha.

"King or no King," said Susanna. "If you put him on a horse again, he will not see the dawn, let alone your King."

Mapitha then had a quick conversation with van Zyl. He would leave Nzobo here, together with four of the horses. Van Zyl gave him repeated assurances that if the posse arrived at the farm, they would not even know of Nzobo's presence and he, van Zyl, would send them off in the wrong direction if he could.

Van Zyl's sons had tended the horses unasked and Mapitha selected the sturdiest of them. He noticed that one of van Zyl's own horses was also being saddled.

"My son Theo will go with you to the local chief's kraal, which is about one and a half days' ride into the mountains. They will not harm you if he goes with you. We are on good terms with them," said van Zyl.

Mapitha nodded and put his head into the outhouse where Nzobo was now resting more comfortably than he had since he had been wounded.

"*Sala gahle*," Mapitha said quietly to his friend, who didn't stir.

All the van Zyls knew the country very well, and even in the dark Theo and Mapitha made good time and climbed steadily into the mountains.

One member of the pursuing posse had been detailed to take the wounded man back to Kimberley. As the dawn broke, the others continued their hot pursuit of Mapitha and Nzobo, who they were now certain was badly wounded. The tracks they were following pointed unerringly to the van Zyl homestead, but before they arrived there they were covered with a mass of cattle tracks. Very soon they came upon the cattle, being driven by a white man on a horse and three Africans on foot.

Van Zyl levered a round into the breach of his Mauser. These were obviously the people that were chasing Mapitha and he did not like the look of them. One of them addressed him rather rudely in the *Taal*:

"Hey, old man, a couple of *kaffirs* on horseback came this way. They were riding two horses and leading another three. One of the men may have been wounded."

"And who speaks?" asked van Zyl in High Dutch.

"Andries Enslin," was the answer.

The other members of the posse looked on silently. They did not understand a word of the exchange although they could tell it was not friendly.

"I have seen no strangers for many days," said van Zyl.

"Their tracks come right up to here," said Enslin now more respectfully, in High Dutch.

"What tribe are they?" he asked.

"Zulus," was the answer.

"If any Zulu wanders into these parts the Sotho will kill him," said van Zyl.

"We'll look about," said Enslin and the five members of the posse started to move off.

Van Zyl stopped in front of them, rifle poised.

"Not so fast, *meneer*, not so fast. Where are you from?" he asked.

They looked at each other.

"Kimberley," said Enslin.

"You realise that this is the independent Republic of the Orange Free State," said van Zyl. "You have no jurisdiction here; you need to be very careful. Do you have any authority to be chasing blacks around in an independent country?"

There was some hesitation among the members of the posse, who looked as if they were about to run van Zyl down. Then a shot rang out from a nearby copse and Enslin's horse fell down dead. Enslin had managed to jump clear but fell into the dust, cursing. Van Zyl by now was on full alert.

"Down all of you, dismount now and throw me all of your weapons. I've had enough of this nonsense. You're all going to jail in Bloemfontein." He dragged one of the surprised members of the posse off his horse and wrenched his rifle from his hands. The rest of the posse followed suit very quickly. They still hadn't worked out where the shot had come from.

Within five minutes the members of the posse were standing forlornly to one side. Van Zyl had a pile of weapons on the ground in front of him and one of his African herdsmen was holding the four remaining horses.

"It's time *pampoene* like you were taught a lesson," said van Zyl. "If you think you can run about here as you like, then think again."

The Africans were directed to take the cattle back to the paddock.

The horses were confiscated and during the two hours that it took van Zyl to organise four of his neighbours, the members of the posse were tied together back to back and were made to sit in the hot sun. The irony of the situation was that they were less than fifty yards from Nzobo's sick bed.

Four of van Zyl's neighbours arrived on horseback and, despite pleadings from Enslin-the posse were roped together and made to walk in the direction of Bloemfontein.

"We'll be back in three days," van Zyl called to his wife.

By nightfall of the second day Mapitha and Theo had arrived safely at what Mapitha had determined was the kraal of an important chieftain. Theo was greeted warmly by Chief Leribe and until the Zulu was introduced and his story told he was treated with suspicion and disdain. Theo stayed two nights and then, as he made preparations to leave, he said to Mapitha, "You will be safe now, they will take you to *Ukhahlamba* (lit. Barrier of spears—Drakensburg Mountains) and show you a path down. You can see the Tugela River from there. After that it won't take you long for you to find your way back to the kraal of the Zulu King."

Mapitha thanked him profusely. He realised that he might not have survived if these whites had not helped him.

"*Hamba gahle*, please look after Nzobo, he is a good man," said Mapitha in halting Sotho.

"*Sala gahle*," said Theo.

The journey across the mountains took almost a week. Mapitha's companions were a man of about his age and a boy aged in his mid-teens, both riding small Basuto mountain ponies. The pair were extraordinarily uncommunicative and Mapitha was never really told their names. He was made to realise that the only reason they were taking him was because they had been told to by the chief. The countryside was almost totally devoid of trees and the tall grasses swaying in the summer breezes gave the fields a benign look. The land would be bleak in the winter, Mapitha thought. They threaded their way through the majestic countryside and paddled through many little streams on their way to the distant mountains. Mapitha shot a buck to keep them in meat, which pleased his companions even if it made them no more communicative.

The little party had been climbing steadily for seven days and looking back southwest from whence they had come, they looked down on the flatter plains of the Sotho stronghold. As they came into the mountains proper, the trails became steeper, until they reached the rim of the escarpment, where Mapitha suddenly found himself on the edge of a precipice, looking out over a vast plain many thousands of feet below. They directed their ponies along an amphitheatre where a stream gurgled its way among the rocks and then dashed itself many hundreds of feet over the mountainside.

"Tugela," announced his guide proudly. Mapitha could see a river threading its way across the plain.

"Tugela?" questioned Mapitha.

The guide nodded. "Tugela."

So this was the source of the mighty Tugela, thought Mapitha. He dismounted and almost reverently knelt down and took a long drink of the clear, fresh water.

His Sotho guide watched impassively. The guides then pointed downwards where Mapitha could just make out a path of sorts. His possessions were unpacked from the ponies and the teenager took the animals and stood twenty yards away. He was smiling. Then it dawned on Mapitha: The path was much too steep for the horse, so the guides would show him the way down but they scored his horse. "Fair enough," he thought. "This could not have happened without them." Mapitha counted his possessions:

his Mauser rifle, his spear, the precious diamonds, his kaross, and a food bag and water carrier.

The guide indicated a path and walked confidently on with Mapitha following. The child was left with the horses. After an hour of descent the guide stopped. He was able to point out the main features of the path, which Mapitha made him repeat two more times.

"The Hlubi people down there," said his guide, "keep away, they will kill you. They hate Zulus." The Hlubi, Mapitha understood were the people who occupied the foothills of the *Ukhahlamba*. He would heed that advice. In fact he decided to avoid all forms of human habitation until he had returned to Kwa-Bulawayo.

The guide left and started to scramble up the mountain. Mapitha went on in the gentle sunlight.

He had planned on returning home in style, the three of them with a horse each and guns and western clothing.

Mapitha reflected that he was on his own. He knew Kulaan was dead. He hoped Nzobo was still alive. He had nothing but what he stood up in, his gun, spear and of course the diamonds, and most valuable of all his three years' experience of dealing with the white invaders.

◇◇◇◇◇◇◇◇◇◇◇◇◇◇◇◇

Chapter 14

There was a silence when Mapitha had completed his story. King Cetswayo and his indunas were all wrapped up their own thoughts. The beer pot was passed around.

The King suddenly asked Mapitha a question, "How many people in this Kimberley?"

Mapitha had no idea.

"As many as there are stars in the sky, *Nkosi*," he responded.

The group lapsed into silence again. The Zulus had had continual contact with the whites south of the Tugela in Natal and the steadily growing white population posed an increasing threat to them. In truth none of them, including the King, had any idea how to deal with this threat. There was already a significant Zulu population resident south of the Tugela, many of whom did not accept the authority of the Zulu King any more and were employed in white owned enterprises, mainly agriculture. Cetswayo felt secure, however, in the fact that he had forty thousand fit and well-trained warriors ready and willing to fight.

"There are also many of these whites going to the land of the Swazis looking for *igolidi*. If they find it many more will come," said one of the *indunas*, as if expressing the thoughts of some of the people sitting there. Cetswayo looked up sharply.

"There is no threat," he said.

"*Yebo! Nkosi*," the indunas grovelled.

"Do we not have agreements with the *amaNgisi*?"

"*Yebo! Nkosi.*"

"Did not *Somseu* come and crown me King of the Zulus himself two summers ago?"

"*Yebo! Nkosi.*"

"Does not this *Somseu* call himself the 'White father of the Zulus'?"

"*Yebo! Nkosi.*"

"Do we not have forty thousand of the fittest, strongest Zulu *amabutho*?"

"*Yebo! Nkosi.*"

"Let the *amanNgisi* come," said Cetswayo. "They will find out what a piece of Zulu steel feels like."

The indunas stood up and, as one, stamped their right feet and shouted, "Bayete!"

They were all dismissed except for Mapitha.

"You will take one hundred of the best and fattest cattle. You have already taken the *isicoco* so you may now marry. Return to your kraal on the Black Mfolozi. I will keep the diamonds," the King pronounced.

"*Yebo! Nkosi*, the generosity of the great elephant is boundless," said Mapitha proudly. One hundred cattle was a prize indeed. He would be a great chief and hero among his own Ndwandwe people.

"The *amaNgisi and Somseu* will come here again. I will send you a message; you must be here to listen to their babble. Please remember *Somseu* speaks Zulu like you and I. You may go now." The King waved Mapitha away.

"*Nkosi!*" said Mapitha. "The wisdom of the great King will prevail." He backed away and left, elated to return to his home.

◇◇◇◇◇◇◇◇◇◇◇◇◇◇◇◇

Chapter 15

Nzobo, drifting in and out of a coma, had been vaguely aware of the departure of his friend Mapitha. He was really too sick to care. The last few days in the saddle trying to escape the pursuers from Kimberley had been nothing less than an experience from hell. The shattered bone in his wounded right shoulder had caused him agony with every movement and his recollections of being strapped to his horse, with Mapitha trying to lead him as fast as possible through the bush, had been agonising hell. He had wished to be left alone in the bush to die—just as long as the pain stopped.

Now he was aware of a white man and woman and two young white men, none of whom he had ever seen before. They were kind and considerate and the woman came every day to examine his arm. Within a week he was able to take in his surroundings, and he became aware that he was on a white owned farm and that the name of the farmer was van Zyl. After another week, he was able to wander about outside and sit in the sun or under a tree. The farmer had cattle, which seemed fit and healthy, and Nzobo also noticed that some of the horses that he had taken from the pursuers out of Kimberley were still at the farm, plus his own horse.

Van Zyl, the farmer, had told him that Mapitha had gone to report back to the Zulu King and that he, van Zyl, had captured and disarmed the posse from Kimberley and they were now in jail in Bloemfontein.

Nzobo gradually started to do small tasks around the farm and by the time he had been there a month, he was looking after all the horses on a daily basis and helping out around the farmyard. Within two months Susanna van Zyl had removed the splint altogether, and he slowly regained almost full use of his arm. As he got better the desire to return home grew stronger, but he still felt a keen sense of duty towards the people who had saved his life.

In the year that Nzobo spent at the van Zyls he developed a respect for the family and the just and humane way they operated. Hennie van Zyl soon discovered that Nzobo knew how to handle a rifle, and he accompanied his employer on many a hunting trip, mostly on his own land. When his arm had fully recovered he also helped his employer design and build some outbuildings for the farm. Once he felt his debt to the van Zyls had been fully repaid, he discussed the matter in some detail with van Zyl, who allowed him to take one of the horses. Theo accompanied him to the village of the Sotho Chief Leribe, as had happened to Mapitha.

Nzobo had made it clear that he needed the horse to travel back to Zululand, so his Sotho guides took him right across the Kingdom, almost as far as the peak of Giant's Castle, where they showed him a path which his horse could negotiate down the mountain.

"Don't go near the Hlubi," he was told. "They will kill you or make you into a slave."

Nzobo nodded. He had every intention of avoiding all human contact until he had found his way back to Zululand, or at least to his mothers' people, the Cele.

The path at the top of the mountain was very steep, and Nzobo had to lead the horse most of the way step by step. On more than one occasion he spent what seemed like hours coaxing the horse down a particularly steep section of the path. After almost two days, including one very uncomfortable night spent under an overhanging rock with the rain teeming down, he arrived at a point where the mountain seemed to flatten out. He was just about to mount his horse and ride out into a well-watered, fertile valley when a dozen or so fierce looking warriors appeared out of the tall grass. Virtually nothing was said; he was roughly pulled from the horse and one of the warriors raised a spear. Nzobo thought he was done for.

"Wait," commanded a voice. "We will take him to the chief."

His hands were roughly tied behind his back and within an hour he was marched into a prosperous looking village. One of the captors had told him that they had been watching his progress down the mountain for the past day and a half. He was unceremoniously shoved in front of the chief, and made to kneel.

"Who are you and what do you want?" asked the chief roughly.

"I am Nzobo of the Ndwandwes, but my mother was a Cele," answered Nzobo.

"All stinking, thieving, murdering Zulus," was the chief's unsympathetic response. "What do you want here?"

"I want nothing from you," answered Nzobo. "I am on my way back to Zululand; all I want is free passage."

The chief laughed contemptuously.

"Where have you come from?" he asked.

"Kimberley, the diamond fields," answered Nzobo. He was about to tell them of his year with the van Zyls, but the chief barked a curt order and Nzobo was stripped naked and a very intimate search was conducted of his own person and his clothes. Of course nothing was found.

"Search his faeces every day," ordered the chief.

Nzobo kept his mouth shut. He was going to tell them that he had been away from Kimberley for more than twelve months, but if they wanted to mess with him they could take the consequences.

In the first few days of his captivity Nzobo was fed copious amounts of food and his every movement was watched twenty four hours a day. After a few days one of his captors went to the chief and said to him, "No *idayimani*; we should kill him."

"Keep looking," said the chief. "We will not kill him yet. He may come in useful if there is a Zulu raiding party."

Nzobo was then treated like a slave. At night he was tied up and there was a guard twenty-four hours a day. For the slightest misdemeanour he was beaten and he was given all the unpleasant jobs to do, such as digging graves and butchering animals. Once or twice he was aware of a visit from an outsider, but on pain of death he was escorted into the bush and hidden until the visitor disappeared. He was fed on food scraps, and over a period of a few months Nzobo became thin and emaciated and there were open sores over much of his body.

One day in the very early winter, Nzobo was finishing off a task and wondering how or if he would survive the winter, when a white woman rode unexpectedly into the village. It was Alice Cuthbertson; she had been into the mountains and had decided to take a detour to check on a patient in the village. When she saw Nzobo and the state he was in, she leapt off her horse and immediately started to examine him. As she examined him she spoke to him and learned most of what had happened to him over the past six months, and before that at the van Zyls. After a few minutes she stood up.

"Malnutrition," she said to herself. A small crowd of villagers had collected around Alice and Nzobo. Soon chief Mahbule appeared. He tried to get Alice to leave Nzobo and attend some of the other sick people. By this time Alice was absolutely furious but she kept her head.

"*Nkosi*," she said respectfully in Zulu. "How many times have my father and I helped sick people in this village?"

The chief looked at the ground.

"How many sick children in this village are still alive that my father and I have made well again?" she asked. There was no reply.

"There, there, there and there," she said pointing.

Still nothing was said.

"Do you want me to leave and never come back?" she asked.

There was a rumble from the ever-increasing crowd. Mahbule knew he was in trouble. If these white people did not ever come back, he would be the first casualty. He would be killed and another chief appointed, not necessarily from his direct family. His family would also suffer; they might even be chased out of the village.

"You and your father have always helped us, *Nkosikazi*. You cannot stop now," he answered with some dignity.

"Then answer my questions," Alice glared at him.

"You have helped many sick people and many sick children in this village," he answered.

"And you treat a person like this?" she indicated Nzobo. "Worse than a dog, worse than a snake or a lizard."

"He is just a stinking Zulu spy, he wants to steal our cattle," said the chief.

"One person, steal your cattle?" Alice laughed harshly. "One person, against all the Hlubi *impis*" She was contemptuous. "Are the Hlubi so weak that they run away from just one Zulu? If I hear any more of this nonsense I will leave, now." She moved to remount her horse.

"No, no, no," murmured the crowd.. "We want the *Nkosikasi* to stay and come back."

Alice stamped her foot.

"This man is being starved. You will feed him now and when it is time for me to leave, he leaves with me together with his horse, his rifle, his clothes and anything else he brought here. Is that clear?" she said.

The chief issued some mumbled instructions and food was immediately rushed to Nzobo. His horse was fetched, firstly without its saddle and bridle. Then an old flintlock was produced. Alice waved it away.

"The man had a Mauser, you know what that is as well as I do," she said firmly. Nzobo's belongings were then accounted for to his satisfaction, and he sat under a tree eating, while Alice spent the next two hours in the village tending the one patient she had come to see, plus half a dozen others.

Before she left she paid her respects to Mahbule; he was clearly not very happy with the turn of events. Despite the fact that he had done everything Alice asked, the villagers were furious that he had risked the one thing they valued from the whites above all else and that was white medicine. He, the chief, would have to do something really special over the next few months to maintain his position. Their anger was not for his treatment of Nzobo, however. The other village elders would have either killed Nzobo or enslaved him, just as the chief had done.

"*Nkosi*," Alice said matter of factly. "I will be back next week. That boy who was bitten by the snake must be kept quiet."

She could see he was not happy, but enough had already been said. Although the Hlubi needed the Cuthbertsons, the Cuthbertsons also needed the Hlubi and the chief could have wiped out the Cuthbertson clan without blinking an eye, although Alice was certain they, in their own self-interest, would not do that.

The chief nodded and Alice collected up all her medicines, mounted her horse and left the village, followed by Nzobo.

They arrived back at the farm well after dark, much to the relief of her anxious parents. When Alice explained the situation, Tom was quite thoughtful.

"Well, he can't stay here long," he said. "After all that, sooner or later they will try to kill him. Tonight he can sleep in the storeroom. They won't find him in there."

"You did well, girl," Tom said to his daughter later at supper. "These people have to start thinking of each other as human beings and behave accordingly."

Alice looked up sharply.

"Our people have hardly set them a good example, Dad," she said quietly.

"True enough," was the response.

Alice nursed Nzobo over the next few weeks. This mainly consisted of keeping his sores clean and making sure he was properly fed.

◇◇◇◇◇◇◇◇◇◇◇◇◇◇◇◇

Chapter 16

After Mapitha's return to Kwa-Bulawayo and his discussions with King Cetswayo, he spent days carefully selecting the one hundred head of cattle promised by the King. He questioned the herdboys about the lineage of each beast. After two weeks he was satisfied and, accompanied by a troop of about fifty warriors from his clan, drove the animals slowly back home to his kraal on the banks of the Black Mfolosi River.

As far as he, Mapitha, was concerned, he had done his duty as a Zulu. All he now wanted was to settle down in his kraal and acquire as many wives and cattle as he could. In time he expected that he would become one of the *indunas* of the Ndwandwe. He had taken note of the King's request that he attend any meetings with whites from south of the Tugela. He looked forward to those meetings but did not think they would amount to much. After all, over many years under Mpande and now Cetswayo, the *amaNgisi* had been confined to south of the Tugela and the *amaBhunu* to the Transvaal. The boundaries were established and there was enough land between the Tugela and the northern borders with the Swazis and the *amaBhunu* for the Zulu nation to operate in much the same way as it had in the past. Mapitha was also comforted by the fact that the Zulu had forty thousand well-trained *amabutho*. Although few of them had seen much action, they were fit and strong and aching for a fight. Mapitha made a point of training with them regularly as a leader of one of the Ndwandwe regiments.

Over the months Mapitha felt he had some catching up to do, so first he married Bibi who was almost eighteen and then within a year Mbweli, who was just sixteen. His father made all the arrangements and paid the *lobola* for Bibi, but he had to give the father of Mbweli five of his precious cattle given to him by the King for her *lobola*.

Sir Theophilus Shepstone, the Natal Native Commissioner, "White father of the Zulu people", called *Somseu* by the Zulu, had a vision of a South Africa unified under the British. There were several problems with this vision, the biggest of which were the independent Boer republics in the Transvaal and Orange Free State and the apparently independent Kingdom of Zululand backed by its forty thousand warriors.

Shepstone also had a few scores to settle with Cetswayo, the King having bested him on a number of occasions since his accession after Mpande's death in 1872. Most particularly Shepstone had intended that by recognising Cetswayo as the Zulu King, he would make him a vassal of the British. In this regard Cetswayo had completely outmanoeuvred Shepstone. Firstly, the Zulus themselves had recognised Cetswayo as their King months before Shepstone did, and they had acted on it, installing him with all the formality they could muster. Shepstone, however, had decided that he would go and crown Cetswayo King in a ceremony that eventually took place on September 1st 1873. The Zulus kept the British party waiting for two weeks to attend to burial ceremonies for an old and faithful adviser. When the day eventually came, Shepstone made a speech including the words in Zulu, which Shepstone spoke fluently:

"Here is your King. You have recognised him and I now do so in the name of the Queen of England."

To the thousands of Zulus watching the event, this was a confirmation of their King by the *amaNgisi*. It was unequivocal and there were no conditions. It certainly appeared that here was the confirmation that the Zulu could continue to rule themselves as they had done and that none of Mpande's other sons (he fathered more than sixty children) would in any way be recognised.

It was only afterwards in a nearby tent that Shepstone suggested to Cetswayo that, since the Queen of England had recognised him as King, it was incumbent on him to behave more like the British Queen, in particular when it came to executing wrongdoers without a trial. Cetswayo had no intention of giving up his powers in such a way. There was no tradition or institution that could have delivered British style justice in the Zulu Kingdom anyway. Cetswayo immediately countered by asking Shepstone what he was going to do about Boer encroachments in the north. The Zulu had every right to expect help from their newfound friends the British; protecting their boundaries was fundamental.

Shepstone went away from the ceremony fuming. He had again been bested by "a naked savage". He had granted him full recognition and all he had in return was a request to sort out the problems between the Zulu and the Boers on the Zulu's northern border. Shepstone never forgave Cetswayo and was determined to put the Zulu King in his place.

Mapitha had not, of course, attended the ceremony where Shepstone recognised the Zulu King but he had heard about it from colleagues who were there. There were meetings from time to time between Shepstone and the King. Shepstone thought his title of Natal Native Commissioner meant that he ought to have jurisdiction over the King. Without going out of his way to snub Shepstone, the King always managed to maintain his own authority and not allow the British to interfere.

An urgent summons came from Kwa-Bulawayo for Mapitha to attend a meeting between the King and Somseu. There were a number of issues needing discussion.

The British had taken a poor view of an incident, which Cetswayo felt was wholly outside their jurisdiction. Two Zulu regiments of maidens had been disbanded and instructed to take husbands from a recently disbanded men's regiment. Many of the maidens, however, had already taken lovers in a functioning men's regiment and they demanded that the King disband that regiment so they could marry their lovers. To have women behave in such a way, flaunting the authority of the King and the male dominated society, was unheard of, and in the ensuing fracas some of the maidens were killed.

Shepstone had demanded that the men involved in the killing be brought to justice and Cetswayo had refused point blank, telling Shepstone that this was a matter for the Zulu people to decide.

Shepstone was negotiating an arrangement with the Boers in the Transvaal whereby they would recognise British sovereignty over their territory, so in addition to his duties in Natal, Shepstone also expected to become head of the new administration in the Transvaal. The border dispute in the north with the Boers had been a problem for the Zulu for many years.

As was usual with these meetings, the Zulu King kept *Somseu* and his entourage waiting for three days after they had arrived. This no longer upset the colonists, but it did cause comment and reinforced the view that the Zulu were uncivilised and needed to be taught some manners.

Cetswayo was careful at the meeting to accord *Somseu's* delegation a similar status to his own. So the King sat in a large chair to one side of the entrance to the *isigodlo*, surrounded by some of his *indunas* seated on the ground. Mapitha was on his left side and one of his chief advisers on his right. *Somseu* was seated on the other side of the entrance to the great beehive hut, with the other members of the delegation seated around him. As was customary, neither the colonists nor the Zulus were armed; the colonists had left their arms outside the great kraal of Kwa-Bulawayo and the *indunas* had done the same. After long discussions about the weather, the prospects for crops and the prevention of disease in cattle, the King looked at *Somseu* and said in Zulu, "White father of the Zulu people, you have some other business with me and the independent Kingdom of Zululand."

Somseu was already on the back foot; his eyes glittered and he thought to himself, "I will get this black bastard if it is the last thing I do." He smiled.

Mapitha leant over and whispered to the King, "He has the eyes of a spitting cobra and the laugh of a hungry hyena; *Nkosi*, please be careful."

Cetswayo glanced at his compatriot.

Somseu answered after a short silence. "You were crowned here four summers ago as King of the Zulu nation."

"*Yebo*. Firstly, I was crowned by the Zulu people themselves, and then, you, *Somseu*, White father of the Zulu people, representative of the great white queen, also acknowledged me as King. You even set off seventeen of the great firesticks as a final acknowledgement," said Cetswayo.

Somseu acknowledged the statement and said, "The great white Queen (Victoria) offered her protection to the Zulu people, under certain circumstances."

"There were no circumstances," said Cetswayo, "but the Zulu people are grateful that the *amaNgisi* and the Zulu are at peace, as they were during the long reign of my father Mpande. You as representative of the great white Queen also offered to protect us from the *amaBhunu* in the north."

"The damned black savage," thought *Somseu*, "he already has one of his issues on the table." *Somseu* smiled again.

"We will deal with the issue of the *amaBhunu*," said *Somseu*. "There are also some other issues that we need to deal with."

Cetswayo inclined his head. *Somseu* continued. "The great white Queen thought that you as King of the Zulu people might acknowledge that some of the more brutal ways of Zulu life could be changed. The great white Queen feels that people should be properly tried in a court of law before they are punished."

"We, the Zulu, do not wish to interfere with the cherished practices of the *amaNgisi*," said Cetswayo. "We would expect that the *amaNgisi* would not wish to interfere with Zulu traditions."

Somseu was stumped but he went on. "Some unmarried maidens were killed when they objected to the husbands you had chosen for them and demanded husbands from another regiment."

Cetswayo held up his hand.

"Did this incident happen in the land of the great white Queen?" he asked.

"The great white Queen would never allow such a thing to happen in her territories," answered *Somseu* triumphantly.

"If it did not happen in her own territories, then why is she concerned about it?" said Cetswayo.

"But it happened here in Zululand and the Zulu are under the protection of the great white Queen," said Somseu.

"Anything that happens here is the affair of Cetswayo, the Zulu King to deal with. Things that happen in the territories of the great white Queen are for the *Nkosokasi* to sort out."

This issue was batted backwards and forwards for over an hour. Beer and food were brought out. It had always been Cetswayo's position that the Zulu Kingdom was separate, equal, and independent from the British. Protection meant just that—nothing more, nothing less. The British always tried to infer that protection meant much more than that: it almost meant ownership, although no discussion or agreements had been held that even implied anything like that. The Zulu King was morally and legally correct, not that *Somseu* was going to let that worry him.

Cetswayo decided that he would raise the question of Boer incursions to the north.

"The great white Queen agreed, as you have now said many times, *Somseu*, to protect the Zulu nation."

Somseu looked up sharply; although he was proud that the Zulus had a name for him, he was not certain that he wanted them to use it as a form of address.

"Yes," he eventually responded.

"The *amaBhunu* are trying to take land away from our people in the north. Protection to us means that you help us send these people away so the Zulu in the north get their land back," said Cetswayo.

"The *amaBhunu* suggest that a boundary commission be set up to make a clear line where the boundary is," said *Somseu.*

"Boundary commission, boundary commission," said Cetswayo heatedly. "There is already a clear line; the *amaBhunu* should stay north of that."

The discussion then moved on to the number of Zulu *impi.*

"Now that the great white Queen has agreed to protect the Zulu people, why do you need so many *amabutho*?" asked *Somseu.*

"We have always had a strong army," answered Cetswayo. "My uncle Shaka showed us the way; there is no reason to change. It is important that the young men have some discipline in their lives before they are allowed to marry. The *amabutho* have not fought the *amaNgisi*, ever. This is an internal matter." Cetswayo paused and then continued. "The *amaNgisi* now have thousands of their own troops south of the Tugela. If the white father of the Zulu people is truly a man of peace, why does he need so many soldiers? There are almost as many soldiers as there are white settlers."

Somseu was furious. "How the hell does this black savage know all this?" he thought.

The discussions went on for several days, with little resolution on any of the issues. The only issue on which the Zulu King said he would consider further was the question of the boundary commission.

In his despatches to Sir Bertle Frere, the sympathetic governor of the Cape, Shepstone was scathing.

"There is only one way this savage can be brought to heel," he told the governor, "and that is by military force." The build up of British forces in Natal continued.

After *Somseu* and his delegation had left, Cetswayo met with his *indunas*, well satisfied.

Mapitha was the only one who urged caution.

"I know these people, *Nkosi*, they want to come in here and conquer the Zulu people. They will make you disband your army and they will allow more *amaNgisi* to come and take land north of the Tugela. That *Somseu*, he wants to destroy the power of the Zulu King, you can see it in his eyes."

Cetswayo was thoughtful but eventually he said to the assembled *indunas*, "Did not *Somseu* himself crown me King of the Zulus four summer ago?"

"*Yebo, Nkosi!*" was the thunderous response.

"Did not the great white Queen give the Zulu people her protection?"
"*Yebo, Nkosi!*"
"Do we have forty thousand well trained *amabutho*?"
"*Yebo, Nkosi!*"
They all dispersed.

◇◇◇◇◇◇◇◇◇◇◇◇◇◇◇◇

Chapter 17

Since his discussion with the bishop in Pietermaritzburg, Charles had made periodic visits to the Cuthbertson property in the 'Berg. Alice always seemed pleased to see him but was still adamant that her life's work was to be among the Zulu and her husband had to be able to contribute to that goal.

Shortly after Alice had rescued Nzobo from his plight, Charles arrived unannounced at the Cuthbertsons. He immediately noticed a change in the atmosphere. He felt much less welcome than on previous visits, in fact his feeling was that they couldn't wait to get rid of him.

While he was worrying about the changed situation and how he should respond he found Nzobo hobbling around the yard and quickly put him at ease. Nzobo then told him his story.

"I am an Ndwandwe and my village is on the Black Mfolozi River, but my mother was a Cele, although I have never seen her village."

"My father's farm is quite close to a Cele village; the chief there is Magaye. I know him almost like a father; I learnt my Zulu at his kraal," responded Charles.

Nzobo beamed. He suddenly felt that his luck had changed.

"That was my mother's village. Magaye's father was the Chief when my mother was born, but she also talks of Magaye."

At lunch, which was rather awkward, Charles mentioned his conversation with Nzobo and suggested that if it suited everybody Nzobo could return home with him.

"He cannot travel for at least another ten days," said Alice sharply, and then seeing Charles' surprised and slightly hurt expression said more kindly: "he was badly treated by the Hlubi and we have nursed him back to health as you can see."

"He told me the story," said Charles evenly. "Anyway the offer remains open."

"He needs to go as soon as possible," said Tom. "His presence has created some tension between us and the Hlubi and as soon as he can he must leave."

There was an exchange of glances between Alice and her mother, which heightened Charles' sense of unease. After lunch, Charles tried unsuccessfully to talk to Alice alone but was diverted by Tom, who suggested that Charles could help him shoe one of the horses.

As they were working Tom said to Charles: "Alice will have told you that she thinks that her life's work should be among the Zulu. She thinks that Shepstone and the Governor are determined to bring the Zulu to heel."

"Yes," answered Charles "she has told me of her plans, and I think that she may be right about Shepstone."

"To do that she will have to marry a priest."

Charles didn't respond; he had discussed his own plans and the progress he had made with the Archdeacon on more than one occasion.

"Well, there is a new young priest, who has joined the church in Estcourt, just out from England. He is now courting Alice. He was educated at Oxford and seems keen to help Alice with her plans to start a mission station there. You will meet him this afternoon."

Charles was stunned. He thought that he was in the middle of a bad dream, but he kept his head and responded:

"I look forward to meeting him."

Charles now understood the source of the tension.

"How long will he be staying?" he asked.

"I think a week," said Tom, relieved at Charles' reaction.

Eric Fothergill arrived on horseback accompanied by two servants, later that afternoon. He was tall, dark and good looking. Charles reasoned that he needed someone to help him find his way around and knew they would have spent at least one night on the way. He wondered about the need for two servants though.

Tom made the introductions. Eric had a firm handshake and looked Charles straight in the eye.

Dinner that evening was a rather stilted affair; Alice was looking her stunning best and was naturally trying to impress the visitor, though she didn't say much. Charles kept his mouth shut and just watched the byplay round the table. Meg was on her best behaviour and was obviously concious of her lowly background and the need not to embarrass the family with her lack of education. Tom considered Eric his social equal and after some discussion on Eric's journey the subject of education came up. Eric listened to Alice saying that she thought that what the Zulus needed was western medicine and education. "What about Christianity, I thought that one of the main objectives was to teach the natives the word of God?" he asked

"Yes," said Alice "Any mission would have to be based on Christianity, but to be of any practical value to the Zulus we must educate them and introduce western medicine."

Eric was surprised at Alice's strong views. He thought correctly that she had had a rudimentary education and had then spent two years in the hospital in Pietermaritzburg training as a nurse. Alice was slightly flushed and looked really appealing and beautiful to Eric. He had expected Alice to be rather shy and in awe of his fine education and accomplishments. He could now see that if he were to win her hand he would have to work at it. He also wondered why Charles was there and, with a twinge of jealousy, what his relationship with Alice was.

Eric thought that he would try to test Charles and started to discuss Shakespeare. He happened to choose Macbeth. This was one of the books that Archdeacon Green had given Charles and indeed had schooled him on. So, much to Eric's amazement, Charles was able to more than hold his own in the discussion.

Eric then changed tack and said: "There is a newish rather controversial author gaining popularity now in England, Charles Dickens. Have you read any of his books?"

Charles mentioned two of the books that Archdeacon Green had given him and said: "He raises some interesting social issues; I had no idea that there was such poverty in some of the big cities like London."

Eric, well aware of Meg's background, responded sensitively saying: "The movement of people into the cities to work in the new factories has created

Rough Diamonds

enormous slums. Hopefully the Church and some education will help in times to come."

Meg looked at Eric gratefully. His presence had brought back some of those awful memories of England where the so called upper classes had made life a misery for those on a lower level, especially in any social situation.

By the end of the evening Charles could see that he had a real rival in Eric for the attentions of Alice.

Charles had arranged with Tom that he would supervise the milking, so, as usual, he got up at five thirty and with Nzobo herding the cows into the portable milking bale, had finished the chore by seven. While he was with Tom the previous day he had noticed that some of the other horses also needed to be reshod, so he fired up the small kiln and had Nzobo operate the bellows. They had trouble between them in operating the bellows, holding the horse and keeping it quiet, and then replacing the iron shoe. Alice came in to the barn quietly and after asking Nzobo how he was, smiled uncertainly at Charles and said: "Here, let me hold the horses." As usual she looked stunning in her riding breeches and shirt, but Charles could barely bring himself to look at her. Charles worked quickly and efficiently and they completed one horse and had replaced two shoes on another one when they were called in to breakfast.

Eric couldn't hide his look of amazement at Alice's attire as he stood up when she entered the small dining room. The ladies glanced uneasily at each other. He helped her settle into a chair. He nodded at Charles.

Tom asked Charles as a matter of routine how the milking had gone and Alice then said:

"Charles and Nzobo and I were reshoeing the horses; we've been meaning to do that for weeks now. We'll finish up after breakfast."

"Don't you have a blacksmith?" asked Eric.

"No," answered Tom. "There's not enough work on this farm for a full time blacksmith, so we do it all ourselves."

"A proper mission station will have to have a blacksmith; maybe one will have to be trained," said Eric.

There was an uneasy silence.

After breakfast Charles and Alice went back to the barn and together with Nzobo had finished the job of shoeing all the horses by lunchtime. Eric came and helped. He was a bit clumsy, but was willing to learn: "I can see that I will need many other skills that I don't really have if I am to run a successful mission in Zululand," he said generously, laughing.

During the afternoon Alice and Meg had a furious discussion about her dress. Meg said: "You saw Eric's look at breakfast, when he saw what you were wearing. I think that while he is here you should dress more conventionally. Ladies are not expected to wear riding breeches and they are expected to ride sidesaddle."

"Mother, I have no intention of behaving in any way different to how I normally am. Frankly he can take it or leave it. This is how I would have to be on any mission station, so he had better get used to the idea."

"You may chase him away altogether; he probably already thinks that you are just a rather unladylike farmgirl."

Alice laughed: "Maybe he's right, that is exactly what I am."

"You'll never attract the right sort of man with that attitude, young lady."

Alice just shrugged: "I am what I am, I have no intention of trying to be something that I am not. All that class prejudice that you have talked about in England is now coming back. You left all that behind when you left England, so please don't let it raise its ugly head again. I now think I understand better what you must have had to go through with Dad's family and all that. I am not going to be victimized in that way. If people don't like it then they don't have to come here."

Meg looked uneasy: "I'm just trying to help you do what's best for you."

Alice hugged her and no more was said.

On the Sunday that Eric was there, he, Alice and Charles decided that they would ride up into the 'Berg for the day. After a brief Sunday service they set out. It was a beautiful clear 'Berg day with a slight wind and only a few wispy clouds in the sky. Much to Charles' surprise Alice took them up to her special pool. On the way Eric suggested that he and Charles jump a few boulders and then he led Charles a merry dance over some bushes and a very dangerous looking *donga*. Charles understood fully that he, Eric, was trying to show Alice that he was every bit as much a man as Charles so obviously was, and he followed with some ease. Charles thought that the game was a little foolish; he had been brought up to value his horse, not as a plaything but as a useful means of transport. He thought that if there had been an accident, many people would be inconvenienced. Nevertheless he continued to follow Eric and refused none of the challenges that Eric presented. After more than an hour of these antics Eric looked with some admiration at Charles, said nothing, and they went on their way. He said quietly to Charles afterwards, with Alice out of earshot: "I've run this type of challenge with a few of my friends, back in England, and they all back off after about twenty minutes. You are an exception." Alice had watched the antics of the men without saying much. She thought that both of them were rather silly, risking life and limb trying to impress her. She was at least as good a horseman as either of them, and could have done everything they did. She didn't let on though. She already knew that both were substantial men. Her reason for taking them both up to her special pool was to see how she felt about each of them in that place, which for her was a sanctuary. They had a pleasant picnic and good conversation, despite the underlying tensions. Much to Charles' frustration he was unable to catch Alice's eye while they were lying on their coats next to the pool.

The pattern of challenges continued for the next few days and somehow Charles managed to keep his end up during conversations over dinner.

"Did you read any Latin and Greek at school?" Eric asked Charles one evening.

"No," answered Charles. "I did learn Zulu and like Alice here speak it fluently. Very few of the natives speak English, as I 'm sure you have found out, and in order to communicate with them one has to speak Zulu."

Eric nodded, "I am starting to learn, but it is not easy." He smiled.

"I am going up to the village in the morning," said Alice to Charles after dinner.

"I said that I would help Tom brand calves, but I'm sure that Eric would be happy to go with you."

She smiled wanly. "I'll ask him."

After an early breakfast Alice, Meg and Eric rode off into the mountains. Eric insisted that one of his servants accompany them. Charles tried to dissuade him:

"He's from a different clan Eric; all you will achieve is to create an atmosphere of suspicion. I think you should leave him here."

Eric was intrigued and he decided to test the situation out and see for himself, he didn't really believe that there could be that much animosity between people of the same tribe, albeit different clans. He thought that the local white population greatly exaggerated the situation to suit their own ends.

"I think that he should come this time," he answered tactfully. "I will be there to protect him if there is any trouble."

Charles, Tom and Nzozbo spent the day rounding up calves and with some of Tom's Hlubi labourers helping, managed to brand more than one hundred of them. By the end of the day they were tired but happy.

"That's a great help," said Tom. "I would have had trouble doing that without you."

"That's a pleasure," said Charles and he smiled. "It could be the last time I'm here to help, of course."

Tom looked at him sharply, but said nothing.

A very grumpy Alice and her mother returned with Eric just before dusk and Eric was unusually silent at dinner.

"I've learnt rather a lot today," he volunteered tiredly, over coffee. "You were right," he said to Charles. "They would not let my servant into the village, although they did him no harm." And then he laughed: "I will listen more in the future; I tried to conduct a service in the village, much against the advice of the two ladies here. The Chief was furious, since I had not asked his permission."

Alice and Meg looked at him gratefully. They had half expected some acrimony.

"Mahbule took full advantage," Alice explained to Charles and her father. "He has been trying to find a way of bolstering his authority, after we rescued Nzobo, and he really laid it on today."

"I'm sorry," said Eric. "They didn't understand much of my rather rudimentary Zulu in the few minutes I had before Mahbule stopped it all. I'm grateful for the experience, and I will listen in future. The clinic that you two ladies ran was a great success though."

"Yes, " said Meg, "over the years we have got to know them all very well and the clinic has improved their lives considerably, especially as Alice has been able to work with their *sangoma* and not challenge her."

Charles was impressed with way that the man handled the situation. It could have been acrimonious, but he took full responsibility for his actions, and he had put both the ladies at ease, at least for the time being.

Before they all went off to bed Tom asked Charles if he would help with a few more major chores, which would take two more days.

"Don't know what I would have done without you, Charles; as always you have been most helpful."

Alice just looked down. Charles changed the subject:

"Alice, I spoke to Nzobo today, and he thinks that he is ready to travel now. Perhaps you could give him the once over just to make sure. I will take it easy though. He is not one hundred percent."

At breakfast, the next morning, Eric announced that he was to return to Estcourt and he asked to see Tom privately before he left.

Charles left the table; he knew that Eric was about to ask for Alice's hand and wondered what he could do to stop it. He thought that it was premature, as far as he could see Eric and Alice had not spent more than a few moments alone together since Eric's arrival. Charles thought that Eric was a fine man but needed to learn a great deal about Africa and the Zulu to have a chance of making a success of any kind of mission. He found a tearful Alice in the barn. She smiled sheepishly at him. Charles decided that bold action was what was needed.

"I have been speaking to the Archdeacon and he seems very happy with my progress," he said to her. "He at least seems to recognize that locally born people have more chance of success in setting up a mission for the Zulus than someone straight out from England. More important than that, we have something special, you and I. I love you with all my heart and together we will make a great team. If you want my opinion, Eric won't last six months on a mission station, and then as a dutiful wife you will have to return with him to England or wherever. He is in there-" he gestured towards the house—"asking your father for your hand right now. Please don't accept. I have a much better chance of getting both Shepstone and the King to agree to a mission in Zululand, and even if Eric did get permission, as I said—and you can see it for yourself—he won't last and that will be an opportunity lost for you and the Zulu."

He then tried to kiss her. She pushed him away.

"Maybe this is God's test," she said. "I can see that he has much to learn, but he seems willing. I know I can help him."

"Do you love him?" asked Charles.

"I can learn to love him, if it God's will," answered Alice.

"This is for life, Alice. You know I love you and you have said that you love me. Unless you are certain of your own feelings don't accept him."

She looked away.

"Promise me one thing," said Charles.

"What?"

"That you won't accept him or marry him for a year. If I haven't got permission to set up a mission in Zululand within that time, then I will have failed and you must do what you must do."

"A year?"

"That's what I said; I think I need a year."

She looked at him.

"I agree; you have my word. I will not be betrothed to anyone for one year from today." She almost looked relieved.

She then flew into his arms and they kissed passionately until they heard her mother calling from the house.

"One year," she said and turned and ran.

Charles stayed where he was. He had what he wanted.

True to form Eric had got down on one knee and proposed to Alice.

Eric looked very handsome and was at his most charming. At that moment he would have been every girl's dream of a fine husband. She hesitated as she thought about her conversation with Charles in the barn a few minutes earlier and then replied:

"I am flattered by your proposal but before I consider it you must have permission from the Church, the Government and the King to set up a mission in Zululand. That is my condition."

He tried to argue. She held up her hand.

"That is my condition. I have a calling to help the Zulu. I will consider your proposal when you have permission to set up the mission. Not before. I need to know that you are committed to the Zulu and not to your own career within the Church, which may take you anywhere in the world."

She left the room.

Eric contained his fury. He had status, he had a private income and he had expected Alice to agree to marry him without delay. He was after all a great catch, and women had been falling for him for years now. He was now more determined than ever to have her as his wife. Women were not expected to have a calling, especially someone like Alice who seemed to Eric to be quite unsophisticated. He thought that he would be a Bishop here or elsewhere in the not too distant future. He was completely non-plussed by the condition of setting up a mission, although he had made positive noises about such a project when he first met Alice in Estcourt. He bade a rather hasty farewell to the Cuthbertsons and Charles and clattered off.

Charles stayed a few more days as he had promised, although much to his disappointment Alice kept her distance. He heard her arguing with her mother.

"I can't believe you said that to him," Meg shouted. "You may not see him again."

"I may not, but he didn't say anything about his feelings; it was almost as if I were some sort of chattel or object that he would possess. Anyway, we have had this discussion before; I will marry someone who can help me with a mission to the Zulus and I am quite happy to wait. I have told

Charles that I will wait for him for a year."

"You what?"

"You heard, Mum."

"This man has status, money, he is very handsome and I am sure will look after you. What more do you want?" asked Meg angrily. "Charles doesn't really compare, he's just a colonial."

"Like me," answered Alice. "I am just a colonial, as you have so graphically described us."

Meg looked her daughter. "Sorry," she said. The anger went out of them and they embraced.

"You have to understand, Mum, I have a calling and I am determined to fulfil it and whether it is Charles or Eric who will help me do that, is in God's hands."

At that point Charles decided that he would speak to Tom and tell what had transpired between him and Alice. He did not want to get on the wrong side of him.

There was a heavy snowstorm in the Drakensburg the night before Charles and Nzobo set off from the Cuthbertsons. They knew that within half a day's ride they would be out of the worst of it and then they would be able to make their way quite quickly back to Greytown. Alice, much to Charles' surprise, came with them for the first few miles, and despite the presence of Nzobo they kissed deeply before they each went their own way.

"I will be back soon." said Charles.

On the way home Charles reflected on his fate. He was in love with Alice; he had no doubt of that. The idea that she should marry a cold fish like Eric Fothergill was just beyond him. Alice was a warm, loving person, maybe somewhat obsessed by helping the Zulus, but Charles could see merit in what she said on the subject. Unlike his fellow colonists and after his conversations with Alice, he had realized even at this early stage that the Zulu would not accept a subservient role for ever and that they should be encouraged to develop their own skills so that they could compete in the modern world.

Nzobo could see that Charles was depressed and said to him when the matter was raised:

"The *Nkosi* will marry the *Nkosikasi* Alice?"

"Maybe," was the curt response.

Despite the brush-off Nzobo persisted: "I can see that the *Nkosi* likes the *Nkosikasi* very much."

Charles said nothing.

"You spoke to her father?"

"Yes."

"Then the matter is settled."

"No"

"No?"

"The *Nkosikasi* wants to help the Zulu in Zululand, north of the Tugela."

"As she does with those stinking Hlubi; that would be good for the Zulu."

"She wants to teach the Zulu as well as run a clinic; there will also be a church."

"What will she teach the Zulu?"

"To read and write and maybe count."

"I saw the *Nkosi* Frank; he was writing and spending time reading books. That *Nkosi* was a good man. Also there were schools in Kimberley, and I visited a mission school in Kuruman."

"She will run the clinic as well."

"The clinic is good; the *abelungu* can teach the Zulu many things about healing people. As the *Nkosikasi* Alice helped me."

They rode on in silence for a while.

"Too much time reading books and writing will make the Zulu people weak," volunteered Nzobo.

Charles smiled. "There will be plenty of time for games and stick fighting; reading and writing will help the Zulu be more like the white man." Then he almost bit his tongue and wished he had not said that.

Nzobo looked at him sharply and said angrily:

"The Zulu have no need to be like the white man. If this reading and writing makes us like the white man, then it will be very bad for the Zulu. Zulus are Zulus and have their own traditions, you white men must not try to change that. There were many bad white men in Kimberley, we spit on them. They tried to steal from us and kill us."

There was an uneasy silence for a while. Charles tried to mollify Nzobo:

"We do not wish to change the Zulu, but there are some things that the Zulu can learn for his own benefit from the white people. We will help as much as we can."

"There are many things that the white people can learn from the Zulu also. The *Nkosikasi* Alice uses her own medicine as well as what she learned from the *sangoma*. She told me that. The *Nkosikasi* would be good for the Zulu. *Nkosi,* you also seem to understand; will you be part of this great plan of the *Nkosikasi?*"

"Maybe."

"Maybe? If the *Nkosi* has spoken to the *Nkosikasi* Alice's father and the father is happy, then you will get married and you will also go to help the Zulus."

"The Good Lord might prefer it if the Reverend Eric married the *Nkosikasi* and went to Zululand with her."

"The Good Lord?"

"Yes, our God."

Nzobo's only contact with the Christian faith was with the Reverend Potts in Kimberley, apart from the brush-offs he felt he had received from the more established churches.

"Maybe this God does not understand the needs of the Zulu. The *Nkosi* Eric is only concerned for himself; he does not see the Zulus as people, just as a source of his own power. He did not say one word to me while he was visiting the *Nkosi* Tom."

Charles was amazed at Nzobo's perception; he couldn't have put it any better himself.

"In Zulu tradition if the father has spoken, the daughter will obey, she has no choice. We do not want that to change. Some of the *abelungu* traditions are difficult for us to understand." Then he brightened up: "Does the *Nkosi* Eric have more cattle than you, is that why *Nkosi* Tom prefers him to you?"

Charles laughed.

"No, we do not believe in paying for our wives in cattle or anything else. If the marriage is blessed by our God and all the parties agree, then it will take place."

Nzobo looked thoughtful.

"If this God you speak of wants *Nkosi* Eric to marry the *Nkosikasi* then he is making a very big mistake. She will not like him. You should challenge him to a fight, you will win easily."

Charles laughed again.

"That is not our way. I must get permission to build a mission in Zululand and then the *Nkosikasi* will marry me."

Nzobo just shook his head.

A few miles later Nzobo asked again:

"This God, this *Nkulunkulu* of yours, you will bring him to Zululand?"

"Yes, he is the basis of our beliefs. The clinic and the education all depend on that."

"He must be careful, we have many powerful Gods. Many of the things that the *abelungu* do are very bad. I don't think that the Zulu will like your *Nkulunkulu* very much and the *Nkosi* Eric, if he is the choice of the *Nkulunkulu* then that will not be good. The Zulu will not like him."

From time to time they had similar discussions along the way, without much change in the perceptions on either side.

Charles knew that there was a very wide gap between his own culture and perceptions and those of the Zulu. He put some thought into it. Alice had it right, he thought. The priority was education and medicine; the religion should come in its own time. The problem was that the only possible way of starting anything in Zululand was through a mission station, which was seen as harmless by the authorities. Many whites thought that education was wasted and possibly dangerous and would give the 'natives' aspirations above their station.

Four days after the start of the journey, Charles and Nzobo reached the Lawrence establishment near Greytown and the next day Nzobo was taken to his mother's clan village and Chief Magaye. When they found out who he was, he was greeted like the prodigal son. Charles left them to their celebrations.

Nzobo's intention was to spend a few days with Magaye and then return to the Ndwandwes but Magaye had other ideas, especially when he witnessed Nzobo's prowess with his rifle.

The British Administration was building up their military strength. Shepstone was determined to curb the power of the Zulus, and from the very first the new governor of the Cape Sir Bartle Frere encouraged these aspirations. Magaye was, therefore, under pressure to send his young men to the British for military training. All the young men north of the Tugela were obliged to join Cetswayo's *impis* as they had been since the time of Shaka, now more than fifty years earlier.

Nzobo had a discussion with Charles before he decided what to do. Usually he would not have been given the choice, but in view of his time in Kimberley and his subsequent ordeal Magaye allowed him to make his own decision.

"If I return to Zululand I will have to join one of Cetswayo's *impis*." Nzobo said.

"Yes."

"I can also join the British and they will pay me and I will have a rifle."

"Yes."

"For many years Mpande stayed at peace with the British, maybe Cetswayo will do the same thing. *Somseu* has already crowned him King of the Zulus."

"Yes."

"I do not think that the Zulus will want to fight the *amangisi,* the Zulus will stay north of the Tugela and the British will stay south."

"Maybe." Charles was thinking of his conversations with Alice.

"What is 'maybe'?"

"*Somseu* does not like the idea of having so many Zulu *impis* all waiting and ready to fight."

"But they have always, since the days of Shaka, been like this. Every young Zulu will spend some time in an *ibutho* until he has permission to marry."

"Yes."

"It is the source of our discipline and strength; take that away and all you will have is many young men with nothing to do. That will bring trouble; we will be weak again, like the Swazi and the Mpondo. The great Shaka taught us that. *Somseu* will make a big mistake if he thinks he can change us by taking away our discipline."

Charles said nothing more. He thought that this would suit Shepstone admirably; the young Zulus would then be available to join the labour force in Natal.

Nzobo listened to all the arguments. He personally thought it very unlikely that the Zulu and the British would ever fight each other. Also the kindness that he had been shown by two white families in the space of little more than a year had an influence. He was aware that on both occasions he would have died had he not been rescued and then nursed back to health. So he agreed to join the British Army.

Charles did not know what to say. It seemed that Shepstone was determined to disarm the Zulus by fair means or foul. He hoped forlornly that Nzobo was right. Whatever he felt, he could hardly encourage someone to join the Zulu army, especially if he thought that there would be a conflict with the British.

Many of the black troops were used as scouts and many others were used in non-combatant roles such as handling baggage carts and as cooks and batmen for the British officers. Nzobo was trained as a scout because of his proficiency with a rifle. The scouts wore their traditional loincloth and had bare feet, much as they would have done in the Zulu army. The big difference was that in the British army they all had rifles and they were trained to use them. Within months, under the guidance of British officers, Nzobo came to understand his role; he had a number of men assigned to him. Generally the black troops were treated well despite the arrogance of their British masters. Nzobo was as happy at this time as he had been since he and Mapitha had left for the diamond fields, now about four years earlier.

◇◇◇◇◇◇◇◇◇◇◇◇◇◇◇◇

Chapter 18

Charles was now more determined than ever to become a priest and he went to see Archdeacon Green as soon as he could.

"The Bishop is away at the moment in England defending some controversial articles he has written. Some in the Church even consider them to be blasphemous, so there is not much I can do."

"I could stay here at Bishopstowe and learn from you. I could respectfully ask you to write to the Bishop to ask him what his attitude might be," Charles answered.

"Yes, both of those options are possible. I would also like you to preach to the locals in their own language; that will be a test of how you will manage as a priest."

Charles stayed for some months at Bishopstowe in Pietermaritzburg and made progress with his studies. He had high hopes that his plans for a mission would be fulfilled in the required time. He also preached in Zulu to the local congregation. Remembering his conversations with Nzobo and others, he explained the values and concepts of Christianity in terms that he thought the Zulu could understand. The Archdeacon was very pleased and impressed with him and wrote to the Bishop, still fighting his own battles in England:

"I think that I have found the ideal candidate for our long cherished ambition of starting a mission among the Zulus north of the Tugela."

He went on to explain Charles' background and his progress over the past few months at Bishopstowe and before that on his own.

The response, three months later was not encouraging:

"I remember the young man you mention quite well. I found him poorly educated and he has a reputation for wildness among the settler population. Not a good candidate I am afraid. I am in correspondence with a far more suitable person in the form of Reverend Eric Fothergill, who is currently at Estcourt. He is an Oxford graduate and says he is progressing his Zulu studies. He also mentioned in one of his letters to me that he is hoping to marry a local girl, one Alice Cuthbertson, who was brought up among the Zulu and speaks the language fluently, I am told." He went on to suggest that the Archdeacon should make some enquiries regarding Alice's background, since he had heard that her father was a remittance man and her mother had once been a barmaid. "The people we send to minister to the Zulu must be from exceptional stock and they must have a feeling for Zulu culture and tradition, not a feature that is predominant among the settler population I'm sorry to say."

The Archdeacon knew that the Bishop had in fact supported the Zulu tradition of polygamy, suggesting that a tradition such as this, lasting centuries, could not be changed overnight. Privately he had some sympathy with this point of view but it had got the Bishop into hot water both with the settlers and the wider Church. With all his troubles the Archdeacon thought the Bishop would be lucky to retain his post; because of his sympathies with the Zulu, Shepstone and the British authorities wanted him to be replaced.

The Archdeacon plucked up courage and a week later he mentioned to Charles that he had had a letter form the Bishop. He told Charles the broad contents of the letter.

Charles showed no emotion during the discussion and despite his inner turmoil he said quietly:

"Archdeacon, respectfully, have you met the Reverend Fothergill?"

"No, for a number of reasons we have not met. I have heard a few complaints from local parishioners though, who say he is high handed and arrogant."

"I've met him at Tom Cuthbertson's place. He is not a suitable person to send on a mission to the Zulus. He won't last six months."

"The Bishop thinks that he will marry Alice, the Cuthbertson girl, and that together they would make a great team for our first mission in Zululand."

Charles' stomach gave a lurch, but he tried to hide his feelings.

"With respect he will not do you or the Church any good in Zululand and he speaks very little Zulu—or at least that was the situation only three or four months ago. Also if the local settlers think he is arrogant, you can imagine how the Zulus will feel."

The Archdeacon looked shrewdly at Charles. There was more heat in his response than he had expected, so he asked:

"The Bishop has asked me to make enquiries regarding the Cuthbertson clan. You say you have been there: what are they like?"

"Hard working, sober, and they have a great relationship with the local natives. Alice and her mother provide some medical facilities for the local Hlubi and they get labour and live in peace with them in return."

"What's Alice like?"

Charles thought he had already said too much. He was not ready to discuss his understanding with Alice, not with anybody.

"She seems very nice," he responded."She speaks fluent Zulu."

"No suitors?"

Charles shook his head. "I don't know."

He then made his excuses and quickly left.

The Archdeacon shrewdly guessed that Charles was in love with Alice but that for some reason his suit had been rejected.

Eric had fallen for Alice despite her apparent lack of sophistication, and he was determined to make her his wife. So he spent every spare moment visiting the Cuthbertson farm in the 'Berg and he tried to charm both Tom and Meg, with only limited success. Tom found him rather heavy going and couldn't help but compare his lack of farming skills with those of Charles. To start with Meg was flattered by his attentions and although she kept her own counsel couldn't help wondering why Alice just didn't accept his marriage proposal, which was renewed more than once. Alice found him interesting and quite fun to be with. She took him up to her special pool several times, but he behaved like a gentleman and on the one occasion he tried to kiss her she gently pushed him away and he apologized for his behaviour. There was none of the passion that she had with Charles, nevertheless she enjoyed his company when he was around, but did not miss him when he returned to Estcourt.

On one of the visits to the pool he told her: "I am in regular touch with the Bishop, who as you may know is in England at the moment. He thinks that he will win his current battles in the Church and return here soon. He has said that when he returns the Church will give me full backing to set up a mission in Zululand, he sees no problem with getting permission from Shepstone and the King for such a venture, but he needs to be here to do all of that."

"How soon will that be?" asked Alice innocently.

"Just a few months," responded Eric. "Look, I am certain that all this will happen, please just marry me and then we will be ready when the bishop returns. Ready to go to Zululand."

Alice was sorely tempted, but he had never said anything about his feelings and when she looked about at the pool she remembered with pleasure the times she had spent up here with Charles. She also remembered her promise to Charles, which still had six months to run.

"You know my condition, fulfil that and the answer will be yes," she answered.

"But it's only a matter of time, as soon as the Bishop returns I am sure we will have the permission you seek."

"We will have to wait until then," said Alice, getting up and tightening the girth on her mount's saddle.

Having considered the matter, Charles decided that the only people he could safely confide in were his parents, so he took a few days off from Bishopstowe and returned to his parents' farm in Greytown, where he explained in painful detail his situation. Almost six months of the twelve months he had asked Alice to wait had passed and with the turmoil in the Church caused by the Bishop's perceived indiscretions, a decision regarding a mission in Zululand seemed a long way away. He had to find a way round the situation; waiting for the Church seemed a forlorn hope.

"I'm in love with her and cannot imagine living the rest of my life without her, and to even think of Eric touching her makes me feel quite ill."

"What about the mission?" asked his father.

"I am absolutely committed to that. If we can find some way of helping both sides value the other then we have a chance." He did not discuss his thoughts regarding the relative importance of education and medicine as opposed to religion. That remained strictly between him and Alice.

They continued to discuss the situation over the next few days and then his father said:

"I know Shepstone quite well and think that he would welcome a missionary presence up there somewhere, especially someone with the 'right views'. I know that he distrusts the 'do-gooders' just out from England and he is very annoyed with the Bishop. He might support the idea. After that I suppose you would have to get permission from the King. The King is being cooperative at the moment, so if Shepstone agrees there is a chance that Cetswayo will also agree. If all that happens, I think that the Church would support you."

Charles kept his mouth shut about the injustices being perpetrated on the Zulus and he said nothing about the Langalibalele affair. He knew that his father would support the government line.

Alice during this time helped where she could with the farm and ran the clinic at the village on a regular basis. She looked forward to Charles' letters and always replied straight away. Often she cried herself to sleep; fearing it was inevitable that Eric, because of his education and acceptability to the Church establishment in England, would get permission to start a mission in Zululand and Charles would be rejected. During Eric's visits he always mentioned that he had the support of the Bishop and that when the said Bishop returned he was sure that permission would be readily granted. He never again tried to kiss her, much to her surprise, and she tried to think about his strengths.

"If this is God's will then so be it," she said to herself. "I will learn to love him and do my duty to the Zulu as well."

She felt that her mother was not much help. Her mother had not warmed to Eric and was now thinking that maybe Charles was a better prospect despite her previous advice:

"Follow your heart, that is what I did and I have never regretted it."

"Even if he is just a colonial," Alice couldn't resist the jibe.

Meg looked up as if surprised: "So you are in love with Charles, after all, then marry him"

"You know my conditions; I will not be swayed by anything else."

"If you marry a man you do not love you will be making a rod for your own back, you may be very unhappy."

"God's will is God's will," said Alice lamely.

When she received Charles' letter telling her that the Bishop's expectation was that she would marry Eric, she was furious and wrote back saying that the arrangement between them still stood. She tactfully did not mention Eric's constant visits.

When she remembered the happy times she had spent with Charles, swimming and kissing up at her special pool, sometimes she glowed with pleasure and at others she was ashamed of her wanton behaviour. "Maybe Eric is God's punishment," she thought guiltily.

During the next month Charles and his father paid three visits to Theophilus Shepstone, the Natal Native Commissioner, self-styled 'White father of the Zulu people.'

To start with he was unenthusiastic, mainly because it was a new idea, but he gradually warmed to the idea of the mission north of the Tugela. Politically it became more and more attractive: it would upset the Bishop, since Eric was his preferred candidate, he had the general support of Archdeacon Green who disapproved of the Bishop's activities and it would create a listening post north of the Tugela. Charles kept his mouth shut as far as possible and let Shepstone assume that he held the same views as Shepstone himself did.

The third meeting with the Commissioner was brief and to the point:

"You will have to get permission from the King yourself; I will send a letter indicating that, subject to anything that Cetswayo has to say, the plan has my approval."

After the third meeting with Shepstone Charles had told the Archdeacon what had transpired and said: "My father knows Shepstone and arranged everything, in view of our discussions I assumed that this would meet with your approval."

The Archdeacon was surprised everything played into his hands very well. He could not be accused of conspiring against the Bishop since he genuinely had no knowledge of the meetings, but it certanly helped advance his campaign of undermining the Bishop.

"I think you can assume that the church will support you," was all he said. "Best of luck with the King."

Charles arranged to take a month off from his studies and in an excited frenzy tore off to tell Alice of his success.

He arrived at the Cuthbertson farm just before lunch and, abandoning his horse, rushed into the house looking for Alice.

"She's out in the barn," a bewildered Meg told him.

Alice was grooming one of the horses when Charles charged up and almost bowled her over. He picked her up and danced round the barn; the horse looked on nervously. "I've done it, I've done it!" he shouted.

Alice was bemused by Charles' antics but she was pleasantly surprised to see him. She had been thinking about Eric's proposed visit in a few days' time, where he was certain to ask for her hand again. "Done what?" she asked, looking down at him. He was still holding her a few feet off the ground.

He stopped dancing round. "Shepstone has given me permission, so has the Church."

"Shepstone?" she couldn't comprehend was he was saying. She had geared all her expectations to coping with being married to Eric, and had almost given up hope of Charles.

"Yes, the Commissioner has given me permission to set up a mission north of the Tugela." He let her down gently on to her feet.

"Oh, Charles, I can't believe it."

He kissed her and she returned the kiss so passionately that they were oblivious of Meg's approach. Meg tactfully gave a quiet cough, causing the couple to part, flushed and flustered.

She smiled.

"Now, now, plenty of time for that later. Come and have some lunch."

Meg was delighted with the news. She wanted some finality and at last her daughter was in a position to make a choice.

Charles told the family of his success and then said: "All we now have to do is to get permission from the King. Alice, I need you to come with me to see him. We will be away for three weeks, I expect."

He showed them Shepstone's letter to the King.

They spent a day at the pool and swam, freezing though it was. It was wonderful to be together. Alice was passionate in her kisses, but firm in allowing Charles no further liberties.

"When we are married," she admonished as he tried to ease his hand into her breeches.

They spent a day preparing for the trip to Zululand and then left for Pietermaritzburg with Tom as a chaperone. His brother was to accompany them the rest of the way to Kwa-Bulawayo. Charles had previously sent messages together with Shepstone's letter to the King, requesting permission to visit.

The four-day ride went without incident and they set up camp outside the great Kraal.

As expected, the King kept them waiting for a week before he would see them. This played into their hands, particularly Alice's hands; she had taken all her medicines with her and ran a daily clinic in the kraal, treating minor ailments. She also assisted at the births of two babies, and on one occasion helped to save the child's life, due to her quick action. Within a few days the couple had caused a stir and made an excellent impression on the ordinary Zulus in the kraal. The Zulus were intrigued with Alice; most of them had never seen a white woman before. They approached her cautiously and fingered her clothes and hair. She chatted to them in Zulu, quite at ease.

At the first meeting with the King, Mapitha, who attended all the King's meetings with whites, was sitting in the background. He was very impressed with the attitude and the demeanour of both Charles and Alice.

After formal greetings and some gift giving the King directed all his questions at Charles. Alice in deference to her white skin was allowed to attend the *indaba*, but she knew that it was beneath the King's dignity to address a woman in such a situation. Alice was thus free to look around. The kraal was meticulously swept. The *isigodlo* was in perfect repair with fresh thatch, and all the huts in the kraal were lined up in rows with almost military precision. The *isigodlo* was much bigger than the others but they were all the same beehive shape. Cetswayo's *indunas* were all there. This was an important occasion, and they were also wondering whether allowing such a mission on their territory would be a further white encroachment on Zulu territory or whether they would gain something from it.

"So, what is this mission station you want me to agree to?" Cetswayo asked Charles.

"Well, *Nkosi*, we are Christians and we believe in one true God. We believe the Zulu people would benefit from understanding the teachings of our God," was the answer.

"What about our own Zulu Gods, will they be neglected or destroyed?" asked the King.

"No, *Nkosi*, we would merely present the teachings of our God. We have faith that many of the Zulu people will in time also believe what we teach," said Charles.

"And anything else?"

"Nkosi will be aware that the *Nkosikasi*, Alice here, will be able to heal people when they are sick. She has many years of experience and has even helped your people these past few days," said Charles.

"Where has this *Nkosikasi* done these wondrous things?" asked the King. He knew perfectly well, of course, he just wanted to put Charles on the back foot.

"The *Nkosikasi* was brought up in the *Ukhahlamba*; she helped the people there."

"You mean the feeble spirited, stinking Hlubi," answered the King.

"The very same Hlubi that pay homage to you as King of the Zulu," said Charles.

Rough Diamonds

"They no longer pay homage since *Somseu* took all their cattle," said the King reproachfully. Alice whispered in Charles' ear.

"The *Nkosokasi* reminds me that it is part of our Christian upbringing to treat all people as equal. Zulus who welcome us, in whichever part of Zululand they live, will have the benefit of our help," said Charles.

"You think the white people and the Zulu are equal?" demanded the King.

"In the eyes of our God all people are born equal," answered Charles.

"So you will bring this religion, this medicine; what will the *isangoma* say?" asked the King. "Will you not take away some of their position in Zulu society?"

"Our purpose is to help the Zulu, not to threaten any part of the Zulu culture," said Charles. "Alice has worked with the local *sangoma* in the mountains; she understands their place in Zulu society."

The King grunted.

Alice whispered again in Charles' ear.

The King looked up alert.

"The *Nkosikasi* has other words of wisdom?" asked the King. All the *indunas* chuckled.

"The *Nkosikasi* has reminded me that we would also set up a school for the Zulu children," said Charles.

"School, what school?" asked the King. He was aware that some black children south of the Tugela were attending school. He was not convinced of the value of this.

"School, to teach the children to read and to write and some arithmetic," said Charles.

Mapitha then whispered in the King's ear, trying to explain the value of school.

"*Somseu* has sent me this letter," said the King. "He only talks about the Christian mission; he does not mention the school or the medicines."

Charles remained silent.

Mapitha leant over and whispered in the King's ear.

"Come back tomorrow," ordered the King. "We have much to discuss." He waved his hand around to indicate and include all his *indunas*.

It was three days before they were called before the King again.

During the three days Cetswayo had many discussions with Mapitha and his indunas.

"These are good *amaNgisi*," said Mapitha. "The Christian God we can take or leave but our people need medicine and schools. This is a start; it will enable our people to get on equal terms with the whites."

"We are equal; what do you mean?" asked the King.

"We do not have the power to make firesticks. Their people have come to our country, but without their learning we may never have the power to travel to theirs. We need people like this *umfundisi* to help us get on equal terms with the white intruders," said Mapitha.

The King was astonished at Mapitha's insight. Mapitha went on, "I have told the great *Nkosi* that this *Somseu* is like a bad dream. He is a hyena that longs to feed on the body of the Zulu people. He is like cobra ready to spit into the eyes of the Zulu people. We need people on our side who speak our language and will help our people."

"You want our people to become like the white man?" asked one of the *indunas*.

Mapitha hesitated.

"Answer him, man," ordered the King sharply.

"Not like the white man, but we must gain some of their skills, otherwise we will be crushed," said Mapitha.

"Where will these people go?" asked the King. "I will not have them here, not at Kwa-Bulawayo, not yet."

There was a general discussion among the indunas.

"I have a place on a small river that flows into the Buffalo River," said one of the indunas. "They can go there, it is near Nqutu."

When Charles and Alice next appeared before the King, he asked Charles, "How many days in each year for the Christian Church?"

"Every Sunday, which is one day in seven, we dedicate to the worship of our God," said Charles.

"And the other six days?" asked the King.

"Those days can be used for teaching the children how to read and write and for giving medicine to the sick," said Charles.

The King nodded.

"You will set up your mission near Nqutu, it is on a river. Mapitha of the Ndwandwes will go with you."

They were dismissed.

Mapitha was aghast.

"You want me to go to Nqutu; what about my cattle, my two wives, my children, my position with the Ndwandwes?" he protested.

"Mapitha, you are a good and faithful Zulu; your children will be the first to be educated by the whites. Take your cattle and wives with you; I have spoken to the local *induna*."

He was dismissed.

Eric spent a fruitless few weeks, writing to the Bishop. He paid several visits to Shepstone and to the Archdeacon. In the end he sensed that he had been outmanoevered and that in the Bishop he had backed the wrong horse. Once he had accepted his fate he wrote both Charles and Alice generous letters wishing them well. He was invited to the wedding and attended with good grace.

The wedding of Charles and Alice, two months later, was the wedding of the year in Pietermartizburg. After a morning service in the Anglican cathedral the five hundred guests retired to Alice's aunt and uncle's magnificent garden on the outskirts of the town.

By mid-afternoon Charles and Alice had changed and said their farewells to family and friends. Two horses were waiting in the backyard, loaded up as if for a long journey.

"Where are they going?" asked one guest. Normally, newly married couples would remain at the wedding party and then retire either to the local hotel or a nearby farm.

"Some crazy idea of Alice's to honeymoon in the Drakensberg," said Meg Cuthbertson. "Tom and I have been told to stay away from the farm for a week."

After much teasing, the happy couple clattered out of the yard and headed for the mountains. Charles was somewhat nonplussed by the arrangements but he went along with Alice's wishes.

"Our first child will be conceived in the 'Berg next to our special pool," explained Alice. "So after the wedding we will ride up to the farm and into the mountains."

"That will take three days," protested Charles.

"Yes," said Alice. "I have arranged for us to be accommodated, separately," she looked coyly at Charles, "in various kraals along the way."

"What about our wedding night?"

Alice smiled: "Just trust me; it will be worth the wait."

"It's still freezing cold up there, even at the end of September," Charles observed.

"Yes," said Alice.

Charles didn't really mind. He found this woman fascinating and would have done almost anything to please her.

They made good time and each night for three nights they stopped in a Zulu kraal. Alice was whisked away by the women, all shrieking with excitement, and Charles was left drinking beer with the men.

Alice knew of a short way to the pool in the mountains and by mid-morning on the fourth day they arrived at the pool. Charles was surprised to see that a solid looking mountain hut, made of logs with a thatched roof, had been built.

"I see you have planned all this," he said.

"Oh, yes," said Alice knowingly.

They tended the horses and tethered them and took their equipment into the hut. The furnishings were simple. There was a large double bed, made up with clean, crisp sheets and thick blankets.

"Ah," said Alice. "They've left all the food as I asked."

Charles then led her down to the pool. He made her sit on the bank where he removed her shoes and washed and dried her feet. It was warm in the soft, spring sunlight. He removed her shirt and riding breeches and then took off all his own clothes. He then picked Alice up and waded into the deep water where, despite the cold, they soaped and washed each other all over. Charles then gently led Alice out of the water and they dried each other off.

"Come, now," said Alice. They were both ready and within a few short minutes Alice cried out. Almost immediately Charles flooded her with passion.

For the next three days they swam in the icy water, made love and ate. Charles shot a small buck so they would have meat. They were alone, quite alone with the beauty of the Drakensberg: the snow covered peaks towering above them and the calm, quiet tranquillity of their own pool.

After three days of bliss they packed up and went back to the farm. Charles had arranged for two wagonloads of equipment in Pietermaritzburg, and he and Alice joined the little convoy supervised by Mapitha halfway between Pietermartizburg and the Tugela.

"The *induna* has given us plenty of land," said Mapitha enthusiastically. Charles knew this. He and Mapitha had visited the *induna* who had been generous with his help.

"My wives and cattle are already there," continued Mapitha.

"Wives?" asked Charles.

"I have two wives already," said Mapitha.

"How are we going to convert these people to Christianity if they already have more than one wife?" Charles asked Alice later.

"Flexibility and patience," said Alice. "These people have practiced polygamy for hundreds, perhaps thousands of years. You cannot and will not change them overnight."

"The Church doesn't like it," said Charles uneasily.

"Then to hell with the Church," said Alice.

Charles looked up sharply.

"How often will the Archdeacon or bishop visit us?" asked Alice.

"Hardly ever," said Charles. "It's too far."

"Then don't worry about it," said Alice. "As for me, anyway, I'm more interested in providing the Zulu with practical help. I hope it's not too late."

"What do you mean?" asked Charles.

"Well, that so called 'White father of the Zulus', Shepstone, seems a bit gung-ho to me. I think he wants to disarm the Zulus. He talked to me about being pleased that locally born people were to start the mission and I quote: 'You understand the native and his place in the scheme of things here.' I didn't disabuse him. He thinks that we are here to help keep the Zulus in their place."

A week later they arrived at the place designated for the mission. It was rather a desolate place. Although there was a strong stream running through the area, there were virtually no trees and the wind blew dust devils across the bare patches of parched ground. The wispy, brown grass thirsted for rain.

Mapitha had built two huts for himself and his wives and children, and a bit further away a larger beehive hut for the newlyweds.

Charles and Alice looked about them. They were young and strong. They knew the task ahead was what they had been put on this earth for.

◇◇◇◇◇◇◇◇◇◇◇◇◇◇◇◇

Chapter 19

St. Augustine's mission was established on the banks of a tributary of the Buffalo River in October 1876.

Charles and Alice, far from being despondent or in any way intimidated by the desolation and the enormity of the task they had undertaken, worked all the hours that God made to establish the mission.

Within days of arrival Charles, accompanied by Mapitha, rode around the district visiting the local *indunas* and headmen. Both Charles and Alice knew that support or at least neutrality from the local population was vital to their success. They knew that whilst they had gone to St. Augustine's with the genuine desire to help the Zulus in every possible way, the Zulus had not asked them to come, and few if any of them thought that they needed help from anyone. In general, the white incursions over the previous forty years had been very threatening to the Zulu nation, who felt hemmed in. Added to this the Zulu had a strong, disciplined society and forty thousand fit, well trained and disciplined young men, all itching for a fight. Despite the white incursions, the Zulu felt secure in their own traditions and did not have any concept of the need for the white man's God or the white man's teaching.

Many of the Zulu had heard that the white man's medicine was more powerful than their own and were intrigued by this. They were dependant on their local herbal remedies and the local *sangoma*, of whom they were often frightened. The witchdoctors had enormous power because of their reputation for "smelling out" witches. The penalty for being "smelt out" was instantaneous death either by way of a spear through the heart or by having their neck broken.

Charles and Alice, having been brought up around the Zulus, were aware of their very strong culture and despite the apparent savagery, had a genuine admiration for the disciplined society that the culture produced. In no way did they feel that their own activities would weaken Zulu society; if anything they felt that they could build on the inherent strengths they saw.

All the local *indunas* received Charles and Mapitha politely, even if they were somewhat sceptical of their activities. They had, after all, been at the meeting with the King when the establishment of the mission had been agreed to. The consensus was one of "wait and see." They welcomed the white man's medicine, mainly because it would help to keep the witchdoctors in line by reducing their power; they could not see the value of education unless it helped them counter the depredations of the white man; and as for the white man's God, it would take much to persuade them to abandon the worship of their own ancestors, whom they relied on to protect them from misfortunes such as drought, locusts, rinderpest (disease in cattle), snakebite, disease, infertility, barren wives and much else.

At one meeting with a local *induna*, Charles realised what an uphill task he had when the conversation came around to education. Charles had started extolling the virtues of being able to read and write. The *induna* tried to relate this to his personal situation.

"When a lion comes to attack, how will this reading help a man?" he asked.

"Well, it won't help, not directly," said Charles.

"And if a cow is sick, how will this reading help make it better?" he asked again.

"Well, if the person reads the right books this can help sometimes," said Charles lamely.

"You have these books here?" asked the *induna*.

"Not yet," said Charles. He only had the Bible, and the Shakesspeare and Dickens given him by Archdeacon Green.

"These books about cattle," asked the *induna* shrewdly, "do they deal in diseases in Zulu cattle?"

"Maybe; some of the diseases in cattle in England are the same as here, some different."

The *induna* grunted, and then chuckled.

"You will have to bring the person who writes these books on cattle to come to Zululand; we can tell him about the diseases here; he can then write it down, then you must teach us to read, so we can read what we have just told you and this man who writes books. Is this the value of reading?"

Mapitha, feeling embarrassed and feeling that the *induna* had made good points, looked at Charles in expectation of something profound, but with this type of logic Charles was rather stumped.

"The value of reading is that people can write down their knowledge and stories so that other people can read it even in other countries," he answered.

"Is it written in Zulu?" asked the *induna*.

"Not yet," said Charles. "There is very little written in Zulu."

"So the Zulu will have to learn the white man's language to be able to read," said the *induna*.

"Yes, that would be the most useful thing," said Charles.

The *induna* sat thoughtfully for a moment and then brightened up and asked, "Firesticks, do they have books about making firesticks?"

"Yes, I suppose so," said Charles. "But I don't have any books about making firesticks."

The *induna* ignored him.

"We can learn to read, find out how to make firesticks and then chase the white men into the sea," said the *induna* enthusiastically. Before Charles could respond he said, "Do they have books about making big firesticks like *Somseu* used at the coronation of Cetswayo?"

"Yes, I suppose so, but it's not as simple as that," said Charles lamely. "Look, I can teach your people to read but I am a man of peace, so I cannot and will not teach you anything about fighting and war."

The *induna* had by now caught a glimmer of the value of education. As far as he was concerned the white incursion was a real threat to his existence and he saw this was one way in which the Zulu could at least be on level terms.

"*Umfundisi*," said the *induna* graciously, "you teach the Zulu to read and we will do the rest. Will you teach this Mapitha, Mapitha of the Ndwandwes, to read?"

"Yes, of course, if he wants to," said Charles. In truth neither Charles nor Mapitha had seen Mapitha as a potential pupil; their focus had all along been on the children. Mapitha then became Charles Lawrence's first pupil.

On his frequent trips on horseback round the local countryside, Charles had noticed outcrops of granite. He examined several sites and found one in particular, not all that far from St. Augustines, that he thought he could quarry. After an approach to the local *induna*, who saw no value in the outcrop of rock anyway, he arranged for a stone cutter to come from his father's farm and within a few weeks there was a growing pile of grey, nine by nine inch granite blocks, which Mapitha gradually and laboriously moved to the mission in the ox cart.

Alice inevitably had first call on the prize stones. She vetoed Charles' plan to build a house and then a church.

"No," she insisted. "The clinic will come first, then the schoolroom; after that you can choose between the house and the church," she said to Charles. "As we have always agreed those are the priorities. Anyway, you can always hold church services outside or in the schoolroom if it's raining."

"I'm sure that the Bishop would like a church," said Charles defensively.

"The Bishop will get his church," said Alice. "He's just going to have to wait."

Within weeks of arriving at St. Augustine's, Alice had set up her clinic. It soon became very popular with the local Zulus, and every morning there was a long queue outside the little grass hut that in the early days was the only facility she had. Most of the ailments were simple to treat: cuts, spear wounds, colds and so on. She trained Mapitha's wives, Bibi and Mbweli, as assistants. As far as Alice was concerned cleanliness was the most critical thing, so she had her assistants keep everything spotless. All her instruments were boiled every day and all of them washed their hands with soap and water between each patient. None of this was easy; the water had to be carried from the nearby stream and was then boiled on an open fire outside the clinic. During her years in the Drakensberg, Alice had adapted many of the plant and herbal remedies known to the local population. Now she tried to write down all her knowledge, and she added to that with the different vegetation in the drier climate they were now living in. She tried her best to avoid conflict with the *isangoma* but over time this became impossible. Whilst many of them had a copious knowledge of herbal remedies, their approach to cleanliness was primitive and they always tried to maintain a sense of fear and mystery in their dealings with the ordinary Zulu. This aspect alone drove many people to the clinic. Also from time to time Alice had to deal with mistakes made by the witchdoctor fraternity, which increased her reputation with the Zulu and further alienated the *isangoma*.

The honeymoon arrangements made by Alice had virtually ensured that Alice was pregnant with their first child. As this began to show, Alice used this to get people to come to the clinic, which after a few months was housed in a brand new stone building with a thatched roof built by Mapitha and some local recruits supervised by Charles. Some of the local communities expected Alice to visit them, which meant a great deal of time, wasted on travel and less time for actual medical work. She was often called on to attend Zulu women in their confinements, which usually involved going to the village in question. For nearby villages she sent either Bibi or Mbweli ahead and followed on horseback with her limited equipment. Often calls for help were late and well into the birth process, which required Alice to gallop off to distant villages, usually accompanied by Charles or Mapitha.

One night when she was six months pregnant, she heard an urgent tap on the door well after midnight. It was raining heavily.

"*Nkosikasi, Nkosikasi*" came the urgent voice. "My *umfazi* is having trouble with her birthing." Charles lit the paraffin lamp and without a word went out into the storm. With some difficulty he caught two of their horses and saddled them up ready to ride.

"How far?" Charles asked the young man who sat nervously in the clinic waiting for Charles and Alice.

He shrugged. "It took me two hours to get here."

"That will mean at least four hours since they decided to call before we get there," said Alice almost to herself. "How long since the baby started to come?" she asked.

He shrugged nervously again. "Some time in the morning," was the answer.

"We'd better hustle, then," said Alice.

They set off into the pitch black with rain teeming down and the Zulu jogging ahead, dressed in nothing but his loincloth and carrying his spear. The going was very slippery in the rain and on a number of occasions both Alice's and Charles' horses slipped and had trouble keeping their footing. Charles in particular became very nervous worrying about his wife's condition and what would happen to the baby she was carrying if her horse actually fell and threw her from the saddle. The journey took almost two and a half hours. Alice and Charles were bustled into one of the neat beehive huts in the village. The hut was full of women, all there to witness the drama, and there was a fire blazing in the middle of it filling the place with smoke. Alice quickly sized up the situation and chased most of the spectators out, including the local *sangoma*, who was furious at Alice's intrusion. She made one of the older women boil water and while Charles was bringing in her instruments and medicines, went to examine the patient. The woman was sweating profusely and looked quite exhausted. Alice gave her a drink of water.

"Looks like the baby might have its umbilical cord wrapped around its neck," she said to Charles. "So we'll have to be ready and quick."

Alice spoke quietly in Zulu to the woman. "Push hard," she said.

With almost a final effort the woman pushed, and with some help from the forceps Alice delivered the baby.

"Quick, scalpel," she said to Charles. With a quick snip she cut the cord and unwrapped it from the baby's neck. Seconds later, the lusty yell from the new baby announced to those standing in the drizzle outside the hut that he had arrived.

Alice with Charles' assistance spent the next forty minutes, by the light of the fire, tidying up and making sure the woman and her baby were as comfortable as possible. The relief on the woman's face was palpable and she beamed as Alice took her leave.

"*Siabonga gakulu Nkosikasi* (thankyou very much, lady chief)," she whispered shyly.

"Come to the clinic at St. Augustine's in two weeks," said Alice kindly as they left the hut.

"I don't suppose she will," she said to Charles in English. That's part of the problem; I don't see them often enough."

By this time the whole village had come out to welcome them and after offering them a meal of *putu* and *amaas*, people started to approach Alice with various ailments. So Alice conducted a clinic with Charles assisting, and it was mid-morning before they were able to saddle their horses and head back to St. Augustine's. As they left, Charles noticed the *sangoma* skulking in the background with a very dark, angry look on her face. "Trouble," he thought to himself but he kept his own counsel.

On the way home as they happily chatted Charles said, "I think you should go to 'Maritzburg in a few weeks for your confinement. I'll arrange a wagon to take us."

Alice stood up in her stirrups with her now large belly sticking out in front of her.

"Maritzburg!" she said incredulously. "Charles Lawrence, I'll do no such thing. I'll pop the baby out at St. Augustine's like any Zulu, thank you very much."

"What about a doctor? What happens if anything goes wrong?" asked Charles.

"The chances of anything going wrong are very low and I'll do the same as the thousands of Zulu women around us," she paused, "take my chances."

"Who is going to attend you at the birth?" asked Charles. Nothing would now surprise him about this woman.

"Why you, Bibi and Mbweli, you're all reasonably well experienced," she answered.

"Me?" said Charles.

"Yes, you, you've attended many Zulu women now; it will be no different with me," said Alice smiling. "Anyway I don't have time to spend six months wasting time in 'Maritzburg. There's so much to do here."

Charles tried to protest but they by this time they had arrived at the developing mission, and after a quick lunch Alice went to attend the long line-up at the clinic.

A few weeks later they were called to the same village again. This time Alice sent Mbweli ahead to boil water and clean up, but when Alice arrived an hour or so later, she found that there was little she could do. Both the baby and the mother died. Alice spent time with her other patients and then she and Mbweli set off home from a very subdued village. To her consternation, Alice had seen the *sangoma* in the background with a smirk on her face.

The incident had almost been put out of her mind when a few weeks later Alice, now eight and a half months pregnant, was busy in the clinic on a cool, windy winter's day. She heard a disturbance outside. One glance told her it was major trouble, so she grabbed the rifle that Charles insisted she kept in the clinic, levered a round into the breech and went outside. Charles was away with Mapitha and would only be back in the evening.

The *sangoma* from the village where the woman and baby had died was about fifty yards from the clinic, backed up by an *impi* of ten young men, including, much to Alice's horror and surprise, the husband of the woman and baby she had saved. The *sangoma* looked her most fearsome; she was dressed in many skins and had a monkey skin mask over her face. She had innumerable gourds and pouches that rattled ominously as she moved. The *impi* were dressed for war, with their heavy buffalo hide shields, their *ixwa* and decorative headrings made of monkey skins. Alice guessed that they had been hyped up by the *sangoma* and would be very dangerous if they got out of control.

The crowd, waiting for the clinic had scattered, and were nervously peering out from behind the mission buildings, waiting to see what developed.

The sangoma yelled, "*Tokolosh*," and pointed accusingly at Mbweli, who withdrew, terrified, into the clinic building. She knew that those accused of witchcraft by a *sangoma* would be put to death immediately, without any kind of trial.

Alice was not intimidated or in the least bit frightened. She could see what the tactics of the *sangoma* were; instead of directly accusing Alice of witchcraft, which would have unknown consequences, as it was unlikely that the Zulu would kill a white person accused of being a witch, she had decided to undermine the clinic and in fact the whole mission by accusing Mbweli of the crime. Alice could see that if the charge were made to stick and if Mbweli were killed as a result, they would not be able to stay, since they would not be able to get the local Zulus to come and work at the mission. The future of the mission depended on how she handled this.

The *sangoma* yelled accusingly, "That *tokolosh* Mbweli killed the woman and child with her witchcraft; she must die."

Alice said quite steadily in Zulu, "You were there at the village, I saw you. You are a very weak *sangoma* not be able to prevent this young wife from causing mischief." There was a murmur of approval in the crowd and looks of uncertainly came over the faces of the *impi*.

Alice went on, "You are the cause of the trouble in your village; it looks as if your witchcraft is having a bad effect on that village. Mbweli is not a witch. Did I not come to your village a few moons ago and save the life of a mother and her child? The husband of that mother is there." She pointed accusingly at the now very nervous warrior.

Alice had clicked off the safety catch of the rifle and was moving forward; the *sangoma* and her entourage were now shuffling nervously backwards.

"You want trouble?" Alice went on, "Then I will give it to you." She raised the rifle and fired a shot over their heads.

The *impi* started to move away, but the *sangoma*, feeling that she was about to be made a fool of yelled, "See, their firesticks will not hurt you, my magic is stronger than the *abelungu* firesticks."

Alice was momentarily thrown by this development. She then drew a line in the red earth just in front of the *sangoma*.

"*Sangoma*, if you or any of your *impi* crosses that line, I promise that I will shoot you," she said.

Mbweli and the witchcraft had now been comfortably forgotten; the deadly contest was between the white missionary and the traditional witchdoctor. Alice withdrew about twenty yards towards the clinic.

If the *sangoma* failed to cross the line, Alice would have won in the eyes of all present and this message would reverberate throughout Zululand, and if the *sangoma* crossed the line, Alice would shoot her; she had no choice.

The *sangoma* danced up and down, up and down, looking for an opportunity but never crossing the line. The *impi* looked on impassively. The longer the *sangoma* waited the less credibility she had. She continued to yell incantations and then, when Alice's attention was distracted for a split second, she launched herself across the fifty yards that separated them. Alice saw the movement from the corner of her eye; she whipped round, took careful aim and fired. With a shriek the *sangoma* collapsed in a pile of calabashes, gourds and skins, blood pouring from a wound in her right thigh. Alice fired three more shots over the heads of the *impi* who, after a short moment's hesitation, scattered and ran for their lives. Alice walked up to the *sangoma*, rifle poised.

"No, no, don't shoot, please, please," she yelled in Zulu. All sense of dignity had left her.

"I can fix your wound, but you must promise not to accuse anyone here of witchcraft again," said Alice.

The *sangoma* was writhing in agony on the ground, with blood pouring from the wound.

"I promise, I promise, no more witchcraft," she yelled.

Then to the amazement of the crowd, Alice stepped back into the clinic and together with Bibi and Mbweli lifted the now semi-conscious *sangoma* onto the operating table in the clinic. Within minutes all the monkey skins, gourds, and calabashes were dumped outside, with a curt instruction to burn them.

Alice looked down on a very nervous, small, non-threatening, middle-aged woman. She got to work.

"Bullet went right through, but I think it's broken the bone," said Alice.

They cleaned the wound and set the bone with splints ready for the purpose. Alice was completely matter of fact. "She will have to stay here for at least three weeks and then we can see about getting her back to her village," she said.

The Zulu were all amazed at Alice's charity. In their society the *sangoma* would have expected another bullet to the head; she would have been shown absolutely no mercy.

Charles was concerned and incensed when he and Mapitha returned later, and he was all for going to the village and rounding up the *impi* that had accompanied the *sangoma*. Alice dissuaded him, saying, "I think they have been totally scared off. Besides, what are you going to do with them when you have rounded them up?"

Apart from fixing her wound, Alice was determined to try to make the *sangoma* into an ally. Alice knew that much of the herbal medicine practiced by the Zulu was sound and she was determined to learn as much of that information as the *sangoma* knew. So, over the next three weeks Alice pumped her for information about local herbal remedies, which she eagerly wrote down. In turn, she impressed upon the *sangoma* the need for cleanliness and gave her a few tips on how to treat minor injuries. When the *sangoma* returned to her village it was as a firm friend and ally. After that Alice and Charles had very little trouble from the *isangoma* fraternity or any of the other Zulus and the reputation of the *Umfundisi* as Charles was known and the *Nkosikasi Dokotela* as Alice was known spread far beyond the confines of the domain of the *induna* at Nqutu.

Mapitha became Charles' first pupil in the newly completed schoolroom. Understandably Mapitha did not want to be an adult pupil among children half his age or less. Charles had decided that if he could get Mapitha to a certain standard of education, Mapitha could act as his assistant. Charles thought Mapitha would need at least a year of extensive tutoring before he would be ready for a wider role. He also felt he himself needed some experience as a teacher to make sure he had sufficient skills to control a roomful of children.

They still had the house to build and of course the church, so apart from Sundays Charles and Mapitha worked from sunrise to midday on building a house for Charles and Alice and the soon to be born child, and after that Charles spent most of the rest of the day tutoring Mapitha.

Charles regretted somewhat that he hadn't built the house first and then the schoolroom, especially now that the child was almost due, but Alice was quite happy with the arrangements so he didn't worry.

Whilst he was in Kimberley Mapitha had learnt to read a little and he did speak reasonable English, so progress was rapid. Also in Kimberley, Mapitha had been exposed to simple arithmetic, and when Charles was able to relate it to everyday things like cattle Mapitha had no trouble. Charles also decided to make Mapitha and then his family his first Christian converts. He went around the local villages every Sunday preaching; although people showed interest, especially if the local *induna* was there it did not develop into much. His conversation and relationship with Mapitha gave him a great deal of insight into what the Zulu felt about Christianity.

The working arrangements at St. Augustine's were generally quite flexible. Charles was able to pay Mapitha a small wage, but the important thing for Mapitha was that he had plenty of land for his cattle and land on which his wives could grow crops. Every few weeks Mapitha would disappear for a week or more. Charles wasn't sure what he went for, but it seemed he went back to his regiment and trained with them during this period. Mapitha was always evasive about this. After one of these absences, Mapitha asked for a week off to build another hut.

"Why do you need another hut?" asked Charles. "You have one for each wife and another for yourself already?"

"My brother, he was killed on a cattle raiding party against those stinking Swazis," said Mapitha.

"Yes, I'm very sorry, but what does that have to do with you?" asked Charles.

"His wife and two children are now my wife and children," answered Mapitha.

"Oh, why doesn't their village look after them?" said Charles. As a Christian he was having trouble with Mapitha having two wives, let alone three.

"The village cannot look after them, it is my duty." Mapitha was becoming impatient.

"As a Christian it is your duty to have only one wife," said Charles defiantly.

"*Umfundisi*," said Mapitha, "do these Christians want my brother's wife to be eaten by lions and hyaenas, because this is what will happen if she does not come here. If I do not look after her she will be thrown out into the veld and made to look after herself."

"She can come here," responded Charles, "but does she have to be your wife?"

"If she is not my wife, then every young *ibutho* will be sniffing round her like a pack of dogs," said Mapitha. "If she is my wife, the only thing they will sniff will be the point of my spear."

Charles sighed; he knew that what Mapitha described was common practice and that it was part of their social security system, ensuring that widows created by raiding parties among other things, were cared for. His main worry was the church authorities, who had no understanding of Zulu society and expected the Christian ethic of one man, one wife to prevail regardless of the consequences.

"Well, they will clear her off into the bush, where she and her children will fall prey to the wild animals," said Alice when he raised it with her.

"That's what Mapitha said," said Charles.

"Also," said Alice, "we don't want young, unattached widows around; they will end up being subject to the attentions of all the young bloods in the district."

"That's also what Mapitha said; have you two been talking?"

"No, but I was aware she was coming; the others are looking forward to having her here, someone to share the chores," said Alice.

"And they don't mind sharing Mapitha, you know, sexually?" asked Charles.

"No, at least they know where he is when he spends the night there. Besides they get tired of being constantly pregnant, I expect," said Alice.

"How do we reconcile all this with Christian faith?" asked Charles.

"Flexibility and tolerance are supposed Christian virtues; it shouldn't be difficult even for the Church to reconcile itself with that—apart from the fact that in this instance we are saving a woman and her two children from almost certain death," answered Alice.

"Her name is Monase," said Charles.

"Yes," said Alice.

Charles was listened to in most of the villages round about, but it frustrated him that he couldn't attract any kind of an audience to his Sunday service at St. Augustine's. Apart from Mapitha and his wives and Alice of course, the only other regular churchgoer was the idiot son of one of the local *indunas*, who had sent him along in desperation.

Charles had started to explain to Mapitha, mainly by drawing lines in the earth, his planned dimensions for the church building. Mapitha was astounded.

"This big building, church you call it, who will come here?" he asked.

"All the Zulus will come when we have a big church," answered Charles.

"But, *umfundisi*, you only have one proper Christian apart from the mission people and he is soft in the head." Mapitha then started to laugh. He knew it was disrespectful but he couldn't help himself, he laughed so much that he fell down in the dust. Charles, slightly piqued, toed him lightly with his boot.

"Get up you silly ass," he said, "come on, we've got work to do."

Mapitha immediately sobered up. He thought he had been paid a terrible insult and went away without looking at Charles to sulk in his hut.

The King had ordered Mapitha to stay at the mission, so he couldn't leave without Cetswayo's permission, but he was determined to make Charles pay for what he perceived was a grievous insult. Charles explained his predicament to Alice, who said the best thing was to bide his time. After two days Mapitha came to see Alice, looking suitably mournful and hurt. After a brief greeting she said, "What's the matter Mapitha, are you sick?"

"No, *Nkosikasi*, but the *Umfundisi* has insulted me badly and I think I must go to the King and ask to be sent back home," he responded.

"Well, what did he say to you?" asked Alice.

"No, no, it is too bad for the *Nkosikasi's* ears, too bad, I cannot say it," was the response.

"Well, I can't do anything unless you tell me," said Alice.

This conversation went on for a full five minutes before Mapitha reluctantly said, "He called me a silly-ass; this is such a big bad word." He looked at Alice expecting her to be totally shocked. Instead Alice just burst into peals of laughter. Mapitha started to look uncomfortable. Wiping away her tears Alice said, "Mapitha, this is not an insult at all, it's something you would say to your best friend or a child who had done something slightly naughty, but it is not at all insulting and you should take no notice of it."

Doubtfully Mapitha listened and then walked off. He kept away for another day and then, much Charles' relief, came back to work the following day as if nothing had happened.

The school lessons progressed and subtly Charles introduced the concept of Christianity into them. Often he was taken aback by some of the discussion emanating from the lessons.

"Your *Nkulunkulu*," said Mapitha one day, "the one who wants the big church here in Zululand."

"Yes," said Charles hesitantly. He was about to argue about God wanting the church but thought the better of it. Instead he listened.

"This *Nkulunkulu*, he loves all the people in the world the very same, the same as each other."

"Yes," said Charles. "In the eyes of God all people are the same and equal."

"Is this the year of our Lord one thousand eight hundred and seventy seven?" asked Mapitha.

"Yes," Charles wondered what was coming.

"And in the land of the *amaNgisi* how long have they had big churches so the *Nkulunkulu* will come to protect them?" asked Mapitha.

"Well, the Romans first brought Christianity to England about sixteen or seventeen hundred years ago." Charles was not entirely certain of his dates but he thought this was about right.

Mapitha looked at Charles quizzically.

"If this *Nkulunkulu* thinks everyone is equal in the whole wide world," Mapitha stood up and waved his arms about expansively, "why did it take him one thousand eight hundred and seventy seven years from the time he sent his son to this earth to find the Zulu people. The Zulu people must have offended him very badly."

Looking nonplussed, Charles tried to respond.

"God works in his own way," said Charles, "he may have decided that the Zulu were not ready to receive him until now."

"The *Nkulunkulu*, did he also decide to send the *abelungu* with their firesticks and their red coats at the same time?" asked Mapitha. "The Zulu had never seen these people before either."

"No," said Charles. "God has nothing to with guns and the army; that is another matter."

"But this *Somseu*, he believes in your God," said Mapitha more as a statement than a question.

"Yes, he does," said Charles, then he added, "almost all the white people who have come here are Christians of one sort or another." A statement he regretted making as soon as it was out of his mouth.

"Your *Nkulunkulu* is for white people only; the Zulu should be left alone and their ancestors will look after them as they always have done. For the Zulu the red coats, the firesticks and the *Nkulunkulu* all come from the same place, and they only want one thing and that is to destroy the power of the Zulu people," Mapitha said sadly. "I have seen your *Somseu*, he is like a cobra waiting to strike; he wants to kill our King and make slaves of all the Zulu people. You, *Umfundisi*, and the *Nkosikasi*, I can see are friends of the Zulu and are trying to help us, but *Somseu* and his red coat soldiers, they are just using you. Your influence will weaken the Zulu because they can see that you are good people and not our enemy but this will not change what *Somseu* and the *abelungu* want. The *abelungu* want our land for themselves and they will send their red coat soldiers to get it."

Charles tried to protest. Mapitha took off his shirt.

"You see this?" said Mapitha pointing to his scarred back. Charles was of course aware of Mapitha's sojourn in Kimberley and the beating he had had at the hands of the authorities.

"This beating was from a bunch of thieving, cheating white men. They were supposed to be the police and an *imanthsi* and they tried to steal what was rightfully ours and then they beat us. Those people were in Kimberley to protect all the people but it seems they did not include black people in that. All they wanted from us was the strength of our backs and our limbs. They wanted all the riches for themselves."

Charles tried to interrupt. Mapitha held up his hand and continued, "It will be the same here; a few white people like you, *Umfundisi*, will try to help us, but this will only weaken and divide us, and then the others who only look on us for the riches we have will come and take everything. You wait and see, the Zulu will fight the British soon and the British will try to take all our power and all our land. We should really kill you and the *Nkosikasi* and all the other white people, right now, otherwise we will be slaves forever."

Mapitha looked off into the distance.

"Maybe it is too late. I cannot kill you or the *Nkosikasi*; I have already become too weak. The Zulu people will be destroyed, but we will fight first."

Charles was taken aback by this outburst but before he could respond, Bibi ran over to the schoolroom and excitedly told Charles and Mapitha, "*Umfundisi*, come quick, the *Nkosikasi*, her baby is coming."

Mapitha looked up and grinned.

"It is my job to keep the water hot."

Charles knew what to do but was exceedingly nervous.

Alice was lying in their bed calmly giving instructions. Charles rushed over to her but she was quite matter of fact.

"Make sure there is plenty of hot water. You, Charles, will cut the umbilical cord. Make sure the child takes a good deep breath as soon as he is born." And so on. Two hours later, with almost no fuss, Rupert Francis Lawrence was born, and he announced himself with as lusty a yell as anyone could imagine. Charles and the two women cleaned up while Alice uncharacteristically lay silent, nursing her child.

Mapitha grinned widely when Charles emerged from the hut that was still Charles and Alice's home.

"The *Umfundisi* has a big strong boy," said Mapitha. "May he be blessed with strong limbs and good health."

"Thank you," said Charles. They then shared a gourd of the best *utshwala*, brewed of course by Mapitha's wives.

Life at the mission returned quite quickly to normal. Alice was up and about within two days and although she spent time with Rupert, she continued to run the ever-popular clinic as usual. The baby was placed in a cot in the corner and attended to whenever he needed it. If the baby needed feeding, she sent the men out of the clinic but allowed women and children to wander in and out at will. The Zulus appreciated this attitude, that she was really one of them and did not put herself and her family on a pedestal.

The house that Charles and Mapitha were building continued to make progress and Mapitha's lessons continued in the afternoons.

Six months after Rupert was born, the house was complete and the family moved in. It was a mansion compared to the hut they had lived in over the past fifteen months, but by any other standards it was modest indeed, with three small bedrooms, a bathroom and a lounge/dining room. The toilet, as before, was a long drop seventy yards away. Charles and Alice's families brought a few items of furniture when they came to visit, and over time their house became a comfortable home.

There had been regular communication with the Bishop in Pietermaritz-burg since the mission had started, but now that the stone home was complete with its pretty thatched roof and the little garden that Alice had started, Charles thought it was time for the Bishop to visit. Alice shrugged when she was told of this plan. Neither Charles nor Alice had any time to deal with the schism in the Church at that time when the 'old ' Bishop, Colenso, had been excommunicated, although somehow he retained the right to preach in the Cathedral, and although the Bishop of 'Maritzburg's situation was made more difficult by the conflict, he continued to support the fledgling mission. Charles had some sympathy with Colenso because of his unrelenting support and understanding of the Zulu, but he did not allow that to interfere with his work. They were little troubled by the Church hierarchy anyway and thought that if the Church was unable to heal its own rifts, what chance was there of resolving the approaching conflict between the British and the Zulu?

"I wouldn't encourage too many visits," was Alice's advice. "I wonder if he has any appreciation of what we are doing here to help the Zulus. My guess is that he will be concerned about the lack of converts and he will blame that on not having a church. I suspect that he will see the clinic and the schoolroom as peripheral issues and that his main objective will be to encourage Christian converts."

When the Bishop did arrive, hot and dusty after almost a week in the saddle from his base in Pietermaritzburg, he was quickly put in a good mood by the welcome given him by the Lawrences and by the hot bath. He was also very taken with Alice, her beauty and her charm.

After having been shown around the mission he immediately asked Charles, "Where's the church? With all this stone being cut I expected to see a church, or at least the start of one."

"Well we've started to dig the foundations; see here, it's all laid out but it will take some time to build," said Charles, showing the Bishop round the foundations which he and Mapitha had worked out and, together with some assistants, were now digging.

"Isn't this rather a large church?" asked the Bishop. "I had no idea you had so many converts."

Charles was not normally given to subterfuge but on this occasion his good relationship with the local *indunas* had enabled him to ask that they send as many people as they could to St. Augustine's for the Bishop's visit. In fact he had arranged for most of them to come to the mission for four Sundays in a row prior to the Bishop's visit so that they could practice hymns that Charles had translated into Zulu. Charles was aware that the Zulu loved nothing better than singing (apart from fighting, of course, but that only applied to the men) so by the fourth week he had more than five hundred people coming to practice the songs, and with the promise of a feast and a beer drink, by the time the Bishop arrived this number had swelled considerably. All Charles said was, "You will see on Sunday, we have few converts but many people will come and sing and listen to the sermon on Sunday."

The schoolroom was proudly shown off to the visitor, whose reaction was less than positive.

"Education? What will these people do with education? You are running the mission, Charles, but in my opinion it will give them ideas above their station," said the Bishop. "Anyway, I'm glad you only have one pupil."

Charles was flabbergasted. "But it's the only chance they have of uplifting themselves," he argued.

"Too soon, too soon," was the response. "It will be one hundred years before these savages are ready for education; we will have to teach them civilisation first."

"One hundred years?" said Charles incredulously.

"Don't you see, Charles, their development is far behind that of the white man, especially the British who really are the leading nation. Their brains will not cope with education. Anyway what are you teaching your man here?"

Charles thanked his lucky stars that they were out of earshot of Mapitha and indeed Alice. He was boiling over in rage with the intemperate words of the leader of his Church. He kept his counsel.

"Macbeth, he's reading Macbeth." It was the Bishop's turn to be astonished.

Charles called Mapitha over. "Mapitha, tell the Bishop what you have learned about Macbeth."

To the bishop's amazement Mapitha then in five minutes gave him a concise precis of the story."Macbeth, like Dingaan, was crazy for power," he concluded.

"Dingaan?"asked the Bishop.

"One of the Zulu Kings; he murdered his brother Shaka and succeeded him as King," answered Charles quietly. He was embarrassed that his boss obviously knew nothing and cared less about Zulu history. These were the people he so badly wanted to convert to Christianity, but he knew nothing of them, nothing at all.

"Comparing this Zulu King, whatever you call him," said the bishop angrily, "to Macbeth is ridiculous. How can a naked savage have any relevance to one of our most treasured stories, written by the best playwright of all time, English, of course. I forbid you to go on with this. Teach him something simpler. Does he know his multiplication tables for example?"

Charles asked Mapitha to recite some multiplication tables, which he did with ease.

"Astonishing," said the Bishop unenthusiastically.

Now that Mapitha had an audience he was determined to show off his knowledge.

"This Oliver Twist," he said to the Bishop.

"Yes," said the Bishop warily.

"This is very bad; these children, their mother and father are dead, you then lock them up and make them work and give them bad food," said Mapitha.

"Yes?" said the Bishop, wondering what was coming next.

"You are coming here to tell the Zulu about your *Nkulunkulu*; maybe it is better if you let the Zulu alone and fix the problems back in your own country before you come here again. The Zulu would never treat children like this."

The Bishop's eyes nearly stood out on stalks. To have what he saw as a semi-civilised savage criticising the soul of the Empire, Queen's Victoria's England, was beyond comprehension.

"Sheer impertinence," was all he could say. Charles thought he was about to have an apoplectic fit.

"Don't you realise," the Bishop eventually blurted out, "that we are here to grant you the benefits of the greatest civilisation that the world has ever seen."

Mapitha looked on impassively.

"And you have the impertinence in your absolute ignorance to criticise us. I will not have it. I simply will not have it," shouted the Bishop. He stormed out and went to his room in the cottage.

Mapitha watched with his eyebrows raised and then he said to Charles, "This one is like *Somseu*, he just wants to make the Zulu into slaves."

"Don't worry," said Charles, "nothing will happen. The lessons will continue."

Mapitha nodded.

The Bishop was pleased with the clinic, which he saw as being closer to his ideal of a mission, which was white people administering what he saw as the benefits of their civilisation to a bunch of ignorant savages.

He was also completely taken in and entranced by the turnout for the Sunday service, the songs in particular. Charles had explained that he had simplified the service somewhat so that the people didn't get restless. This fitted precisely with the Bishop's view of the simple savages he was dealing with. "Quite so, quite so," said the Bishop understandingly.

During one of the evening meals the subject of the large Zulu army came up.

"Shepstone is determined to make the Zulus disarm; having forty thousand warriors under the control of that King, what's his name?" said the Bishop.

"Cetswayo," added Charles.

"Yes, that's the fellow, well we can't tolerate that."

"Its part of the discipline, part of their culture," said Charles. "They have had a similar army for the past forty or fifty years with no trouble, that's especially true under this King and his predecessor Mpande."

"Mm, quite so, quite so, but don't you see this is a threat to the stability of Natal to have this black horde sitting on our doorstep, all thirsting for blood," said the Bishop.

"They're not thirsting for blood and have done the whites south of the Tugela no harm in generations. If they are attacked they will of course defend themselves," said Charles.

"And the savagery up here; there are many stories of girls being murdered because they won't accept husbands that have been selected for them. And

Rough Diamonds

there's no trial by a magistrate. If one of their headmen decide someone is guilty of something, punishment is meted out, often death. We can't accept that. It will have to change."

"Maybe it has nothing to do with us," said Alice quietly. "Shouldn't they be allowed to run their country as they see fit? If over time the colony of Natal is a demonstrably better place, maybe they will adapt some of its more forward thinking policies."

The Bishop was too taken with Alice to be rude.

"We don't have time. Shepstone is already building up an army in Natal. There will be a showdown sooner or later and I'm certain we will win. A bunch of half naked savages against the British army, it's laughable. The Zulus would be well advised to lay down their arms now. It will save a lot of trouble."

It was a great relief when the Bishop eventually left.

"Maybe we can keep him away for another couple of years," said Charles reflectively, "or even better, maybe he'll get promoted to New Zealand or somewhere out of harm's way."

Before departing the Bishop left Charles and Alice with his thoughts:

"Hurry up and build the church; you'll make permanent converts out of those people when you do. Keep the clinic going but please don't spend too much time on educating these people. It's wasted, their brains have not developed far enough to absorb higher education and it will be many generations before they have. And one more thing, as the superior race, keep your distance. My observation is that you are becoming too integrated with these people; they are still savages, you know. You need to keep yourselves a bit separate."

"Well, there is talk of a small Roman Catholic mission about ten miles west of here," said Charles helpfully. "It will only have one priest, but we could fraternise with him."

"No, no," said the Bishop hurriedly, "keep away from them, they're poison."

Not much more was said but the prospect of a British—Zulu war worried both Alice and Charles. They were also horrified by the attitude that emanated from the Bishop's visit.

"Almost makes you want to become a Catholic," said Alice. "Or something else. This man expects to come in here, ram his own philosophy unthinkingly down these people's throats and then expects them to be grateful. It's unbelievable."

Little changed at the mission. Mapitha and Charles and a gang of helpers gradually built the church. The clinic continued.

Mapitha's lessons proceeded and between them Charles and Mapitha recruited three six-year-old boys, for whom they started lessons. Generally the Zulu were sceptical about the need for education; as far as the children were concerned, it prevented them from doing the manly things expected of them as young Zulu boys, like helping their elder brothers herd cattle and practising stick fighting, which would help to determine their status in their teens. Neither Charles nor Mapitha considered girls worth educating. It was not even discussed, and Mapitha would not have stooped so low as to consider educating girls. Mapitha, though delighted with his own progress, worried about the effect that education would have on the Zulu population at large.

"What will these people do with this education?" he said to Charles one day.

"Can they become an *Umfundisi* like you and maybe teach young Zulus how to read and write?"

"Yes, I hope so," said Charles.

"Maybe they can teach young white boys too?" said Mapitha mischievously.

"I think the whites have enough of their own teachers," said Charles diplomatically.

"And if they can't become teachers or priests, what then?" asked Mapitha. "They will not be strong enough to join the *amabutho* since they will have been sitting indoors all the time. What can they do if they go to *Thekwini*?"

"Well," said Charles. "Maybe they can work in an office or a shop."

"Maybe all that will happen," said Mapitha, "is that they will learn some of the white man's ways and forget their own. They will wear white man's clothes and shoes, they will try to be like white men but the white men will laugh at them. If you white men came and tried to be a Zulu it would be the same; you can wear a *bheshu* like a Zulu, you can carry a spear, but you will never be a Zulu. Maybe this education will just confuse the children and make them feel stupid and inferior to the white children."

"That has not happened to you," said Charles.

"No, maybe there is some good, but I can see it will take many years before our people have the same education as the whites. I think *Somseu* will have his way; we will all become slaves." Mapitha walked sadly off into the distance.

◇◇◇◇◇◇◇◇◇◇◇◇◇◇◇

Chapter 20

Periodically Mapitha returned home to the Ndwandwe homeland north of the Mfolosi. Specifically, on instructions from the King, he was to help train and instruct the Ndwandwe *impi*. He was aware that gradually the Zulu nation were readying themselves for war and that all the clans were doing the same as he was doing. The one time that the King was present during a week of training he was really impressed by the Ndwandwe.

Mapitha had the three thousand Ndwandwe divided by age group into ten separate *ibutho*. During the two weeks that Mapitha was there they each had to run fifty miles through the bush without food, although they were made to carry water. They were then told to dance for an hour in front of the King. Mapitha had strewn thousands of three-pronged thorns on the ground where they danced. Not one of the warriors even flinched, although many had bleeding feet when they had completed the dance. They were made to lie quietly under their shields for hours at a time. Mapitha participated fully in all these exercises and was as fit as any of them. He showed them how to creep through the bush unseen and they spent many hours practising hand-to-hand fighting. He showed the few Ndwandwe how to use the firearms they had, much as Frank had shown him in Kimberley.

The King and his generals were impressed and said to Mapitha when they left:

"The Ndwandwe are among the best of the Zulu *impi*, surely no *amaNgisi* can match them."

Every three months Mapitha spent ten days or so with his Ndwandwe and by the end of 1878, they were fit and thirsting for a fight. He never told Charles where he went and what he was doing. He just made the excuse of reporting to the King.

From time to time he was witness to the training taking place among the other clans, and he was optimistic that the Zulu would hold their own against anyone. He had of course never seen a British soldier fight, and he could not imagine how they could fight if they wore the red coats he had seen them wear in Kimberley.

◇◇◇◇◇◇◇◇◇◇◇◇◇◇◇◇

Chapter 21

Towards the end of November 1878, The King summoned Mapitha to Kwa-Bulawayo.

"There is to be a big *indaba* with the *amaNgisi*," Mapitha told Charles. "I will return when I can." It was almost three months before he returned, and by then the whole world of the Zulus was in the process of being turned upside down by the British.

Sir Theophilus Shepstone had been determined for some time to take control of the Zulu state. He saw the overtly military stance of the Zulus as a threat to the developing colony of Natal. He and the other settlers were apprehensive about the strong Zulu army and Shepstone, the self-styled "White father of the Zulu nation," was frustrated by the fact that Cetswayo had bested him in every confrontation and had maintained the independence of the Zulu state, with its own laws and culture.

The settlers' fear had had little or no foundation. Zulu policy under Mpande, Cetswayo's father and predecessor, and under Cetswayo himself, was one of peace with both the Boer to the north and the British in the south. Cetswayo was distrustful of the Boer and urged the British to protect

Zulu territory from Boer depredations. There had been no notable clashes between the Zulu and the British since the foundation of the colony of Natal.

Shepstone had found an ally in the new Governor of the Cape, Sir Bartle Frere, a man who had spent most of his working life as a British colonial administrator in India and had no knowledge whatsoever of the problems in Africa before his arrival. Both Frere and Shepstone had determined that the Zulus would be disarmed and "civilised government" would be introduced. London, in the form of the colonial office, was not so enthusiastic, but they either turned a blind eye to what was going on or they were informed after the event.

Shepstone had in 1877 successfully negotiated the annexation of the Boer Republic of the Transvaal partly by telling the Boers that Cetswayo's *impis* were massed on the Transvaal border ready to attack. This was patently untrue, although Cetswayo had offered military assistance to the British in any confrontation with the Boers, which of course was declined.

By late 1878 Shepstone thought he had everything he needed in place to finally sort out the Zulu problem. He had 18,000 troops under Lord Chelmsford in Natal, trained and ready to fight; half were native levies and half English troops. The boundary commission determining the boundary between Zululand and the Transvaal was due to report.

There had for some time been distaste among the British settlers in Natal and the British administration of some of the more violent practices in the Kingdom of Zululand. One of these incidents was exactly the excuse that Shepstone and Frere required. Two wives of Sihayo, a chief whose territory was on the northern bank of the Tugela, had committed adultery and escaped into Natal with their lovers. One of Sihayo's sons pursued the wives, forcibly returned them to Zululand and put them to death. Cetswayo refused to send either Sihayo or his son to Natal to stand trial; claiming that the women were put to death in Zululand and according to Zulu law.

Cetswayo and his *indunas* were summoned to a meeting on 11th December1878, ostensibly to hear the findings of the boundary commission. The meeting was held on the Natal side near the mouth of the Tugela. Sir Theophilus Shepstone's younger brother John spent an hour reading the boundary commission's report, which was entirely in favour of the Zulus. There were sighs of relief on the Zulu side; perhaps everything would be all right after all.

"*Nkosi*," Mapitha whispered to Cetswayo, "This is only the beginning. The bad news will come now; I can see it in their eyes. The cobra is about to strike."

"These people are my friends," replied Cetswayo. "They do not want war, you will see."

"*Nkosi*, I hope you are right but from tonight every Zulu will be sharpening his spear," replied Mapitha quietly.

The British roasted an ox for the Zulu monarch and his entourage.

It took John Shepstone three hours to read the ultimatum, which amounted to nothing more nor less than a declaration of war by the British on the Zulu nation. In essence it gave the Zulus thirty days to disband their army and accept a British Resident (effectively, a governor), and twenty days to hand over Sihayo's son. There was also to be a fine of six hundred head of cattle.

The Zulu went straight from the meeting to gather up their *impis* and prepare them for the forthcoming confrontation.

Mapitha immediately went back to his beloved Ndwandwe *impi*. He did not question the inherent injustice of what was about to happen; in his dealings with the white invaders this was the sort of the thing that often happened. He was determined to defend his homeland to the utmost.

◇◇◇◇◇◇◇◇◇◇◇◇◇◇

Chapter 22

The Festival of the Fruits celebration at Kwa-Bulawayo that year was a sombre affair. Cetswayo had gathered his whole army of forty thousand men to the great kraal. Instead of the usual ceremonial finery of plumed headdresses and leopard skin loincloths the *amabutho* came ready for war: they each had their *ixwa*, and their six foot tall cowhide shield, and of course they wore their normal loincloths. Many of them had rifles; there were a few Mausers like Mapitha's but most of the others were Martini-Henry rifles favoured by the British.

After a few ceremonial dances Cetswayo addressed the throng, all of who were buzzing with excitement. The *amabutho* were trained to fight, but in the last twenty years or more none of them had seen any action apart from the odd cattle raid against the Swazis. Not one of them had ever fought against a white man.

Cetswayo told them, "I am sending you out to fight the white invaders, who have now, despite all their promises, sent their army against us. They will cross the Tugela in three weeks. You have enough men to "eat them up"; when you have defeated them you will stay on this side of the Tugela; you may not cross the great river."

Nobody was more surprised than Nzobo when he found himself on the march with the British army towards Zululand. To his eyes they were slow, with endless delays due to wagons breaking down and getting stuck. He could see that the cumbersome nature of the operation made them vulnerable. In contrast he knew that the Zulu army could travel fifty miles in a day and could come in, strike a blow and then disappear.

After they had crossed the Tugela at Rorke's Drift, Nzobo went to his officer and said, "Send me and the scouts out to find the Zulu *impis*. I know these people; they will be well hidden. I will be able to tell you where they are."

He received a very unsympathetic response. "Your job is to obey orders; I am sure we will have no trouble with that ragtag army of the Zulus. Within days they will be running for their lives all over Zululand."

He knew better than to argue.

"*Yebo, Nkosi*," was all he said. He thought of deserting there and then, but he had made a commitment so he stayed.

After the conference on the Tugela, Mapitha had returned to his Ndwandwe clan and had gathered up the three thousand Ndwandwe *amabutho*. He and his fellow commanders drilled them to perfection for three weeks. They then made their way to Kwa-Bulawayo for the Festival of the Fruits and the King's speech.

The Zulu army of twenty thousand made its way slowly towards the point of the British incursion. Cetswayo had kept the remaining twenty thousand in reserve. The leadership, which consisted of Ntshingwayo, Mavumengwana and Dabulamanzi, a full brother of the King, were probably not the best choice. Ntshingwayo was sixty-eight and one of the last links to the era of Shaka, the founder of the Zulu nation. Dabulamanzi was a hot head and his influence was later to prove a disaster. The best choice would have been Zibhebhu, but as leader of the rebellious Mabhuda clan his loyalty was questionable.

The Zulu army arrived in the vicinity of Isandlwana on the evening of January 21st. The bulk of the army moved north, leaving Mapitha and his Ndwandwes on the east.

The British were surprised that they had seen not a single sign of the Zulu army. They had been camped under the great rock at Isandlwana now for two days.

Nzobo went again to his officer.

"Yes, any more of your wonderful advice?" he was asked.

"*Nkosi*, I have a very bad feeling about this place; the Zulu are not so far away. If they came here," and he swept his arm across the landscape, now dotted with British soldiers and native levies, "we will all be killed. Please, *Nkosi*, I can smell the killing; we must pull the wagons together and build defences. The Zulu have forty thousand men."

The officer laughed as he took another sip of imported French wine and bit into a thick piece of beef.

"What did I tell you before, you black baboon?" he said harshly.

"You told me to obey orders," said Nzobo.

"Then, obey orders, you silly bugger, before I have you up on a charge. The commanding officer has told us that the Zulu have all run away, they are too scared to fight. This little picnic will take us three months. We'll capture that wretched Zulu King Cats-something and then we'll all go home; now fuck off."

"*Yebo, Nkosi*," said Nzobo sullenly and then under his breath, "The Zulu have not run away and you silly, white-faced baboon will find that out when the moon comes up again in two days." (Zulu preferred not to fight when the moon was in its "dead" period).

Zulu discipline was strictly maintained. There were no fires of any kind and a minimum of talking; only those giving orders were allowed to say anything. During the night they lay under their great shields and those who could, slept. Mapitha, having made sure his precious Ndwandwes had settled for the night, urged calm, making sure that they all had eaten something and drunk some of their water.

"Tomorrow is the day," he told them, "when you will wash your spears in the white man's blood, when you will chase them back across the Tugela. Be strong, be brave and be patient, your time will come."

He could feel the tension, the buzz of excitement and he knew the discipline would hold.

When he was certain that his own *impi* was settled, Mapitha went with one of his scouts to the top of the ridge. The great rock of Isandlwana stared starkly out of the moonless night sky and he could see hundreds of campfires scattered all over the plain in front of it. The Zulu did not fight at night, believing that the spirits of the dead would never escape if they died in the night. Mapitha shook his head, "If we went down there now, we would kill them all." He knew he would have to be patient and wait for the dawn.

The Zulu plan was based on the original plan of battle devised more than fifty years earlier by Shaka. They attacked in the form of a set of buffalo horns, with the bulk of the army in the centre (the boss) and with two horns spreading out to right and left to drive the enemy into the centre. The bulk of the army of twenty thousand had gone to the north and were hidden in the valleys and from there, another three to four thousand strong *impi* had been sent round to the west. Mapitha's Ndwandwes were the eastern horn of the great plan.

The British were frustrated that they had seen no sign of the Zulu and their main concern was that the Zulu army would escape north before they had had a chance to fight them. The idea that there might be twenty thousand Zulus hidden in the valleys within a few miles of the main British force was unthinkable and anyone who suggested that fortifications should be built was scoffed at. Chelmsford, the British commander, left at dawn with some mounted troops to examine reports that some of the enemy had been seen to the east. The rest of the British force stayed in camp, scattered all over the plain waiting for something to happen.

Mapitha was up before the dawn. He knew the main Zulu force would move just after the sun peeked over the eastern horizon. Mapitha and his scout went up to a vantage point and there, not more than three hundred yards away, was a column of British horse making its way purposefully to the east. He knew that it would be foolish to attack men on horseback and since this was clearly not the main British force, he skipped back to his men and made them lie down in the long grass. The troop passed not more than two hundred yards from three thousand watching Zulu, of whom they were totally unaware.

When Mapitha was certain that the horsemen were well out of the way he gave the signal and the three thousand Ndwandwes silently rose as one and crept forward to the brow of the hill. Not fifty yards away they saw a small outpost of the British force.

"Bayete!" yelled Mapitha and within minutes the small force had been eliminated and his Ndwandwes were streaming down the side of the hill towards the British lines.

At the same moment, jogging in formation came the bulk of the Zulu force, almost ten thousand men running from the north. Any escapees who went west round the Isandlwana hill would be picked up by the other horn of the buffalo, which had moved into position overnight.

Mapitha led his Ndwandwes straight into the plain. The British and their cohorts had no chance and almost all of them were caught out in the open. Within an hour Mapitha's spear ran red with blood and by midday he was covered in blood. The way the Zulus worked was simple; they just moved from encampment to encampment slaughtering everything in their path. It was not the Zulu custom to take prisoners.

Nzobo had also been up before the dawn. As soon as he saw the Zulus coming over the hillside he ran to his officer and pointed.

"There, and there and there, *Nkosi*, are the Zulu you could not see."

The officer turned a deathly pale shade of grey.

"Holy shit!" was all he could say. Nzobo and the officer then tried to arrange defences as best they could; with a few rocks and ammunition boxes and food bags they did their best. Nzobo kept firing at the approaching enemy but it seemed to make no difference, they just kept coming. The encampment he was in had just over one hundred men, split evenly between white English troops and native levies. The Zulu hordes just kept coming; in the first rush they lost twenty men and then the first Zulu *impi* moved on, to be followed by another and another. Nzobo's British officer tried to keep his men together but they started to run short of ammunition and further supplies were one hundred yards further up the hill. As the third wave of Zulus came upon them, the officer stood up and fired his revolver uselessly at the approaching warriors. Nzobo fired his rifle until it was almost too hot to hold; twice he hit a Zulu who was just about to stab the officer. His main concern was his own survival, but thoughts flashed through his mind: "Why am I here, why am I fighting for the white man? I should be part of the *impis* coming down from the hills and valleys of Zululand." When he had joined the British forces he had had no idea he would end up fighting his own people. He was almost disgusted with himself for standing by his officer. "This fool," he thought, "he calls us baboons and knows nothing about my people." A further rush from another Zulu *impi* overwhelmed the little group; this time Nzobo was not quick enough to save his officer, who noisily took a spear in the throat and collapsed and died. A few of the troops had managed to escape southwards and joined other escapees from the debacle in making their way back to the Tugela. Nzobo by now was relying on his bayonet to fight off the wave after wave of Zulus; he felt an excruciating pain in the side and then everything went black.

Mapitha continued to lead his Ndwandwes from encampment to encampment. He surprised himself with his own ferocity and complete lack of compassion; he could see his companions were almost in a state of trance. The native levies were dealt with even more harshly than the whites; they were traitors helping the invaders.

By mid-afternoon the Zulu army had fought itself to a standstill. The remnants of the British army were struggling to escape back towards the Tugela. From the British point of view, this was the worst defeat in colonial history. From the point of view of the Zulus it was an absolute triumph.

Mapitha collected his Ndwandwe *impi* together and along with the rest of the *amabutho* they started to pick their way through the debris of the British camp. They carried off what they could and smashed and burnt the rest. They buried their own dead and left the British.

In one of the small encampments that they picked over Mapitha saw a slight movement, and was just about to finish off a native levy when a flash of recognition came across him. He bent down. "Nzobo," he said surprised. "*O bani lo* (What are you doing here?—lit. Where are you going?")

Nzobo looked up, barely able to see; he thought it was his friend Mapitha but could not be sure. Mapitha wasted no time; he gave Nzobo some water, tore off the few remnants of identity with the British and he and one of his colleagues helped Nzobo to the camp of the Ndwandwes, where Mapitha tried to deal with Nzobo's severe wound with leaves, having cleaned it up.

Charles and Alice could hear the noise of the battle from the mission at St. Augustine's: the shots, the yelling and the occasional louder bang of British cannons.

Without saying much, both Alice and Charles were of one mind. They started to load up the scotch cart with all the bandages and medicines they had.

"We'll leave just before dawn tomorrow," said Charles. "The battle will be over by then. We'll take all the people we can from here." Rupert was left in the care of Mapitha's wives.

The scene that greeted them when they came over the brow of the hill from the northwest would haunt both Charles and Alice for the rest of their lives. There were literally hundreds of bodies scattered about the vast plain, as well as wrecked wagons and shredded tents everywhere. A few remnants of the Zulu army were still picking through the debris. And the animal scavengers had arrived; vultures were circling overhead and a few hyenas and jackals were sniffing dead bodies.

Alice set herself up under a tree.

"I'll deal with the live ones first," she said. "I suppose you and whoever you can find to help you should start to do something about the dead."

Nzobo had had a very bad night; Mapitha knew that if he wasn't treated soon he would die. First he arranged for the Ndwandwes to go home with all the loot they could carry. Mapitha knew that the only chance Nzobo had was somehow to get him to the mission under Alice's care, so he carried Nzobo across the plain towards St. Augustine's. Much to his surprise, he saw Alice with the scotch cart under a tree. He rather sheepishly approached. Alice looked up, surprised.

"Nzobo…" he began.

"There's no time for explanations," she said taking one look at Nzobo. "He will die soon if he's not treated. Leave him here; see if you can help the *Umfundisi*."

Mapitha reluctantly left Nzobo and found Charles collecting bodies, piling them up and then building rock cairns over them to keep the wild animals away. After some explanations Mapitha was persuaded to recruit two hundred of his Ndwandwes to help with the process. It took them almost a week, with Alice tending to the wounded, mainly Zulu and Charles burying the dead, mainly British and native levies.

Nzobo was kept under Alice's care in a shelter made from branches and grass. While she was treating him she suddenly recognized him. "Nzobo, What are you doing here?" she asked. "You do seem to get yourself into a lot of trouble, don't you?"

Nzobo was able to explain his relationship with Mapitha haltingly as he got better.

When they had finished their grisly task the little group, carrying Nzobo in the cart, made their way back to the mission. Alice had treated hundreds of Zulu wounded. Despite their white skin, there had not been any sign of hostility towards Alice and Charles from the Zulu; they were accepted as part of the scene.

As the cart wound its way over the rough track to the mission, Charles and Mapitha looked back over the battlefield of Isandlwana, with its dozens of burial cairns strewn over the valley floor.

Mapitha should have felt elated over the victory, but he knew that things would never be the same again for the Zulu. Charles couldn't help but reflect on the waste. Both of them had by this time heard the news of the defeat of the Zulu at Rorke's Drift a few miles away, where the hothead Dabulamanzi with four thousand Zulu had unsuccessfully attacked just over one hundred British troops in a well fortified position, and had been slaughtered in the process. The British had lost twenty-five men and the Zulus several hundred before they withdrew.

After they arrived at the mission, Mapitha had a chance to discuss the situation with Nzobo. After hearing his friend's long, convoluted story he came to an understanding of the reasons why Nzobo had been persuaded to join the British forces.

"The Zulu have had a great victory here at Isandlwana," said Nzobo. "Maybe now the *amaNgisi* will stay in their own place south of the Tugela." He looked forlornly and hopefully at Mapitha.

Mapitha shook his head. "They will not, they will come again and this time we will both fight for the Zulus."

Nzobo nodded.

When he was shown round the mission Nzobo was animated and excited. "We, you and I, have all that money in the bank in Kimberley," he reminded Mapitha.

Mapitha had completely forgotten. Money still meant nothing to him. As far as he and most other Zulus were concerned, the only real source of wealth was cattle. "So?" he asked.

"Well, with that money we could buy a farm and maybe with the help of the *Umfundisi* here we could run it like the *amaNgisi* run their farms in the south."

Mapitha was only mildly interested. "Buy a farm—we already own all the land. The Zulus own this land; who would we pay?"

Nzobo remained silent.

Over the next few days the idea came up again and again. Mapitha could see that there was merit in adopting some of the white man's ways and getting the Zulu to use their land more productively; he also understood that due to Frank Devereaux's generosity they had the wherewithal to do something constructive. But he had bigger issues on his mind. When he was certain that Nzobo was well again, he said, "You help the *Umfundisi* here; I am going to visit the King."

When Mapitha arrived at Kwa-Bulawayo about a month after Isandlwana, he found the King and his royal entourage in a state of semi-euphoria. The triumph of the victory at Isandlwana, only slightly soured by the disaster at Rorke's Drift, had convinced the hierarchy that they were now safe and that the British would leave them alone. Cetswayo's generals gave him no other advice; Ntshingwayo was still basking in the glory of the victory at Isandlwana and Dabulamanzi, who had hotheadedly led the Zulu into the disaster at Rorke's Drift, was not too keen to emphasise any weaknesses and had certainly not admitted to any failure on his part that could have resulted in a change in Zulu strategy.

When he was admitted to see the King, Mapitha approached the subject of Zulu military strategy cautiously. Both Ntshingwayo and Dabulamanzi were there to listen to him.

"The great King Shaka," he began,"he taught the Zulu people discipline and how to fight."

Cetswayo nodded.

"He had many great victories, and the Zulu became the most important nation."

The King urged him to continue.

"Shaka taught us the value of the *impi* being organised in the form of buffalo horns," Mapitha said.

More vigorous nods from the King and his entourage.

"This strategy has always worked when the enemy is prepared to fight us in the open." Mapitha then recited the names of many famous Zulu battles of Shaka's era. "Also Isandlwana was where the British were out in the open and in this case the buffalo horns worked very well."

Ntshingwayo started to relax; he had been worried that Mapitha was about to criticize Zulu military strategy.

"But in the case of the battle at the Ncome River (known to the Boers as Blood River, fought in December 1838) where the Boers were in well defended positions, the Zulu army was not able to wash their spears in Boer blood," said Mapitha.

There was a sharp intake of breath from Dabulamanzi and Cetswayo shifted uncomfortably.

"Maybe the battles at Ncome River and Rorke's Drift have something in common," said Mapitha bravely.

Dabulamanzi rose to his feet and said heatedly, "We should have continued with our attack at Rorke's Drift. We now know that the British had run out of ammunition and if we had attacked once more we would have killed them all. I should never have listened to those lousy lieutenants of mine."

Cetswayo waved at him to sit down. Privately he thought that Dabulamanzi was a high risk and he was irritated by the setback at Rorke's Drift.

"So what is your idea?" said Cetswayo to Mapitha.

"The great *Nkosi* knows of the power of the white man's firesticks," said Mapitha.

"Yes, of course, you yourself have demonstrated that to me," said the King.

"I can get enough firesticks to arm the whole Zulu army," said Mapitha.

"Forty thousand firesticks?" asked the King.

"Yes."

"This is not the Zulu way," chorused Dabulamanzi and Ntshingwayo. The King waved his great hand and they quietened down.

"I can teach them how to shoot," said Mapitha.

The King nodded.

"The military strategy will have to be different," added Mapitha. "The buffalo horn strategy is for close combat."

There were hisses from the entourage.

"Tell me," said the King.

"The Zulu should operate in small groups of fifty to one hundred *ibutho*," said Mapitha.

They all looked at him.

"The British are very clumsy and take a long time to move from place to place, and the Zulu are quick and they can move into place quickly and then disappear again," he said.

"So?" said the King.

"We should split our *amabutho* into small groups as I was saying," said Mapitha. "They can then use their firesticks to attack the *amaNgisi* when they are on the move. As soon as the British start firing back they can withdraw and then another small group can attack from another direction."

Cetswayo could see some sense in this.

"We should never, never attack them when they are stationary in fortified positions, but if they ever set up a fortified position, we can attack supply lines and shoot at them from a distance. If you do this, they will never take Zululand. When they have had enough, they will leave and go back south of the Tugela."

Cetswayo looked admiringly at Mapitha. He admired the courage that it must have taken to confront him and the Zulu military hierarchy with his ideas. A furious discussion then took place, in which Mapitha was ignored.

"It's not the Zulu way..."

"This is the way of cowards to sit behind a rock..."

"Who will train the *amabutho*?"

"Where will the guns come from?"

"The *amaNgisi* need to feel the cold, hard steel of a Zulu spear..." and so on.

After an hour, Cetswayo brought the discussion to a halt.

"Mapitha of the Ndwandwes, you have brought many things to the Zulu people. We will discuss this further another time," he said, and then he went on: "The *amaNgisi* have withdrawn south of the Tugela and my emissaries are right now talking to *Somseu* about peace. There will be no more war, neither I nor the *amaNgisi* want it."

Mapitha tried to speak but Cetswayo held up his hand. "I know your views in respect of *Somseu*; you think he is a dishonourable man. I, your King, do not agree. Your King has spoken. Now go back to your *umfundisi* and learn more of the ways of the white man."

Mapitha spent another day at Kwa-Bulawayo and then made his way home sadly to St. Augustine's. He knew the British would attack again and that the Zulus would not change their tactics. He did not expect to hear from the King again.

◇◇◇◇◇◇◇◇◇◇◇◇◇◇◇

Chapter 23

Mapitha and Nzobo unexpectedly left St. Augustines in mid-June 1879.

Charles did not know where they had gone but he did know that a very strong British force had crossed the Tugela again and were making for Ulundi.

This time the British had armed themselves with Maxim machine guns and were determined not to be caught out in the open as they had been at Isandhlwana.

On July 4th, Mapitha and Nzobo were among the second wave of Zulu *impi* to attack the fortified British position. Mapitha could see that they were in a hopeless position compared to the situation at Isandhlwana; there they had had the advantage of complete surprise and the British were caught unawares. In this situation the British were well prepared and he could see that they had provoked the Zulu army into attacking on a narrow front right in the British field of fire. When the murderous fire of the Maxims started up Mapitha could see that the battle would not last long, and the first wave of the Zulu *impi* was cut down in their hundreds. The Zulu had not seen the Maxims before and despite the carnage continued to charge the British position.

Nzobo was running easily alongside his companion; both carried their rifles, cow-hide shields and *ixwa*; they were not more than fifty yards from the British lines. Nzobo could see that the Zulu were being cut down in swathes and Mapitha suddenly disappeared from sight. Nzobo dived to the ground and after a few minutes found Mapitha; his body was riddled with bullet marks, he had had no chance and had taken a burst from a Maxim right in the chest. The Zulu charge had petered out and late in the day Nzobo, who, along with hundreds of his fellow warriors was picking through the bodies of the Zulu dead, carried his dead friend's body off the battle-field.

A few days later Nzobo arrived at St Augustine's in a small ox-cart, which he had borrowed, with the now decaying body of Mapitha. Mapitha's wives were totally in shock when they saw what had happened and spent the night wailing and rubbing sand in their hair and all over their bodies. They had been used to Mapitha disappearing for weeks, even months, at a time but he had always come back.

Charles was stunned; Mapitha had been his helper, friend and companion since they had set up the mission and he was immobilized. Alice came to the rescue and said to Nzobo:

"He will have a proper Zulu burial. Slaughter an ox and we will bury him in wrapped in the hide, sitting up and facing the dawn."

Nzobo did as he was told and Mapitha was buried as a Zulu chief. The people and *indunas* from round about came to the funeral, Charles was persuaded to roast the ox for them and he and Mapitha's wives provided quantities of the best *utshwala*.

When all was said and done Charles, Alice, the wives and Nzobo held a short Christian service over the grave.

"What will become of Mbweli, Bibi and Monase, and the children?" asked Charles once they had all had time to come to terms with the situation.

"Nzobo is like a brother to Mapitha," answered Alice. "He has told me that he will marry them and stay here and carry on where Mapitha left off. He told me to ask you if that was all right with you."

"What, the marrying or staying here?"

"He will marry Mapitha's wives whatever you say. If you want him to stay he will stay. All three of Mapitha's wives are now very useful to me in the clinic," Alice responded.

"He can stay," was all Charles said.

◇◇◇◇◇◇◇◇◇◇◇◇◇◇

Historical Note

The triumph of winning the battle of Isandlwana was relatively short lived from the Zulu viewpoint. For the record, the Zulus killed 858 whites and 471 black troops; more than 1000 Zulus died. This was by far the worst British defeat in its colonial history.

The next day the skirmish at Rorke's Drift left several hundred Zulu dead and some twenty-five British.

There were other skirmishes during the next six months. On July 4th 1879 the Zulu army was provoked into attacking the British in well-established positions at Ulundi. In two hours more than 1000 Zulus lost their lives and only thirteen on the British side. This was the final battle of the Zulu/British war. The Zulu had learnt nothing from the history of the previous fifty years in clashes with the whites. Every time they attacked well-defended positions, they lost heavily, and so it was at Ulundi. Within weeks Cetshwayo had been captured and sent into exile.

Shepstone appointed thirteen chiefs, whom he regarded as "safe" but who did not necessarily have any Zulu royal blood. This British dictum of divide and rule formed the basis for the apartheid inspired mini-state of KwaZulu in the 1960's and beyond and kept the Zulu people in a state of subservience until the political change of the 1990's came about.

Glossary

(Z = Zulu, A = Afrikaans)

Z   abelungu—whites (pl)
Z   amaas—curdled sour milk
Z   amaBhunu—Boers (pl.)
Z   amabutho—regiment, warriors (pl.)
Z   amaNdiya—Indians
Z   amaNgisi—British/English (pl.)
Z   assegai—throwing spear
Z   Baba—Father
Z   bayete—Zulu war cry
Z   bheshu—loincloth
A   biltong-dried meat
A   blerry—colloquial Dutch speaking pronunciation of bloody
A   Boer—lit.farmer; Dutch speaking white settler in South Africa
A   Buffels-buffalo
Z   Cetshwayo—Zulu king 1872-1884, son of Mpande
Z   dagga—marijuana
A   dankie-thankyou
Z   Dingaan—Zulu king 1829-1840, half brother of Shaka and Mpande
Z   dokotela—doctor
A   dominee—priest
A   donga—gully
A   dop—measure
A   Engelsmans.-the English/British
A   Griqua—people of mixed blood who had escaped from the Cape and created their own homeland in the Northern Cape
Z   hamba—go
Z   hamba gahle—lit. go well; farewell greeting
Z hlobonga—sexual intercourse among Zulu youth without penetration occurring.

Z   iBhunu (pl. amaBhunu)—Boer
Z   ibutho (pl. amabutho)—regiment/warrior
Z   idayimani (pl. amadayimani)—diamond
    IDB—Illicit Diamond Buying
Z   igolidi—gold
Z   ihashi (pl. amahashi)—horse
Z   imantshi—magistrate
Z   impi—army
Z   indaba—meeting
Z   induna—local chief
Z   iNdiya (pl.amaNdiya)—Indians
Z   iNgisi (pl. amaNgisi)—British/English
Z   ingwenya (pl. izingwenya)—crocodile
Z   inyoka—snake
Z   isagila—club
Z   isicoco—Zulu head ring signifying maturity
Z   isigodlo—king's royal enclosure
Z   ixwa—short, stabbing spear
Z   izingwenya—crocodiles (pl.)
A   Kaapstad—Cape Town
A   kaffir—derogatory term for black man
Z   kaross—mantle or blanket of animal skins with the hair on
A   Kgama's country—Bechuanaland. (Now Botswana)
A   kloof—ravine
A   knobkierie—short stick with knobbed head, weapon
A   kopje—small hill
A   kraal—village of huts enclosed by a fence
A   leeu—lion
Z   lobola—bride price
A   mealie-pap—porridge cake made from maize meal.
A   meneer—mister, sir
A   mevrou—madam
Z   Mfecane—the name given to the Zulu depredations of the early nine-
    teenth century, where they attacked and either killed or absorbed all
    their neighbouring tribes.
Z   Mpande—Zulu king 1840-1872, half brother of Shaka, Dingaan.
A   nee—no
Z   ndodakazi—daughter

Z   nkosi—chief

Z   nkosikasi—lady chief, a term of respect used to a married woman

Z   nkulunkulu—God

A   oom—lit. Uncle. Used as a term of familiarity.

A   oke—man (slang)

A   pampoen—idiot (lit. pumpkin)

Z   putu—maize cake

Z   sala gahle—lit. Stay well, farewell greeting

Z   sangoma (pl. isangoma)—witch doctor

Z   Shaka—Zulu king, founder of the Zulu nation.

A   skellum—undesirable, dishonest person.

Z   Somseu—Zulu name for Sir Theophilus Shepstone, Natal Native Commissioner

A   spoor—tracks

A   spruit—gully

A   stoep—front verandah

A   Taal—lit. Language, precursor to the Afrikaans language

Z   Thekwini—Durban

Z   tokolosh—witch

A   uitlander—foreigner

Z   Ukhalamba. Drakensberg

Z   umfazi—wife

Z   umfundisi—teacher

Z   umlungu (pl. abelungu)—white person

Z   usuthu—Zulu warcry, rallying cry of Cetshwayo's supporters

Z   utshwala—beer

A   veld—grassland

A   vragtig—lit. Truly

A   voorloper—usually a young boy leading the oxen pulling a wagon

A   vrou—wife

Z   yebo—yes

◇◇◇◇◇◇◇◇◇◇◇◇◇◇◇◇

Bibliography

Dent, G.R. and Nyembezi, C.L.S., *Zulu Dictionary* (Saphrograph Corp. USA, 1975).

Else, D., Connolly, J., Fitzpatrick, M., Murphy, A. and Swaney, D., *Southern Africa* (Melbourne: Lonely Planet, second edition 2000).

Fitzpatrick, Sir Percy, *Jock of the Bushveld* (London: Longman, 15th impression 1976).

Herd, Norman. *The Bent Pine* (Johannesburg: Ravan Press 1976).

Lonely Planet, *Southern Africa Road Atlas* (Melbourne: Lonely Planet Publications 2000).

Pakenham, Thomas, *The Scramble for Africa* (London: Abacus 1992, first published by George Weidenfeld & Nicolson 1991).

Pearse, R.O., *Barrier of Spears* (Cape Town: Howard Timmins 1973).

Reader, John, *Africa* (London: Penguin Books 1998, first published by Hamish Hamilton 1997).

Roberts, Brian. *The Diamond Magnates* (London: Hamish Hamilton).

Roberts, Brian. *The Zulu Kings* (London: Hamish Hamilton 1974).

Taylor, Stephen. *Shaka's Children* (London: Harper Collins 1995, first published 1994).

Thomas, Anthony. *Rhodes* (London: BBC).

ABOUT THE AUTHOR

Guy Hallowes was born and brought up in Kenya of South African born parents. He lived for many years in South Africa and Botswana.

St. Augustines, Nqutu was founded by Guy's great grandfather Charles Johnson in 1879, sometime after the battle of Isandlwana when as a young curate he was instructed to bury the dead from that battle. The many whitewashed cairns, still visible on the battlefield, are the result.

Charles Johnson is buried in the crypt of St. Augustines The Charles Johnson memorial hospital in Nqutu was founded in 1930 in his honour.

Guy now lives in Sydney. Australia.

www.ingramcontent.com/pod-product-compliance
Lightning Source LLC
Chambersburg PA
CBHW070011120726
47909CB00003B/879